BUCHI EMECHETA was born in Lagos, Nigeria. Her father, a railway worker, died when she was very young. At the age of 10 she won a scholarship to the Methodist Girls' High School, but by the time she was 17 she had left school, married and had a child. She accompanied her husband to London, where he was a student. Aged 22, she finally left him, and took an honours degree in sociology while supporting her five children and writing in the early morning.

Her first book, *In the Ditch*, details her experience as a poor, single parent in London. It was followed by *Second-Class Citizen*, *The Bride Price*, *The Slave Girl*, which was awarded the Jock Campbell Award, *The Joys of Motherhood*, *Destination Biafra*, *Naira Power*, *Double Yoke*, *Gwendolen*, *The Rape of Shavi* and *Kehinde*, as well as a number of children's books and a play, *A Kind of Marriage*, produced on BBC television. Her autobiography, *Head Above Water*, appeared in 1986 to much acclaim.

BUCHI EMECHETA

DESTINATION BIAFRA

Heinemann

Heinemann Educational Publishers
A Division of Heinemann Publishers (Oxford) Ltd
Halley Court, Jordan Hill, Oxford OX2 8EJ

Heinemann: A Division of Reed Publishing (USA) Inc.
361 Hanover Street, Portsmouth, NH 03801-3912, USA

Heinemann Educational Books (Nigeria) Ltd
PMB 5205, Ibadan
Heinemann Educational Boleswa
PO Box 10103, Village Post Office, Gaborone, Botswana

FLORENCE   PRAGUE   PARIS   MADRID
ATHENS   MELBOURNE   JOHANNESBURG
AUCKLAND   SINGAPORE   TOKYO
CHICAGO   SAO PAULO

British Library Cataloguing in Publication Data
A catalogue record for this book is available from the British Library.

ISBN 0435 90992 4

Cover design by Touchpaper
Cover illustration by Synthia Saint James

Phototypeset by CentraCet Limited, Cambridge
Printed and bound in Great Britain by
Cox & Wyman Ltd, Reading, Berkshire

94 95 96 97   10 9 8 7 6 5 4 3 2 1

CONTENTS

I dedicate this work to the memory of many relatives and friends who died in this war, especially my eight-year-old niece Buchi Emecheta, who died of starvation, and her four-year-old sister Ndidi Emecheta, who died two days afterwards of the same Biafran disease at the CMS refugee centre in Ibuza; also my aunt Ozili Emecheta and my maternal uncle Okolie Okwuekwu, both of whom died of snake bites as they ran into the bush the night the federal forces bombed their way into Ibuza.

I also dedicate Destination Biafra *to the memory of those Ibuza women and their children who were roasted alive in the bush at Nkpotu Ukpe.*

May the spirit of Umejei, the Father founder of our town, guide you all in death, and may you all sleep well.

Author's Foreword

The episode that was Biafra happened. But the major characters here are fictional and have been chosen to portray the attitudes of many countries and individuals to the Biafran war. People like them may have existed, but those in this book are all conjured up by my imagination to suit the message this work carries.

For me this book, like my novel *Second-Class Citizen*, is one that simply had to be written. I was not in Nigeria during this war, but was one of the students demonstrating in Trafalgar Square in London at the time. I have tried very hard not to be bitter and to be impartial – especially as I hail from Ibuza in the Mid-West, a little town near Asaba where the worst atrocities of the war took place, which is never given any prominence. Records and stories have shown that Ibuza, Asaba and other smaller places along that border area suffered most; but we are glossed over, not being what the media of the time called 'the Igbo heartland'.

Yet it is time to forgive, though only a fool will forget.

There are so many people I have to thank for helping with this work, but it would not be possible to mention them all here. I simply must mention some names: I have to thank Peter Shepherd for arranging my visit to Sandhurst and the lecturers there for showing us around; my friend Chidi Ekeke for giving me all his Biafran papers; Mrs Nwukor for telling me of the Ibuza incidents and the story of her son Boniface and his kettle; my brother Adolphus Emecheta for narrating his journey on foot along the Benin–Asaba road and all the killings he saw; my brother-in-law Charles Onwordi for accounts of the Igbo massacres in Lagos and his harsh experiences from our brothers in the Eastern part of the river; Mr Luke Enenmoh for details of the killing in Asaba town hall; Alex Obi Ebele for information about how our people organised their own militia as protection against the federal forces and the Biafran ones; and last but not least to Wole Soyinka for writing *The Man Died*, which gave me the idea that some non-Igbos suffered with us. From that I developed my heroine 'Debbie

Ogedemgbe' who is neither Igbo nor Yoruba nor Hausa, but simply a Nigerian.

I must not fail to mention my sons Sylvester and Jake Onwordi, who corrected my basic mistakes about guns and aircraft. This shows how little I know about wars – but who wants wars? I hope we do not have another experience like this again.

Lastly, my enduring gratitude will go to my original publishers Margaret Busby and her partner Clive Allison.

Buchi Emecheta, 1994

Note to the reader

There are three main tribes in this novel, each with its leaders and political party.

The major tribe numerically is formed by the Hausas in the North, who by religion and culture are Moslem and more feudalistic than the other tribes. Their party is NEPU, some of whose members form a political alliance with the NCNC party in the East. The Hausa leaders in this book are Nguru Kano and the Sardauna in the North.

The Igbos are from the East. The majority of them belong to the NCNC party and their leaders in this book are Dr Ozimba and Dr Eze.

The Yorubas are from the West. They form the Action Group, and in this book their leaders are Chief Durosaro and Chief Odumosu.

All these parties existed at one time in Nigeria but they have all been disbanded. However, all the leaders in this novel are fictional characters invented to portray some of the attitudes of these parties at the time in which the story was set, though no character in this book is intended to represent any actual person.

PART I

1 *The First Election*

The governor's residence stood majestic in its Georgian elegance. Its front pillars gave it the air of a small palace, the marble shine the result of decades of careful polishing and pampering. The floor leading to the main entrance had a blue and cream marbled effect that gave one the illusion of walking on a man-made ocean. The windows of the building faced the nearby Lagos marina where at night the music made by the lapping of waves along the artificial shore and the swish of the palm fronds in the breeze seemed any man's birthright.

Moving barefoot in and out of the collonades and indoor plants were the governor's servants who were made to look diminutive by the vastness of the place. Some of them wore squarish police caps, others wore khaki military uniforms topped by headgear of such size and colours that the men resembled large African dragonflies going silently about their work.

Governor Macdonald was playing a thoughtful game of solo golf in the shade near the swimming-pool, watched by his guest Captain Alan Grey, son of the previous governor-general. Grey was there in the South for a couple of days, on his way to the Military Academy in Abeokuta, in the Western region. From there he would be going to help organize the Peace Corps that was needed in the Congo; the trouble in this newly-independent state was beginning to cause concern.

In contrast to the peaceful atmosphere inside the governor-general's compound, outside the gate Nigeria was in a fever of excitement. The country's first general election was to take place soon, an election that would decide the first prime minister of independent Nigeria, its first president and members of the Federal House. It was not surprising that Macdonald was playing his golf alone. He knew the great responsibility that lay on his shoulders. He had to make sure that the right man was elected who Britain would accept as head of state, the

3

man who would offer the least resistance to British trade yet would be accepted by the majority of the natives and ensure stability. He had been given enough loud hints as to the choice of his employers in London. But now there were so many problems, problems which he could not tackle without losing sleep. He stopped and looked at the neat profile of his thirty-five-year-old visitor, and something told him that the handsome Sandhurst-trained army officer would be an invaluable ally. His near-fleshless face displayed the jutting cheekbones, firm chin and pointed nose of the old aristocratic breed. His eyes were of the greyest blue and his hair the colour of corn ripened by the African sun.

The governor stopped playing and walked up to him. It was getting cool and they had not taken a siesta; though it was a luxury Alan Grey allowed himself once in a while, army life had disciplined him to do without it, especially when there were important things to discuss. Macdonald signalled to one of the turban-wearing footmen and ordered some cold beer. Then he sat by Grey. The footman poured their drinks.

'Enjoy your game, sir?' Grey asked.

'Not bad, not bad at all.' Macdonald took a long sip from his frothy Star lager.

'You don't look too happy, sir, if you don't mind my saying so.'

'You're right there. Have you ever seen a man as old as myself underestimating a situation? What is it they say about a fool at forty?'

'I don't think you'll be a fool forever, sir,' Alan Grey replied, his eyes dancing with amusement. 'But we do tend to underrate the natives sometimes, and great men have paid dearly for it. You remember the case of Captain Cook and the aborigines?'

Macdonald threw back his head and laughed uproariously. 'You mean the man who endured the tribulations of sailing all the way to Australia, only to lose his life on account of a miserable old goat?'

'Same man. And to think that before he was killed the natives were dancing with a great show of merriment.'

'Hmm, he should not have ordered their huts to be burned, though, just because of a stolen goat,' Macdonald added thoughtfully.

'Yes, sir, but he thought he understood the natives and intended the burning of their huts as a kind of warning. The poor man also thought he would be able to stamp out pilfering forever among them.'

'Well, that was a tall order. A man's home is his castle in England; do we really have the right to regard an aborigine's home as of less importance to him just because it's made of thatched leaves? No, with due respect to the memory of a great explorer, his attitude was too arrogant. I would not have done that, though I may be a fool at forty.'

4

Grey was at a loss for what to say. One could never tell with a Scotsman. Was the governor siding with the Nigerian leaders? Was he against them? His stand seemed so ambivalent. So Grey simply sipped his drink, his eyes darkening with concentration.

Macdonald heaved a sigh and remarked, 'Yes, the Nigerian situation is much more delicate. And we have more at stake. If it is badly handled, we will pay for it for a very long time. And the blame will forever be on me, a Scotsman. Why didn't Whitehall send an Irishman, so that if he failed there would just be one more Irish joke to add to the thousands of others?' The task of handing Nigeria back to the Nigerians was obviously weighing heavily on him.

He seemed suddenly to realize that Alan Grey was watching him studiously and saying nothing. 'I am sorry. This weather makes one feel sorry for oneself sometimes. Have you heard what the Sardauna said?' he asked Grey all of a sudden.

Grey sat up in all eagerness. He had not heard. The governor-general had access to such information before it went to press. 'What did he say?'

'He said that he was not going to leave his palace to come and live with the "kaferis" – non-believers – in the South. He would rather live in his palace there in the North. Now what do we do? Force the man to come and rule his own country? It will be announced on the radio at six o'clock this evening.'

'Good heavens, the man really means what he has been saying all along. I thought he was only playing politics. You know he did not want Nigeria to be an independent nation – that was one of the reasons why the North was the last to get regional independence. He probably needs someone to tell him that if he refuses to rule he will be selling his people to the Southern politicians.'

Alan was reminded of the first time he and his father had met Macdonald and of their conversation that evening at the Queen's Hotel in London. It was after the Nigerian delegates had finished the serious part of their visit to negotiate independence. Sir Fergus Grey intended to use the opportunity to introduce the Hausa leaders to the new governor who would be taking the post after him. Alan was there since he had lectured for some time at the Army Depot in Zaria and knew all the Northern leaders.

Macdonald had arrived early, a heavily-built man with red face and neck, who would have looked much better in khaki shorts and helmet than in the dark suit and striped tie into which he had forced himself. There was no doubt that this man had stayed long in the tropics.

Maybe after his four-year contract in Nigeria it would be one of the West Indian islands. He had come up to his hosts and boomed, outdatedly, 'Dr Livingstone, I presume.' Luckily for him, the joke went down well, but he did not miss the fact that Sir Fergus was studying him closely. He did not mind though, for he realized that in the diplomatic field some of the most successful men were the greatest actors; their profession needed a touch of the theatrical. When he shook the younger Grey's hand, he knew that the man would not be obstructive to his stay in Nigeria. He in turn would let him have his way with the army and would let him continue the sideline his father had started, buying up the bronzes, carved elephant tusks and moulded animal figures which Western culture had dubbed with the name 'primitive art'. By the time Nigerians came to appreciate the worth of their own products, irreplaceable valuables would have been sold to adorn the homes of English aristocrats or rich Americans.

'I have asked you here half an hour before our other friend arrives on purpose,' explained Sir Fergus as he followed the eyes of their guest. 'There are a few points I would like to explain before we confront them.'

'Ah,' said Macdonald, lowering himself into the soft cushioned chair that seemed to enfold one as if it were one's mother gathering one into her ample bosom.

Alan had ordered the first round of drinks and told the hovering waiters that they would order the food when the other guests came. The waiters brought the drinks and bowed themselves away into the lush background of thick carpet and muted lights.

'To England and the Empire,' toasted Sir Fergus.

'The Empire?' Macdonald laughed looking uneasy. 'I thought that was something of the distant past.'

'I say that because after the charade of this morning I cannot imagine people like them ruling themselves. They still have a long, long way to go.'

'That is true,' Macdonald condescended. 'But, as they say in China, a journey of one thousand miles begins with one step.'

'Well, why don't we drink to the past Empire and the beginning of a workable Commonwealth?' Alan put in, raising his glass.

'Good idea, marvellous,' Macdonald replied.

They toasted and drank deep.

'There is more to being a statesman than just acquiring some signed papers giving one the authority to rule a certain area,' Sir Fergus persisted in his argument.

'Yes, but these people haven't even been given that paper yet and they behave as if they already own the whole world.'

'They are still very young in diplomacy,' Macdonald observed. 'You heard how disappointed the Sardauna was. It even showed in his speech. I felt sorry for him in a way.'

'They won't have long to wait, that I know. But as far as I'm concerned, the whole exercise has been a great mistake. Those people don't need independence, they need guidance,' Alan said.

They had continued this animated banter for a while. The jokes were mainly at the expense of the African delegates. Macdonald was amused by the Sardauna's great headdress.

'Does he wear that in Nigeria? It must be very hot for him, poor soul.'

'Yes, he does, actually. I've seen inside his palace many times. Everything about him has that Arabic feudalistic majesty. But he is a very kind man,' Alan said.

'Kind? Kind to his people, you mean?' Macdonald wanted to know.

'Yes. Beggars line his palace walls and he makes sure that their begging bowls are never empty. His servants are delegated to fill them with cornmeal every Friday, their day of prayer.'

'Ah, that kind of kindness,' laughed Macdonald. 'And was he not the man who placed an order for an exact copy of the Rolls Royce used by Her Majesty and later had it returned because the dust from his desert country entered the car?'

The Greys laughed heartily. 'Right,' agreed the elder statesman. 'Same man. Disgustingly rich, this Emir of the North, as they call him.'

'And after this Independence he's going to be even richer, because the man will be able to control a greater share of the mines in Jos, of the groundnut farming in the North and the tin deposits in Bauchi Plateau. The Northern region is a vast place, fairly rich, and the people are mainly Hausas, comparatively ignorant and happy in their ignorance,' Alan pointed out with regret.

'My son does not subscribe to our granting independence to Nigeria. He thinks it's too soon,' Sir Fergus explained to Macdonald.

'But nine-tenths of the country is still to be thoroughly mapped, to say nothing of being tapped,' Alan continued, becoming quite heated in his argument. He fished out a map of Nigeria which he spread on the polished table, almost knocking over the whisky glasses in his enthusiasm.

'Look,' he expanded, indicating excitedly the whole of the Eastern region and the regions around Benin. 'These vast areas are full of oil, pure crude oil, which is untouched and still needs thorough prospecting. Now we are to hand it over to these people, who've had all these minerals since Adam and not known what to do with them. Now they are beginning to be aware of their monetary value. And after Independence they may sign it all over to the Soviets for all we know. Well, you have seen them, the best of them, the cream of Nigeria. Any fool with a few thousand pounds' "dash" and some yards of shiny cloth can get anything from them. Their type of corruption is built into their system.'

'With the right education, don't you think, Mr Grey, that some Nigerians will come to reject these corrupt practices?'

'Yes, but it will take a very long time. And the corrupt ministers are very powerful, you know. They can buy anything.' Alan was reminded of Samuel Ogedemgbe, whose daughter Debbie was a close friend of his. But he was determined to press home his point. 'I don't want Nigeria to go Communist. That would mean gaining independence from us and becoming dependent on another power. And I do not pray for the kind of situation we now have in the Congo.'

'Ah,' drawled Macdonald, furrowing his brow, 'I'm not thinking about the moral side of anything, but I think it's about time we let them go, but not completely. Since we are committed to handing over a peaceful government to them, now is the right time to introduce the type of government they should have. I mean our type of democracy, maybe adjusted here and there to suit the local people. All Independence will give them is the right to govern themselves. That has nothing to do with whom they trade with.'

'The situation is not as simple as that,' Alan Grey began. 'It would be easy if we had only the Hausas to cope with. But there are the other tribes – the Yorubas have been dealing with us for decades. And then there are the Igbos. They are ambition personified. Every beggar boy in Enugu or Owerri wants to be a doctor.'

'A witch doctor?' Macdonald asked, trying unsuccessfully to inject some lightness into Alan's seriousness. 'The Igbos, I have heard so much about them,' he went on. 'One of their leaders was that tall, well-spoken delegate with glasses. He impressed me very much, I must say.'

'There is no doubt that they are extremely intelligent. But they are greedy as well, and their arrogance could lead them into trouble. Also, the greater portion of the oil areas are in their region; so one has to be very careful how the country is divided constitutionally,' Sir Fergus observed.

'But are the Hausas not greater in number?' Macdonald asked.

Alan Grey nodded.

'Then there is no problem. Introduce democracy, and let the Hausas rule forever. You did say that they are not so ambitious, and that they are happy in the Moslem faith?' Macdonald felt triumphant.

Sir Fergus smiled slowly. 'We must show the Hausas that we are their friends, and that the country will be divided in such a way that they will be the rulers of Nigeria, and that there will be little interference with their religion. Dr Ozimba, the Igbo leader who impressed you so much, has seen to it that his party has its Hausa ally, in the person of NEPU's Alhaji Manliki.'

'You think a Hausa man will be loyal to a party at the expense of his culture?' Macdonald asked thoughtfully.

'The Sardauna probably encouraged Alhaji Manliki to go along with Dr Ozimba in the hope that some Igbos and those minority tribes surrounding them might turn and become NEPU in support of the Hausas,' put in Sir Fergus.

'Tribe, tribe, tribe. How that word can consolidate and yet still divide,' Alan Grey said, looking into the distance over the heads of the other guests in the Queen's.

'During the course of the conference, one man said he was speaking on behalf of the minority people. What in the name of the gods did he mean?' asked Macdonald.

'Oh, him.' Sir Fergus laughed lightly. 'You know that there are three major tribes in Nigeria. That said, one must not forget that there are smaller groups with slightly different language structures surrounding each major tribe. For example, round the Igbos you have the Efiks, the Ijaws, the Binis; and around the Hausas you have the Tivs, the Fulanis – oh, so many of them. After the election, their interests will be taken care of by the governor. It will be in your power, Macdonald, to nominate officers to represent these people. They can vote for whichever party they like, but their men will be nominated by you. You will also nominate the first president, who will sign the treaties binding the country after its independence. But they don't have to know that yet,' Sir Fergus murmured in an undertone, his eyes roaming the foyer to make sure he was not being overheard.

The other diners and visitors were taking no notice of the three men sitting there, looking deeply engrossed in their deliberations.

'The first president must be someone popular with all three major tribes . . .' Macdonald began.

'Not necessarily. These people have no real experience of democracy. We shall have to introduce proportional representation. They won't know it isn't practised in Britain. Three-quarters of the people won't know what voting means, and even after they've voted they still won't know. It is good for Mallam Nguru to be popular among the Ibos, though I doubt if the Igbos will nominate anybody other than their own Dr Ozimba. All the same, numerically speaking the Mallam won't need their votes, since the Hausas are greater in number than the rest of the country put together, even not counting their women.'

'Good,' Macdonald concluded. 'Then we have nothing to worry about.'

'Hmm,' mused Alan, 'there are some dynamic people among the Northerners called the Tivs. They could be a future political threat to the powers of the North, because they are along the borders and, more importantly, some of them have been converted to Christianity. These Tivs are very keen fighters. I met a lot of them in Zaria where I teach them basic weapon familiarization. One young man, I remember him now – Saka Momoh – was even one of those recommended to be sent to Sandhurst for training.'

'Well,' said Sir Fergus, 'you're going to continue training them in Zaria, recommending them to the military academy at Sandhurst, and staying there with them for a while. So see that they become familiar with the way things should run.'

'Well, the thing is to back the Hausas with everything we have . . . Look, here are our guests,' Macdonald announced.

They all looked up and saw Mallam Nguru Kano, with two other Hausas who were acting as his bodyguards, bowing and asking their way from the equally bowing and respectful waiters. He was tall, this Mallam, a picture of magnificence in his tailored robe, his small skull cap like a halo on his closely shaved head. With slow, deliberate steps he approached his hosts and apologized in perfectly modulated English.

'The Sardauna sends his apologies. He thinks you should be his guests, and not he yours. It is one of His Highness's rules.'

Sir Fergus, with a practised diplomatic smile, told the Mallam that he had thought the Sardauna might need a change of air after staying so many days cooped up with his country's problems. No offence was meant in inviting him to a common place like the Queen's Hotel. The Mallam slowly smiled his thanks and accepted Sir Fergus's apologies for his presumptuousness, while Alan Grey and Macdonald gaped in wonder. They all sat down to eat. By the time they had worked through the jellied meat and a mountain of exotic vegetables mixed with creamed prawns, Mallam Nguru Kano had been told how powerful the Hausas were and how they would be even more important in the new Nigeria.

'Do you think that in the not so distant future your women will be allowed to vote?' Macdonald had asked. Seeing the warning glance from Mallam Nguru Kano that told him mutely to mind his own business, he went on haltingly, trying to explain himself: 'I mean, it would secure your hold on the country further. After all, the women in the South are all going to the polls. It seems unfair to you Hausas.'

The Mallam's smile broadened to include all of them at the table. He slowed down his movements, as if to gain time. Then he said, 'In England you had democracy for years before your women were allowed to vote? I presume this is so?' The dour smile was still fixed on his face, a glass was poised in his hand and his brow arched artistically like that of a practised actor. The whole setting had a touch of the theatrical.

Sir Fergus Grey had changed the topic quickly and their guest soon left.

All that had taken place in London months previously. Now in the governor's residence in Lagos, Alan Grey told Macdonald of the recent visit he had made to Zaria in the North, which seemed more relevant. There he had watched like an audience in a theatre the type of election campaign he knew he would never again witness in his life. Grey had been amused at first but on second thoughts realized the gravity of it all, and felt he should acquaint Macdonald with it. The British were working on the impression that two-thirds of the country belonged to the Hausa-speaking and Fulani peoples, whose common Moslem religion cemented their intimacy. The Fulanis had once been the conquerors, and the Emir of the North was their leader. The British thought that the only slight opposition they would face would be from the Igbo party led by Dr Ozimba. But now Alan Grey was not so sure.

He had gone to Kano to see the man chosen to represent Ozimba's NCNC party in the North, and it was apparent that at least this man would win his seat for like his constituents Alhaji Manliki was a Hausa – a clever touch. Grey was cautiously welcomed and in the Alhaji's courtyard, where he was served honeyed spiced meat and cool beer, he tried to persuade the man to talk of the burning topic of the day.

'It seems your NEPU/NCNC alliance could get a slice of the North, thereby reducing the majority of the Northerners' party in the Federal House,' he said invitingly.

Before replying, the Alhaji had got up from the goatskin on which he sat, gathered his white robe around him and then called one of his servants to bring some kolanuts. He gave his visitor some large pieces and took a generous bite himself. Grey was by now accustomed to the tangy taste of which the Hausas were so fond, though he did not like the fact that the northern kolanuts stained one's teeth and lips. The Alhaji chewed thoughtfully like a goat for a while and then spat the red liquid out, a habit that had long ceased to nauseate Grey.

'Would you like that, Captain Grey?'

When Alhaji Manliki said 'you', he meant the whole of Britain. But Grey intended to answer as if he was quite alone.

'I don't know,' he had said, smiling uneasily.

Manliki had smiled too.

'Well, my friend, if you don't know, you who come from a country where such democratic government has been the order of the day for centuries, how am I to tell, who has not tried it before? We must wait and see. There's only four weeks to go.'

They were interrupted by men who came in dragging large cows, and Grey gathered from what was said that one of these animals was to be killed each day and the meat given free to would-be voters. He looked at his host enquiringly, and the Alhaji chuckled and spat more kola-coloured saliva into a corner.

'The trouble with Dr Ozimba ... our party,' he added as an afterthought, 'is that we haven't any funds. And Dr Ozimba was saying until recently that we should not bribe the voters. "If they are convinced of our cause, they will vote for us."' Alhaji Manliki began to laugh. 'Have you seen our opposition at work, the Action Group? Most of the local heads have been given loans to buy new cars; and tomorrow, you watch: they even distribute leaflets from the sky.'

'But surely after eating all these cows people should vote for your party?'

'Well, we hope so. The cows are nothing; Muhammad the servant of Allah said one must feed one's poor. I've been too busy running to London and Lagos to do that for some time now.'

'So at least if you don't win this election you'll have made your peace with Allah.'

Alhaji Manliki did not miss the irony, but he simply assented gravely with a slight nod of the head.

When he showed his visitor out of his courtyard, the whole neighbourhood outside had a festive air. By the mud walls of the compound, beggars sat cross-legged, many of them blind as a result of the dry desert sand blowing for a considerable part of the year. A few were lame and had sticks. All of them had big empty begging bowls. When they saw the Alhaji walking with Alan Grey, pandemonium broke out and they swarmed around like bees. Sticks flew in the air, begging bowls were thrown about and there were shouts of happy expectation.

The Alhaji gave a penny to this one, a penny to the other, telling them in his low, calm voice not to forget to go and vote on election day. He told them that the food would soon be dished out to them. 'This kind of life will continue if you say so. Just put your votes in the box my servants will show you, then come here every Jimoh day, every Friday, for your alms. I shall provide for you . . .'

The effect on the swarm of beggars was spectacular. They went obediently to their places by the wall, positioning their bowls in front of them. They behaved as if hypnotized. Even a lame young boy of about thirteen who wanted to get some extra pennies from the white man was pulled away by a blind woman clad in rags who seemed to be his mother.

Alhaji Manliki wished his visitor goodbye. Grey walked away quickly, fearing that he would be mobbed if the Alhaji went into the courtyard before he reached his car; but he looked back once and saw that the people who moments before had been so infused with energy now sat there, docile and seemingly lifeless.

All he had seen that day worried him – not so much the begging, which in this part of the world was seen as no disgrace, being the will of Allah, but that the election should be fought on that issue: 'I shall feed you every Jimoh day.'

The following evening he made time to visit the Teteku family, who lived in the Sabon Garri, the 'strangers' quarters', in Kano. The Tetekus were good friends of the Ogedemgbes, whose twenty-three-year-old daughter Debbie had become a close friend of Alan's in England. They had known each other for years, since she was introduced to him at a party, and their relationship had developed to the point where they were lovers.

On his way to the Tetekus' he heard the voices of the imams calling the faithful to prayer. The mosques were filling quickly as men snatched their toilet kettles in their rush to give thanks to Allah. The looming election and any campaigning could wait as far as these people were concerned. Grey wondered what the Sardauna in his palace was thinking. Was he so sure of his success that he was not bothered to do any campaigning at all? How was the Sardauna getting his message to these Hausa believers? Perhaps it was through the mouths of the imams in their Arabic tongue . . .

Then the noise rang out. It came from a jet plane flying so low that one could almost see the occupants. It was letting out thick smoke that

13

shaped itself into letters – the initials of the Yoruba Action Group party.

'Did you see that?' Grey shouted to his friend who was in the jeep with him.

'Yes, old boy,' Sergeant Giles Murray replied laughing. 'What a waste! Most Hausas can't read. Look at what it says in the clouds: "Vote AG.".'

'Ridiculous. How in the name of all that is sensible can one write political slogans for people who only understand the message of Allah?'

'Maybe the leader of the party, Odumosu, wants them to think the message is from Allah. Well, look at his timing – just when people are going to pray; and the message is written in the sky where Allah lives.'

'You may be right,' Alan agreed. 'But he would reach them better if he could rain chunks of meat, the way the local Alhajis do.'

'Do you know which foreign company was given the contract to mount this expensive campaign?'

'I can't say for sure, but that plane looks like one of ours,' Alan Grey replied, squinting his eyes at the sky.

'Then what are we moaning about, old boy? Let's just pray the Sardauna gets his people to vote for him.'

'He'll have to,' Grey said firmly.

They watched children chasing the flying pieces of paper that came from the aircraft, and heard them crying out excitedly, 'Indikpenda kpaper, indikpenda kpaper!'

When they approached the Sabon Garri, the atmosphere was different. People shouted abusive language at the plane and some were even trying to throw stones. Most of the strangers there were loyal to the NEPU/NCNC alliance, the opposition party headed by Dr Ozimba, whose 'eye' in the Hausa North was Alhaji Manliki. The Yoruba Chief Odumosu was only confusing the bemused Hausas by coming to the North to campaign in this impressive and extravagant way. As the two Englishmen drove slowly past a school, they heard a very angry teacher shouting at the disappearing plane, 'Who will vote for you Yorubas? All you know is mouth-mouth and so much show-off!' In desperation he began to ring the community school bell to drown the noise of the aircraft.

At the corner of the street that led to Sokoto Road where the Tetekus lived they were met by an enthusiastic group of drummers, mainly young men and women. Judging from their accents they were not Yorubas or Hausas but were Igbos and from other tribes. They sang, or rather shouted:

'Freedom, freedom!
Everywhere there must be freedom,
Freedom for you, freedom for me,
Everywhere there must be freedom!'

The music-makers and the dancers and the placard-carriers moved on and, to the onlookers' surprise, went into the inner city, the Hausa quarters.

'God help them,' Giles murmured to his superior officer.

'Yes, you're right there. They will need Him,' Grey replied slowly, as they came to the Tetekus' house.

Mr Teteku was lyrical in welcoming his guests. His wife, a plump woman in her late forties, embraced Alan like a member of the family and began straight away to pile food on the visitors. She would not accept their excuses that they had already eaten. They must eat. And they did, until Grey could feel his stomach distending like that of his host and hostess. Having recently returned from his annual home leave he was able to bring the couple up to date with news about their daughter Barbara, who was at Oxford with Debbie Ogedemgbe, and the conversation drifted to the politicians' last visit to London to ask for independence.

'I understand that Stella Ogedemgbe was the best-dressed wife of the whole lot. Lucky woman,' observed Mrs Teteku enviously.

'She swept the London streets with her trails of velvet,' Grey agreed. 'Still, she has to do that because of her husband's position.'

'Of course, of course,' put in Mr Teteku quickly. 'I only hope Samuel Ogedemgbe gets in as minister of finance after this election. If that happens I shall leave the North and go to the West. I want to work nearer home in Benin or Sapele.'

'This isn't a bad place, though. The Hausas are easy-going people,' Mrs Teteku said, recovering her composure.

'What do the Hausas think of all this ballyhoo going on around them? The Action Groupers throwing pieces of paper from the sky, and the NCNC dancing "Freedom for you and freedom for me" in the streets?' Grey asked in a tone he wanted to sound indifferent.

'I doubt if they do think about it, and I'll be surprised if they vote at all. But for the Southerners, the election is something worth fighting for. The Action Group is going to win three-quarters of the North, mark my words,' Mr Teteku predicted.

Alan Grey felt uncomfortable. No doubt the Tetekus wanted the Yoruba Action Group to win, for like the Ogedemgbes they were of the small Itsekiri tribe which claimed to be of Yoruba stock, and indeed

15

their language was similar. Ogedemgbe was Action Group too. None the less, if they should win, Macdonald in Lagos would find the country impossible to manage.

'The Sardauna will be very displeased if that happens,' Grey said.

'I don't think so,' Mrs Teteku replied. 'He is rich and powerful anyway, so he isn't interested in this new craze for power. He has everything money can buy and such a large family of Moslem preachers and leaders.'

Alan Grey said no more on the subject. The one thing he was certain of was that any profit to come out of Nigeria should go to Britain rather than to other countries. Having said that, he did not want to see the poor of the country poorer through power being handed to a few greedy politicians. To achieve the first objective, he had to ensure that the first prime minister was a Hausa man, preferably the Sardauna. To achieve the second aim would be more difficult. How could one curb the power of people like Samuel Ogedemgbe and Alhaji Manliki?'

Mrs Teteku's talk had reverted to the topic that never failed to delight her – her daughter Barbara. Babs was in the same class as the daughter of Ogedemgbe, the Nigerian money-man, as all Mrs Teteku's friends in Kano knew for she would talk for hours about the Ogedemgbe household. They were from the same minority tribe, and people knew that if all went well for the Ogedemgbes in the general election their relatives and tribesmen would not be forgotten. As a responsible person in Nigeria, one did not just go into politics to introduce reforms but to get what one could of the national cake and to use part of it to help one's vast extended family, the village of one's origin and if possible the whole tribe; at least in this way much of the ill-gotten money returned to the society.

Alan Grey told the Tetekus all they wanted to know about their daughter, about the party some firms had given for the Ogedemgbes, and of how he had brought Babs and Debbie from Oxford to see the Nigerian delegates in London. But he did not mention that at the party Ogedemgbe had concluded many important contracts with British whisky distillers or that Debbie had confided in him her anxieties about how her father came by the money he spent on her so lavishly . . .

Now, two weeks later in the governor's residence where they waited to hear the Sardauna's broadcast, Macdonald said, 'Whatever you do, Grey, keep the army on the alert. We may need them to keep

16

the peace. It's five-thirty now. Let's listen to some of the radio campaigning.'

The phone rang in another room and Macdonald was called away. Grey sat by the mahogany boxed radio listening to the greatest string of gibberish he had ever heard. One candidate claimed that the mother of his opposition member used to sell cocoyam leaves. Another burst into song on the air and, to the accompaniment of talking drums, told his constituents that if they voted for a person from a different tribe they would be selling their soul to the devil: 'If you offend a man from your own tribe you can beg him through the gods of his family. But if you offend a man who does not even understand your language, how can you tell which is his god? So I beg you to vote Action Group for your own good. The party of your tribe, your people!' The NCNC candidate for one of the Lagos constituencies appealed for national unity. Their party would fight for the independence of all Nigerians. Nigeria would then be an example to the whole black race . . .

The tone of the campaigning seemed very light to Alan Grey. However, it changed rather dramatically with the Sardauna coming on to make his announcement. He was not coming down to the South, whatever the result, and that was that. Macdonald entered the room at that moment.

'You see what I mean?'

Alan Grey nodded. 'Just in case, sir, do you have another person in mind to nominate?'

'Yes. Mallam Nguru Kano. But it would be so tidy if the Hausas could win, then no force would be used. And the government would last a long time since people would always convince themselves they had voted them into power. Our partiality would not be so blatantly obvious,' the governor concluded.

'My only fear is the Southern politicians, especially the Igbos whose party representatives in the North are all Hausas. That will delude people into thinking that if one of them can be chosen for the NCNC party then there can be nothing wrong in voting for him. As I said, I saw one of these men aping the Sardauna, feeding his voters and promising to go on doing so after the election.'

'That's not all. The Alhajis and their Emirs and Mallams are doing absolutely nothing to campaign for their cause. And while our chosen candidates are praying in their mosques, the Action Group has been well financed by some dubious companies and the Yoruba societies have borrowed thousands of pounds for their campaign.'

'Don't forget that for a long time the Yorubas have been very wealthy timber magnates, cocoa exporters, kernel and kolanut producers. The Ibos have never been as well off as the Yorubas, but maybe their time will come now that all these oil men are exploring their area. But at the moment their NCNC isn't half as rich as the AG.'

'I only hope the Hausas turn out to vote for their own men. If not, we'll have a great deal of explaining to do. All I know is that a Hausa man must be prime minister. That is the only way to maintain peace in this place.'

2 'Bakodaya'

After the Sardauna made his statement, parties in the South intensified their political campaigning. The Action Group changed their tune. Now they declared was the time for them to go to the North, to re-educate their brothers so that they could be in a position to share the national cake. The NCNC, on the other hand, were not as agitated as the AG. They felt smug in a way. They congratulated themselves on having foresight in their choice of candidates for the Hausa North and they kept reminding their opponents of their previous derogatory remarks about the Hausas.

Two days before the actual election, five hundred Hausa infantry descended on Lagos. The army barracks in Abeokuta, Lagos, and in other parts of the country, were drilled and put on alert. Brigadier Ene Onyemere had to return with his regiment from keeping the peace in the Congo and they were stationed at the Army Depot, Yaba, in Lagos. The air was tense with excitement, apprehension and even hope.

The election day itself was an anticlimax, after all the ballyhoo and the preparations. There were a few fights at the Lagos polls, where at least a fifth of the population knew or had a little idea of what it all meant. For those who did not understand, the political candidates simply hired canoes to bring voters to the polls. The fishermen around the creeks in Lagos and Badagry areas were persuaded and then bullied, by men who dressed like water policemen, into coming to vote. Their wives screamed in terror, not knowing what was happening. A woman was smoking her herrings peaceably and breastfeeding her baby when the party workers paddled to her bamboo hut which stood precariously on stilts. They told her that she was to come and vote for her freedom. She replied that she did not want to, and could they please tell her what she had done to warrant the visitation of such strange men in European uniform. One party worker got fed up with

19

trying to explain to her what it was about and merely gave the order that all the Ilaje people living along the creeks should be bundled into open canoes and taken to St Jude's School in Ebute Metta to cast their votes. They were screaming, thinking that they had done something wrong. At the polling station, voters' cards were quickly improvised and they voted for whichever party had taken the trouble to bring them into town. They were fed and calmed and then paddled back to their huts in the swamps. This pattern was not unique to Lagos. Market women were collected in big American cars and taken in droves to the polling stations. Most of them did not know which party they voted for; all they knew was that they were given VIP treatment and had a ride in the leader's car.

As for the educated but unemployed Nigerians or the partly starved school-teachers, it was their day. Their reason for voting was mainly tribal. They hoped that if their tribesman got in as an MP then he would secure them more lucrative posts.

Towards the evening there was big confusion. Most of the party workers did not know whether they were coming or going. Most of the actual candidates were too tired to say or do much. They just watched helplessly. They knew it was not a case of 'one man, one vote' but of forcing as many ballot papers as possible into your box in the short time allocated. Many people voted not twice but three or four times for whichever party leader had given them most money.

The highlight of the day came in the early evening, when the voting booths were packed with manual workers who had been at work all day. Then from Yaba came the heavy sound of army trucks. Soldiers perched inside them with guns held in position. People ran for their lives, and amidst the noise and confusion women's cries could be heard. These women, it was said, had rigged votes. They were said to have had about a hundred ballot papers each, nicely tied in their enormous lappa cloths, and to have simply poured them into the ballot boxes. Fifty of these women were rounded up and brought to Lagos prison. The soldiers terrorized them into confession, and it then came out that they had each been given a 'dash' of twenty pounds. They were jailed for a month, but any attempt to trace which names they used in voting was useless. It came out much later that more people voted in some constituencies than were registered. But still a kind of shaky order was forced on people at the end of it all.

People did not hear much about the North. But the Southern politicians were further shocked when they learned that the Hausas were voting to the last man. Dr Ozimba of the Eastern region breathed easier; his NCNC alliance would do well in the North. Stories were told of polling booths belonging to some Action Group candidates disappearing or being openly burned. Still their leader, Chief Oluremi Odumosu, did not despair. All his party needed to be in the majority was a few Northern seats.

On the second day, it was as if the entire country had gone to sleep. All was so quiet. The politicians were exhausted. But the radio stations came into their own as they began to announce results. By evening, the fate of the South had been almost decided. The East went solidly to Dr Ozimba's NCNC party.

Though the NCNC had started as a national party to combat the tentacles of colonialism, in this election it had been pushed into becoming an all-Igbo party. It was able to gain all the Igbo seats in the East, and a large slice of the Benin area, and many votes even in the thick Yoruba towns, such as Ilesha, and some parts of Ibadan. Before the fate of the Hausa North was decided, many thinking Nigerians expected Dr Ozimba to be the first prime minister of the whole federation, for he was one of the most prominent Africans of those days. He was well educated in all branches of political ideology, a firm believer in Pan-Africanism, a charismatic leader, and an everlasting scholar, philosopher and idealist. He himself took it for granted that there would be little dispute about it. The fact that many of the elected candidates for the Northern section of his party were Hausas seemed to seal the issue. So no one thought it wrong for him to move to the capital, Lagos, before the results were known.

But when the election results started pouring out from the excited radio announcers, the Action Group knew right away that the best they could gain would be to be in the opposition. They could not form a coalition with the Hausas, because of the insults they had heaped on these people, and moving in with the Igbos was out of the question for they suspected that with the Igbos they would not see the light of day any more.

In the early hours of the third day, the results coming from the North were shaking everybody in the country, most of all Dr Ozimba. It was becoming clear that while the NCNC looked as if they would gain a handful of seats there and the Yoruba party none at all, the NNP Hausa party was sweeping the whole North. The Nigerian Broadcasting Corporation kept the announcement of the decisive results to the last minute, perhaps to taunt the over-confident Southern leaders. Then the results of about twenty Northern candidates came to the ears of stunned Southern Nigerians:

'The Sardauna of Sokoto, 500,000 votes; his opponents, *bakodaya*.

'Alhaji Mallam Nguru Kano, 4,000,000 votes; his AG opponents, *bakodaya*.

'Alhaji Latifu Bello, 600,000 votes; his AG and NCNC opponents, *bakodaya*.

'Alhaji Tajudeen Zungeru, 5,000,000 votes; his AG opponent, *bakodaya*.

'Alhaji Usman Madagari, 4,500,000 votes; his AG opponent, *bakodaya*.

'Alhaji Sikiru Momoh, 400,000 votes; his AG opponent, *bakodaya* . . .'

After about ten minutes of these singsong results, the boys at the broadcasting station had turned it into a song ending with the refrain '*bakodaya*'.

Governor Macdonald laughed heartily for the first time, and so did all the expatriate guests there with him in his elegant high-ceilinged residence.

'What is *bakodaya*?' asked the wife of one of the managers of the Esso company.

'It means "nothing, nothing at all",' Alan Grey answered, displaying his knowledge of the Hausa language.

'What?' asked Macdonald, his face red with amusement. 'Not even one single vote?'

'I'm afraid so.'

The night was pleasantly warm. The only noise in that part of Lagos where the governor and his previously worried guests were was the gentle lapping of waves on the marina close by. The few muted electric lights were not really necessary on an evening like this. They were all outside in the large lawn-covered garden that was full of perfectly tended wild roses. Looking at these people, from whom laughter floated lazily as they sat in this beautiful atmosphere, one would think that the passport to a happy life must surely be to persuade one's maker to colour one's skin pink. Black male servants, in heavy headgear and khaki uniform trimmed in red, padded barefoot among the guests giving ice to this one, gin to that, and tonic to another. Even the servants noticed that the forced hush of earlier in the evening had somewhat gone. Happiness rippled not far from the surface.

Macdonald stood up and toasted to the Commonwealth. The others followed suit, amid almost unnatural laughter. Alan Grey laughed the longest, remembering his father's toast in London.

Macdonald downed another glass of whisky, then walked briskly into his office. He made two telephone calls. One was to Mallam Nguru Kano, telling him that he had nominated him as the first Prime

Minister of Nigeria and that he had every right to start his term of office at once: 'And let me be the first to congratulate you, Mallam Nguru. I am announcing it to the Nigerian Broadcasting Corporation straight away,' which he then did.

Macdonald's guests in the garden stopped talking when the radio they had installed there boomed a news-flash:

'The governor-general has nominated Mallam Nguru Kano to be the first Prime Minister of Nigeria.'

Dr Ozimba, in his large sitting-room in Yaba, in another part of Lagos, threw up his hands. His assistant Dr Eze felt like crying for this man who had done so much for Nigeria. The imprisonment, the self-denial and the sleepless nights of planning speech after speech – all for nothing.

Mrs Ozimba could not help shouting: 'But this is unfair. What have the Hausas done for Nigeria? They sat there in the North while we Igbos did everything. Who introduced this way of choosing leaders, anyway? I can see no peace in this country with this kind of treachery.'

'Keep quiet, woman . . .' Dr Ozimba began.

'But the Madam is right, sir,' said Dr Eze, his mouth tasting bitter. 'How does that man know the Hausas are going to win? We have had only forty results out of a hundred and ninety from the North. Suppose the tide turns? Oh, dear!' Dr Eze slumped into a cushioned chair, and he saw the leader of his party shaking his head. It was true that there had only been forty results so far, but apart from the two seats gained by the NCNC the rest had gone to the Hausas, and the AG candidates had lost their deposits.

'No, Eze, we are dealing with a power greater than we are . . . Listen, listen; the Sardauna is talking.'

The rich voice of the Sardauna repeated what he had said previously, that he did not wish to come down to the South, but was sending his 'right eye' down to be his presence in the South.

Yorubas all over the federation were shocked at the speed of it all, how everything seemed to fit neatly as if planned and rehearsed to the last letter. But they accepted defeat quickly, while planning how to circumvent it. If it had to be a choice between two evils, the Hausas were the better, being Moslems like three-quarters of the Yoruba-speaking peoples of Nigeria.

Chief Oluremi Odumosu of the West, the leader of the Yoruba party, said to his deputy, 'This is just the beginning, you know. As I see it, the great battle is still ahead. Then we will have the Nigeria we dream of, where we will really be free, where we will be ruled by our own people, not by these *gworo*-eating wanderers from the North. We must get to work forthwith. We must change our image to the Hausas, meanwhile I will go to the Federal House in Lagos to see how we can change this method of voting. Otherwise, we shall be ruled by the Hausas till the end of time.'

'I am sorry, I am very sorry,' said Chief Durosaro, the assistant party leader. 'But this is very bad. Nobody is going to be satisfied with this. Yes, I share your dream. We shall have a new Nigeria. But it must be called something else – maybe after one of the early Yoruba kingdoms, like Ife or Oduduwa – a name we choose for our country by ourselves. These English people have their fingers in very pie. Look at all the party money we paid their boys for that aeroplane campaign. Oh, God, how silly we must have looked to the Hausas!'

'To think those people made us believe we were contesting an election, when they knew the result in advance because they planned it.'

The results still poured from the radio, and the word '*bakodaya*' was in every sentence. Soon all the children in the street started to sing along:

'*Inakuana, Inagejiya, bakodaya!*
Inakuana, Inagejiya, bakodaya!'

Dr Ozimba saw his guests out. He switched off the radio and as he did so he saw some shadows moving in the compound. He called his wife, and when they put on their street lights they saw four heavily armed men walking away from their home.

'What is it? What does it mean?' Rosita Ozimba asked her husband with fear.

He smiled wearily and covered her mouth gently with his moist hand. 'Shh,' he cautioned. 'Don't say anything. You know why those soldiers are outside? Someone has got it into his head that I'll be so unhappy about the turn of events I might be tempted to try and mobilize our Igbo people. Those behind this know our people would not hesitate to fight. But I am a man of peace, Rosita, you know that. So they will be disappointed. I am not going to fight with bullets.'

Mrs Ozimba let her self-control slip and gave in to anguished tears. 'Everyone thought it was a sure thing. I never dreamed you would even have a rival, to say nothing of being in opposition. Oh, if only we had insight into the future, I would have advised you to give up the struggle and let the British rule us forever.'

'Stop crying,' he said, idly smoothing the glossy, still black hair on his wife's head. 'Well, how do you know they are not going to rule us forever? I mean the British. Anyway all is not lost. At least we are independent, on paper maybe, but it is a beginning.'

If Dr Ozimba and his wife were hurt by the events of that evening, the soldiers, especially those in the senior ranks of officer and colonel, were more than hurt; they were baffled at how things had happened, while they were helpless to do anything about them. But the saddest of all was Colonel John Nwokolo, when he was commanded to go with four soldiers to keep an eye on the movements of his political idol:

'If he shows any move to organize a force on his side, he should be arrested, and if there is any kind of resistance, he should be eliminated.'

Nwokolo prayed fervently in the damp bushes surrounding the Ozimbas' residence that such a move would not be necessary. God heard his prayers, for Ozimba had quickly rationalized the situation; he was a practical politician, not an emotional type. So John Nwokolo's duty was not as difficult as he had feared. In moments of solitude after that night he asked himself many times whether he would have shot Dr Ozimba dead if he had organized a civil uprising. He still did not know what he would have done, but he thanked his personal god that the situation had not arisen.

At the barracks he ran into Saka Momoh and the latter said by way of salutation: 'You see that we will have to stay in Nigeria to defend the ordinary people from this kind of corruption. They call this an election? Pooh!'

'It is not an election but a time bomb. It will explode soon, you mark my words. How many of us are going to sit on our backsides and let this happen? Mallam Nguru Kano the first Nigerian Prime Minister indeed! This result is like playing *Hamlet* without the prince. Can you imagine a Nigerian government without the great Dr Ozimba?'

'Well, at least we have the majesty of Nguru's hooded eye-lids and his pope-like gestures,' Momoh replied sarcastically.

Nwokolo saluted his senior officer and marched away angrily into the greying night.

'A time bomb . . . a time bomb . . . how very apt! Maybe, my dear young officer, the answer is to elect a new prince – not necesarily your Dr Ozimba,' Momoh murmured to himself as he made his way to his temporary home in Lagos to spend a quiet night with his wife Elizabeth, who was expecting their first child.

3 The Republic

Samuel Ogedemgbe rolled this way and that on his cool white-sheeted bed. Then he opened his eyes to the pale green walls and large French-curtained windows. He heaved a big sigh of relief. Yes, it had all been worth it. Now he could really sleep, rest and do his bit of the job of keeping the country out of trouble. It had all been worth it. He tried to lie on his stomach, but it was not possible; he was too fat, the bed too soft, his surroundings too rich. He heard a car pull up in front of his magnificent house. He tensed himself for a moment, wondering who it could be so early in the morning. In any case, there was no reason to worry, the ministerial guards by the door would ward off any unwanted intruders. He should get up, though; he did not want the poor people in his constituency to start saying, 'Look at him, we voted for him only a month ago, now he sleeps all day long.' He pulled the bell cord near his Victorian brass bed and his personal male servant came in.

'Morning, sah!' He saluted like a soldier.

Ogedemgbe ignored him, preoccupied with freeing himself from his tangled bedclothes and carefully finding the carpeted floor to put his plump feet on.

'Good morning, sah!' the over-enthusiastic servant shouted again, clicking his bare heels to attention.

'Oh, go to hell!' the new minister shouted back at him.

Sikiru Lemomu, the veteran Hausa man, smiled quietly. He went to the aid of his master and together they were able to put the bulk of Samuel Ogedemgbe on the floor. Sikiru was a servant in a million who had been with Ogedemgbe since he was just an ordinary timber trader. The man could neither read nor write, but he had all the good qualities which distinguish the Hausas. He was loyal to near stupidity. He was very protective of his master to the extent that Ogedemgbe would rather trust his life to him than to his own people. Sikiru had fought in the 1939–45 war, one of those huge Hausa army guards popularly known as 'Korofo Gwodogwodo' who, it was said, would only obey the first word of command from their masters, not bothering to think that there might be a second word or another command coming. So if the master said, 'Shoot!' the Korofo would go on shooting until he had emptied his gun. Sikiru was not a young man; he was about the same age as his master though one would not think it looking at the two of them struggling to get the latter dressed and ready to face the public. Sikiru was agile and had shaved his hair off completely to reveal a head that seemed too small in proportion to the rest of his body. His eyes were sharp and dark, and looked as if they were outlined with some dark pencil. He was a solid, silent man and all secrets were safe with him.

'Whose car is that?' asked Samuel Ogedemgbe from the bathroom where he was taking his shower.

'*Bature*,' Sikiru replied in his monosyllabic way, as usual touching the front of his skull-like head first.

'Hmm,' grunted Ogedemgbe, wondering what white man would come to him so early in the morning. Did these people not realize that the politicians had spent almost a year preparing, campaigning and winning the election – could they not have some peace now? One needed time to recharge one's battery before taking up the staff of office. He had been fortunate in not having strong opposition in his constituency in the Mid-West. He was too well known, and the few 'don't knows' were bought with money, gifts and promises of better things. And he had got the post he wanted of Minister of Finance. But others had not fared so well. Chief Odumosu, for example, had not dreamed of finding himself in opposition, thinking that at the very worst he could form a coalition with the Northern Hausa party. Not in his wildest imaginings did he think the Igbo NCNC would join forces with the North. Ogedemgbe knew that for everybody's sake they had to make it work.

His wife Stella came into his dressing-room, looking immaculately beautiful as usual.

'You slept well?' she asked casually, looking not too friendlily at Sikiru who stood motionless like a rod. She knew he would not move an inch unless ordered by his master. She continued in a whisper, 'There's a Mr Shepherd to see you.'

'Shepherd? I don't think I know him.'

'Of course you do. He came to see us in London about the whisky, remember? We should have charged him a good ten per cent to start

27

with, you know.' She came closer and wiped the shaving cream off his rough chin.

'Wasn't he to pay your "company" ten per cent after the first batch sold?'

'Yes, but we didn't keep a record of the number of crates in the first batch. The crook now tells me he hasn't sold any of it yet, since he was waiting for the election results. So how come we bought whisky of the same brand in Sapele during the campaign, if he claims he hasn't begun selling it? At this rate there'll never be an end to the so-called first batch,' she pointed out impatiently.

Her husband made a sign to Sikiru to leave the room. 'Sit down, Debbie's mother.' He looked seriously at her and then continued: 'This is Lagos, you know. I am now at the height of my ambition. You must help me see to it that there is no breath of scandal near the name Ogedemgbe. You saw what's been happening over ministerial posts – lifelong friends like our colleagues Chief Odumosu and his tribesman Durosaro have quarrelled so much that I'm sure they wouldn't hesitate to kill each other. That's what politics does to people. Something tells me that there's trouble ahead. The Igbos are very angry at the way Alhaji Nguru Kano has been elected.'

'But the governor has the power to nominate whoever he likes, doesn't he?'

'He has the power to nominate from the party that gained most seats.'

'The Hausas gained most seats, and Nguru Kano is a Hausa. I don't see what all the trouble is about. The Igbos are too greedy for my liking. Isn't it enough that their man has been tipped as first president? Must they leave nothing for the other tribes?'

'Shh,' Ogedemgbe hushed his wife. 'We have much more to worry about than that ten per cent which will eventually be paid anyway. That stupid governor has made a mistake. He should have waited for the final results. This way, it looks as if it was planned. He must apologize to the nation and hold a press conference soon. Then we can all sleep better.'

'Oh, it will be all right,' Stella said, sweeping a jewelled arm in the air with abandon. She had prayed for her husband to be elected a federal minister and he had been lucky; coming from a minority tribe, he could not hope for more. 'The Igbos will quieten down when they get used to the fact that the Alhaji can be as good a prime minister as their beloved Dr Ozimba.' She moved towards the door and then turned. 'Incidentally, Madam Osajofo has been sent to Warri prison, Mr Shepherd was just telling me.'

'What was she caught doing this time?'

'Oh, the same thing, her illicit gin trade. But she added a touch of drama this time. She put gallons of her gin in a coffin and got her two male helpers to carry it. She followed, with her hands on her head and her hair completely shaved off so that no one recognized her. She had the audacity to carry out this charade in the market, crying that her cousin who came to visit her had died suddenly. She said she was taking the dead cousin to her husband's village in Effurun area, and her sorrow was so great that people didn't stop her.'

Ogedemgbe was so convulsed with laughter at this point that the bath towel round his expansive stomach almost fell off. 'Who in the name of all that is holy discovered she was faking?'

'A group of children playing outside a hut on the fringes of the town remarked that the chief and only mourner looked like Madam Osajofo. She must have thought she had passed the danger zone and lapsed into her usual way of walking. As soon as her carriers heard the children mention her name, they dropped their 'corpse' and ran. She's been jailed for eight years, and most of her stalls and valuables confiscated.'

'Poor woman.' For a moment, conscience pricked them both and they were quiet, knowing that the ban on local alcohol enabled them to import the foreign liquor and take ten per cent of its profit. As if to justify himself, Ogedemgbe said, 'Our local gin is not well treated. It burns into one's system and isn't good for any living thing. People like her who think they are above the law must be shown up as public examples. Sentences should be so stiff that it won't be worth anyone's while to dabble in it again . . .'

When he eventually went down to see his guest he left all jocularity behind, reminding the Scot that he was only acting for the good of his country, not wishing his people's insides to be burned by local gin. Shepherd began to say that the liquor sent for export was even stronger than that on the British market, and here they both stopped like thieves who had inadvertently caught each other out. But Ogedemgbe was conceded the point that the Scotch whisky was definitely cleaner than the Nigerian brew, and he laid down his terms: that the first batch of imported whisky was to end twenty-one days from then, whether or not it was all sold. He, Samuel Ogedemgbe, was a busy man. After that, his percentage should be paid to a named Swiss bank account. The whisky man from Britain, having been reminded that he was being greatly favoured, bowed himself out, but not before leaving a case of twelve large bottles of whisky with the new minister of finance's guard.

A few days later, the House of Representatives in Lagos met. The ministers' disappointment again dominated the topics of the day. There was no doubt about it, many were very bitter. Chief Oluremi Odumosu called on Governor Macdonald to resign and go back to his country. Many supported this motion, but the Igbos under Dr Ozimba, though the most offended, were more cautious. It was decided that the governor should be given a chance to say his piece on why it was that he had nominated Alhaji Nguru Kano before the final result was heard. They wanted to find out from him if he had known beforehand what the outcome of the election would be, how his prediction had been correct.

Macdonald was hurt by this reaction of people he thought he was saving from slashing each other's throats, as he said to Alan Grey later that evening.

'Do you know what would have happened if I had waited for the last slow-moving Alhaji to crawl tortoise-like to the polls, when it was apparent that they would win eventually? There would have been complete anarchy. The Igbos thought that whatever happened I was going to invite their man Ozimba to form the government. As for the Yorubas, they still believe that money can buy everything. Well, it did not buy the Hausas this time.'

'Look, sir, tell them that you're sorry – '

'Sorry! You must be out of your military mind. Would your father have done that?'

The senior Grey would have been too proud to apologize to Africans, but would he have got himself into a situation like this, Alan wondered? Still, it was about time people like Macdonald started treating the natives as equals.

'What is the world coming to?' raged the governor, puffing furiously at his fat cigar. 'Good Lord, these people don't even know what democracy means.'

'Do we know what democracy really means ourselves?' Alan asked, a mischievous smile on his narrow face.

Macdonald stopped in his stride. 'Do you know, you should be in the diplomatic service, instead of wearing that ridiculous uniform.'

'Well, I don't think I am far from being in the diplomatic service. My colleagues and I are here to give friendly advice on the use of arms.

We don't want them shooting each other in the streets, do we, especially as they would have to do it with guns bought from England?'

'And no expatriate wants to be shot down in the street. You take care of that side of things. There are five of you, aren't there?'

'Yes,' Alan nodded, 'but only two in the army. The rest are in other professions.'

There was a pause in which Macdonald realized for the first time that he simply had to do what this innocent-looking young man said. He was glad he would be leaving after the swearing-in of Dr Ozimba as first president, but meanwhile he would have to explain his nomination of Mallam Nguru Kano to the useful post of prime minister.

'We are very lucky that the Hausas eventually won the election, don't you think, sir? Suppose after Nguru Kano had been chosen the results showed that they had lost? The situation would have been chaotic.'

Macdonald started to smile into the smoke he was puffing out of his cigar. Yes, the younger man was right. If the Igbos or another tribe had won, how could he have explained his move? Or had he hurriedly put Nguru Kano there just in case the others won? He could have told them that he had the ultimate authority as the Queen's representative to nominate anybody he liked as prime minister. Either way, it would have been very nasty. Yet apologize to them? No, it would be a matter of telling them why he had done what he did, and that was a small price to pay for what might have happened.

The next evening Macdonald held a press conference in the governor's palace, during which he congratulated the Nigerian people on their civilized behaviour in the recent election. He told them that the black race all over the world was looking to countries like Nigeria and Ghana for inspiration and for liberation. He encouraged them to keep their green and white flag flying. He had chosen Alhaji Nguru Kano, a very noble and respected Hausa man from the North, after he knew from the first results that the North was going to win. The results from the Northern hinterland took too long to be announced in Lagos. It was unsafe to leave the seat of prime minister vacant until the last Hausa vote was counted. That might have tempted any irresponsible group to seize power; he had seen it happen in other countries. He was not saying that there could be such a nonsensical civil war in Nigeria, for he knew that the people of Nigeria were too level-headed. Yet he had not wished to take any chances. Their well-loved politician Dr Ozimba would be the nation's first president, and the Honourable Chief Oluremi Odumosu from the West would be the opposition leader in the Federal House. Macdonald said he was sorry if these decisions had caused misunderstanding in certain quarters; they should please bear with him. He was only doing what he knew was good for Nigeria, and his decisions were backed by Britain, which was the mother country of all Nigerians by right, both as colonial subjects and now as citizens of a member of the Commonwealth of Nations. He invited all Nigerians to celebrate with him the birth of this great nation, and he congratulated them all on this great and historic occasion . . .

After such an eloquent and heartfelt speech, who could blame Nigerians for feeling ten feet tall? They felt they must be worth something for the governor-general to apologize.

The Nigerian people love celebrations, whether of the birth of a baby or the death of an old beggar. Now they were going to celebrate their freedom, and celebrate in style, after their long and hard time with the British oppressors, and any political dissatisfactions were pushed aside. The jobless young people were given the work of painting the streets and hanging up flags. For the newly appointed senior servicemen it became the thing to own an Independence car. These cars had originally been ordered from America to take visiting dignitaries about the country during the celebrations, but the Nigerian senior civil servants would not be left behind. There were families who had little to eat yet must be seen in one of these vehicles that looked more like winged aeroplanes than cars, painted the colours of the Nigerian flag. Many streets that had been named after British missionaries, diplomats, kings and queens were renamed to honour members of the political parties of the day.

When eventually Princess Alexandra, the Queen's representative, came and the British flag was lowered, the celebrations reached a feverish peak. If one could not afford one of the long green and white cars, at least one could afford a few yards of cotton material with 'Nigeria' and 'Independence 1960' printed all over it. Here you saw a whole family turned out in the same cloth, there a musician was singing the ballad history of the country. Some of the soldiers, the elite who had managed to leave the peace-keeping force in the Congo and come home, were glad that they had for there was no need for them to work. People were too happy to fight each other. This euphoria lasted a long time.

The Moslems shouted thanks to Allah until they went hoarse. The Christians went to their different churches and cathedrals to take part in thanksgiving services. It was towards the end of one of these services that the politicians knew that trouble was not far from the surface. Chief Oluremi Odumosu's wife was well turned out for the service in an expensive lace outfit which she had thought would be seen on her and nobody else. But during the service who should turn up in the same material but the wife of their former friend Chief Durosaro.

'We must do something about this,' she hissed to her husband.

Odumosu's appointment as leader of the opposition gave him little power in the Federal House. To go back to his former constituency and ask his former friend and supporter to give way because he wanted his old post back would seem ridiculous. Yet that was exactly what his wife and his people wanted him to do. Nor was this all. Chief Durosaro suspected that he was expected to step down gracefully for his former friend and politicial leader, but he was not going to do so. It was not his fault that the leader of the Yoruba party left his regional post to go to the Federal House in the hope of becoming the first prime minister. Well, Macdonald and the Hausas had outplayed him at his own game. That was politics; one could not expect to win all the time. But the leader of the party knew what he would be missing. The Yoruba West was a very wealthy and easy-going region for any political leader. He would lord it over all those political chiefs, and of course the important contracts would have to go through the regional premier. Odumosu must have been made to give up all that in the first place. When he had the idea of being prime minister, his wife – now standing beside him, angry that someone was wearing the same outfit as her – had not bothered to stop him or tell him that he might not succeed. But who could blame her? They had all been so confident of their success. 'I bet that treacherous thief knew it all along. I bet he is laughing at us. Now his wife has the audacity to wear the same outfit as my wife. Yes, this must be stopped, or people may start preferring him to me as leader of the party which I founded,' Odumosu mused.

He jolted himself to sensibility when he noticed that all eyes were on him in the middle of the church. His wife nudged him, reminding him that he was to read the first lesson. He rushed to the pulpit and began to read haltingly but with growing confidence. When he returned to his seat he was somewhat taken aback when his wife told him that she had ordered Mrs Durosaro to go home and change her outfit. But though Mrs Durosaro looked really angry she did not leave the church. Chief Durosaro gave the leader and his wife a black look as he went to read the second lesson.

The CMS bishop of the federation, not knowing that a battle was going on under his nose, remarked in his sermon that unity was going to reign in Nigeria. He invited the congregation to look at the two leaders of the party who though they had not won and become the party to form a government yet came to church with one mind wearing the same clothes. Chief Odumosu nearly choked in suppressed anger and was determined to push his lieutenant from that post.

Two of the army brigadiers sitting at the back of the church with their different officers guessed that all was far from well. Outside the church, Saka Momoh, now a colonel, shook the hand of Brigadier Onyemere who, like him, had been allowed a short leave from the Congo for the Nigerian celebrations. Momoh grinned from ear to ear and remarked:

'Sir, do you see a cloud in the sky?'

'I think I am beginning to see it very clearly, Colonel.'

They and their troops formed a guard of honour for the newly appointed President Ozimba and the other senior ministers to pass through.

'A president without any power,' murmured Captain John Nwokolo, as the men walked past to their various Mercedes cars and the especially built limousines.

4   *The First Confrontation*

Alan Grey woke up to an avalanche of noise coming from the bush near the small hotel in Ikeja, on the outskirts of Lagos. He could distinctly place the lone song of a bird he had come to regard as his friend. It would start on a high note, then would go very low, and then in jerks like someone trying desperately to subdue a painful sob. It sounded as if it was calling a lost mate. The poor bird had been going on this way for the three days he had been in the hotel. It did not monopolize his thoughts for long today, for a group of frogs suddenly awakened, drowning its voice in their croaky calls. Cocks from nearby farms seemed determined to outdo the other animals. The noises soon jammed together in one confused harmony. What a contrast it was to his mornings in England, where even the birds were much more polite and had a gentle way of waking one.

He switched his attention away from the African morning sounds and looked at himself, naked to the waist. He stretched his arms and opened his mouth to yawn, but chuckled when he saw the saliva shooting from his mouth like that of a frightened snake. He checked his amusement in order not to wake his partner. He looked at her now, still asleep and breathing gently. He stared at her high forehead, proud even in sleep, the smoothness of the arm that lay outside the sheet and the richness of the shapely lips which looked as though they would burst into a smile at any moment. He wondered why he had always been attracted to the brownness of the African woman. To his own people he knew that this colour meant primitiveness, backwardness and savagery. But to him it was excitement, richness, moistness, newness. He wondered what his father would say if he knew Alan had waited two whole nights in this hotel so that Debbie Ogedemgbe could come all the way from Oxford to join him. He could imagine his father

35

saying, 'The native woman is only an adventure, dear boy, don't get too involved with her.'

Was he getting too involved? Would Debbie now that she had finished her degree want him to be more involved with her? She was such an independent soul who did not look forward to being tied down yet ... Well, who could blame her? With her father's millions in Nigeria and in Switzerland, why should she, until it became absolutely necessary? Alan did not wish to be tied down either until he had seen enough of the world. And whatever happened, he was not going to do his tying down with a girl like Debbie, for all her Oxford knowhow. She was slim and pretty, but arrogant. She was intelligent, nice to be with, but independent. She was too English for his liking. If he was going to go native, he might as well do it properly. The way he saw it, people like her were building themselves big identity problems. 'Poor Debbie,' he murmured as he ran his fingers over her body under the sheet.

She woke at this, and her smile was wide as she stretched. She had lost a lot of weight and was still tired from late nights studying for her final university exams. As soon as they were over, she had left college early, so that she and Alan could be together for a few days before she let her parents know she was back in Nigeria.

She turned to him and sat upright, her straight back tantalizing. In a moment of carelessness, he asked:

'Have you ever thought of marriage, Debbie?'

She burst out laughing, though there was gentleness in her laughter.

'Definitely not to you! My parents would kill me, and your father's grey moustache would never stop quivering. But right now I would bless you forever if you can convince those people downstairs that there's an invalid up here who would appreciate breakfast in her room.'

Four days later, he saw her to a taxi that was to take her home, very much refreshed. Alan looked round the room to make sure they had left nothing incriminating, then checked out and returned to his barracks.

He learned that Chijioke Abosi, whom he had known since Sandhurst, had been looking for him to invite him to his forthcoming wedding. Then he found himself faced with the fact of some of the rumours he had read in the newspapers. There was a battle of words going on in the Western region. The two chiefs, Odumosu and Durosaro, were at each other's throats and had gone as far as organizing thugs to bully each other's relatives and friends. It was necessary to recall as many Nigerian soldiers as possible from the UN forces in the Congo, and there were signs that the size of the standing army would have to be increased, headed by a Nigerian brigadier or colonel. So there was a great deal of work for Alan Grey.

In addition, Dr Ozimba was to be officially sworn in as president. It would be virtually a public holiday, on which he would make a speech to wind up the Independence celebrations. Everyone, even the Hausas who formed the majority in the government, seemed somehow ill-at-ease at this show-piece of an appointment. Dr Ozimba had fought for the independence of Nigeria. His NCNC party had started as a national party which cut across tribes, but it had been pushed into becoming one mainly for the Igbos when a rival predominantly Yoruba party sprang up, appealing to its members' ethnicity. Nobody had guessed that the post of prime minister of the new nation would go to the leader of the Hausa party that did not even exist when the diplomatic wranglings for Independence were taking place.

Now Alan Grey and Saka Momoh found themselves arranging the transfer of regiments to the North, in case the millions of Igbos there should start making trouble for this slighting of their leader. Some were sent to the West under Oladapo, another of Grey's former students from Sandhurst, and the rest remained stationed in Lagos. No trouble was expected from the Igbos in the East.

But Dr Ozimba grew in stature on that day he was sworn in at the biggest square in Lagos. He preached peace, to calm his Igbo followers, and reassured the whole nation that he was not bitter. If his speech was a purely diplomatic exercise, then it was well staged, for few doubted his sincerity though he sounded a little tired. His listeners were reminded of the biblical story of Moses leading his people for forty years, only to realize in the end that he would never set foot in the Promised Land of which they had all dreamed and for which they had suffered, since the time they were slaves. Ozimba, like Moses before him, took it philosophically. What else could he do? Had he wanted to try to take up arms, how many soldiers would have supported him? Only the socially disadvantaged went into the army, those who were failures financially and academically. For him to stoop to ask for the help of such social rejects was out of the question. Even if he had swallowed his pride, it was well known that the Nigerian army was nothing but a regiment of the British one; the greater part of the expense of maintaining it was borne by the British taxpayer as part of Britain's foreign-aid policy. Most of the Nigerian soldiers were employed directly by the British officers. Dr Ozimba would have been fighting against a bigger power than the whole of Nigeria could overcome.

So he accepted his humble position with superficial gratitude and promised to be the adviser and father of the nation, as if it were possible. Many people went home with mixed feelings, though pacified over all.

If there were lingering doubts in the minds of the thousands packed in the square that day, they were overshadowed by the military display. The police and soldiers marched past the new president while he took the salute in his white robe, grinning without joy, like any Western diplomat would. The national anthem, the words of which were given to the nation by an English housewife, was sung and schoolchildren waved their newly acquired flag with its green and white bands.

Afterwards an open car slowly drove the new president and his wife out of the square, smiling and waving at the crowd who bowed as they passed. The Ogedemgbes, like most of the ministers, followed in their limousine, standing up to acknowledge the cheers of the hordes of people who saw in them a dream of richness come true.

An announcement had been made at the ceremony that Mallam Nguru Kano had also been knighted, though he was not cheered, for his name was still too new; Ozimba, on the other hand, who had been at the game of Nigerian politics for almost thirty years, was enthusiastically acknowledged with the shortened form of his name, 'Zimmm!' Sir Nguru Kano, standing in his open car without a wife, since as a Moslem woman she was not allowed to take part in such outward show, sensed that his appointment was not liked, and his unmoved look seemed to challenge anyone to say a word against it. He was as always tall, majestic, silent and distant. People looked at him with awe.

Away from the crowd, the Ogedemgbes relaxed their public face.

'Wasn't it lovely?' Debbie enthused. 'The schoolchildren, the police officers, and as for the soldiers – they really excelled themselves today.'

'Well, everybody smiled when they all felt like crying. Look at Ozimba. I've never seen such a great actor,' Samuel Ogedemgbe said.

'Nguru Kano looked so thoughtful, as if he was seeing a ghost,' Debbie said.

'The funny thing is, he is the only one who ought to be laughing, yet he looked not only serious but unhappy too.'

'I quite liked the army display,' Stella Ogedemgbe remarked.

'They should be good, for the amount of money they are costing the government. They are a luxury we can do without. Imagine employing grown men just to march up and down on occasions. Even ants do better.'

'Oh, Papa, look what they did in the Congo. Look at how the

illiterate soldiers in Ethiopia helped restore Haile Selassie to his throne. Now educated men are going into the army for the love of defending their country. Surely you should be proud of them.'

'Since the general election over a year ago, we've only had a few small disturbances. You don't need an army for those. What we need is a good police force doing its job well, and we have that. Yet we keep enough soldiers to defend the whole of Africa.'

That evening at the state banquet the Ogedemgbes as usual surpassed everyone in their turn-out. There was such a big show of wealth, and the women came in the latest lace designs. Stella Ogedemgbe and her newly qualified daughter wore shoes heavily decorated with real gold. Politicians congratulated each other and ate too much against the background of music played by the latest fashionable orchestra, though most of them were either too fat or too lazy to dance. The few young people present, however, and some youthful foreign diplomats danced to the Nigerian rhythms. Chijioke Abosi was there with his fiancee, as well as his millionaire father, Sir Ike Abosi. Nearly all the top people in the ministries were represented. From the army came Brigadier Onyemere, whose promotion to General had been announced that week. Alan Grey was also there. It was a gathering of the very top cream of Nigerian society. The grass was lit by artificial candlelight, and the food was rich. People drank champagne like water. Nigeria was an independent nation at last.

'Can I get you a drink, ma'am?' Alan Grey asked Debbie, noticing that she was left to herself for a brief second.

'Oh, it's you!' she said, laughing.

'Yes, it's me again. I saw you this morning, waving like a princess.'

'I had no choice. Do you know, Father had to order that car just for today. Poor man! If he dies tomorrow, it'll be his wealth that's killed him. I thought things would have changed. But no, even though the crowd today came in their best clothes, I saw that three-quarters of them had no proper shoes. While my father bought a car costing almost ten thousand pounds just to drive through that crowd. Do you know what I kept thinking? Suppose those people had decided to mob us? Oh, I feel so guilty about it all.'

'I think you need a drink,' Alan said, taking a glass of champagne from a male servant who wore a white tailored jacket and black velvet trousers yet walked barefoot. Noticing this, Alan smiled.

'That, for instance, is very humiliating,' Debbie said, following his gaze.

39

'Hold on, now. You yourself were wearing gold shoes that the papers have already written about. You didn't have to do that.'

'Father's press secretary was responsible for that. It's not enough that we own so much but we must noise it about the country. And you can't argue with Father. You know, I think I'll tell him I'm going to join the army.'

'Oh, no!' He was laughing now and she joined him.

Then she asked: 'Do you think Nkrumah really wants to rule the whole of Africa?'

'Why do you ask? It's true that he wants to unite the continent, and somebody would have to be at the head.'

'Well, I don't mind if it is Nkrumah. At least we would have someone who is really doing something, unlike all these corrupt politicians.'

Someone soon claimed Debbie for a dance and she could not refuse without appearing rude. As Alan stretched out his hand for another drink, the senior Abosi waddled towards him in his native Igbo outfit which seemed to consist of yards and yards of colourful material wound around his big body.

'Good evening, sir,' Alan said. 'Would you like a drink?'

Abosi waved his hand to show that he had had enough. 'Come, let us talk.' They found two cushioned cane chairs and sat down. 'Tell me, young Grey, how is my friend your father? He hasn't been back to see us as he promised. He collected a lot of carvings and bronzes before he left. He seemed to think he might make some money from all those.'

'Ah,' Alan drawled cautiously, 'he, er, decided not to sell them.'

'I told him they wouldn't be worth anything. Some were dug up from old burial places. Enough to scare one to death. There are still thousands of them among the Mid-Western Ibos, in places like Ibuza, Asaba, Ogwashi and, of course, in Benin.'

'I must go there again when all is settled at the barracks. I'll pay John Nwokolo's family a visit before the UN back in the Congo sends for us.'

'Ha! You think there won't be enough trouble here to last you the next decade? You mark my words: we're going to need every Nigerian in uniform to protect us from each other. Let Nkrumah and the others mind affairs in the Congo. Nigeria needs her men.'

'You believe there's going to be trouble?'

'Well, do I need to tell you? A first Nigerian cabinet without Dr Ozimba? Chief Odumosu wanting to get rid of his lieutenant Chief Durosaro? No, my boy, there's big trouble looming. You just stay here and put more men in uniform. And get well-educated men, like

Chijioke. We want an army like the British one. Stay here and see to that. Forget about the Congo.'

'I see you have faith in the army, sir.'

'No, I don't,' Abosi senior laughed. 'Think of all that money I spent educating my son your friend, hoping he would go into business or politics, anything but the army, and then he comes to his mother and me in uniform . . . It was a shock, I can tell you. Now that we've come to accept it, he'll probably change his mind and become an actor or some such terrible thing.'

They laughed heartily at the expense of Chijioke whom they both loved and respected.

'You know he's getting married to his woman friend next week?' the seventy-year-old millionaire said. 'I'm glad he's made his mind up about her. I don't want her having babies for him without a proper marriage . . . Ah, there's the Ogedemgbe girl coming for you. Are you two just friends or is it more serious?' He chuckled and gave a knowing wink then, acknowledging Debbie's greeting with a stiff nod, he moved on with his hands clasped behind his back, as though he had not uttered a word to a soul all evening.

Dr Ozimba danced past Alan and Debbie with his American secretary. He wore his famous smile and the gold-rimmed spectacles which served as his professional mask, beyond which it was difficult to penetrate.

'He didn't look too unhappy,' Debbie commented when they were out of earshot.

'Well, that's where his political statesmanship comes into play. He realizes that not being prime minister isn't the end of the world. Maybe he's glad of the rest, and that he's giving way to younger people . . .'

'Oh, come, come. Is Nguru Kano younger than Dr Ozimba? Why did your people do it to him? Is it because he's too intelligent for an African? People are thinking that it was all pre-arranged by these so-called 'friends of Africa' – including, I'm sorry to say, your father. They say that with the Hausas on top you think you can continue to rule the country indirectly forever. Anyway, thank goodness Ozimba realizes that to fight for his rights would only make you people say, "See, they can't rule themselves." Was that why you did it, to trap us into starting a war among ourselves?'

'Honourable ladies and gentlemen . . .'

Debbie did not get her answer. Alan could not give any; and there was a timely interruption by Governor Macdonald, who told his illustrious guests that this was his last public appearance to them since

41

he would be leaving the country the next week. He could not keep it a secret from people who had been so kind to him. He was happy to see the peaceful close of a historic Nigerian chapter.

The guests cheered and about a hundred of the governor's countrymen present that evening sang 'For he's a jolly good fellow'. Dr Ozimba, like a good sportsman, proposed a toast to the great friendship between Nigeria and Great Britain. Everyone drank to that, and the music resumed in earnest. It was a glorious moonlit garden party and many stayed and danced until the early hours of the morning.

The following days were filled with newspaper publicity about the wedding of the year, between Chijioke Abosi and his barrister girlfriend Juliana. Chijioke's life history was traced in all the news media until almost everyone in the country knew it parrot-fashion. His bride's background was kept a little quiet, since she had been married before and had a thirteen-year-old daughter. Many wondered why such a rich man who could have chosen any girl in Nigeria should go for a woman nearly the same age as himself; some cynics even said she was older. Yet they would have thought nothing of a man of seventy marrying a child of seventeen. To Nigerians, in marriage the male partner was superior and the female must be subservient, obedient, quiet to the point of passivity. But people shrugged their shoulders; Chijioke Abosi had always been a rebel. His father had prepared an easy-going job with great prospects for him, and what did he do? He came to his father in a khaki army uniform.

On the day of the wedding, however, the glamour of it all silenced even the cynics. At thirty-two, Juliana was slim and beautiful. She wore a plain white silk dress and her short black curls were held back with white roses strung on a broad satin ribbon. To the surprise of some onlookers, her young daughter and Debbie were her bridesmaids. The older women among the oceans of people watching the wedding procession shook their heads at her audacity in letting her child openly address her as 'Mum'. Other women were either jealous or praised Juliana's boldness. There was a strong suspicion that a new breed of Nigerian woman was in the making.

The guard of honour was mounted by men from Abosi's regiment. The Cathedral Church of Christ was packed with relatives, friends and acquaintances. There was no vacant seat among the choiristers. They all sang lustily, honoured that they were privileged to be at the wedding of one of the most eligible bachelors of the time. Most of the ministers and important members of the House of Assembly were there; although Abosi senior was not a politician as such, they knew that money was power and that people like him could make or unmake any political party, to say nothing of individuals. It was noticeable that Chief Oluremi Odumosu and his deputy Chief Durosaro of the Western region, who were still at each other's throats, were not represented.

The reception was in the grounds of the spacious Palace Hotel, most of whose hundred rooms were booked by visitors who came from all parts of the country to honour the Abosi family. As for the army, one would have thought all the newly established barracks had opened their gates wide to let the young recruits have a free day. Army boys in smart starched uniforms and shining boots ushered the guests to their seats. Among the VIPs surrounding the bride and groom there were more men in the dark green army officers' uniform than in civilian clothes. The groom was majestic and immaculate in his; he spoke very little and laughed only occasionally, yet one had the feeling of being beside a very contented and confident person. Next to him was his best man, Brigadier Onyemere, with Colonel Saka Momoh on the other side.

The Prime Minister as usual looked remote, seemingly uninterested in what was going on. People were becoming used to his still, mask-like face which, either by accident or design, never betrayed any emotion. One of his eyebrows was perpetually arched as though asking a question no one would ever answer. He was a difficult man to entertain; being a Moslem, he did not drink or eat pork and would not bring any of his wives to such a gathering. Yet his steely coldness held an attraction for the Lagos society women, who fluttered around him like butterflies in search of rare flowers, ministering to all his needs.

Debbie charmed everyone, playing the dutiful daughter of Samuel Ogedemgbe. The climax for her was when she confidently gave the bridesmaids' toast, her accent perfect and her smile unwavering. That was what most fathers wanted: a daughter who not only was a been-to but who could talk and behave like a European. Everyone applauded, and even the Prime Minister almost smiled. And when someone shouted, 'A chip off the old block!' Ogedemgbe and his wife were in seventh heaven as the whole gathering roared into happy laughter.

'She should go and join them in the House of Assembly,' Saka Momoh put in sardonically.

'Yes, as a secretary,' the old Abosi commented in a lower tone, but not low enough for him not to have been heard.

As far as Ogedemgbe was concerned, all was laughter. 'If my daughter is to go to the House, she will be nothing less than a lady prime minister!'

Nguru Kano's features wavered slightly yet perceptibly, his full lips moving as if in the beginning of a smile. Debbie quickly excused herself from the centre of the gathering. If her parents thought they could advertise her like a fatted cow, they had another thing coming. She would never agree to a marriage like theirs, in which the two partners were never equal. Her father always called the tune. She did not hate him; on the contrary she loved both her parents very much. It was just that she did not wish to live a version of their life – to marry a wealthy Nigerian, ride the most expensive cars in the world, be attended by servants . . . No, she did not want that; her own ideas of independence in marriage had no place in that set-up. She wanted to do something more than child breeding and rearing and being a good passive wife to a man whose ego she must boost all her days, while making sure to submerge every impulse that made her a full human. Before long she would have no image at all, she would be as colourless as her poor mother. Surely every person should have the right to live as he or she wished, however different that life might seem to another? She felt more and more like an outsider, and told herself that she must make a move to fashion a life for herself. Yes, she would join the army. If intelligent people and graduates were beginning to join the ranks of the Nigerian Own Queen's Regiment; she intended to be one of them. It would be much more difficult for a woman, she knew, and the daughter of a minister at that, but she was going to fight. She was going to help the Nigerian army – not as a cook or a nurse, but as a true officer!

Chijioke Abosi, his beard shining with sweat, began making his speech, telling the story of how he had met Juliana. He suspected that he was boring his listeners and felt that such personal experiences should be kept to himself; but his family wanted him to narrate it all so that no one could be in doubt that he had been to public school in England and to Oxford University, and that his wife had been at the London School of Economics and Gray's Inn. If those millionaires suspected that they could be awakening the spirit of jealousy instead of admiration among the ordinary people who flocked outside the Palace Hotel to catch a glimpse of the overfed and overdressed guests, they were not letting it worry them. But the ill-paid soldiers and their officers were also watching all this wealth display, and they had what the ordinary people did not have: they had guns.

The noisy atmosphere continued after the bridegroom's speech. The orchestra, the best in town, played at full blast; it was rumoured that the Abosis had ordered the group's outfits from the UK. The leader called the newly-weds to dance by weaving their names into the song they were playing, a great hit at that time called 'Bonsue'. So moved was the senior Abosi by the praise the musicians showered on his son that he took out a wad of money, undid the wrapping and began to stick five-pound notes on the players. Amidst applause he said he was giving each of them six notes because he foresaw that his son's new wife would have six children for her husband.

Gently and with grace, the couple went to the centre of the floor and moved slowly to the music, Chijioke being careful not to tread on the hem of his wife's gown. Money was showered on her too and the guests clapped until their hands were red. The white diplomats, the Syrians and all the Abosis' business associates threw pound notes, and even Alan Grey did the same. The crowd of nobodies whose mouths had been watering at the food being served cheered as each VIP gave his money. Juliana managed to free herself from the notes and made her way on her husband's arm to their seats, while the bridesmaids collected the money in large brass trays to be counted. The music started up again and the floor was open to everybody.

All of a sudden there was a hush from the crowd outside, many of whom had been there three hours in advance in order to gain good viewing places. Then the loud screeching of army trucks could be heard, followed by the heavy tread of soldiers' boots. Instinctively all the military men at the reception stood to attention. Then twelve soldiers marched in led by Colonel Oladapo, who was in charge of army headquarters in the Western region. They halted abruptly in the centre of the gathering, the colonel saluted and went straight to Brigadier Onyemere, bending down stiffly to whisper something to him. The silent stare of all present felt almost solid.

The whispered conversation lasted only a couple of minutes, minutes which hung in the air like a dark cloud suspended over the celebrations. The smiles of the band seemed fixed on their faces. The bride's daughter ran to her mother and held on to her gown. Brigadier Onyemere's attitude, the way he pushed his stomach forward and clicked his heels, betrayed the fact that, whatever he was being told, all was far from well. As soon as the muttering ended, the colonel took a couple of soldierly steps back, saluted his superiors, barked orders at the men he had brought with him, who with their boots pounding on the cemented hotel grounds marched out as if on parade. They were without doubt proud to have such an appreciative audience.

Momentarily the brigadier furrowed his brow then, after tightening his military belt and adjusting his cane of office under his arm, he spoke in a low voice to his friend and colleague Chijioke Abosi. The latter did not seem at all pleased and made a sound of involuntary exasperation which was loud enough to break the trance which had held everyone spell-bound. There was puzzled movement everywhere. Onyemere felt it was time to make an announcement.

'We are all sorry but we have to go back to barracks. This should not stop your enjoyment at all. So sorry.' He looked at the politicians, who were sitting on the edges of their seats, and considered giving them an explanation. However, he changed his mind. Time was too short and maybe it was a good thing to let them stew in their own juices for a while. It would serve them right after all they had been saying about the army.

At his command of 'Fall out! Quick march!' soldiers, suddenly infused with energy, extracted themselves from the wedding guests and made their way out, high boots hitting the macadam with such force that the crowd outside dispersed like ants as soon as they saw them. Chijioke, not even bothering to kiss his new bride, took up his cap and cane and followed his brigadier.

Alan Grey remained behind and moved closer to the Prime Minister and his bodyguards. Nguru Kano looked with suspicion at the departing uniformed men; he was not amused at not being told what all this bustling was about, but he did not wish to look more stupid than the situation warranted by going to ask them what the matter was. Alan, somehow always at the right place at the right time, moved quickly to rectify the neglect of his African army colleagues and in grave words he addressed the Prime Minister. The Hausa man, retaining his feudal pride, nodded darkly at what the Englishman was saying, his grey eyes darting from side to side. The fact that Nguru Kano was being given the message by a white soldier somewhat restored his dignity since, in the eyes of those present, it was presumably because he was too important to be approached by an ordinary black soldier. After all, should he not as head of state be informed if anything had gone wrong in his democratic society? Yet the poor man was living in cloud-cuckoo-land to be thinking of the kind of democratic society the British had been practising to perfection in their own country for hundreds of years and which they now thought should work instantly in the colonies they had ruled for so long. At the moment that kind of democracy was like a borrowed robe that one had to learn to wear. There was no easy way out.

All this was too much for the father of the bridegroom who bellowed in anger, shaking with rage:

'What type of country is this to be? One ruled by young boys who have not even learned to do up their trousers properly? They have no respect for their elders any more. Shouldn't they have consulted us and then waited for us to advise them what to do? Since when did young men start holding secret talks – '

'Abosiiii . . . Abosi, please, you cannot argue with a man holding a gun to your head. You are not even a politician. Leave them be,' his old wife wisely warned him. 'They may have disrupted our son's wedding, but we still have our lives.'

Everyone knew that Mrs Abosi was speaking the truth. How could they oppose men with guns?

Nguru Kano and his entourage made hurried and muffled excuses and left. Stella Ogedemgbe made a sign to her daughter that it was time for them too to go. The soldiers' shouts could still be heard in the distance, but the streets outside were deserted.

At home, the Ogedemgbes switched on the television, and it was then that they heard what at the time sounded comical and childish, as the squabbles of the two Western chiefs were reported. But then the horrific news started to come. Over thirty people had been killed . . . thugs had been employed by both sides and innocent people were being killed in the streets . . . many market places had been emptied as rival thugs looked for their opponents.

'Honestly, could not Chief Odumosu have given in gracefully? Whose fault was it that he didn't become a minister in the Federal House? And after all, five years isn't forever!' Stella Ogedemgbe spat in anger.

'All those innocent people killed for nothing,' observed Debbie mournfully.

'That's politics, my dear. I only hope our Prime Minister acts in time to stop more atrocities. Now I'm glad the soldiers have been called in. The police could not cope. A state of emergency will have to be declared,' Ogedemgbe said, his voice sounding distant.

'Power, just greed for power,' his wife started again, her anger mounting.

Debbie felt like laughing despairingly whenever her mother mentioned the word 'greed'. Could she be so blind as not to see that all of them, especially her family, were equally guilty of that greed? Her father was trying hard to convince himself that the corrupt side-gains he made were his entitlement. She knew how his argument would run: 'The Europeans who ruled us for so long did it, now it's our turn . . .' Her mother likewise saw nothing wrong in the proverbial ten per cent from all contracts signed by the federal government going into the Ogedemgbes' private purse, paid into the Swiss account her husband had opened for her. She only felt angry when others tried to do the same and, what was more, quarrelled over it.

But Chief Odumosu, too, had debts to pay. His people were used to his squandering money to impress and also to help some of the underprivileged in his extended family – it had to be so, since there was no state welfare money to take care of them. That was one of the tragedies at this time in Nigeria. If a man became an MP, it was his duty to see to the well-being of all members of his extended family; he must show his wealth by helping this ageing farmer, that clever boy born of poor parents, make sure that his village had the best amenities, the largest buildings and all the paraphernalia of modern living. Of course, no government minister was paid enough to be able to afford this, and so as not to lose face they would go behind the scenes for their percentage. Some posts carried greater rewards than others. If Odumosu had been a minister in the Federal House he would have been sure of a large share; but no, he was not elected a member of the cabinet, nor was he chosen to be a minister. He had been so sure when leaving the provincial Western House that he would be elected that he had not bothered to make an arrangement that his best friend and assistant would step down, if all failed. What annoyed him the more was that he had invested all the party funds and most of his own private money, saved from his previous political posts, in campaigning. To think that it had all failed!

The rift between him and Chief Durosaro had become open; it was clear that his life-long ally was determined to sit tight and sit pretty in that post as if by right. 'Good Lord, I put him there,' Odumosu would say, 'now he is making fantastic sums of money, building up his name while I am . . . am . . .' It was always too painful to complete a sentence like that; one must never admit to oneself that one was a failure. Indeed, if anyone else dared suggest such a thing, that person should either be physically or mentally eliminated. And that Chief Oluremi Odumosu was prepared to do.

The rest of the party thought the way their two leaders were exposing each other in the media was shameful. For they were all of the same tribe, Yorubas, so why couldn't they settle it between themselves like brothers? However, they did not realize how deeply the wound had cut into Odumosu's pride.

He had agreed to come to the Western House that day, having made adequate preparations: he had seen to it that the topic of his returning to the West would be discussed and voted upon. He was certain that as the nominal leader of the Western party he still commanded the respect and loyalty of most members. But he had forgotten that Durosaro, his now enemy, had been schooled in his own 'Bribery Academy' and had spies who paid Odumosu's 'seers' to acquaint them with all his plans. Durosaro was determined to deal with the matter in another way.

He knew that he did not stand much chance of winning against the immediate presence of the party leader, who had that charismatic bearing of a man for years used to telling others what to do and who demanded instant obedience. The loyalty of Durosaro's own followers would be stretched to breaking-point if they were asked to choose between the leader and himself, the assistant leader. He suspected his mentor would ask for an open vote, saying: 'Secret ballots belong to the English parliament. Here we are brothers of the same tribe, the children of our ancestor Oduduwa, so why play a game of duplicity with one another?' This archaic appeal never failed. So Durosaro was taking no chances.

After the preliminaries that afternoon the topic was introduced, and as soon as it reached the voting stage Durosaro stood up. Folding his voluminous robes around him as if readying for a fight, he shouted in his thin voice: 'Fire, fire on the mountain! Run, run! Fire, fire, fire!' Of course, the few who knew that their fate depended on his remaining premier of the West pretended to be frightened of the invisible fire and took up the shout of 'Fire, fire!' The paid thugs outside began to shoot into the air and at the sound of gunfire all the members ran for their lives. The House could not vote at all, to say nothing of voting against Chief Durosaro.

Chief Odumosu fumed with rage as he dashed home through the streets, inciting his own thugs. The whole town found itself in a mini civil war. Bullets sang in the streets of Ibadan. The police could do little, faced with groups of armed hooligans. Most of them were normally unemployed but had been given large sums of money and promised more if they saw the operation through.

That was why Chijioke Abosi had to leave his new bride, and why their wedding cake was uncut; and that was how the country was made aware that the honeymoon after Independence was over.

After the extreme heat of the afternoon, the evening breeze fanned the young army officers and their soldiers as they carried their weapons ready to shoot at anybody who defied the curfew. They took an impressive stand as their jeeps moved into Ibadan, the largest city in West Africa, to restore order. The situation had reached a point where the only workable order involved guns. The politicians had failed; the military was gradually taking over. It was the first confrontation.

Debbie Ogedemgbe watched all this on television that evening until she could take no more. With decisive steps she walked up to her father and said, 'Father, I'm joining the army.'

49

5 Emergency Action

Two army cars swerved at neck-breaking speed into a quiet street in Oke Bola, Ibadan, and screeched to a stop in front of a modest bungalow with a neat cement front. This was the civilian home Oladapo rented away from the barracks. He was lucky in being stationed in Ibadan after Sandhurst and the Congo. Like most of his colleagues he had thought that life would be easy after Independence, and that people like himself would if need be willingly take up arms to defend this great, new and promising country of theirs. If it had been suggested to him that there would ever be a time when he would be called upon to protect one Nigerian citizen from another, he would have taken it as a joke in bad taste. Yet that was what had been happening for over twenty-four hours now.

The Nigerian army heads did not sleep. They were in all parts of Ibadan, commanding the still untrained local recruits, keeping an eye on the residences of ministers and important businessmen, patrolling the streets. The few shots they fired were only to scare; a stray bullet did hit one man in the leg but the injury was not too bad. Those who died did so as a result of beatings by their opponents. Some of the ringleaders were captured and taken to the army barracks, since it seemed the police had played a disappearing game. As soon as they saw the spirit of the thugs and guessed that some of them were on a suicide mission, the police ran for cover. But meanwhile the soldiers were everywhere like locusts.

A young man, scarcely nineteen, in new khaki uniform, was holding a gun almost as big as himself, marching up and down the street with a high-stepping swagger. His greenish-brown felt hat was folded on one side of his face like that of a sailor. Those soldiers native to Ibadan made sure they paraded down the streets or lanes in which they were born or brought up as youngsters. To them it was like a big game; they

50

had never had so much power, they had never felt so important. These young people were left almost unsupervised for the dayshift. The colonels and officers who had been out in full force to quell the uprising when it first erupted now felt that danger had been averted and all that was needed was simply a show of strength on the streets. The young soldiers with their loaded guns could do that.

Inside Oladapo's house, Chijioke Abosi sank his huge body. Others followed his example, less dramatically but achieving the same ends. They were bone tired. Outside in the streets they had maintained an unflagging profile, yelling out orders, calling the thugs to give themselves up, screaming searching questions at ordinary people whose feet jellied with fear as they stammered their answers, swearing innocence by whatever gods or goddesses they worshipped. None the less a few suspects had been rounded up, to be openly treated as scapegoats at the appropriate time. Meanwhile the officers needed their rest, and what place more welcome than Oladapo's small yet comfortably modern bungalow.

It was usually very difficult for people to feel sorry for Chijioke Abosi: his confident carriage, sheer bulk, the luxuriant beard and moustache, all seemed to exude strength, and the fact that he was a man born and reared in luxury did not help. Yet the others, sitting there weary-eyed, did feel a little sorry for him now. Oladapo, being the flattered host on this morning after the first uprising in the West, felt it his privilege to speak his thoughts:

'To think that last night was to be the beginning of your honeymoon.'

Abosi's eyes registered pain mingled with righteous anger, but he quickly got over it and replied in joke: 'Do you know, I had forgotten all about that. This was my wedding suit, wasn't it?'

'And this was my guest suit at your wedding. How crumpled they look. How muddy, just because of a . . . a set of greedy politicians.'

'Well, Juliana won't be too upset. She has been honeymooning with me ever since I set eyes on her. Anyway, she is a soldier's wife now and might as well get used to our way of life,' Abosi added, with suppressed emotion.

A houseboy in old khaki shorts padded silently in to find out what they would drink. With the exception of Saka Momoh, they all went for a long cool glass of beer. Momoh asked for Fanta.

'I've had my bellyfull of this political nonsense,' Onyemere said. 'If they can't govern then they should say so and let us try our hand at it. At least under us there would be peace. I wouldn't have minded if Durosaro and Odumosu had ended up killing each other; but getting innocent citizens involved . . . I don't like it,' Brigadier Onyemere said judiciously.

'Ah, Brigadier, we think along the same lines,' Momoh replied. 'Afrifa did the same thing in Ghana when the young soldiers felt that Nkrumah wanted to unite Africa and elect himself the first emperor of the continent. They said that the domestic demands of the people in Ghana were sacrificed for the rest of Africa. They had to plan a coup.'

'I don't think it will ever come to that here in Nigeria,' Oladapo said optimistically. 'We are born cowards. No one wants to get killed. People here are more cautious.'

'Didn't you see the faces of the thugs when we came in yesterday? We may be cowards, but those were the faces of people determined to die for what they believe to be right. Most of them were not just unemployed but unemployable because of their past records. So they would do anything for money.'

'I still feel sorry for the families of those killed, all for a few pounds. It's not worth it,' Abosi said dreamily.

'We are not all born into the lap of luxury,' Momoh bawled.

This made Abosi open his eyes lazily to look at this man from the Tiv tribe who had never bothered to hide his hatred for him, believing whatever the evidence he heard that Abosi regarded soldiering as a rich man's sport.

'Those who died weren't all innocent,' persisted Momoh. 'They knew there was a chance of being killed. Same as us. They gambled and lost. We could be killed at any moment. A soldier must face that fact.'

'I hope our Prime Minister wakes up and faces facts. Surely he must have heard the news by now. Why doesn't he say something? Twenty-four hours is a long enough time for any head of state to react to an emergency of this magnitude,' Brigadier Onyemere observed.

'He's hurt that we didn't wait for him to tell us what to do before we rushed down to Ibadan to keep the peace. I don't think he liked that,' Oladapo reminded his brigadier as he sipped his drink.

'Well, it was an emergency. People were killing each other in the streets. If we hadn't stepped in, I'm sure there would be more than thirty dead, and the whole nasty mess would have continued. Abosi, later you and some of your soldiers should go and interrogate those prisoners. I want to know who paid them, how much and why. If they refuse to talk, bawl it out of them.'

'Sir, do you think they will respond to being questioned by an Igbo? After all, Chijioke doesn't speak Yoruba,' said Momoh. 'And an interpreter would have to understand the language thoroughly to know what they mean. Ibadan Yoruba can be confusing even to another Yoruba person from Lagos. And you are Igbo, sir. John Nwokolo who is still there in charge of the barracks is also Igbo, Abosi is Igbo . . .'

The brigadier looked closely and thoughtfully at this small Tiv man. He was indeed speaking the truth, although it had never occurred to Onyemere that he was choosing only officers from his own tribe. Yet to an outsider it must seem deliberate.

Aloud he said humorously, 'John Nwokolo is not a real Igbo, you know. He's what we Eastern Igbos call "Hausa Igbo".'

This brought laughter. It was a good thing the quiet hard-working Nwokolo was absent, for he regarded himself as a full Igbo. His people from Okpanam were Igbo-speaking, like those in many towns in the West, towns like Asaba, Ibuza, Ogwashi Uku. These Igbos had at some time in the past emigrated to the West simply by crossing the great River Niger. Now those who had not emigrated looked down on them as stupid and easy-going, while the Western Igbos saw their brothers from the East as uncultured bush people who loved money more than their souls. However, the curious thing was that whenever there was a threat to the core Igbos of the East their brothers in the West would take up arms in their defence. Whether the reverse would be true had never been tested by history.

'All right, Saka the son of Momoh, you go and interrogate the prisoners. I want to know where they got our brand of arms from, and where their opponents got Russian-made rifles. If they resist, you know what to do. Frighten the living daylights out of them but, please, no beating or any kind of torture.'

'Yes, Brigadier.' Momoh stood to attention and saluted.

Abosi and Oladapo smiled knowingly.

Brigadier Onyemere said that he was going to the nearby hotel at Lafia to have some proper sleep. It was all right for him, the others thought; the army would pay his expenses. He gave orders that he should be contacted if there was the slightest disturbance, pausing by the door to express what had been worrying most thinking Nigerians on that day:

'I wish we had a prime minister who would act quickly. It's all very well for him to be dignified, but we need someone quick-thinking to deal with this kind of situation. Let's hope it will be the last.'

In Lagos many people were expressing that wish as well, although the city was calm. People spoke of the previous night's frightening incident in whispers and many felt embarrassed. They had had

Independence only a little over a year and look what was happening. The future looked grim.

Nguru Kano was going up and down, consulting first of all with the now redundant governor-general and then, on Macdonald's advice, his master the Sardauna in the North. And while these consultations were taking place, the soldiers were enjoying their new-found power. Orders had gone round the barracks in the North, in the East and in Lagos to be on the alert for easy mobilization, and in less than three days, while the prime minister was still hesitating about what to do with Chiefs Odumosu and Durosaro, the soldiers were prepared. After a while, people stopped whispering about it and began to speak openly.

What she saw and heard frightened Debbie Ogedemgbe. She had declared defiantly to her parents that she was going into the army. She knew it was a masculine preserve and did not underestimate the ridicule her announcement would engender once she dared make it public. Yet she must make a move, before her shocked parents could recover from their anger and try to talk her out of it.

She had thought of going to join Abosi and the others in Ibadan, not only because that was where the action at the moment was but because there her father's strong moneyed tentacles would be less able to prevent them from accepting her. But she could as easily enlist in Lagos. At first she had thought Alan Grey would understand and put in a word for her, but she realized that at heart he would subscribe to her father's concept of what a woman should be. For her, joining the army was not a matter of going into action to shoot. She would be trained in military familiarization, but what she really hoped to achieve was to be a lecturer in one of the military academies. Alan himself was getting ready to go to the North to help in keeping the young officers on their toes ready for any eventuality. 'Coup begets coup,' he had said, 'and it's the same with civil uprisings. One has to be prepared.'

When she learned that Chijioke was back from Ibadan, Debbie went to the Abosis' Lagos villa. The newly-marrieds, whose honeymoon in the Bahamas had been cancelled, seemed happy enough in their own introspective way and not upset about their disturbed plans, although Juliana did admit that she had been looking forward to the trip.

Chijioke patted her hand. 'Last month we vowed to remain married until death parts us. So there's plenty of time. One has to be realistic, you know.'

'I knew I was marrying a soldier but not that he wouldn't have

54

permission to complete his wedding,' Juliana said, half seriously, so that it was impossible to tell whether she was proud of her husband for answering the call of duty or really bitter to have missed the celebrations. Debbie judged that it was the former and smiled. The way the couple looked at each other made her feel that she was probably an unwelcome third, though they were too nice to say so. She must hurry and tell Abosi her plans.

'Chijioke, I want to join the army. Could I start in your regiment? I'd like to enlist as soon as possible.'

'The army!' Juliana allowed herself the luxury of raising her voice excitedly. 'You'd be the first Nigerian woman graduate to join up. You could sign on for five years, and by the time you're thirty you'd have – '

'Just a minute, Juliana,' Abosi cut in. 'One thing at a time. Debbie, what does your father say?'

'My father? Don't be funny, Chijioke. You know he's like your father. Have you forgotten the fight you had to put up a few years ago to get what you wanted?'

'Then he must be really angry; he'll throw his weight about, and you know your father's weight: it can crush anything – to say nothing of the size of his purse. In the army we try to stick together, and not bring tribalism into it; that was why I went to the West with the others even though it was a minor Yoruba uprising. Yet I don't think any colonel would want a confrontation with your father. That's asking too much of any regiment or recruiting officer.'

'But you did it successfully,' Debbie argued.

Abosi put on an expression which might have been a smile; one couldn't be sure, since the lower part of his face was fully covered by a beard.

'I'm a man.'

'You make it sound as if that explains everything. I want to join the army and I intend to do it.'

'I'm sure you will if you are determined enough. But it will be extremely difficult. I'm not saying that because I am a man I can handle guns better. It's just that my father gave up the fight when he realized he wasn't indispensable in my life. Parents treat their daughters differently. Besides, you wouldn't want to hurt them too much. I'd gladly take you, Debbie – it would certainly add glamour to our regiment. There would be problems, though; we have no women's quarters. Are you ready to be a pioneer? Pioneers always suffer. Well, I'll bring the matter up when I go back to barracks next week.

55

Meanwhile you stay at home and work on your parents so that they don't go around blaming innocent officers for seducing you into uniform. They must at all costs recognize that it was your own idea.'

'Thank you, Chijioke. You know, you're the first person I've told about wanting to be a soldier who hasn't laughed at me.'

'Why should I laugh? Army life, like the priesthood, is a calling. Have I told you why I gave up an easy life in administration? I didn't want to go into politics . . . I have a suspicion that those in it are not playing an honest game.'

'Few games are honest, Reverend Father,' Juliana mocked.

Debbie knew what Abosi was trying to tell her about her father and she also knew that Juliana was trying to hush him out of respect for her feelings. She had to check herself from confessing to her friends that she felt the same way; it would be disloyal to her father and an open admission of his guilt. People might even misconstrue her actions and think that her decision to join the army was simply to spite Samuel Ogedemgbe. So she smiled and promised that she would try to soften the blow to her parents.

Within a few days of that meeting in Lewis Street, Lagos, more portentous events began happening in Nigeria. People were fed up with the government's inactivity and of being kept in the dark. And they started to riot.

For reasons that were not clear, the Igbos living in the North felt a vague belief that the Hausas had tricked them out of a say in the country's affairs. It was also being noised about that the Igbos were striking it rich from the oil that was being discovered in the Eastern region, and one of the new legislations was that the nation's wealth would be shared almost equally between the regions with only a slightly higher share going to the areas from where the wealth originated. This the Igbos regarded as unfair. During the cocoa and timber days of the West, they reasoned, all the money went to the Yorubas there; and the revenue from groundnuts went to the North. So why should the East now be deprived of oil revenue? There were demonstrations in the East itself. The university students had a field day, protesting about everything from the cost of living to the corruption of ministers. In the West where the disturbances had started, people died in riots in the streets, women were waylaid on their way to market, all in the name of politics. There were shouts from all quarters for the Prime Minister to wake up.

He eventually did, amid the chaos, and put the warring Yoruba chiefs under house arrest. A state of emergency was declared in the West.

Once again the army officers met in Oladapo's house in Ibadan.

'Last time we dispersed the crowds with tear-gas, now we have to use guns,' Abosi said exhaustedly. 'The politicians can't govern with this chaos, can they? We are kept just to do their dirty work for them, and still no word of thanks. If the army were in control, at least we'd know we had a military government. I don't know what we have at present, or what we're going to have in the future.'

'I know what we'll have,' put in John Nwokolo. 'More corrupt people at the top.'

'The best thing would be to have a completely new set of people. These have failed, and they will go on failing,' said Momoh.

'But with the system we have now, how will we ever get a new set of younger people at the top?' asked Brigadier Onyemere.

'Put all this lot in jail, lock them up for five years, while a new group we can trust takes over for a time, and restores the fabric of our society after all this devastation. A new Nigeria, where there would be no corruption, no fighting in the streets, where traders need not fear being waylaid by gangs of armed robbers and there would be jobs for everybody,' enthused Momoh.

If he was surprised that the others were looking at him seriously, he did not show it. He was an intense person and took everything he did to heart. Abosi was temporarily alarmed that this might indeed be the only solution, though Momoh was always coming on too strongly. To dispel the heaviness, Abosi said in his slow, deep voice:

'And what name would you give this new nation, Bight of Benin or Biafra?'

He achieved the desired effect and the atmosphere relaxed.

'I think you have a point, Chijioke. We should name her after one of the old lost kingdoms of West Africa. The Gold Coast has reverted to Ghana, why shouldn't Nigeria be either Benin or Biafra?'

'There still is a town called Benin, so it wouldn't be advisable to use that; we'd be accused of partiality. But Biafra is a good enough name for me,' said Oladapo.

'So when we lock them up we'll say it's in the name of a new and happy country called Biafra,' Nwokolo said.

'I would rather say our destination is "Biafra", since as far as I am concerned we're not yet independent. We sent away one set of masters, without realizing that they had left their stooges behind. Even the matches we use in our kitchens come from abroad. I think this country needs a military respite, and so to Biafra we will go. Destination Biafra!' Abosi finalized.

57

The conversation grew increasingly serious and they all became more determined to make a decisive plan. After careful thought they reached the conclusion that imprisoning politicians who had enough money stored in Swiss accounts to buy the whole of Nigeria would be fruitless. They would soon bribe their way to freedom and eliminate those who had planned the operation. The only sure solution must be for all the politicians, the ministers including Dr Ozimba himself and Nguru Kano, to be killed – instantly and without pain if possible, but it had to be done. The decision was taken. All that remained was to organize the details.

'Look,' said the brigadier cautiously, 'I wouldn't want this to look like an Igbo affair. So, Nwokolo, you take care of the Sardauna. You have lived in the North and know the people there. Momoh, you delegate a regiment to deal with the leaders in Lagos; Oladapo, the West. Left to myself, I wouldn't really subscribe to such extreme measures, but I do see the reasoning behind it . . . And, Abosi, see that the Eastern ministers are properly taken care of.'

Then the arrangement was again changed. It was agreed that the Yoruba soldiers were to take care of the corrupt Eastern Igbo politicians, while the Ibo soldiers would see to the Yoruba West. That way, there was no danger of any of the politicians being spared or escaping. Nwokolo, from the Ibo minority in the Mid-West, was to take care of that feudal hangover, the Sardauna.

It was with a heavy heart that Brigadier Onyemere left the group that day, after they had fixed the date and time. It was all to happen simultaneously and unexpectedly, so secrecy was of the utmost importance.

To this they all swore on their word of honour, as soldiers and gentlemen.

6 Coup

It was the early hours of the morning, when the air was exceptionally cool, when all was so quiet that it almost seemed unreal. The type of quietness would have encouraged deeper sleep but for the extremity of it; it forced Debbie Ogedemgbe into a gradual wakefulness. In the past two weeks, since she had been at loggerheads with her father, sleep had invariably eluded her. The humid air hung thick and tangible like fog, ready to be dispelled by the first rays of sun. That would not be for hours yet, Debbie knew by glancing at the bedside clock.

She got up and went near the large French windows. If only she could stop worrying about her future, about the unhappiness she was causing her parents, about the uncertainty which seemed to cling to her like a leech. Involuntarily she moved the heavy green cotton curtain. Then she stood there looking puzzled. It was not just the dew hanging in the air that she saw, it was something else. Why was she reminded of that scene in Shakespeare's *Macbeth* that described trees as walking? No, she must be hallucinating; the walking trees seemed to stop on seeing her. She gave her eyes a good rub, pinched her cheeks and touched her chest. She was wide awake, of that she was sure. She did not doubt it now: something strange was happening in their compound among the lantana bushes. For when she had diverted her gaze, in that split second during which she made sure she was not dreaming, the bushes had moved nearer the side door of the house and two or three clumps of them already seemed to have gone somewhere into the house. They moved so quickly, so orderly, so determinedly, like soldiers on an exercise . . .

Debbie decided to raise the alarm. Flinging on her housecoat, she ran lightly towards her parents' bedroom. She expected to find the faithful Hausa bodyguard lying by the door, like a friendly loyal dog. She did not in her wildest dreams think possible the ghastly scene that met her eyes in that dim early morning light. The silent giant Sikiru Lemomu, their friend of many years, was lying sprawled in his own oozing blood. He had been shot in many parts of his body. He must have struggled in the agony of death, but this had not prevented the bullets of his assassins from driving home.

Frozen with fear, Debbie stood there shivering, as though rooted to the spot; her shaking palm over her mouth, her eyes bulging, she swayed from side to side. When the voice came behind her, very near, when she felt something being pushed against her back, she behaved as if she were expecting it.

'Move, move on! If you resist or raise your voice, you are dead, girl.'

She obeyed like a zombie and was half pushed into her parents' bedroom. She would never forget the sight that greeted her there that morning.

Her father was on his knees, wearing only his pyjama trousers, sweating, and it was if he was sweating blood. He had been hit on one side of his head and blood from this deep cut mingled with his sweat. A young soldier was amusing himself by ordering her mother to undress and Stella Ogedemgbe was resisting. Then Debbie found her tongue.

'Please leave my parents, please. They have done you no wrong, please, shoot me instead . . .'

'Listen to the Oxford-trained daughter of Ogedemgbe saying that her father has done no wrong! Let's finish him now, that would save us a lot of trouble.'

'No, don't!' barked another voice, more authoritative than the others, the same voice that had commanded Debbie before.

She whirled round to look at him, and saw that the man, this very soldier, had danced with her only a few months before at Abosi's wedding. It then dawned on her what was happening: the soldiers were taking over. Doing some quick thinking, she tried once more.

'I support you, you know. Ask my parents, I have been wanting to join the army. They are just victims of circumstances. Please don't kill them. Please don't harm my mother. Take all the wealth they have. After this they will have learned their lesson.'

'Please,' Samuel Ogedemgbe's voice cut into that of his daughter, 'I will write you a cheque for a hundred thousand pounds this minute . . .'

The army leader looked at him kneeling there praying, begging for his life, and burst into derisive laughter, in which the younger soldier joined. Another marched into the room, saluted and declared:

'All the members of the household have been taken care of, sir. We only had to shoot one, because he refused to leave his post. The other servants fled.'

'Hey, you there, leave that old woman alone. I don't want to see her body. Tie his hands and lead him out. Quick, we have no time to waste. We'll deal with him like the other one in the jeep.'

'Yes, sir!'

Debbie watched unbelieving as her father's hands were forced behind him and tied with a long cord. He could hardly stand and at the moment Debbie wished they would kill him there and then, for she guessed that they intended to amuse themselves with him first. If only something could be done to stay their hands. Ogedemgbe took a last look at his family and managed to say.

'Keep the boys in England as long as possible. Don't let them come home for holidays. Tell them I love them and you too.'

He was pushed out of the room.

'Tie up the women as well and lock them inside. Have you cut the telephone?'

'Yes, sir!'

Stella Ogedemgbe, dressed only in her underskirt, was forced to sit on the floor. Her hands were tied to the bedpost, and Debbie was treated likewise. The soldiers were in a hurry so did not force her to strip, but they toyed with her breasts and made rude remarks. Debbie did not mind that; what she minded was that her proud father was seeing all this. She could hear him whimpering and still trying to bribe the soldiers into sparing him. The poor man had never in his life faced a situation in which money, however acquired, could not save the day.

Despite his valedictory statement to his wife and daughter he did not believe that was the last time he would see them. He still had it somewhere in his mind that money would buy the officers. The killing of his personal guard had taken him aback, but he thought respect for his own person would not allow them to carry out their threats. Why, he was wealthy enough to buy the whole army if he wished. He would be all right. After he had gone, his wife and daughter would raise the alarm. Yet the rough manner in which they treated him on the way to the jeep made his faith begin to waver. When he lagged behind a little, he was given a sharp hit on one arm, so painful that it was almost paralysing. Were it not for the layers of fat flesh that covered him, his bones would surely be broken. He protested weakly and the harsh voice of the leader told him to shut up and called him a pig.

Ogedemgbe started to cry, and he had reason to cry the more when he was half carried, half pushed into the jeep. For sitting there on the damp floor of the jeep with his hands tied behind his back was his friend in politics, Alhaji Sir Nguru Kano, the prime minister. The two did not exchange any words. There was no point. Although Nguru Kano had not been physically beaten, Ogedemgbe knew that emotionally he had taken it worse than he had.

Nguru Kano was a man of dignity whose approach to everything in life was through calmness, and even here, when he was so humiliated, that was reflected. He did not beg for his life. He wore a look of utter control and submission to the inevitable, a look that said: 'If it is the will of Allah.' The soldiers during that short ride were jeering and laughing at Ogedemgbe and his pleas but they said little to Nguru Kano and whatever they did say was said in an undertone.

They reached an open farm, a place which seemed miles from Lagos though the prisoners could not tell where they were. They were ordered out of the jeep. Nguru Kano suspected what was about to happen and was taking it with quiet resignation. But his body seemed unwilling to obey him; he was tired, very stiff and in great fear; during their bumpy ride to this out-of-the-way place he had felt his heart stop many a time. Then he made his one and only request:

'If this is the will of Allah, please let me thank him for having given me life.'

At this one of the young soldiers almost took to his heels, saying to himself, 'I hope we are not killing a prophet.' But another officer pushed him with the butt of his gun.

'Have you thought what will happen to you if we leave them alive now? Guard him until he finishes praying.' Then the leader turned to Ogedemgbe.

'Do you want to say prayers to your bank account, Mr Minister of Finance?'

'No, oh, no,' Ogedemgbe replied shakily. 'I will give you all my money and say nothing of this. I give you my word of honour that you and your men will not be punished – '

'Sorry, Mr Money-man, but we have our orders. There, take that spade and dig.'

Ogedemgbe, who less than twenty-four hours before was folding and refolding his organza lace robe, and convincing the Federal House of the importance of the bill he wanted them to pass, was now reduced to a mound of wobbling flesh digging a hole he was told would be his own grave. The leader of the regiment walked up and down, bawling orders to him to hurry up. Then there was a shout from the young soldier who had been asked to keep watch over Nguru Kano while he prayed.

'Sir, sir! I think the Prime Minister is dead, sir. I think he is dead.' The young boy of barely twenty burst into tears.

Nguru Kano had died of heart failure. Not a single blow had been dealt him. He simply died. Those watching knew that there was no going back now. Ogedemgbe was still muttering but was exhausted. The grave he had managed to dig was very shallow. The leader of the operation could wait no more. It was nearing five a.m. and soon the whole country would be awake to the happenings of the night.

There were eleven of them. They formed themselves into a firing squad and together shot at the tired man. Ogedemgbe fell into the shallow grave. They placed the body of his colleague on top of his and covered them up. The Lagos part of the coup was completed.

At the same time as Debbie had thought she saw lantana bushes walking, the Sardauna was also having a premonition. His was so strong that he had tried to make for safety. It was while he was trying to escape that he was killed. Most of the soldiers that John Nwokolo had led there were from the tribe bordering the Hausa heartland, who had no love for the Sardauna and his pomposity. At first Nwokolo had not revealed to them the true nature of their operation, saying only that they were going on an early mission, but when he had told them the truth they had cheered and looked forward to a new order of things. To his surprise he met with no opposition and Nwokolo felt triumphant. The operation was short and swift.

That morning, as the average Nigerian was waking up, the radio began to pour out news which made almost everyone jubilant. The corrupt ministers had been eliminated. People must not panic, the army was in control, people should go on with their normal duties. This announcement was followed by military music and the Nigerian national anthem, repeated over and over again.

There were soldiers everywhere, at the newspaper offices, at the House of Representatives, at all important buildings in the capital and the regions. The relatives of the murdered politicians were too afraid to show their sorrow; it seemed they were the only Nigerians who had not wanted the deaths of these men.

But what was not then known was that not all the operations were complete, to say nothing of being successful. A major hitch was that not a single top Igbo politician had been killed. So unsettling was this that the officers who had spearheaded the coup had to meet. At that meeting Oladapo, the Yoruba man due to carry out the Eastern Igbo operation, reported that when he arrived in the East he had been surprised to learn casually while having a drink in a local club, that the

President Dr Ozimba who topped their list of those to be killed had gone to the United Kingdom for health reasons.

'For health reasons!' exclaimed Saka Momoh, feeling very bitter. 'See what we've done? One would think we carried through this coup only to the advantage of the Igbo politicians. What of Ozimba's deputy, Dr Eze?'

'He was in the president's Lagos house. Before we realized that, he had heard about the killings and he's been in hiding ever since. We've searched the house and he wasn't there, nor was any member of his family.'

'Look, my friend,' said Brigadier Onyemere gently, 'do you know that one of the chief culprits responsible for our first republic's wrongs, Chief Odomosu, is still alive and in jail? It seems he was arrested on the recommendation of Nguru Kano, in the hope of corruption charges being brought against him.'

'Shouldn't we go and finish the operation then?' asked Oladapo.

'No, enough is enough,' said Abosi deliberately. 'We have taken over. The most senior officer among us should be head of state and we'll work at re-establishing law and order and building the confidence of our people.'

It was unanimously agreed that Brigadier Onyemere be made head of state as a temporary arrangement, until the country had settled and could elect a new civilian government. Chijioke Abosi was to be the caretaker of the Eastern region; he accepted the post with grace and as much humility as a man like he could muster. The devout nationalist Saka Momoh was caretaker of the North while Oladapo was to look after his people in the West. John Nwokolo was content to be Abosi's right-hand man and also to help with the running of things in the Mid-West.

After these decisions were made, the small group of army officers were very solemn. It was easy to criticize those in government, it was another thing to shoulder the yoke of governing oneself, particularly after this kind of takeover. With eyes red from sleeplessness they looked at each other, all ignoring the cool beer Oladapo had provided.

'Well, we have taken over,' drawled the brigadier, aware that he had been reluctant about the coup in the first place. He felt like a Judas even though he had seen on his way to Ibadan how happy the whole nation was; but if their jubilation was lasting, he would rest at ease. He went on, 'Public opinion is a difficult horse to ride. We must be determined to win the people's confidence, to make them take pride in us, we must not incite their envy as the rulers of the first republic did.

We must make this second republic work, as an example to the newly elected politicians.'

Noble and well-meaning words. Under that bold exterior, however, he knew that the fact that the Igbo politicians were alive and that he as an Ibo was taking over leadership from a Hausa would be used against him. So to counteract this, Onyemere made up his mind to try to curb tribalism. To save his own skin and to impress upon people that they should take pride in being Nigerian rather than Igbo or Yoruba or Hausa, the brigadier abolished the tribal meetings for which the Igbos in particular were notorious. The nation, the new Nigeria, should come first. States would be created to cut across tribes during the period of reconstruction.

'We must not omit one important thing,' Abosi said in his deliberate way. 'We must work for outside recognition. At the moment we are not popular with the British. As you all know, Nguru Kano was their man and they will never forgive us for eliminating him.'

'Is their recognition really necessary? After all, we're not forcing their embassy to close its doors. All I'm asking them is to mind their own business. This is an internal affair,' said Saka Momoh heatedly.

'That is so. But you don't know the Big Powers; if they minded their own business they wouldn't be where they are today. This coup is the first step we Nigerians have taken without consulting them. Apart from that, they are already here and would find their way back in if we try to force them out. Look at the biggest chain stores in the country, Kingsway for example.'

'What I wish to suggest is this,' Abosi went on. 'You know that girl Debbie Ogedemgbe? Well, she came to me weeks ago wanting to join our army, but I hesitated. Now I don't see why she shouldn't join us, especially with her education and her connections with the white officers in our national army. We need arms, a lot of arms. Through her English boyfriend she could see that we have a more than adequate supply. Even if we don't use them, the mere fact that they are there should prevent the type of sectarian uprisings we have been having recently.'

'Why should she join forces with people who killed her father?' Oladapo asked. 'Do you really think she will ever forgive us?'

'Ah, with that so-called sophisticated foreign education, she will have realized why her father had to be killed. I happen to know that she herself did not see eye to eye with him; but being a dutiful daughter she stayed loyal to him in public at least. Yes, she will naturally be upset but it will soon pass, especially if I invite her to come and help us build the new nation.'

'Well, if she can be a useful tool I don't see why we should not use her and others like her,' Onyemere finalized. And then he suggested something which gave his listeners the first clue that he was probably afraid. He suggested that they should pray.

Having asked God or Allah for His support, they left for their various posts in a lighter spirit than they had been in when they arrived. The faith of all of them in their ability to achieve their aim of making Nigeria a better place to live in was unwavering. But they did not count on the ripples created by their behaviour.

Many Igbos living in the Sabon Garri quarters of the North regarded the coup as an Ibo success and were arrogant in their joy. The banners, placards and slogans thrust up where Igbos lived in Hausaland jeered at the death of the Sardauna. Alhaji Manliki, the Hausa representative in the North of Dr Ozimba's Igbo national party, was disturbed about this. On hearing that Captain Alan Grey was in the North for a short while, on his way to visit one of the villages in the Mid-West, he invited him to his palace.

When Grey arrived there with his friend Giles and another officer, a chaplain from Northern Ireland, he was surprised at the changes that had taken place since his visit there just before Independence. There were still one or two beggars but they were far from Alhaji Manliki's palace walls. Instead, young soldiers paraded up and down, enjoying the new power of the guns they carried and the importance of their khaki uniforms. They barked at you like mad dogs, they asked you your business before you even stepped within the outer palace walls. There were now barricades and barbed wire where there had been only desert sand and baskets and calabashes containing kolanuts.

A turbaned guard bowed the white soldiers in to the open courtyard, where more armed men strolled up and down. Rather stiff formal pleasantries were exchanged and the Alhaji offered the usual kolanuts and honeyed meat before going straight to the core of the matter on his mind.

'Look, Captain, what is your country doing to our country, eh?' he asked agitatedly, the words rushing out. He was nervy and his erratic gesticulations betrayed a worried mind. 'You see, the army boys trained in your country come back and forget our tradition. No anointed king's son was ever killed without great bloodshed following. I wish those Southern kaferi soldiers had consulted me, as their man in the North. I would have advised them to leave the Sardauna out of it. Now to rub salt in the wound they are making fun of us, while we are still shocked at our spiritual leader being murdered like a beggar. And the Ibos are claiming it as their victory. They may think we Hausa are fools, but there is a limit to human patience. See how I have to guard myself against my tribesmen and against people of the same faith as myself because I am associated with Dr Ozimba? I don't like it, I don't like it at all . . .'

'Please, Alhaji,' Alan cut in, suspecting that he might not otherwise be given the opportunity to speak, 'I do sympathize. I am very sorry for the deaths of Nguru Kano and the Sardauna. But, believe me, Britain had nothing to do with it. It came to us as a shock.'

'Believe you?' Manliki's voice was so thunderous that many of his soldiers stopped pacing and held their guns in position ready to fire at Alan and his friends.

The Irish officer looked nervously around, but the Alhaji waved reassurance to the soldiers, smiled a little and regained his calm.

'I am sorry to be such a bad host. But I think you understand my fear. Are you sure the British government cannot bring their soldiers back like in the old days?'

'No, Alhaji. Our Foreign Office no longer pays the Nigerian army. We stopped that over four years ago. You are an independent nation now and if we intruded openly the OAU, the UN and all would raise a protest.'

'But the Belgians went into Katanga during the time of Lumumba and then the United Nations came in.'

'Well, it hasn't come to that here. Thousands were killed in the Congo. Only a few people have died here.'

'A few important people,' the Alhaji echoed him sarcastically.

'I shall try and warn Onyemere. I don't know when I'll be seeing him but I'll be visiting Nwokolo's village; his brother has collected some artistic pieces for me to see.'

'I can't understand what you want with those devilish things the kaferis used in their pagan worship. I don't know how you can touch them, to say nothing of packing them up and shipping them to England.' He laughed hoarsely.

Alan Grey smiled politely. He was concentrating his search in and around Benin where there were many images – carved from wood, modelled in clay, sculpted in bronze – associated with the personal gods each person was supposed to have to worship in times of difficulty. He had taken carvings representing twins, important chiefs, the gods of crucial crops such as yams. He had no moral qualms about it, knowing

67

that in Nwokolo's household, now they had all been converted to Christianity, such things were regarded as embarrassing and anti-progressive and would be destroyed but for his interest in them. On his previous visit Nwokolo's mother brought him all the bits and pieces she could find in the burial bushes, ransacked every corner of her old hut, flattered that her son who had trained as a soldier in the United Kingdom had as a personal friend this white man who condescended to eat their village food and accepted gifts of broken wooden images and calabashes.

The British men thanked the hawk-like Alhaji for his hospitality and returned in silence to their jeep. Outside the palace they saw the usual file of the faithful hurrying to the mosques, jumping to the side of the road at the jeep's approach. In the distance they heard the local imam, his practised voice rising and falling like evening sea waves; but it held a kind of haunting pathos that was not there before and the faces of the faithful seemed more serious and unsmiling. Alan felt uneasy. One or two old Hausas stared at them through half-closed eyes with a suspicious frown. He remembered their talkativeness and generous laughter on the way to their mosques from his previous visit. Now silence hung in the air. Only the plaintive voice of the imam, like a ghost from the past, continued to remind him of what life used to be like inside the Hausa city of Zaria less than two years before.

They had not turned many sandy roads when they were confronted with some of the Ibos' provocative graffiti: a drawing of Dr Ozimba treading on the crumpled head of the late Sardauna. Alhaji Manliki was right to be alarmed. If nothing was done to restrain the Southerners then the Hausas would be aroused to the point where a holy war might result, with human blood running down the streets like tropical rain. No, this must be prevented.

In fact it was not long before the first wave of Northern rioting began. A small group of Southern demonstrators were carrying a mocking placard and unfortunately had come face to face with a group of Hausas returning from their mosque. A knife fight had ensued in which many of the demonstrators were wounded and about six killed. This incident triggered off a tide of 'Kill the Kaferis' in Northern towns, before the police and armed forces intervened to halt it. But the horrible seeds of violence had been sown.

Brigadier Onyemere made a radio broadcast praising the efforts of the police and army. He reminded his tribesmen that the soldiers had freed the country from the corruption of the politicians not for the benefit of any particular tribe but for the betterment of the whole nation. He begged all concerned to help him work towards achieving a more peaceful Nigeria, in which people would be free to live the way they liked, a new Nigeria to which everyone would be proud to belong and in which words like 'tribe' would have no place.

However, Onyemere did not know what he had let himself in for. Yet he thought that by praising the spirit of nationalism he would abolish tribalism, blunt the sharpness of imported religion, convince people to let bygones be bygones and start afresh. His false belief that he had been successful in his broadcast to the nation was fuelled by the praise the newspapers heaped on him. He was convinced he was doing the right thing. He had explained the reasons for what had happened and felt that every rational Nigerian should be able to understand and not hold it against him that the Igbo politicians were alive. The army would hold the ruling position for a while, until the country was ready to go back to civilian government, with leaders of a completely new breed. The brigadier was going to follow his supposed verbal success with a tour of the country, destined to show he favoured no particular people or tribe. A tour of unity, a tour of peace.

During the first flush of Onyemere's political triumph, Alan Grey and the Irish chaplain O'Hara managed to arrange an interview with him. It was the first time Grey had seen him since the coup.

At the building that had formerly been the governor's residence, the first thing Grey noticed was that the barefooted house servants with enormous headgear had gone. Now there were booted young army officers, smartly dressed in jungle green uniform. They spoke good English and were confident and alert. What a contrast to the sleepy-eyed servants who were there during Macdonald's term of office. Yes, Grey reluctantly agreed within himself, Onyemere had imbued a new confidence into the young people. But the Englishman, despite his avowed love for Nigeria, still felt that the country's wealth should be shared with the powers of the West, preferably Britain; but with the ambitious Igbos at the helm, trade agreements with the Russians might be signed. Though he congratulated his old friend upon being head of state, Grey's congratulations were too brittle to hide his mistrust.

Onyemere in his happy mood did not fail to notice this. He tried to tell Alan why this was all necessary; he talked and talked, like someone who felt he had to justify himself. Alan let him talk himself almost dry, listening without interruption. Then after a long pause Grey injected his poison.

'Do you know that the Hausas in the North are very displeased with

69

you? Why, for example, didn't you let Manliki know your moves? After all, he was and still is a supporter of your Dr Ozimba.'

Onyemere would have ordered the man out of his palace but for the fact that they were both army officers.

'We did not take over in order to hand back power to any of the old politicians. Have I not made this clear? So what has Manliki got to do with me or I with him? The Hausas were displeased at the taunts and jibes of some Igbos in the North. But have I not stopped that? Haven't I even stopped my people from holding their tribal meetings? And how come it is any business of yours, eh?'

'Brigadier, Brigadier, if I may interrupt a minute,' O'Hara said in his shifty way, his spectacles shimmering as if he was finding it impossible to focus on his audience. 'I personally don't think it would be right for you to go to the North now. Not while the Hausas are in this mood. They are very bitter. Some people, especially in the North, are beginning to regard the army as politicians too. So I'd advise you not to go.'

'But I want to make them understand that the old politicians will not even smell the type of lucrative posts they had before. I want to hand power back to the people,' Onyemere maintained convincingly.

This kind of outburst was not new to the two white men. The new leaders of many other nations had had the same noble idea but had found it impracticable, to their cost.

'When I return,' the brigadier went on, 'I shall see that the new Nigeria we are creating is recognized by Britain, otherwise most of the nation's industries will be nationalized.'

Alan Grey exchanged glances with the Irishman sitting by him. The British diplomats in Lagos must be informed of this. He still maintained to Onyemere that it was too dangerous for him to visit the North, nevertheless he promised to cooperate and be in charge of the Apapa barracks for the three weeks the brigadier would be away. He would have to shelve his visit to the Mid-West until the brigadier's return.

'I know my people better than you ever will,' bragged Onyemere. 'Leave this matter to me, if you don't mind.'

The two white officers shrugged their shoulders.

It was at this time that the first two female recruits were enrolled in the Nigerian army, as officers in training who would teach the fast-growing army population the English language. One of these was Debbie Ogedemgbe – some of the senior officers were not sure whether she was set on avenging her father or on being commissioned for patriotic reasons – and the other was her friend Babs Teteku. As soon as it was announced that these two girls from illustrious homes had joined the army, three girls from the Igbo East applied, not to be outdone.

Onyemere was well known, since the early days of the UN forces' presence in the Congo, for talking his way out of trouble. He had a pleasant personality and a trusting attitude to life, and in fact his visit to the North proved to be a triumph. He had grown up in Hausaland, was schooled there and though he joined the army from the Umuahia government college in the East he had joined as a Northerner. He could even recite part of their Koran and he now blessed his childish curiosity which had led him into the darkest Hausa homes and sometimes into their mosques. All this knowledge he now put to considerable advantage. And because he could speak their language, the Hausas loved him. They showered him with presents, regarding him as the saviour of the whole country. A few trouble-makers still held the Sardauna's death against him, and against the Igbos in general; he promised them that such a calamity would never happen again and that any Igbo who behaved badly would be publicly dealt with by the army. Had he not banned the usual tribal meetings? What the country wanted was national unity. He was going to let them elect new representatives who would not lord it over them. With his own brand of trust, coupled with boldness and charm, Onyemere visited all the local dignitaries, bowing to them, promising one thing to this one, something else to the other, listening to their boring accounts of their aches and pains and already behaving like a seasoned politician in pledging to alleviate all these wrongs in the new Nigeria. He begged everyone, including the lowest beggars in the streets of Kano and Zaria, to believe in him and help make the slogan 'Destination Biafra' come true.

On Onyemere's last but one night in Kano, a rather disturbing letter reached him from his wife. She warned him to go easy on curtailing the freedom of his own people, the Igbos. His moves were making him unpopular among them. She asked why he surrounded himself with Hausa and Yoruba bodyguards. Had he forgotten that the day of blood relatives, friends would go? Had he forgotten that a person with relatives was richer than one with money? He should please not anger his people any more. She knew that the coup was not planned to be an Igbo success, but since he had already convinced the Hausas of the sincerity of his apologies for what had happened, was it too much to ask to allow his tribesmen to claim part of the success? She begged him to cut short his visit and quickly come back home.

The letter stirred something in him somewhat. His wife knew him well. She was silent and passive whenever he was around, but in her shrewd retiring way she had discovered methods of getting round him. But Onyemere felt that on this score she was wrong. There was nothing to fear in the last lap of his tour. After all, the Yorubas and the Igbo soldiers planned and carried out the coup. It was the Yoruba soldiers who in not killing the Igbo politicians had failed to carry through their assignment. Moreover, in the army there was no tribalism; the Nigerian army had been discriminated against for so long, because of their unenviable beginning, that they were forced to seek comfort among themselves. And his people – well, he would see to them when he returned to the East and when he had had a good talk with his man there, Chijioke Abosi. How else was he to convince the Hausas that he was sincere, if not to show them that he was prepared to go against his people?

On his last day in the North, Hausa horsemen performed acrobatic displays on their decorated horses. He was flattered and full of gratitude when the Ibo-speaking people there gave him a token in the form of a giant pipe, but his bodyguard showed him a note stuffed into the stem of the pipe and reading: 'You have done well so far, but please don't go to the Yoruba West.' He looked straight and for an uncomfortably long time at his literate Hausa bodyguard, then suddenly, to cover his pounding heart, burst into laughter, a laughter that sounded like the baying of a hound even to his own ears.

Brigadier Onyemere decided to change his route. But that was something he was keeping secret; no one must know, then if people had planned to do him evil they would be foiled in their attempt. But why should they try?

At Kano airport he surprised his lieutenants by declaring: 'I am going by road. Get the armoured car out. I want to see the countryside.'

The junior officers knew better than to remind him that there was a big reception laid out for his arrival in Ibadan and that the officers there would be disappointed. Their duty was to obey and not question. They all arrived in Ibadan ten hours later than the scheduled time. And that was not the last of Onyemere's surprises: he was now going to stay with his friend and colleague Colonel Oladapo.

Mrs Oladapo did not know whether she was coming or going. She kept stammering, 'But there is a big reception for you at the army headquarters . . . they've made elaborate arrangements.'

'Do you object to my being a guest in your house?'

'Oh, no, sir, not at all. We are flattered. It's only that our modest home is not what you are used to. Please forgive our slow servants . . .'

Onyemere laughed his embarrassingly artificial laugh to mask his apprehension. Maybe being head of state was going to be too difficult after all. He decided to rest for the remainder of the day and then go to the barracks the next morning. It was still only three o'clock in the afternoon, hot and very bright. The Ibadan earth was white and the sky cloudless and blue. The sun directly overhead was intense and he sought refuge in the shade Oladapo's house offered.

Oladapo's wife busied herself in making their illustrious guest comfortable. She had telephoned for her husband and he would soon be with her to help her cope with this big job. Onyemere, Saka Momoh, Abosi, Nwokolo – she had entertained them all when they were ordinary soldiers. But now things had changed, and they were soldiers who ruled. She and her husband would be moving to the premier's lodge soon, since Durosaro had been eliminated and Oladapo was now the Western head of state. The official swearing in was to be after the brigadier's tour, and meanwhile they had kept their old bungalow. But nobody told her that it was in that bungalow, where they had drunk and made merry many, many times in the past, Onyemere would choose to stay; even if he did not like staying at the governor's palace, which had been made adequately ready for him, he had more illustrious Igbo relatives at the University of Ibadan where he could have stayed. Well, maybe the man was just exhausted and wanted a real home where he could put his feet up. If so, she was going to do her very best, for Onyemere had been generous to all the colonels under him.

She ordered the maid to get the best bed sheets from the linen cupboard, she sent for the best cut of meat and vegetables, and she supervised the pounding of the yams herself. Amidst all her busyness her husband arrived and quickly took in the situation. Brigadier Onyemere was sleeping on the couch in the front room, and Oladapo sent his men to the barracks to rest after their rough journey, deciding not to wake the brigadier until the food was ready.

Oladapo spent the next thirty minutes answering calls from various people who wanted to entertain the brigadier. Many wanted to thank him personally for bringing about such a coup. As for the Ibadan businessmen, they were furious because elaborate gifts and dinner parties had been arranged for the new head of state. Eventually Oladapo unhooked the phone, after making sure he let the barracks know of his action.

In this way they had their meal in peace. Onyemere was relieved and looked relaxed. They exchanged light-hearted reminiscences about life in Sandhurst and were laughing heartily when they heard a determined tread on the drive. Instinctively, Brigadier Onyemere got up, suddenly on the alert. Oladapo tightened his army belt and stood at attention. A young officer of twenty-eight, who was sitting with them, put on his hat ready to salute on hearing the march of soldiers outside.

They came in unceremoniously and their leader barked at the brigadier:

'You, get into the jeep!' He looked round the room and saw Oladapo's wife. 'If you raise your voice, my men will rape you here and then shoot you dead. So move out of the room. And you, good host, are you willing to be the new head of state, or do you wish to be shot with your Igbo benefactor?'

'The brigadier is my guest and while he is in my house I am responsible for his safety. What has he done to warrant this treatment?'

'As you wish,' the leader of the group said with a sly smile.

Onyemere's hands were quickly tied behind his back, as were those of Oladapo. It seemed that they were going to leave the young officer who was with them, but the leader changed his mind. 'Take him as well.' But they forgot to tie his hands.

Brigadier Onyemere and his loyal Yoruba host were never seen alive again.

One of the early attempts to make friendship cut across tribes thus ended that evening. It was a noble act for a Yoruba man to stand by his Ibo colleague. The young officer, however, was lucky. He escaped, and despite the thorough search of his pursuers he lived to tell the tale. His people smuggled him out of the country into the neighbouring West African state of Dahomey.

With the death of the brigadier, Nigeria was plunged into the bloodiest carnage even seen in the whole of Africa. And the greater part of the blood that flowed was Igbo blood.

7 Chaos

'Everyone stand up and put your hands on your head. Any false move means death. Shoot to kill any soldier who moves. You there, take all their guns and ammunition. You, search them! Unarm the soldiers, unsoldier them all!'

Debbie Ogedemgbe screamed at the bemused men sitting around at the Ikeje barracks mess. It took them so unawares that for a very long time most of the officers thought they were seeing visions – younger soldiers creeping up on them and unarming them, and all under the command of a woman! Debbie's large eyes sparkled with excitement and fear; to make her voice carry any weight she had to yell at the top of her voice until the sinews of her thin neck stood out in relief. One or two of the officers on recovering from the shock made as if to laugh and shots rang close to their ears, making instant holes on the walls behind them. There was no doubt that this small detachment of twenty soldiers meant business. Everybody behaved accordingly after this demonstration. One or two of the officers who had briefly contemplated fighting their way to freedom gave up the idea and took refuge in staring at Debbie Ogedemgbe and her small group with undisguised amusement as if to say, 'Whatever you do, however much you are armed and in command now, you are still a woman.'

They were ordered to stand against the wall where they waited in baffled expectation for her next command. When it came, fear started for the first time to creep into the minds of the officers who only a few minutes before had been enjoying a quiet chat and drinks together.

'All Igbo officers stand to this side,' Debbie barked. 'Western and Eastern Igbos, all Igbos!'

The officers looked at each other in confusion.

'You, what is your tribe? Yoruba? Then move, move out,' Debbie's shrill voice went on. 'You, what is yours? Ijaw? Then quick, move . . . Now you Igbos, tell me your names – you and you.'

The Igbo officers shouted their names as they were ordered. Some showed signs of anger mingled with fear. Then one officer, unable to stand the suspense any longer, demanded coldly:

'Since when did it become a disgrace to be an Igbo?'

For a reply, the younger soldier standing near Debbie landed the butt of his gun on the man's stomach, so that he doubled up in pain and then sagged. He had to be propped up by his astonished friends. The few who had been told to move away looked on and wondered what was happening. Only a few officers belonged to the other tribes. As the standard of living of the soldiers improved, so did the standard of entry, and it happened that those most qualified for the officers' grade were Igbos and the minority tribes surrounding them; of the twenty-five officers relaxing at the Ikeja barracks' mess that evening, fifteen were Igbos.

They were unceremoniously stripped to their underwear and commanded to march into an inner room which was kept for punishing disobedient young recruits. The room had a very small wired opening for a window and was meant for five soldiers at the most, never fifteen. They were pushed and the injured officer was dragged in along with the rest. Debbie whispered orders to two soldiers who were left to guard the door. As soon as she left, the young officer shouted:

'I have been ordered to shoot to kill anybody who makes a sound. And you,' he addressed the man who had been moaning '*Nnem-o-o, Nnemoo*', 'if you don't stop moaning for your mother, I shall finish you. So absolute silence, please.'

As there were no chairs, no mats or anything, they sat on the cement floor. It did not take long for the stuffiness to hit them. Although it was evening, when the weather was cooler, Lagos coolness meant at least seventy degrees Fahrenheit. The officers started to sweat, and during this short ordeal they were able to establish the movements of the soldiers outside their prison door, managing to communicate with one another at the risk of losing their lives.

'But what is happening? Why are we suddenly singled out for this barbaric treatment? What have we done?'

'Maybe there's been another coup,' an officer named Ejiofor whispered behind his palm.

'And all Igbo soldiers are to be . . .' Another one could not bring himself to finish the sentence.

'No, if we were to be killed they would have done so straight away.

And I don't think they would have sent a woman to do their dirty work.'

The others were quiet but none was so sure. One started to whimper and the others hushed him. 'Do you want us all killed?'

Lieutenant-Colonel Ejiofor, who had assumed the role of leader, hissed: 'Those boys out there, there are four of them. They are very nervous and will shoot immediately if they think we are disobeying them. Bear it like a man.'

After a long silence, another voice from the corner asked, 'I wonder if the brigadier knows anything about this. I wonder if the orders came from him?'

'Maybe, maybe. Perhaps in his enthusiasm to show the other tribes that he is impartial he has ordered his own people to be detained.'

'They say that power corrupts, now I see it.'

'I would like to go to the toilet,' an officer by the name of Madu murmured, little knowing that the others were all feeling the same. He got up and by sign language indicated his desire to the guards.

Two of the guards looked through the small hole, their guns at the ready, and when they heard Madu's pleas to be allowed to relieve himself they laughed.

'I was not given an order about that,' one of them said, and they continued patrolling in front of the door. It was clear that these new recruits were going to humiliate the Igbo officers.

By the middle of the night, the small room was choking with the smell of sweat, human droppings and urine. But the men boosted each other's morale. They made signs to each other to use one corner of the room for their toilet, and hoped that humanity would prevail. However, they were too optimistic. The following morning, another soldier marched in holding his nose against the stench of human waste.

'You all look rather hungry,' he teased. 'Well, I can see that you have made yourselves a delicious dinner. So start eating it up!'

'What? Eat what up? Our excrement? We are not Yorubas, or from whatever tribe you belong to,' Ejiofor said indignantly, staggering to his feet.

'Is that so?' the soldier asked, with counterfeited graciousness, bowing and still holding his nose. 'I think you should be the host and show your brothers how to behave. Now be a good boy, and start eating.'

So saying, he pushed the tired lieutenant-colonel towards the heap of faeces, commanding him again but now in a voice like that of a mad hound. Ejiofor refused, and a shot rang out, tearing part of his shoulder blade. He looked at his tormentor in surprise and asked, 'What have we done to deserve this?'

The soldier laughed again, his derision echoing round the whole building. 'An Igbo officer asking me what he has done? I will tell you. You people want to rule the country, don't you? You rushed into the army, into the government, into all the lucrative positions in the country, not satisfied with that you killed all the politicians from the other tribes and then your man the brigadier became self-appointed head of state.' At this he laughed again and the other guards joined in. There was something singularly chilling in their laughter.

The mocking soldier looked like a Northerner but it was difficult to tell whether he was Hausa or not. The others with him could neither speak English nor any Southern language, so appealing to them for mercy was out of the question.

'Your leader,' he went on excitedly, 'thought he was clever, going round the regions preaching "One Nigeria" after he had made sure all the comfortable posts were held by his own people. He is dead now. They killed him and his friend Oladapo – that stupid man, dying for an Igbo. Would an Igbo die for a friend? I ask you. Come on, eat up your shit and don't annoy me further. Otherwise I will shoot parts off you, piece by piece. You start!' he finished. He went away, leaving the guarding of the door to his subordinates.

About an hour later he looked in and aimed his gun point-blank at Ejiofor. It coughed. Ejiofar sagged and died instantly.

'If I order you to eat, you must eat and ask no questions,' the soldier said.

The Igbo officers did exactly as they were ordered, but none of them lived to tell the tale. They were lucky that at least their agonies and humiliations ended within five days; not so for their brothers in places like the North, in Lagos, in the bushes of the surrounding Igbo heartland, in towns like Ibuza, Asaba, Okpanam. While those officers were agonizing and dying little by little in their airless one-room prison, the country was plunged into the kind of bloodbath it had never seen before.

Ugoji lifted his tired eyes from the counter and greeted Mr Idowu, a well-known Yoruba businessman in Kano. They exchanged the usual pleasantries, then Ugoji asked in his usual cashier's voice, 'And what may I have the pleasure of doing for you today, sir?' This was followed by a smile which was meant to be professional; he had a thick neck and when he smiled he was wont to sink his puffy chin into his chest, making himself look neckless.

'I want to take out all my money. Every penny,' Mr Idowu said in a voice that was a near mumble.

'Every penny, sir? Surely you can't mean that . . . Oh, I'm sorry, sir, it's just that you are a rich man, and if everybody did that there'd be no money left here in the bank.'

'I mean what I say,' Idowu persisted, banging his palm gently on the counter. But when he removed his jewelled hand, twenty pounds stared Ugoji in the face. He gulped in confusion, looked around quickly as he put the money aside, to slip into his own pocket at an opportune moment.

Meanwhile he stammered, 'But, sir, it's against the rules of the bank. All I can do is get you as much as you can lawfully take with you. You can arrange to come in a week's time for the rest.'

'I won't be here in a week's time. Get me the maximum possible today.'

'Yes, sir, right away.' As Ugoji busied himself in the next hour with Idowu's vast accounts, checking and rechecking, he wondered why the wealthy Yoruba man was making this drastic move. Was he in trouble? He stole furtive glances at the man waiting patiently, determined not to leave without his money.

'There you are, sir,' Ugoji said after they had both counted the several thousands of pounds in cash. Then he remarked jokingly, 'Another big business venture, sir?'

Idowu shook his head negatively. His expensive gold-rimmed glasses shimmered in the sunlight. He lowered his voice once more and imparted: 'Brigadier Onyemere has been kidnapped.'

'Kidnapped!' Ugoji mouthed. 'By whom? God, this will mean big trouble.'

'Shh, it is still a rumour,' Idowu said as he made his way out of the bank, leaving the counter-clerk in a state of confused shock.

It couldn't be true, he argued with himself, disregarding the waiting customers. Why, the man was so popular, and had won the hearts of the difficult Hausas when he came to Kano. Who would harm such a man?

Ugoji walked like a man in a dream for the rest of the day. He had a restless siesta, and heard his girlfriend Regina moving about in the kitchen they shared. He did not wish to talk, in case he blurted out this rumour. It must still be simmering unofficially about the town, but it had not been announced on the radio, and it would be another twenty-four hours before he got his copy of the *Daily Times* from Lagos. Because he was Igbo, although a Western Igbo, he did not want to think of what would happen to Nigeria if Onyemere had been killed. For Yorubas were well known for putting tragic news euphemistically, and saying that a big man had been kidnapped or that he was very ill usually meant that he was dead.

In the evening, when the Islamic worshippers were hurrying to their mosques, he decided to go the Yankee Bar in Sapele Road in the local Sabon Garri. There he would meet his Igbo friends and find out if there was any truth in what Idowu had told him.

'Just look who is coming to buy us drinks this evening,' shouted the loose-limbed easy-going Joseph Duru.

Ugoji rolled in, in his swaying walk, but this evening instead of wearing his ill-fitting smile he looked forlorn. His friends noticed this at once but assumed he was looking sad because Duru had said he was to buy the drinks. They could understand that, for as a salaried clerk Ugoji was paid only once a month and most of the Igbo men sitting round the table at the front of the Yankee Bar were either businessmen or self-employed artisans. They made their money any day of the week.

'Oh, sit yourself down, we'll buy you a drink instead. You don't have to dramatize your approach like a white-coated doctor coming into a ward full of patients. We're your friends, man. Take that woebegone look from your face,' Mr Uju, a contractor, admonished.

Ugoji thanked them. He drank long and deep of the local barley drink, *burukutu*, then said inconsequentially, 'Do you know, I keep telling Area Mama and her husband to mend that sign at the front. Have you noticed that the "K" has been missing for months?'

'Has it?' asked Joe Duru. 'I didn't notice. But I know you are feeling better now. What was that earlier look about? Had a row with your Regina? I told you two to get married so that we can come and drink at your place.'

'No, it's not Regina. It's something very serious but I pray it isn't true.' He told his friends of his encounter with the wealthy Yoruba Mr Idowu, omitting mention of how much money the man took from the bank and the 'dash' of twenty pounds he had given.

There was an involuntary silence after Ugoji imparted the unwelcome news. They all became suddenly sober, despite the fact that most of them had been drinking for hours, since the bar opened that evening. Then Duru, who could not put up with a moody atmosphere, said in an unnecessarily loud voice, as if to convince himself:

'Maybe Onyemere is hiding in the harem of one of those Hausa women he flirted with when he came here, singing in their language and everything.'

Uneasy laughter followed this. The proprietress of the bar, locally known as Area Mama, bustled out, greeting everyone in her happy voice. 'Who is in a harem?' she asked.

'Oh, Onyemere, who else?' Mr Uju said.

'Well, I wouldn't be surprised. Anything is possible in the name of "One Nigeria". Now, forget about him. I've finished cooking, and there's fresh okro soup and tuo, nice cornmeal or yam flour, or garri. Take your choice,' she announced as she bustled back inside, her rolling posterior like two large pieces of dough.

After filling themselves with Area Mama's yam flour dough and her spicy okro soup, it was unanimously agreed that most Yorubas were cowards.

'Fancy running away like that at an unconfirmed rumour!' Duru exclaimed.

'Even if it were true, the Igbos should be the last to go. I've never even been to the East,' said a young man who had joined them. 'I would lose my job and my livelihood if I left here.'

'Maybe the Yorubas are spreading such rumours so that we'll all get scared and run away and then they can take our jobs,' Duru said darkly.

'It's not beyond them,' Uju said.

'Anyway, rumour or no rumour, we should have heard about it by now,' put in Area Papa, who was as dry as stockfish. One would have thought that his wife ate for both of them. She was loud and had lots of dancing flesh while he was thin, quiet and spoke with deliberation.

Ugoji's head sank deeper on to his chest as he tucked into the big bowl of *amala* yam dough, as if he was not the bringer of the unsavoury news.

Area Mama shouted to them that the news was on the radio. But the men were all so mellowed with beer and *burukutu* that when it was announced that Onyemere was missing they laughed it off, saying that he probably was having a good time somewhere with a woman.

Ugoji left them to it. When he got home, Regina was waiting for him. The night air had miraculously cleared his head.

'Have you heard?' she wailed. 'They have kidnapped him. The Hausas are going to start slaughtering us again. I wish I had gone back home before.'

'How were you to know this would happen? The Okonjis, who went home following the rising after the Sardauna's death, lost all their

81

belongings. The father is still jobless, because his employers said he left without giving notice.'

'Yes, but at least he saved his life.'

'Don't fret. It will blow over. The Hausas all believed Onyemere when he told them that the Sardauna and Nguru Kano died by accident. They could not help but be convinced by his speech.'

Regina shook her head. 'The pain is still there. The Sardauna was their spiritual leader, their Pope, and Nguru Kano his messenger from Allah. Onyemere waved a kind of magic wand over them with his presence, but now that presence is gone . . . I think we should keep a low profile until we see how things turn out. I'm frightened, Ralph. These people have seen how vulnerable we are. They won't hesitate to strike again. They are like sheep, and we Southerners have taken their shepherd from them. It's trouble.'

There was no sleep that night. They watched and waited, like most Ibo families trapped there in the North, praying that common sense would prevail. By morning, people were beginning to face life with cautious optimism; maybe Onyemere was only kidnapped after all, not dead. But it was too much to hope for.

The Hausas were at first sorry for the demise of a man who only a few days previously had almost been successful in consoling them for their loss. Less than forty-eight hours after the announcement, the radicals again started up their cries about a holy war. They carried clubs and machetes, tore down from their own areas into the Sabon Garri shouting, 'Death to the kaferi infidels!' At the Barclays Bank, they hacked humans to death and those who tried to escape were clubbed and battered to death. 'Down with all Igbo infidels! Down with the enemy!' they screamed, and the bank workers stared horrified. Anybody who did not have a tribal mark on his face was regarded as Igbo. That was what saved Ralph Ugoji; his conservative Western Igbo mother had seen to it that he had little tribal dots on both his cheeks because she did not like a man having such a moon-like face and these marks were meant to relieve the broadness.

'I am not an Igbo. See the marks on my face,' Ugoji shouted as one man lifted his blood-dripping club.

'Then move, Tofi,' he screamed, showing teeth that looked like the fangs of a wild dog.

Ugoji ran for his life out of the building. He passed the Yankee Bar on his way to his home and he saw with horror, out of the corner of his eye, what they were doing to Area Mama. She was stripped naked and was being dragged by two madmen who were tearing her feet in opposite directions. Area Papa was still alive, but only just. One of his shoulders had been completely hacked away. Ugoji ran, the animal cries of those being slaughtered in broad daylight following him. Inside his house he found Regina under one of the beds, whimpering and shivering as if she had malaria.

Only God knew how those who survived achieved that great feat. Igbos were hounded from their homes, from the market places, and many were killed at the airport on their way to the East. Then the witch-hunt began. The murderers started combing every dwelling. It was only a question of time. The Hausas did not distinguish between Eastern and Western Igbo, and whenever an Ibo was caught in the street, maybe going in search of food, he was forced to tell the killers where fellow Igbos were.

Then one Sunday afternoon, barely two weeks after Onyemere's sudden disappearance, Ugoji heard people breaking down the door of the house where he and his girlfriend were hiding. There was no way out except to climb through the small high window at the back of the room, on to the roof and then jump down into the sugar-cane bush. Even if there were any time to think about helping Regina escape he knew she could not manage it. He would have to leave her behind, and trust to their compassion.

'They are here,' he said to her in a sad, gruff voice. 'They won't kill you. Just play the dumb woman. But if it comes to it, please don't resist rape; that may save your life.' He gave her a wordless hug, took off his bulky clothes, and in so doing his fingers touched the twenty pounds Idowu had given him. He pushed the money into the hands of Regina who was shivering with shock, then he scrambled through the window, jumped down outside and ran for it. As he ran he heard Regina's cries of fear and he could only pray they spared her life. There was nothing he could do for her now.

He lived in the bush for three weeks, existing on nothing but the cane sugar that grew wild around the area. He lost so much weight that when he touched his sides he could count his ribs. Then he developed diarrhoea, and he suspected that if he did not do anything to help himself he would certainly die due to the progressive inability of his system to cope with an empty stomach. 'How can politicians be preaching "One Nigeria" when a tribe of people is being massacred?' he kept asking himself. 'When the Europeans ruled us, few people died; now we rule ourselves, we butcher each other like meat-sellers slaughtering cows.' It was in that state of bitterness that he crawled back to his apartment to see what he could get, before trying to make his way home to the Mid-West, to his tribe and to his own people. It still pained him to remember that he was only alive because he had denied his tribe.

The sight that confronted him in that twilight was one he would never forget. He thought that the smell that assailed him to the point of making him retch was the result of his exhaustion, until he stepped on something that exploded and let out a slimy liquid. He jumped to one side. But when his eyes became accustomed to the darkness he saw that he had stepped on pieces of human body. He stared for some seconds, dazed and almost fainting. He got hold of himself, looked round and asked aloud, 'Why did I come back?' He made his way to where his water cooler was and scooped some water into his mouth. Even the water seemed to have collected some of the human smell. Although it was to look for food that his feet had instinctively carried him into the house in the first place, he did not wait to do so now. He found the portable radio he kept beside his bed, took a warm sweater and left, this time through the back door. He had no energy to climb through the window, he did not care any more. 'Poor Regina, poor beautiful Regina. I wish you had insisted on following me. But you could not climb through the roof. People who could murder such a beautiful woman in cold blood are not worthy of being called members of the human race.'

He tottered along, knowing that his best bet was to go home by train; something warned him against going to the airport. He took cover again in the sugar-cane grove, for the road was too open, and he smiled bitterly when tuning in the radio he heard Chijioke Abosi encouraging all Ibos not to leave their jobs.

At the railway station Ugoji wondered whether perhaps Regina had not been lucky. The passengers on the platform were still alive – just – but the killers had made sure that those Igbos who went back home would always remember their stay in the North. Nearly all the women were without one breast. The very old ones had only one eye each. Some of the men had been castrated, some had only one arm, others had one foot amputated. All were in a shocked daze, their eyes staring as if from skulls of the long dead and buried.

One boy of about fifteen, who had long taken leave of his senses, rushed up to Ugoji and started to blubber, with saliva dripping from both corners of his mouth, 'My mother, my father . . . we were made to watch while they pounded them like yam with their clubs. My mother, she begged them for our lives and they promised her they wouldn't kill us, but they made us watch our parents die. Then as we neared the door they noticed that my older sister was pregnant . . . they pounded on her, spread her wide and pushed the sharp edge of their club inside her, pounding her and the baby . . . My mother, they – '

One of his brothers came and pulled him away, apologizing and saying to Ugoji, 'He has been like this since the night of the incident.'

Ugoji simply gaped. He could not take it in. In fact he did not remember much of that journey back to the East. Many people who had been hiding in the nearby bushes, still afraid to show themselves, ran out and filled the train when it came. Some bled to death on the way, but most of them arrived at Enugu, where those who were in a state to eat were fed. The doctors and nurses there wept as they performed emergency operations, soothed the demented and gave hope to the bewildered and forlorn.

A journalist approached them and asked what they felt. Most were not in a state of mind to talk; but Ugoji spoke out fearlessly.

'Tell Abosi to forget talk of "One Nigeria". Tell him to forget about his colleague Saka Momoh in Lagos; that man will not help us. Nigeria does not want us. Look at our innocent men and women. Thousands were mauled in broad daylight, thousands who can never get away are still to be killed. And Abosi is there talking about our jobs. You have to be alive before you can hold down a job. Why should we sit and let our people be killed this way without raising a finger to defend ourselves, just because we are waiting for an ordinary army recruit in Lagos to make up his mind? If he can't do it, we should nominate another man. We may be called the Jews of Africa but we don't want the same fate as the Jews in the last war.' Ugoji paused for breath, surprised at himself.

But the small crowd who surrounded him encouraged him to go on, fanning his rage by their looks and silent gestures that told him he was speaking for them all.

A canoe ferried Ugoji to his native Ibuza, where he saw more casualties arriving from all parts of Hausaland. It was said that over thirty thousand Igbos died in that first part of the troubles.

In Lagos, a place as cosmopolitan as any modern capital, things were even more chaotic. But whereas in the North the massacre was carried out openly, here it was done discreetly. People who had the remotest connection with Igboland started disappearing. Many dead bodies were found floating along the Lagos creeks.

In the middle of this chaos Alan Grey paid Debbie Ogedemgbe a visit. He had heard that she was at her family's former luxurious home, packing away the furniture, for she had been told that the house would be handed over to Saka Momoh who had now been appointed leader of the army in the West and Lagos. Debbie was feeling very low, although she still tried to hide her grief.

Tears came as she folded an old cotton rug which her late father had insisted on carrying with him wherever he went, saying that it was the best in the world. It used to be placed in the bathroom just before he bathed, then hung out to dry in the sun during the day and returned to the cool bedroom in the evening. No amount of protestation from his wife, no cynical remarks from the rest of the family could make him buy another rug. As Debbie held it in her hands, with her thoughts so far away, she did not hear the bell ring.

Alan stood by the doorway, army hat in his hand, hesitating. His attention was momentarily caught by Debbie's overfed black cat, which was stretching and lazing in the warm evening sunshine. It yawned with boredom and fixed its yellow and black eyes on Alan. He imagined it saying, 'I used to know you, you used to visit us here. Now what has happened? Why is the whole place so deserted? Why didn't you do anything to stop all this mess?' It gave another yawn, looked away from him and coiled itself again on the warm grass.

'They say that black cats are witches – do you believe it, Alan?' Debbie asked all of a sudden, making him involuntarily jump to attention. He had not realized that she was aware of his presence.

'I'm sorry, Debbie . . . er, the officers told me you were here so I've come to – '

'You've come to say goodbye. You're going back to your country. Everybody is leaving Nigeria but the Nigerians; the Americans are evacuating their people, all the British females have already gone. I get the message: we got ourselves into this mess, we have to stew in it and clear it up ourselves. Then you foreigners will come back and befriend the winner. I get the message.'

'You are wrong, Debbie, I am not leaving Nigeria, though God only knows why. I was planning only to go to John Nwokolo's place. I've been promising myself to go to the Mid-West again for so long. I very much want to preserve those artistic works.'

'Oh, come off it! Who do you think you are deceiving? Those old relics you claim to be saving are going to adorn your museums and art galleries.'

'Yes, yes, maybe.' Alan gritted his teeth to control his rising temper. 'But if I leave them here they will be destroyed forever, in the name of what your country calls modernization. Do you know that John Nwokolo's brother is threatening to burn them all, just because he's been ordained a vicar after spending a couple of years at your country's fifth-rate university?'

Debbie looked up sharply at him. Her eyes seemed hollowed out of her face, her cheeks sunk in like those of old people without their dentures. It was clear that she was under strain, and Alan felt protective.

'Sorry, Debbie. I shouldn't have said that. We are all under pressure and – '

'Oh, forget it. I don't know why you don't go back to your own country and forget all about us.'

'I could never do that. Forget you, I mean.'

Debbie laughed quietly, a ghost of her former charming laugh. 'What do you think I feel like doing now?' she asked. 'I'll tell you. I feel like going straight to Iddo bridge and plunging myself into the water underneath it, never to be heard of again.'

'But why? I know things are not as they should be, but you have borne your father's death bravely . . .'

'My father, my father. He was just one man. Haven't you heard how first I betrayed him by joining the army? Then when I got there what did I do? When soldiers were needed to go and make a surprise arrest of all Igbo soldiers at Ikeja barracks, after Onyemere was kidnapped and I suspected he was dead, I jumped at the opportunity. I think Saka Momoh allowed me because he thought I wanted to avenge my father's death, though that didn't occur to me at the time. Oh, Alan, you should have seen the eyes of those men, whose only crime was that they were Igbos. No one told me they were going to be killed, though I admit that I did enjoy making those men obey me, Alan. Now . . . they are all dead, and I was the one who arrested them. I put them in a position where they could not lift a finger to defend themselves. And you stand there talking to me about guilt.'

'Look, all that is past now. It may take time but you will forget. The whole country will forget soon anyway. Here, look at today's papers. The headlines are very hopeful. Ankrah of Ghana is offering to mediate and there's to be a meeting at Aburi with Saka Momoh and Chijioke Abosi. I don't think Momoh enjoys being called an ineffective leader. He wants this opportunity to make it up with Chijioke.'

'I hope and pray the two of them sink their differences and come to a settlement.'

'Momoh only wants Abosi to recognize his leadership; as soon as that's been achieved, the rest will follow easily. Chijioke was born with the proverbial silver spoon in his mouth, whereas Saka is an aspirant, a social climber. He wants to stay at the top, and he wants peace to enjoy being there. This will be a great test for Abosi. If he really is for his people, he'll give in and let Momoh keep the federal capital, while they come to an agreement over the East.'

'But doesn't Abosi want a united Nigeria? He can't cut the East away from the federation. Even Momoh wouldn't allow that,' Debbie said.

Alan nodded, thoughtful. 'Debbie, are you quite sure Onyemere is dead? No one seems to have a clue where his body is.'

'Have they told us where my father's body is? To reveal such a thing would badly incriminate some people. But I'm sure Saka knows the man is dead, otherwise he wouldn't be so confident as to step into his shoes so readily.'

'Well, all should be revealed at the meeting in Ghana.'

Debbie continued packing while Alan watched.

After a time he asked, 'What are you going to do, Debbie?

She shook her head. 'I don't want to think about that yet. I would like to stay in the army and go to the East, but I'd be a wanted person for the part I played in the deaths of those men. I don't want to go back to civilian life, and don't talk to me about getting married. I'm in no mood to start breeding. Right now I have to clear out our things from here to make room for Momoh.' She burst into joyless laughter. 'To clear out Samuel Ogedemgbe's things for the likes of Saka Momoh, that raw specimen who hasn't the faintest idea how a statesman should behave! Oh, poor Nigeria, that you should be reduced to this. You have ruined yourself, you have lost distinguished and irreplaceable men of bearing and breeding . . .'

'Ah, but what about a man like Chijioke Abosi? Whether he likes it or not leadership is being thrust upon him. He is cool, well educated, a gentleman and determined. Maybe a little spoilt, but that is to be expected.'

'You forget that he is Igbo, and once our national hounds have tasted Igbo blood all Igbos will be hunted from their hiding places and led sacrificially to the slaughter.'

'Don't think that way, Debbie. All this will pass. I'm sure Saka will halt the butchery at this end at least. After all, like you, he is neither Igbo nor Yoruba, nor even Hausa proper. He will bring calm, you'll see.'

'I hope you're right, Alan.'

Suddenly there was the screech and door-banging of army lorries outside and the sound of orders being yelled. Debbie moved to the window and saw young privates jumping down from the lorries and marching into the house.

'Did you know the soldiers would be coming so soon, Alan, while I'm still here packing? Are they coming to arrest me or something?'

'Why should they arrest you? As far as the soldiers are concerned there is still only one national army. Abosi and Momoh may have their differences but those will be settled. And you are still in the army . . .' He paused. 'Are you sure you really want to see this army bug through? Because if you do, you may soon be actually killing people, not just ordering others under you to do it. If you mourn so deeply the deaths of men you didn't yourself kill and whose deaths you didn't even order, what will happen on the battlefield?'

'In other words you think I'm weak because I am a woman? Hmm. My secret is safe with you. Well, if there is to be division in the Nigerian army, I'm making my way to Abosi.'

'You'd do well as a peace ambassador between the two warring leaders, since they both like and respect you.'

'I'd soon be declared redundant, if our prayers are answered and the two men settle their differences at Aburi.'

At this point the soldiers, their guns at the ready, marched into the main room where Alan was standing with Debbie. The young officer leading six recruits saluted, clicking the heels of his shiny boots. Alan returned the salute.

'I was here to see Miss Ogedemgbe,' he said. 'She's just about to leave. The packed cases are to be sent to the address she will give you and I'm sure you won't need to tamper with any of them.'

'Yes, sir,' barked the young officer, and saluted again.

Debbie picked up a few pieces, then the cat, and walked along the long open veranda to the main road where her car was parked.

'Thanks, Alan. I don't know when I shall be seeing you again. But pray all goes well at Aburi so we can all go back to proper soldiering.'

Alan smiled and kissed her lightly on both cheeks. 'I'll keep in touch,' he promised as he went to his landrover and ordered the driver to wake up.

Debbie's white Mercedes headed towards the mainland, while Alan went to the other side of Ikoyi.

That very evening Saka Momoh made his maiden speech to the nation. It seemed from his halting manner that he had not had time to rehearse the script which had been clearly typed out for him. He stumbled over simple words and most of the long political ones had to be repeated to make sense to him, to say nothing of his listeners. None the less he muddled through. Like a politician, he made many promises: the people responsible for killing the Igbos would be severely and promptly punished. And like a soldier he made liberal use of such words as 'severely' and 'promptly'. Chief Odumosu, the politician who was in detention, would be released forthwith. The harassment and killing of Igbos would stop. Those who wished to return to their villages of origin should not be hindred. With everyone's help, he intended to keep Nigeria one country.

It was a desperate speech of hope. But how, in reality, was he going to prevent Igbos being killed in the remote Northern parts of the country, being taken from their sleeping places and slaughtered in the dead of night? There was little likelihood of Momoh's being able to do anything, apart from releasing Chief Odumosu. Northern soldiers were pouring into the South, so men were being quickly and sketchily trained to counteract this. As soon as Odumosu was released, his voice joined forces with those of the thinking people of the country calling for peace. He was alarmed at the number of Northern soldiers from Momoh's part of the country parading along the major roads of the Yoruba lands.

Meanwhile frightened refugees of Eastern origin were daily streaming down to Abosi. Two weeks after Momoh's speech, it became clear that he could do little to halt the Northern invasion. Eye-witnesses were summoned to Abosi's house in Aba, and among them was Ralph Ugoji, the bank cashier who had spoken so eloquently at the railway station in Enugu. The most moving witness was a young woman from Lagos who gave an account of how her husband was murdered a few yards from their house.

'We had heard rumours that our people were being molested, but we did not believe them,' began the young mother, tears welling up in her eyes and spilling all over her face. Her nine-month-old baby boy was astride her back, unaware of all the sadness about him. 'Most responsible Igbo men started sleeping outside their houses. My husband did the same. But on the night they took him away a Yoruba child, one of our neighbour's, was ill and called around nine o'clock for a bottle of dysentery tablets. My husband was a chemist and we owned our own shop. As he was locking up, I heard the heavy footsteps of soldiers. I thought they were just passing but they banged on our house door and forced me to open up. They asked where my husband was, and I told them that I did not know. My husband saw from outside, but he was more worried for us. I wish he had not come in. Of course they grabbed him, and he promised to give them everything. They threatened to kill me and our two babies. My husband ordered me to do what they said. As he said so, one of the soldiers landed the butt of his heavy gun on his back. He called for help as they started to drag him out of the house. Our neighbours heard him calling for God's help, calling his mother and me, but none of us could help. We all heard the firing, and I disobeyed him and ran out . . . I was alone in the dirty muddy street where his bullet-ridden body, still warm, was left. I realized later that the soldiers knew we were Igbos through some Yoruba people who owed my husband money; they could never afford to pay him back so the only way was to eliminate him. I brought his body home for burial the following day. I do not wish to see that town Lagos again.'

All the women present, including Juliana Abosi who was sitting in the corner listening to this story, began to cry.

Then Ugoji repeated his own experience from the North, and when his story was not only confirmed but expanded by his friend Duru from the Yankee Bar, who had also miraculously survived, the anger of those listening was stirred to fever point. Many urged Abosi not to bother to wait for Aburi but to declare war immediately.

Abosi was attentive and begged his annoyed people to give him a few moments to speak. 'Nobody wins a war. Please try to remember that. If this can be settled without our having to fire a shot, I shall be the happiest man alive. But since you have unofficially elected me your leader in this time of our need I must consult my advisers. This misunderstanding is not just between the Igbos and the rest of Nigeria but between Igbos from the West (you heard Mr Ugoji), Igbos from the East and the minority tribes in the East, against the rest of Nigeria. So before I make any move, all these people must be fully consulted. We must also be patient. After all, Momoh made his promise only two weeks ago. You know the speed of communications in our country at the best of times, to say nothing of now when there is chaos in every town and village. If all else fails, I am sure Aburi will set everything right.'

Abosi's voice was deep yet calm. After these heartfelt words he sat down. He looked tired, his wide shoulders stooped and his watchful eyes were almost closing from lack of sleep. His wife, knowing the private unhappiness that hovered over their marriage, felt the more sorry for him. She found it difficult to conceive and when eventually she did become pregnant the signs of miscarriage were always looming. She had begun to feel them now, just as with the two previous miscarriages, and she and her husband had scarcely slept at all the night before from worry. Juliana hoped Saka Momoh would do something soon, if only to save Abosi from the early grave she suspected would be his lot if he continued this way.

Many of his listeners did not agree with him, and showed their impatience in loud yells and a great deal of muttering.

'If that is the case, my brothers and sisters, will you let me consult our elders? Brigadier Onyemere has gone, I know, but don't forget that Dr Ozimba and Dr Eze are still with us. And if Aburi fails, well, we can break away after that. That much I promise.'

On this solemn vow the meeting closed. Abosi had given hope to the despairing and joy to the sorrowful and the recently bereaved. He had hoped he would not be pushed to the wall, and he was still pondering all this, and waiting for the elders who had been sent for, when a young soldier was brought in. After the heel-clicking salutes, a note was given to Abosi. As he read the contents a slow smile spread on his dark face. He thanked the officer and went back to the main part of the house.

His wife was lying in bed as she had been ordered to. He had meant to ask why she had come to the main hall earlier on to listen to the refugees' horror stories, but for one reason or another he had not had time to speak to her. The smile disappeared from his face as he saw her tossing in pain.

'What is it, Juliana?'

'We are losing the child, Chijioke. I am sorry.'

'Can't the doctor do anything?'

'He thinks I'm imagining it . . . and in any case, if the child is going, it is going. There is little he can do about it.'

She began to cry deep touching sobs, and Abosi sat by the bed. After a few seconds he knew that she needed a doctor and quickly. For the rest of the day they watched helplessly as the little life, whose heartbeat they had already begun to hear, drained away.

He did not have much time to mourn the loss of his unborn child, however, for the business of his people took over. His advisers were there to meet with him and it was to the elder politicians that Abosi read the note the young soldier had given him. In it the released Chief Odumosu confirmed what the refugees had said – that there were now army camps springing up all over Ibadan. He was worried, but if the Aburi talks failed he intended to declare the West a separate state; Abosi should do the same in the East. So if the worst came to the worst, any war would be between the North and the South.

This pleased Abosi indeed and he went on to enthuse, 'At least I now have reason not to declare war immediately. Our people will understand in the face of this evidence.'

'Don't forget,' drawled Dr Ozimba, 'that Chief Oluremi Odumosu is a politician and not an army man.' This statement provoked laughter.

Abosi noticed that these men, who were colleagues of his father's, were all getting on in age. Eze had grown so obese that he seemed to be carrying someone else's body along with him; he was slower, more cautious. As for Ozimba, whose charm and charisma had once earned him the foremost position in Nigerian politics, he seemed to have been plunged eternally into a ditch of perpetual doubt. It was a difficult time for all of them. But, as Abosi reminded them, it would be the height of irresponsibility to wait until the Northern soldiers came to their door before doing anything. Yet though Abosi consulted these politicians, he knew he would rely more on the logical if sometimes abstract advice of the university lecturers and academics. He was not going to betray the people who had trusted him.

Abosi was urged not to go into detailed arguments at Aburi. There were few points he had to put to Saka Momoh, and if Momoh agreed to them then Abosi should let him be the supreme commander of the whole country if he so desired.

'Supreme commander without any power at all,' mocked one of the delegates.

'Well, he wants the name more than anything,' said Abosi.

They all became light-headed and there was no doubt but that the East would gain its autonomy within Nigeria after Aburi. Someone raised the problem of the Western Igbos, considering the fact that it was John Nwokolo who had led the band that eliminated the Sardauna; but it was agreed that it was not yet an important issue. They could even be given the choice of joining the Eastern Igbos or following the rest of the country.

Prayers were said in many churches after the announcement that the two leaders were willing to meet at Aburi to settle the differences, and speculation abounded in the newspapers. The descriptions of what they imagined would happen and be said made very entertaining reading, but the message was clear: every thinking Nigerian wanted peace, and time to enjoy the new-found oil money.

It was in this spirit of optimism that Abosi, flanked by his learned friends, went to the elegant palace situated on top of a hill at Aburi in Ghana. The beauty of the place could be seen for miles around. Through the high-ceilinged and chandeliered hall the army men marched to their seats. The former politicians were there in their various impressive ethnic outfits. Their host, Ankrah, was very hopeful and it showed in his welcome. He greeted the two leaders together, referring to them as brothers.

Abosi was relaxed but watchful. Momoh was jumpy and apprehensive, like a schoolboy who had neglected to do his homework; if he failed at this important meeting, in which so many Nigerians put so much hope, he could not foretell what would happen. He had brought fewer advisers than Abosi and gave the impression that he was going to make all the decisions by himself. It was clear that he trusted no one.

It was remarkable how many foreign journalists had flocked into Ghana, in spite of the screening and security checks imposed at the airport to limit their number.

'One would think this was a European congress or something,' remarked Dr Ozimba to Dr Eze at the sight of so many white faces.

'They don't want to miss anything. Have you seen our "supreme commander"? He's shaking like a water lily.'

The meeting soon started and telegrams from well-wishers like the old governor-general Sir Fergus Grey were read. The delegates did not have to be reminded that the whole world was watching and listening for the outcome of this historic meeting.

Abosi dispensed with any frills or drama. Momoh could keep his capital, Abosi said, all he himself asked was for the butchery of Igbos to stop, for the Hausa soldiers to go back to their barracks and for the East to be granted autonomy within the federation.

The atmosphere was tense. Surely Momoh would refuse, surely he could see the catch, surely he would know that this was too easy?

But Momoh wanted peace. He saw nothing wrong in letting the East manage its own affairs. He was the more relieved that the worries he had entertained about Abosi acknowledging his leadership were unfounded. He wouldn't even have to deliver the long defence speech that had been written for him and that he'd spent the night rehearsing, learning how to modulate his voice, pause at the right places, twist his neck in a certain way – to think all that was no longer necessary. Let the East go, if they wished to; after all, they would still be the same country and he, Saka Momoh, would be the supreme commander of the army of Nigeria. That alone was worth everything.

His excitement was unconcealed as he bubbled out his thanks and relief. He agreed to the proposal:

'I always knew that Aburi would settle our differences. We are all brothers really, and when brothers quarrel they make it up. I am only sorry to announce officially the death of our beloved Brigadier Onyemere, who was killed in the active service of his country. His widow and relatives will be amply compensated, and I beg them to accept our sympathy.'

As the journalists gaped and the Western diplomats present bit their nails, suspecting a trap somewhere, they heard Abosi's ponderous voice acknowledging Saka Momoh as the supreme commander and, in the same breath, asking him to make arrangements to have Onyemere's body flown to the East, and to compensate the refugees for their losses. Abosi begged him again as the supreme commander to lose no time in making a declaration of what he had promised to do, so that the troublesome Hausas would go back, so that the Igbos would feel safe.

Chief Odumosu, looking greyer and thinner, answered on Momoh's behalf that the commander should be able to make his declaration within forty-eight hours. 'It is not only the Igbos who are frightened of the Hausa soldiers; our Yoruba people are as well. They do not understand our language, and their guns terrify innocent people.'

Momoh, wearing the bright smile that seemed to be carved out of his face, nodded in agreement.

Abosi looked at the advisers that flanked him and from their grave nods he knew that he had gained all they wanted.

At the end of the conference, congratulations were given to the two army officers, Saka Momoh and Chijioke Abosi, the former accepting it all with studied calmness, the latter very exuberant. They toasted to the future peace of their country. They embraced, trying to convince themselves that they had nothing against one another, as the whole world could see. It made a good front-page photograph.

While the big men were busy celebrating the end of the civil misunderstanding, Alan Grey was standing and admiring the beautiful setting of the palace. He was joined by his friend Giles who had been present throughout the proceedings.

'What do you make of the charade that went on in there, Giles?'

'I think that man Momoh is a fool and Abosi knew it,' Giles laughed. 'It wasn't really fair, Abosi taking advantage of the man's foolishness. How can he rule as the supreme whatever-he-calls-it without any money? The country is in debt and her only hope is from the oilwells in the East. Yet he is letting Abosi take all that. Well, that's their business, so long as they let Britain have the greatest share.'

'You must be kidding. You think Abosi is a fool? Even if he were, those shrewd advisers of his would see to it that they join hands with the Arabs in the Middle East to tighten their squeeze on the West.

With Momoh controlling the oil there might be hope of trade with Britain.'

'Hmmm, you're right there. Momoh has been ordering all his weapons from us whereas the tricky Igbos have been getting their supplies from China and France. I must say I find that a bid odd.'

'It's not so odd when you remember that Abosi lived most of his life in England and knows what we actually are.'

'Then Momoh is not going to make that declaration!'

'Of course not, and we are starting on him straight away. Remember, you don't tell the likes of Momoh what to do, you advise them. They are too sensitive about their own inadequacies.'

They soon joined the other Western jounalists and Alan began chatting animatedly to a young female photo-journalist. They were all hoping that the men of the day would grant them an interview for their various papers. Abosi, however, refused to say anything, claiming that he was in a hurry, and his advisers quickly followed in his wake. But the trim girl gave Momoh a bewitching smile and asked sweetly:

'Your Excellency, how come a quarter of the country will be keeping most of the oil money?'

'Oil money, what oil money?' Saka Momoh asked, a nerve on his forehead beginning to twitch, as realization began to dawn.

'Well, since you granted Abosi the East's autonomy – '

'Autonomy! Autonomy!' Momoh gave her a quizzical look, no doubt uncertain what the word actually meant. He gazed around him helplessly, and saw that the smile on the face of Chief Odumosu was frozen.

Then Alan Grey, the friend of Nigeria, stepped in: 'His Excellency will doubtless work out the details of all that later. What we have seen agreed on today is a framework for peace. The details will be filled in later.'

'Yes, a framework for peace,' Saka agreed quickly, smiling his thanks to Alan as he made his way to the waiting limousine.

When Abosi reached Aba and broke the good news to the eagerly waiting crowd, there was jubilation. Children danced in the streets, messages of congratulation poured in from Igbo leaders and the leaders of most of the minority tribal groups. Later people glued their ears to their radio sets, waiting for the declaration. Abosi's wife Juliana gave him progress reports from time to time as he tried to snatch some sleep. The feeling of happy anticipation was heavy in the air, filling all the houses, the streets and everybody's hearts. They were going to be free at last.

A feeling of disappointment started to replace the thrilled expectation as hours rolled into days. Radio Nigeria was saying many things, but not a mention was made of Aburi, to say nothing of any kind of announcement about the autonomy of the Igbo East.

On the third day, Abosi and his advisers knew that they must meet, for they all felt they had to share their sense of failure with fellow sufferers. And throughout that short meeting the question that kept cropping up was, 'What are we going to do if this man Saka Momoh goes back on his word?'

'He did promise to make the announcement as soon as he got to Lagos,' Abosi said dogmatically. 'I've known him longer than any of you. Momoh has many faults, but going back on his word is not one of them. He's a dedicated soldier who likes to regard himself as a gentleman as well.'

'We all know that soldiers should keep their promises,' Dr Ozimba said with caution, 'but Momoh is now a politician as well as a soldier. He has to be diplomatic and listen and act upon advice given him.'

'I know this couldn't be Momoh's doing alone. Somebody must be behind him in this. But it beats me who that is, who would want to see this country awash with the blood of her people.'

'Could it be one of his new foreign friends?' Dr Eze asked tentatively.

'Maybe, maybe. But I'm sure of one thing: that foreign power can't be Britain, nor would it ever be America. I know the way these people think. I grew up among them,' Abosi said. 'They would never encourage a war of separation in a place like Nigeria. Perhaps the communists are at the back of all this.'

Dr Ozimba's dry guttural laugh echoed soulfully in the makeshift corrugated-iron bungalow where the meeting was being held.

'The poor communists are fast becoming the scapegoats for anything that goes wrong in the Western world. So you believe the British are above such two-faced activities, even when it would work to their advantage?' he asked cynically. 'Well, maybe so. Those people knew what they were doing when they encouraged us to educate our elitist sons and daughters in their country . . .'

Abosi whirled round and his piercing eyes bore deeply into Ozimba's face. 'Are you suggesting that I am brainwashed, Dr Ozimba?' he growled.

'No, no, no,' declared the elder statesman. 'On the contrary, I am just making a general observation. After all, didn't I have my own boys educated there? We have much more important things to worry about, Chijioke. Listen, none of us here want to fight. But since we have talked ourselves into this corner, we have to be prepared for anything. Momoh, for all his outward obstinacy, can be easily swayed. Let us hope and pray that it is just that they are still making their minds up. Anyway, didn't Chief Odumosu promise to declare a separate Yoruba state if Momoh did not act quickly enough? Well, he hasn't made a move yet; so, brothers, let us wait. We don't want to be accused of being the first to divide the country, do we?'

On this cautious note they dispersed, hoping to hear favourable news from Lagos soon.

Days rolled into weeks. Then after a fortnight they did hear from Lagos, but it was not the news they wanted to hear. It was news of more mutilated Igbo bodies being brought home by stunned relatives, relatives who were too bemused to recount what happened as members of their families were dragged from sleep to be shot in cold blood, or beaten out of their hiding places to have their throats severed with blunt cutlasses. The survivors made their leaders painfully aware that if it was not to continue being a shameful thing to be an Ibo in Nigeria there was only one sensible solution: secession.

Around four o'clock in the morning Abosi lay awake on his back sleeplessly staring at the whitewashed ceiling. His thoughts were tortured. He knew every member of his inner circle wanted the Eastern region to secede. He wanted it too, if it would work. But what of the rest of Nigeria, would they take it calmly and simply do nothing? He doubted it. But one thing he knew, when it came to fighting to defend his territory, the Igbo man was more determined than anyone else. Yet somehow Abosi was still uneasy. Suppose there was a war and Nigeria decided to prolong it, how would they hold out? They were tough hard-working people, but could they bluff through a long period of deprivation and maybe a series of blockades?

Abosi tried not to dwell on these doubts and rolled to one side, away from Juliana, in order to get a few hours' sleep before day. The next thing he heard was the rumbling of a car along the driveway that led to the temporary home where he was staying with his family in Enugu. He got up slowly and peered into the still young day and saw the sentry in front of his house saluting an officer. Something must have happened to warrant the officer's early visit. Abosi padded towards the sitting-room, covering himself with a dressing-gown as he went.

Colonel Nwafor, one of the senior Igbo officers left alive after the Ikeja massacre, came up to him and saluted.

'We have received official news from Lagos, sir,' he announced crisply.

Abosi smiled benignly, rubbing his tangled beard. He was about to say that he had known Momoh would not go back on his word and that common sense would prevail and prevent him pushing the people of the Eastern region into such a tight corner that they would have to fight for their survival. But before he could give voice to his relief, he saw that the officer before him, who was still standing to attention, looked so serious that his seriousness could only be unhappiness. No, this officer had brought no good news.

'What is the news?' Abosi murmured.

'Saka Momoh has divided Nigeria into twelve states, sir.'

'Ah . . . so that's the game.' Abosi did not permit himself to say any more, not in front of Colonel Nwafor. He only thanked him and walked back into the house.

He saw Momoh's tactics clearly: to divide and rule. His dividing the nation into twelve states would mean putting wedges between the united people of the Eastern region, Abosi thought. And this must not be allowed to take place.

'I have to be ready to take up the mantle,' Abosi said to himself as he paced nervously in his dressing-room, waiting for the morning of 28 May 1967. 'Now we have no choice but to fight for our right to live as a nation.'

The Igbo leaders could hardly restrain the joy and celebration of the people of Eastern Nigeria when the state of Biafra was declared on 30 May, three days after the news from Lagos about the division of the country.

This was a major move against the first republic of Nigeria.

PART II

8 *Divide and Rule*

Debbie Ogedemgbe's eyes flew open with the suddenness that one usually associates with bad dreams, but she had not been dreaming. She wondered why she had woken at that early hour. It was still partly dark and she could not claim to have been disturbed by the teasing glimpses of sunlight that had a way of working themselves into the bedroom through the tiny openings in the curtain. 'Perhaps Mama's snores woke me,' she reflected with affection as she looked at her mother lying curled up like a centipede on the corner of the bed. Poor woman, to be reduced to having to share a bed with the daughter she had done with nursing over twenty years before. Life must be intolerable for her, since her husband's death. No, this could not go on. After all, they still had their house in Sapele, her mother could stay there; she had nothing to do with this horrible war.

Debbie walked to the end of the room, a bare room with one all-purpose table. They were grateful to the Teteku family for giving them this shelter; Barbara and her parents had proved dependable friends. But it was time to talk to her mother seriously about going back to the Mid-West, or finding a way to reach England, until this whole episode blew over.

'All Igbos in this area, come out . . . come out! All Igbos in this area, come out . . . you have to be counted . . . All the Igbos in this area . . .'

Debbie peered out into the still dark street and made out two men who looked like army men in civilian clothing, gonging their announcement. What was it all about?

A gentle knock on the door made her jump. She could not have been mistaken for an Igbo woman, surely. They were Itsekiris, neither Igbos nor Yorubas, although their language was something of a mixture. But it would take a long time to prove that to these novice soldiers. The fastest language was always that of the gun. Although she had never yet killed anyone, if a group of army teenagers with shaved heads and snotty noses was going to come in here and demand to take her mother away, just as they had her father, Debbie was not going to stand for it. She would shoot to kill if necessary.

So determined, she dashed under the table and fished out the rifle she had taken to carrying since joining the army.

'Who are you? Shout out your name or I'll shoot!' she barked, her voice assuming the screaming quality she had been taught at Yaba barracks. 'Speak up!'

'Oh, for God's sake, Oritsha Debbie, what's come over you?'

Debbie put the rifle down and smiled slowly. 'Come in, Babs. I'm so frightened.'

'What is all this, Debbie?' asked Mrs Ogedemgbe who had woken up. She looked quickly round the room. 'What are you doing with that gun? I've told you so many times to return it until you make up your mind what you really want to do. How can a well-brought-up girl like you go about carrying guns, eh?'

'Oh, Ma, please go back to sleep. We're sorry we woke you.'

'But why are you up anyway? Are you going to kill somebody?'

Debbie took the time to light a cigarette. 'No, Mama, we're not going to kill anyone. I had a bad dream, that's all. Come on, Babs, let's go into the living-room.'

She gave Babs a cigarette and started to cough as she smoked, which made Mrs Ogedemgbe wring her hands.

'I don't know what has come over you girls. We all want freedom for women, but I doubt if we are ready for this type of freedom where young women smoke and carry guns instead of looking after husbands and nursing babies.'

Before the argument developed into a full lecture which they had both heard many times before, the two girls quickly left the room. Babs was still in giggles when they got to the front room.

'Your mother never gives up, does she?'

'No,' smiled Debbie. 'She must be wondering what kind of daughter she has raised.'

The distant sound of the gong could still be heard. Both women were quiet for a while.

'Do you think the Aburi conference has failed? No one's saying anything. I rush to buy the newspapers every morning hoping to read about the outcome, but nothing.' Debbie spoke into her cigarette smoke, her large eyes looking a little reddened. Her voice was subdued, reflecting the doubts she had begun to have.

'You're an incurable optimist, Debbie Ogedemgbe. I gave up after the first excitement. I've suspected since last week that we're in for a big war. Look at the way everyone has been behaving as if Aburi never happened. Momoh and his group simply returned and said nothing to anyone. And now this morning, just listen to those bastards, calling Igbos to come out and be counted – for what, eh? Why should one be counted in one's own country?' Babs stopped to take a breath.

'What I'd like to know is this: in a true democracy, have Momoh and his advisers the right to withhold any decision they have made from the people of Nigeria? After all, what could be more convincing than that photograph which was released of the two leaders embracing. So what's holding up the implementation of their decision?'

'Maybe he changed his mind. Maybe they convinced him on the flight back that he was wrong to want peace,' Babs said sarcastically.

'That doesn't make sense. What is he going to do, declare war on Abosi and everyone in the East? That would just mean killing more innocent people. The East alone can't fight the rest of the country, any fool can see that.'

'Any fool of a woman, perhaps, but not men, least of all army men turned politicians. The women and children who would be killed by bombs and guns would simply be statistics, war casualties. But for the soldier-politicians, the traders in arms, who only think of their personal gain, it would be the chance of a lifetime. And the politicians who started it all can pay their way to Europe or America and wait until it has all blown over,' Babs said cynically.

The gonging in the street, though now faint, was persistent like the determined death knell of a nation bent on destroying itself.

'I must look for a way to get Mother out of here,' Debbie said. 'Then I must go back to the army.'

Babs smiled slowly. 'You never left the army. You can't leave that easily, otherwise you would be a deserter.'

'Oh, Babs, you make it sound as if we are already fighting a big war. The most it would be would be a civil war, between two peoples of the same country.'

'Wake up, Debbie, my friend! Didn't you see that picture taken at Aburi, and didn't you see that all the faces in the background were white? Since when have we had white Nigerians? And the guns, even your rifle there – are they made in Nigeria? What about the oil – are we going to refine it here, use it here? You know the truth as well as I do; and believe me, I don't like what I think is coming. Yes, your mother should leave the country.'

'What about your parents, Babs? Aren't they equally vulnerable?'

Babs got up with a noisy yawn. She walked towards the window and looked out. Then she turned to face her friend. 'My parents haven't got the Ogedemgbe tag, remember. Your dead father was a politician. People take it for granted that your mother shared the same opinions as he. That's why she would be better off out of this mess.'

'You're probably right, though I don't think Mama ever had an opinion about anything except her wardrobe.'

'You're not being fair. Imagine what you'd be like if for twenty-five years you'd been the wife of a domineering man who took it upon himself to have the last word on everything that went on around him, including his wife.'

They both laughed. 'That's not very complimentary to my father,' Debbie said, still laughing.

'I'm sorry; but I'm sure he would like to be talked of in those terms.'

'Poor proud Papa . . .'

'I know. But look, girl, we're still alive, what are we going to do? How are we going to find out what is happening?'

'I'll find out, don't worry. My boyfriend is an Englishman, remember, and he should know.'

Alan was not unhappy when he saw the note on his desk that afternoon to say that Debbie had telephoned. He had had enough of male company for a while. Apart from everything else, it dawned on him that Momoh was not going to be as easy a customer as he at first appeared. He had to be flattered, cajoled and pampered before one could get him to see anything. Why, the man could not be less prepared for the role in which he found himself. He did not realize his immense responsibility, thinking of the country as no more than a barracks full of new army recruits. Still, Alan felt he had done his job, and could do with a little break. He phoned Debbie and told her he would be coming to take her out to the Island Club for a drink, or a quiet walk along the beach.

By the time Alan left his temporary abode at the barracks in Yaba it was past the rush hour yet there was still a slight hold up in traffic flow, locally known as 'go slow.' He inched his way along until he crossed the railway line into Ojuelegba. He had escaped the 'go slow' now he was in a region of uneven roads; his army Austin pumped and jumped as it made its way round this hollow and that stone or that broken bit in urgent need of repair. He was relieved when he was eventually in front of the Tetekus' house in Itire Road, Surulere.

He didn't have to wait long for an answer to his knock. He was expecting the family's fifty-year-old servant – incongruously still known as the 'small boy' – to let him in, but Babs opened the door with a wide grin and a warm welcome.

'It's nice to see you, Babs,' Alan said quickly in slight confusion. 'I thought you were still at the military camp in Abeokuta.'

'Yes, I am still there officially, but I came home a few days ago to celebrate the Aburi peace initiative.'

At the mention of Aburi Alan reddened, unguardedly displaying embarrassment. Barbara kept her wide smile as she led him into the front room, waiting for some comment about the Aburi affair. He said nothing, instead he worked hard to control himself.

'How long are we to be kept in the dark about Aburi? You attended the conference, didn't you, Alan?' Babs probed.

'Yes, I did, but like you I am waiting for the outcome and hoping for the best,' Alan replied noncommittally.

'I'm sorry to have kept you waiting,' breathed Debbie as she sailed in wearing a brightly coloured Itsekiri outfit, with two pieces of vivid cotton George material tied round her. Her flaming red silk headtie was intricately and artistically knotted, so that for a moment Alan thought that the beautiful woman standing in front of him was Mrs Stella Ogedembgbe transformed. She looked very like her mother but with some touches of her own: her bold smile, the confident thrust of her head, the way she looked him straight in the eye when talking, were gestures which Mrs Ogedemgbe had never acquired. When Debbie walked in her native attire she seemed to move with measured grace; it gave her an air of still formality, almost bordering on artificiality, but all told it added grace and femininity, qualities which were lost when she put on the shapeless green army trousers she had insisted on wearing of late.

'See you soon, Alan,' said Babs, making her way out of the room, 'and maybe then you'll have something tangible, maybe good news, to tell us.'

Alan and Debbie drove slowly towards the island and to the beach, which was adequately illuminated by some lights from the residential quarters and from the nearby Palace Hotel. Debbie settled herself on one piece of her wrapper, spread on the golden-white sand, remarking,

'One thing I like about our native clothes is that you can take one layer off without upsetting the whole outfit.'

'Yes, but don't they say that women who are still unmarried aren't supposed to wear that second waist piece?' Alan asked, sitting down by her.

'The trouble with you, white man, is that you know much more than is good for you. Anyway, nobody observes such traditions these days. When those taboos were made all girls married before they reached the grand age of twenty, so that wearing one piece only would enhance a girl's slim figure,' Debbie explained easily. 'But when you're over twenty and have been through what I've been through, yet are still expected to play the innocent, there must be something really wrong.'

Alan rolled on his back and laughed at the moon, while Debbie began to pound his chest in playful anger. After a while she became serious.

'Alan, I want to ask you something. What's really happening? I would have gone to ask Momoh himself, but it's easier to reach the moon than talk to him these days. How things have changed!'

'Well, Momoh is a big man now. You have to book an appointment even to see his secretary. But he's not putting on airs, it's just his new office.'

'He'd be silly to put on airs. He's in a very hot seat, so he has to play safe.'

'I think he is aware of that. And, if my guess is right, he will stay in that hot seat for a long time yet, as soon as he has settled with Abosi.'

'Why do you say that?'

'He's young, still in his early thirties, he comes from a minority tribe, not one of the major warring ones, he claims to be a Christian though he has a Moslem name and lived in the Moslem North. And he is a frightened man . . .'

'And your country approves of him,' Debbie said lightly, and then went on: 'I thought the two men settled their differences at Aburi. What went wrong, why is there so much silence?'

'Debbie, I hate having to keep anything from you, but at this moment all I can say is that things didn't work out as we thought they would. The fault is more Saka Momoh's. He didn't do his homework thoroughly before going. Well, you know Chijioke Abosi.' Alan had completely ignored the first part of her claim. 'And those advisers of his. Momoh is suspicious of any advice, very nervous of taking any. So he slows down and bungles things . . .'

Debbie jerked herself away from him. 'Wait a minute – I think I'm beginning to get the picture. You know, I've always wondered how a tiny place like Britain came to rule so many people. Now I can guess: divide and rule. Is that why you are here? What part are you playing, Alan?'

He stood up and walked a few paces away, towards one of the

coconut palms that grew in great numbers at that part of Victoria Island.

'Alan, what happened at Aburi? What part did you play in changing Momoh's mind? Alan!'

He turned back angrily. 'Look, stop being hysterical. Why must you blame everything on Britain? Remember we once talked about you being a kind of ambassador of peace? Well, now's the time to play your part as peacemaker, instead of standing there blaming others.'

Debbie knelt down and sobbed bitterly. 'I thought after people like Father were killed things would be all right. Now God help us. Innocent children are suffering – many of them have already been deprived of their parents. And now I see more bloodshed coming.' She faced Alan squarely. 'Why can't you be the ambassador for peace? You people started it. Both Abosi and Momoh were once your students, why can't you go and talk to Abosi?'

'I would love to. But as I said earlier Momoh is still very nervous of his position as head of the army and it would be dangerous to leave him at the moment, with those Chinese and Russian "friends" hovering about. Any false rumour would set him on the wrong path.'

'At least you are frank.'

Somehow, Debbie allowed Alan to make love to her, there on the bare sand. There was desperation in her behaviour and uncertainty in his; but at the end each felt calmer, seeming to accept situations which they thought were beyond them.

'I'll have to take Mother home before I come back to Lagos to re-enlist,' Debbie said drowsily on their slow drive back to the mainland. 'Trouble is, I want to continue as a Nigerian soldier and at the same time still feel like helping Abosi.'

'Why don't you concentrate for the time being on keeping your mother out of it, for who knows what goes on in Abosi's mind? If he should declare that the East is now Biafra, as we hear he might, then your sympathizing with him would make you an enemy of Nigeria.'

'You mean there may have to be two countries, Nigeria and Biafra? That would take some getting used to . . . But I hope Chijioke Abosi doesn't do that. He hasn't got the military might.'

'You think so?' Alan asked, his interest really aroused.

'Yes, can't you see? It's very obvious. How can a quarter of a nation fight the other three-quarters and win? It's sheer common sense.'

'Debbie, Debbie, look, if it really comes to the crunch, could you make the journey to the East and remind Abosi of that simple fact? That would be all you'd have to do. You know how the man adores you, because his father and yours so respected each other. You can use that to try and save the situation. Mind you, it's more complex than that; I'm only suggesting a simplistic solution to a very complicated problem so that at least a start will have been made. Please, Debbie, do this for your country.'

'You men make all this mess and then call on us women to clear it up. I'll come to headquarters tomorrow, get my new uniform and go to the Mid-West in the uniform of the Nigerian army. The antagonism can't have gone so far that a woman in Nigerian army uniform would be regarded as an enemy of the East. Why, Abosi was wearing the same uniform in that photo taken of him and Momoh in Aburi. In any case, this is just conjecture. Abosi may not even declare a separate nation. He's much more rational than that.'

'He has to take the advice of his followers if he wants to stay in office. That's why I said that it's a very complex situation. Your going may make him think up a way to convince his advisers.'

'War costs a lot of money. Does he think he will get enough from the oil revenue to finance it?'

'He may be able to, especially as he too has now collected "friends" from France, Ireland and Eastern Europe who would jump on the bandwagon of drilling oil from the East.'

'But all those people – France, Ireland and the rest – are at the moment on friendly terms with Britain. Why can't Britain support Abosi then?'

'That would be against our national policy. How can we want to maintain a United Kingdom, with the hope of joining a united Europe, and then come to Africa and disunite another kingdom?'

Debbie's laughter was low. 'When you put it like that I want to believe it. I'm not doubting you as a person . . . but it's just the attitude of your government and what you stand for. I just can't reconcile the two.'

'As individuals we can only do our best,' Alan said finally.

Mr Teteku stirred the thick spinachy soup carefully, peering into the bowl through his heavy horn-rimmed glasses. His weak mouth worked itself into different shapes as he stirred. His wife smiled knowingly at Mrs Ogedemgbe who was sitting opposite her at the table for their evening meal. Debbie and Babs watched the three of them from the other side.

'Father, you'll mash up all the fish if you go on like that,' Babs remarked lightly. 'By the time the soup bowl reaches this end of the table it will be a porridge, and you know I don't like porridge with fufu.'

The two older women winked at each other.

'Don't worry, Babs, not even an iron bar could break these hard things your mother and the cook have piled in here. Are there no longer any fishermen at the waterside of the Lagos lagoon, that we should eat this hard stockfish all the time?' Mr Teteku said as he passed the soup to his wife after giving up the attempt to find fresh fish in it.

'I'm sorry, dear, but this is the best we can do. Here, Stella, take your share. The Igbos are leaving Lagos in great numbers so the stockfish that used to be a great luxury here is now going cheap,' she explained to her husband. 'And the young boys who used to fish are all being urged to join the militia. Besides, you used to like stockfish before, when it was expensive.'

'Not when you have to eat it every day,' Teteku said between mouthfuls, 'and in this quantity. I think those Igbos are making a big mistake in leaving. They'll have lost their good positions when they come back after this scare.'

'I wish I could agree with you, sir,' Debbie said, 'but I don't think they are running home because of empty scares. I suspect there's more to it than meets the eye.'

'Hmm,' he agreed grudgingly. 'I hope something productive was agreed at the much-publicized Aburi talks. It's taking those army boys an unnecessarily long time to come out with their decisions.'

'I think there's going to be a secession anyway, any day now. I'm sure of it,' Babs said pessimistically.

'You always come up with outrageous declarations,' Mrs Teteku said warningly.

'It's not really so outrageous,' Debbie said. 'If all these people leaving should go to Aba and report the secret killings to Abosi he will come to the conclusion that Aburi didn't matter.'

'So you are now beginning to see it from my point of view,' Babs said, getting up from the table. 'It's nearly seven o'clock, we might as well listen to what Momoh and his men will be telling us on the radio.'

There was an uneasy silence as they went on eating. Then a loud, harsh voice came through the radio, commanding and intense. It was the voice of someone used to giving orders; it was the voice of the Nigerian soldiery: 'To keep Nigeria one is a task that must be done. To keep Nigeria one is a task that must be done.' This was followed by a gun-salute, and the national anthem was sung with such fierceness that one would think some invisible god was challenging the country's determination to remain one.

The Tetekus looked at each other, then at their guests, aghast. No one spoke for a while. Then Mr Teteku left the table and went over to where the radio was on a bookshelf in a corner of the dining-room.

'Why do we have to be reminded in this dramatic way about maintaining our unity? That is what we all want. Nobody's disputing the fact.'

Debbie too got up and made her way towards the living-room. 'Funny, we can all guess what is happening but are too tactful or too afraid to say it. I think we all know that Abosi has seceded.'

'Debbie!' Stella Ogedemgbe called sharply to her daughter.

'Yes, Mother, I think the country is at war with herself. Civil war, eh, Babs?'

'Trouble is, how long will it remain a civil war, with those foreign vultures hovering ready to pounce on the mess we leave behind? Our natural resources, our oil, will be the end of us. Can't those two men see the forces are wedging themselves between them to encourage the rift?'

The shrill ringing of the telephone cut short Babs's outburst and she dashed towards it. From what she said into the receiver, it seemed the other person was surprised to learn that she was still at home.

'. . . In that case I shall leave for Abeokuta tomorrow. But can it really come to that?. . . All right, all right, I'll get Debbie.' Babs covered the mouthpiece and said in a stage whisper, 'It's Alan, he wants to talk with you.'

As soon as Debbie began to speak it was clear that she wanted to talk with Alan privately. Her voice was low, her back turned, stiff and uncompromising, towards the others.

'What beats me about this sham independence they say we have is how that man Grey is allowed to come so close to the ruling parties of our government when we are never allowed to do the same to theirs,' Mr Teteku remarked.

'He is one of the friends of Africa, Papa,' put in Babs, cynicism ringing in her voice, 'and they can always say that no African is cultivated enough to be regarded as a good adviser to the British government. And we are still young in the art of ruling ourselves.'

'We've been ruling ourselves for centuries, and what does a skinny thirty-year-old Englishman know about government to make him a self-appointed adviser to a country like Nigeria?'

'He's closer to forty, Father. I don't like his being there, but Momoh is hardly the person to cope with all the diplomatic twists and tangles that ruling a vast country like Nigeria involves. If Alan wasn't there, men from those new foreign embassies would take over. Momoh will listen to anyone whose skin is white and who can flatter him enough. At least Alan and his family know about Nigeria,' Babs commented.

Debbie left the telephone and came over to them, her face aglow with a feverish excitement. She first looked away, as if she had an unsavoury piece of news to impart, then she turned to her mother. The likeness between the two was striking. They were both dark with narrow faces; their eyes, almond-shaped, were large, expressive and beautiful, Stella's outlined with black tiro. The older woman's face seemed more relaxed and comfortable, for worry lines had formed themselves on Debbie's forehead which her excitement now accentuated.

Then she announced, 'Mother, I think it would be best for you to leave Lagos.' Trying to stem the protests, she hurried on: 'They think Abosi has seceded . . . Mother, you know you can't stay here forever. Our house in Sapele needs looking after; the servants will have neglected it, thinking we may never come back.'

'Why can't Stella go to the UK and stay with the boys?' asked Mrs Teteku.

'It's rather late for that now. If Abosi has seceded, the airport will be under constant surveillance. And if they find out that Stella Ogedemgbe is trying to leave the country – well, all hell would break loose. When things have deteriorated this far, any known person can be made a scapegoat.'

'But not a woman, we don't treat women like that,' maintained Mr Teteku.

Babs and Debbie laughed almost involuntarily and Teteku suspected he knew the reason. In the distant past in that part of Africa women were treated almost as men's equals, but with the arrival of colonialism their frail claim to equality had been taken away. Now, with the coming of independence, young women like these were determined to play their part in the new nation; and this in turn was making the army boys more brutal to unlucky women caught in any helpless situation. There were stories of women being beaten and sexually assaulted by soldiers, whose commander would only say, 'It is war, and in a war situation men lose their self-control,' as if that were explanation enough. Teteku looked at the women around him, shrugged his shoulders and walked away, his head bowed.

'Mama, we have to start packing,' Debbie began, then gave a short, nervous laugh: 'But I think we shall need a man with us. We can go in

113

Father's old Rover, that won't attract too much attention. I'll ask our driver Ignatius to get ready.'

'He is Igbo, isn't he? What will happen to his family here?'

'Oh, his wife and children left three weeks ago. Funnily enough, he must have suspected that Aburi wouldn't work out, because when I told him that the danger had passed he shook his wise head and said he'd only have peace of mind if he knew they were all safely in his home town Ibuza. You know that Nwokolo is from that area, don't you?'

'Yes,' Stella said. 'Where is he now, by the way?'

'I think he's in the East with Abosi. I have a feeling that this is going to be the real fight for Independence. What we've had up till now was a sham – the Europeans leaving but putting greedy "yesmen" in the government. Now the young men are fighting for our real freedom, and Biafra may hold the key to that freedom.'

As the conversation grew more idealistic, the older people drifted nearer to the radio to catch the latest news while Babs and Debbie continued in a corner of the room. Babs yawned and remarked:

'All this is fine in theory but in reality sounds like a dream. Yes, we were partitioned and bulked together, but that was a long time ago. Personally I believe we should concentrate on making the way of living we are used to work, and not spend the little energy we have in destabilizing further our shaky nation. If Abosi secedes, I'll have to be convinced that there was nothing else for him to do before I forgive him. The rest of the country will think he's doing it because of the oil.'

'The oil will no doubt help, but the Igbos have been embittered by their massacre in the North. Any group of people would be.'

'That is true,' Babs agreed, 'but nothing's to be gained by going over that now. I say let bygones be bygones.'

'Wasn't that the point of convening the Aburi meeting? That the two should agree to start all over again? Now the Igbos are being hunted out of their homes even in Lagos.'

'Yes, that's what is puzzling about the whole thing. The country blames the Hausas for the Northern killings, and now the same situation is being repeated here in the South, and in the federal capital at that.'

The phone rang and Mr Teteku walked briskly over to pick it up. From the way he deferentially repeated the phrase 'Yes, sir,' they deduced that he was talking to someone in authority. Then he said, 'Debbie, it's for you,' before covering the mouthpiece and mouthing: 'It's from Odumosu in Ibadan.'

The two older women rose at once from their seats and drew nearer to Debbie, and as they listened eagerly, gesturing to one another, it transpired that Debbie was being asked to go to the East to attempt to talk to Abosi. And it seemed that Debbie had agreed to do it by the time she replaced the receiver.

'Oh, no, you don't!' protested Mr Teteku. 'They made their own uncomfortable bed, let them lie in it. Why implicate an innocent girl like you?'

'Thank you, sir, but I talked myself into this, you know. I've always said that should a situation like this arise I'd want to play some role as a peace-maker. Don't forget that though Momoh is a new friend Abosi and his family have been our family's friends for a very long time. I hope I'll be able to reach him . . .'

Mr Teteku, with eyes averted, brow furrowed, his total demeanour studious, asked, 'Have those two boys really split our beloved Nigeria?'

Debbie nodded limply. 'The rest of the federation will be informed tomorrow.'

'A stupid and very, very irresponsible move,' Stella Ogedemgbe said heatedly. 'I wonder what his nice mother would say to all this. Why should he secede?'

Debbie turned to her with surprise; so her mother had a mind of her own after all. She wondered what her father would have said had he been there to witness it.

'I don't think Abosi's move is as stupid as it looks. You know what Momoh did – he divided the country into twelve. Not only that, he made sure that through the way it was divided the richest oilwells in the East fall into the hands of the non-Igbo-speaking people. In other words, he declared war against Abosi and his people.'

Why didn't he bring up such an important topic at Aburi?' Teteku asked.

'Momoh probably only just thought of it. Now the non-Igbos have been told that they can form a separate state. Divide and rule,' Babs observed.

'There may still be hope. At least Chief Odumosu thinks so. We hope to be able to talk Abosi out of it. The question really is how long could they hold out? How long will the non-Igbo-speaking peoples of the East rally round Abosi, knowing that they can have their own state and that the richer oilwells lie in their villages? The seeds of doubt have already been sown; and if Abosi shows any signs of weakening, those seeds will germinate, and they too will want their independence,' explained Debbie. Momoh and Abosi should be made to see their folly, she thought; she was not going to be committed to either of them, but to justice and the prosperity of the country.

'If I were in Abosi's shoes I would give up right now, and renounce the secession, before firing a single shot in self-defence,' said Babs.

'There are a great many things one has to do before declaring a new nation, you know. Abosi would need recognition, and I'm sure no sovereign state in its right mind would recognize a nation like this, a nation born out of mere revolution,' Teteku concluded somewhat illogically.

'But, Father, so was America.'

'Yes, but Nigeria is a black nation. The Western world will not treat her problems as sympathetically as they treated America's, remember that.'

The others looked at each other questioningly, each with her own thoughts about the implications of what he was saying.

9 A Delicate Mission

Breakfast with the Tetekus was unusually quiet that morning. A landrover had come for Babs at five a.m. to take her to headquarters in Abeokuta where she was to supervise new women recruits. Debbie could sympathize with the unease of her friend's parents.

'Babs will be all right,' she volunteered.

Mrs Teteku burst into tears. 'I wish that girl hadn't gone to England to learn all this talk of women behaving like men.'

Debbie knew she was in the minority. She didn't feel the expensive education they had been given was just to prepare them for life with the first dull rich Nigerian man who came along. 'Marry one of them and start breeding and continue bleeding till menopause,' Babs often said. There was plenty of time for domesticity and motherhood; at the moment their country was in trouble and they should help. Debbie got up and walked towards the door, as if in need of some fresh air. She could hear her mother's voice beginning to intone her own woes, but she was in no mood to listen or argue.

Just then the front door bell rang and she answered it. It was a messenger from the military governor's palace. He presented a card on which was a black and white drawing of the house she knew so well. To think that Saka Momoh and his wife now lived there in the opulence of what was once the Ogedemgbe home, while they stayed in this cramped place, arguing with the Tetekus . . .

'Miss Ogedemgbe?' The young man's voice cut into her thoughts.

'Yes,' she replied in a small voice, taking the sealed official stamped envelope from him.

Before leaving, the young soldier touched his cap in salutation and clicked his heels.

Debbie returned to the dining-room to give the others the sudden information that she was required to present herself to the 'Military

117

Governor' Saka Momoh at three o'clock that afternoon. Then she went to prepare one of her green khaki army uniforms which she had not worn for quite a while.

She could not believe the transformation that had taken place in her former home. There were soldiers marching this way and that, there were huge impressive flags of many African nations, with that of Nigeria holding place of honour in the centre. Everywhere there was an atmosphere of brisk, quiet efficiency. Heels clicked and hands flew to the foreheads of young officers as she was taken through into the main hall and into the large side hall where her father used to welcome visitors. It all seemed so cold, so remote and so bare without the familiar soft furnishings. Even the drapes at the window seemed stiff like the soldiers. The pictures on the walls were now of armoury and soldiers on parade at Sandhurst. It was hard to imagine this as the elegant banqueting hall it used to be.

Debbie turned her head sharply towards the door as the light but soldierly step of Momoh echoed down the hallway. She could hear the officers on guard jumping to attention. Then Momoh came in, smiling. He looked so alien in this ambience, she thought, and he was thinner, nervier. When he began to talk, the smile disappeared completely and he spoke rapidly and restlessly.

'I want this country to be one,' he maintained. 'Why should we divide her? We may be different peoples but for over fifty years we have stayed together. Fifty years . . . think of that – long before you were born. Then Abosi came and ruined it. Why is he so arrogant, just because he's the son of a millionaire and went to Oxford?' Here Momoh checked himself and said rather apologetically, 'I know you went to Oxford too, but you don't put on false airs. At any rate, we think you would be the right person to reach him. Your family and his were friends for a very long time, and of course you were both at Oxford, although you're a woman . . . Not that that should be a handicap. It might help: you can use your feminine charms to break that icy reserve of his.'

A picture of Chijioke Abosi with his luxuriant beard loomed into Debbie's imagination. To think that she was being delegated to go and convince Abosi that a united Nigeria was the thing to be fought for, just to keep alive the whims of the ambitious Saka Momoh! Well, it would not be because of Momoh she was going but because she personally believed that keeping the country together was a good thing.

But Momoh was still talking: 'Tell him that we do not want to fight him. Why kill innocent people just to pander to his foolish dreams, eh? Tell him the Igbos have suffered enough and that I also do not want to see them go through such hard times again. He would be forgiven for seceding and all his people welcomed back into the federation.'

'Maybe he seceded because of the twelve states you declared . . .' Debbie had hardly finished this sentence before she knew she had put her foot in it.

Momoh whirled round and stared at her intently. His eyes were red-rimmed. He had so worked himself up and his body was so taut that Debbie was momentarily frightened for him. The man was liable to break.

'What was that? What did you say, enh?'

One look at the vein twitching on his forehead told Debbie that it was time for her to be quiet. He was not the old Saka Momoh. He had risen politically and militarily, and for her own survival she had to play along.

He was impatient, he wanted the whole world to hear his part of the story. Maybe he was feeling guilty for going back on his Aburi promise, but he did not think Debbie too inferior to be confided in. The man needed someone to listen.

'The minority peoples in the East have to be protected, you know. You do realize that there are many groups who are not Igbos living in the East too? We seldom hear about them, because Abosi and his Igbos are busy shouting as if they own the whole world. Those silent minorities have to be considered. We had to create the twelve states to protect those people.' He added the last sentence as a kind of reassurance to himself.

He strode to the window that opened on to the marina, looked out a second, then jerked at a cord by the curtain. A tall young soldier entered and Momoh gave him orders to take Debbie to get her outfitted with a new uniform. A letter would be given to her when she was ready to leave. Momoh wished her luck, and marched out of the room.

During their short drive to Apapa barracks where she was to be fitted with a fresh uniform, the soldier, who Debbie realized was a sergeant, volunteered crisply and suddenly: 'My name is Salihu Lawal, or Lawal Salihu, it doesn't matter which you put first. Don't bother to tell me yours, I know it. And I am sorry for your father's death. You must miss him very much to make you want to join the army, just to revenge his death.'

'Thank you very much. I was close to my father, but time heals everything. I wanted to join the army long before he was killed.'

The officer nodded and then went on dangerously, as if Debbie had not spoken: 'I still think those men ought not to have been killed. Who in this world can replace Nguru Kano? We belong to the same area in the North.'

Debbie looked at him sharply. The man was undoubtedly Hausa, a Hausa man in authority, and she was not going to let his sympathy overwhelm her to the point where she would let go of her tongue.

He started to whistle, and then tried again. 'Seen your friend lately?'

'Which friend?' Debbie asked cagily.

'The Bature.'

'He has a name, hasn't he? How would you like being called "the Black"?'

The sergeant started to laugh huskily. 'They call us so in their country. His people taught me to refer to people by their colour. So don't blame me, white man's girl.'

This annoyed Debbie. Why should her private life be public property? It was her affair who she chose to be her friend.

'So what is bad in being the friend of a white man?'

'Nothing, nothing at all. I only wish to know of his welfare. We are still in Nigeria, you know, where people ask after one another's welfare – or is that too old-fashioned for you and the Bature? I won't ask of him again.'

By the time they arrived at Apapa, her anger was simmering, nearing boiling point.

Salihu smiled and wished her luck. Then he remarked, 'I don't understand why you black girls think that when you are well educated your black men are no longer good enough for you. To the Bature you are just a whore, to be used and discarded, just as they are doing to our country. May Allah forgive you!'

With that he turned the car and sped out of the barracks, leaving Debbie there, dumbfounded. She shrugged and went inside the building.

Feeling rather strange and uncomfortable in her new uniform, she stared silently at the quiet outskirts of Lagos. Her mission to Abosi was known only to a few high-ranking officers and one or two of the old politicians. It could not be seen as an offical initiative. She was to give Chijioke Abosi an opportunity to back down without losing face. She suspected that despite Momoh's noisy explanations he feared that if the quarrel were prolonged other countries would start cashing in on the situation. She also suspected that one of the reasons for these men choosing her was that they guessed that were it not for Alan Grey Chijioke Abosi might well have married her. That, Debbie smiled to herself, would have been an arranged marriage which would have made both her own father and Papa Abosi so happy. So now these men thought she could use her sexuality to make Abosi change his stand. She was to use her body, because Saka Momoh did not want to get into a war with the Easterners, because no one knew what such a move would precipitate.

But there was another thing Debbie had discovered only that morning, that in the media Abosi seemed to be growing very strong. She would not have tuned into the BBC World Service but for the fact that she had read in one of the Lagos papers that such an act was now illegal. Illegal indeed! But when she heard the news, she knew why. Well, Momoh would have to fill his prisons with offenders, for she knew many families would be committing the same crime. It was like telling a child not to peep through a door which before had been innocent-looking; if nothing had been said about it, people would probably have dismissed the news as the propaganda of Nigeria's enemies. As it was, however, Debbie tuned in not only to the World Service but to the East as well and learned to her horror that the people of the East already regarded themselves as members of a different nation. There was talk of their poets submitting words for their new national anthem. Young people were flocking into the army of the East, which regarded itself as unconquerable. If anything, patriotic zeal among the Igbos was twenty times more than that of the rest of Nigeria.

Debbie sighed sadly. What was her position in all this mess? She was neither Igbo nor Yoruba, nor was she a Hausa, but a Nigerian.

'Ignatius, you're driving from one lane to another and avoiding the main road as if we are criminals on the run,' Stella Ogedemgbe remarked, echoing her daughter's thoughts.

'At this rate we won't get to Ibadan in time for me to have an audience with Chief Odumosu. And I intended to call on Babs in Abeokuta too,' Debbie added.

'These are hard times. I am only trying to avoid the road checks. As you know, it is now unpopular to be an Igbo.'

'Whoever checks this car will see that I am an officer, Ignatius. I am not going to the East on a pleasure trip,' Debbie said.

Ignatius looked round from the driver's seat and smiled wryly. He had known her since her school days, but she must maintain her distance and command.

'You'll have to go on the main road, Ignatius. I can prove to anyone that you are my driver, and what's more I am on secret army business.'

121

'But why didn't they let you have an army car?' her mother asked.

'That would have been too obvious. And it wouldn't be proper for me to use the army car to pack our linen and bedside lamps.'

They both laughed.

At Abeokuta Debbie was only able to spend an hour with Babs. Ignatius at first refused to leave the car, but after a few minutes he came to join them in the visitors' lounge.

'Those officers at the gate don't believe that I am not an Igbo,' he announced unnecessarily loudly for the benefit of the people sitting by and drinking beer.

Taking the hint, Babs remarked in a low voice, 'I hope you aren't going to have a difficult time after Ibadan.'

'Oh, I don't think so,' Debbie replied. 'I am in uniform, and in the uniform of the only Nigerian army. We haven't got two armies, have we? Well, not officially.'

Babs sighed. 'I wonder if they realize how dangerous this trip to the East could be for you. Abosi and his people seem so determined to form a new nation that sometimes I think all negotiations should be suspended for a while, until we see what their moves are.'

Debbie looked around at the soldiers lounging about and relaxing. She knew that some of them had recognized her as Ogedemgbe's daughter when she first came in, but apart from that they went on drinking and throwing their darts.

Debbie lowered her voice. 'Don't tell me you've been listening to the "Voice of Biafra" too.'

Babs's smile was wide. 'Mind you, I do admire the Igbos' spirit,' she said. 'The programme I got – I don't know if you heard it – the young people at the University of Nsukka were voicing their opinions openly and offering their services and even their lives for their fatherland. I don't think we in the rest of Nigeria feel like that. From the whole of the Western region I have only five girls who are willing and suitable to join the militia. The other women who came up were those well know locally as women of easy virtue, few of whom went beyond Standard Six. And what we need is women who are better than the average. We are in the minority and I don't want them to attach to us the type of stigma that female singers and actresses have been given – you know, that they all sleep around. It worries me that the good girls don't come forward, while in Biafra all women with degrees want to fight.'

'Biafra seems rather symbolic to me. The ideal that we should all aim to achieve: a nation that has been detribalized, a nation where wealth will be equally distributed . . . But it's early days yet.'

The two women walked out of the barracks, embraced and wished each other luck in their different missions.

Chief Odumosu had nothing special to add to what Momoh had already said to Debbie. But it was from him that she learned that Alan Grey had crossed to Benin on his way to Nwokolo's place.

'That man and his primitive art,' Odumosu remarked indulgently. 'Is he an archaeologist?'

'No, he is simply a soldier. Collecting those objects is just his hobby,' Debbie explained, 'though I think he'd risk his life for them.'

'Hmm, interesting hobby. But if you ask me, no Englishman does a thing like that for nothing. Try and find out about it. I am intrigued.'

'Yes, sir. And, sir, do you want me to tell Abosi that you've changed your mind about declaring a Yoruba kingdom?'

Debbie sensed the chief stiffen. She saw the glint of panic behind his gold-rimmed glasses. She had known even before she began the question that he would not like her asking, but she knew what she was doing. He was indirectly asking her to spy on her friend Alan, so she wanted to know where the chief himself stood.

'We all read about it in the foreign press after Aburi, sir,' she tried to soften the blow, but she felt that the man was playing a double game.

'Well, you know the media. They'll publish anything to fill their stupid papers. I am for one Nigeria . . . I should say nothing to Abosi about that, if I were you,' he went on. 'Don't meddle in things bigger than you and don't forget, my dear, that you are a woman. That is why we are giving you this delicate mission.'

They left Ibadan very late, hoping to reach Benin before midnight. In the half light, which was not made better by the moonless sky, they could make out someone waving a piece of material in the middle of the road.

'That man wants to get killed,' Ignatius said under his breath.

'See what he wants. Be careful,' Stella Ogedemgbe advised.

'He could be a soldier, ma'am. We have not come across any so far because I've been avoiding the main road, but here there is only one major road to Asaba.'

Debbie sat up and cocked her shotgun. Her hands were shaking. In the dim light the man could not have seen that she was a woman but he saw the gun and began to shout in Western Ibo language, as Ignatius stopped the car by the roadside:

'My wife, the baby – we are very tired. We left Yaba two days ago,

123

walking only at night. Please, I didn't know you were a soldier ... please, my wife can't walk any more.'

'Where is she?' Debbie asked suspiciously, her gun still at the ready.

The man waved in the direction of a thick cluster of wild palms, and a young pregnant woman staggered out, holding an ill-looking child in her arms. She struggled with the sick baby and a bundle of clothes.

Seeing Debbie's cocked gun she was about to run back into the forest, but her husband called her sharply and said:

'Are you not ashamed of yourself? Why, she is only a woman holding a gun.'

Ignatius doubled up with laughter, and the other man gave him a conspiratorial wink. The woman came closer, and though she was obviously weak she was none the less amused at Debbie.

'You mean you dress like a soldier on purpose to guard your car and your belongings? But you have a man with you – why didn't you let him wear the army uniform and carry the gun?'

'I am a soldier and he is not. But where are you going?' Debbie ask crisply. There was obviously no point in trying to convince these people that she was indeed an army officer; she also had to be careful not to reveal too much and jeopardize her sensitive mission.

'We are going to Asaba. We left Lagos when we heard the rumour that our people may take Ore at any moment and that the state of Benin will be established to protect Western Igbos.'

Ignatius could no longer contain himself. He came out of the car and asked, voice exuberant, eyes glowing, 'You mean our Biafran soldiers are in Benin already?'

'Oh, yes, Benin has surrendered. The Nigerian soldiers ran for their lives when our men marched in. Hail Biafra, hail Biafra!' The two men's joy was obvious.

Suddenly, as if conjured up by a magician, two army cars swooped on them, screeching to a dangerous halt. Before they could recover from their surprise, soldiers jumped out and the leader ordered: 'Stop, or we'll shoot!'

The young woman with the child screamed and was about to run back into the bush when one of the soldiers fired. Luckily he missed her, but her husband made a dash for him and was hit with the butt of the gun. He doubled up in pain. His wife's reverberant screams seemed to infuse ominous life into the dark forest beyond.

Other soldiers swarmed out of the car, the darkness exaggerating their number. Their voices were unnecessarily loud and they were in a state of excitement; it was clear that they meant trouble.

Debbie walked up to the first soldier to emerge, her gun cocked, and using her harshest voice shrieked, 'I am a Nigerian soldier.'

This was greeted with laughter. The leader looked derisively at the crumpled man on the ground, then at Ignatius, and asked in undisguised mockery, 'What is this? A battle fought by women? Is that how you intend to maintain your so-called invincible Biafra, eh?'

'I am a Nigerian soldier, not a Biafran. As far as I am concerned, Nigeria is still one.'

The leader waddled up to her and mimicked her voice: '"I am a Nigerian soldier."' His laughter was like the roaring of many fierce lions.

Debbie knew she must look ludicrous; her trousers were baggy and her shirt's shoulders were too wide for her slim frame. But she was determined not to be made a fool of by these men. 'I will shoot, and shoot to kill, if you don't let us alone,' she threatened. 'And don't think I'm not going to report this.'

The leader shrugged and seemed about to amble away when Debbie added:

'Don't move until we are safe in our car.' She pointed the gun menacingly.

At that point one of the other soldiers grabbed and twisted the arm of the young mother, making her cry in pain. Then he addressed Debbie: 'If you don't put that gun down, I'll shoot your friend.'

'Leave her alone, she has nothing to do with it!' Stella Ogedemgbe screamed. 'What outlandish home did you come from, treating a woman like that?'

The woman was pleading for mercy in Igbo and her husband was doing the same. But Debbie steeled herself and still refused to lay down the gun.

'Hand it over to me peacefully, then your friend can go,' the leader said.

'No, I am not giving this gun up, and if you move your hand you're a dead man.'

There was a brief stalemate, but it was obvious that Debbie could not keep watch on them all at once. She could hold only the leader to ransom. The other soldier started to pull the woman with the child along towards the edge of the forest.

'Give them the gun, please, miss,' pleaded the woman, 'give them your gun. After all you are a woman, and we are outnumbered.'

'Do what you're told,' the husband cried to Debbie, hatred on his face.

'Miss Debbie – ' Ignatius called softly.

'Shut up, Ignatius,' she hissed, then said to the leader of the group: 'If I give you the gun you must not hurt us. You must let us go. We are innocent, and although I am a soldier I am also taking my mother home. If you promise that, I will do as you say; if not I will shoot you. I know we are outnumbered but you would be a dead man.'

'All right,' replied the leader, grinning. 'We'll do as you say. You women rule the world now, don't you? We'll let you go.'

'OK, now you leave that woman alone. Let her go. You get into the car.'

Still whimpering and clutching her baby to her bosom, the woman ran towards the car, while Ignatius went to sit behind the steering-wheel. The woman's husband was helped up and, when they were all seated and Ignatius started the engine, Debbie realized that she was trapped; all eyes were on her. If she handed over the gun, how were they to defend themselves? If she tried to shoot her way out, there were at least eight of these men, all armed, who could shoot her, her mother and the rest of them in no time.

'I am not an Igbo, you know,' she began, 'I am a Nigerian soldier. I know that because communications are bad those of you in the provinces don't know what is happening in the cities. We have started enlisting women; even if you go to Abeokuta you'll see women in the militia. I'll hand my gun over, to prove to you that I am speaking the truth. It would be wrong for us to begin shooting at each other.' With that she gave the leader her gun.

He took it and roared with laughter. Debbie's heart sank. As Ignatius started the car, shots rang out, smashing the windscreen. The woman began to scream again and so did Stella Ogedemgbe.

'You promised to let us go, you promised,' the woman tried to remind the soldiers.

'Promise to let Igbo soldiers who we saw hailing Biafra go? Oh, Mother, think of another one,' one of the soldiers said, to the amusement of the others. Then he addressed the leader, 'Bale, do you want to take care of that chick in uniform?'

The leader eyed Debbie, who was now struggling fiercely in the arms of two hefty army boys. 'Take everything off her,' he commanded.

'And you, madam,' he said, turning to Stella Ogedemgbe, 'take off all that finery. We won't hurt you unless you give us trouble.'

'What are you talking about? What are you doing? Do you know who I am? What do you want to see, eh? You want to compare my nakedness to your mother's?'

126

The leader slapped her on one side of her face and barked, 'Leave my mother out of this.'

Ignatius pounced on one of the soldiers and in the struggle that followed a gun went off, hitting another of the group in the leg. His cry of agony incensed his friends and with no warning Ignatius was shot several times. He struggled in death as each bullet burned into his body until at last it was a still twisted heap, oozing blood like unwilling tears.

The others were too shocked to say a word. Mrs Ogedemgbe methodically undressed herself then, with her head held high, walked to the leader addressed as Bale and begged: 'Do whatever you want with me, and afterwards kill me. But, please, in the name of your mother, leave my daughter out of it. Don't let me live to see my daughter humiliated, and please don't kill her.'

'This is war, madam. We are not killers of women and children. Take them into that bush,' he ordered the soldiers. 'It is more hidden. Leave the old lady alone, you hear, don't touch her. Her clothes and those large golden earrings are worth something.'

Debbie was following all these happenings with her eyes. They had torn off her clothes and stuffed her undergarments into her mouth. In her distress, she could not fail to admire her mother's courage. The pregnant woman now began to wail as she was dragged from the main road to the side bush, pushed mercilessly with the butt of a gun; the woman was falling and getting up again, and calling to her husband Dede to help her. Debbie wondered what had happened to the child. She heard the tired, strangled voice of the woman calling out in Igbo, begging for mercy as they took her to a different part of the bush, and then Stella Ogedemgbe's voice cut in:

'Leave the woman alone! She is pregnant – don't you people fear God?'

Debbie heard the slap on her mother's face and it burned into all the nerve fibres of her body. She kicked out at one of the men holding her and heard him cry in pain. Her punishment was that the man fell on her.

She could make out the figure of the leader referred to as Bale on top of her, then she knew it was sombody else, then another person . . . She felt herself bleeding, though her head was still clear. Pain shot all over her body like arrows. She felt her legs being pulled this way and that, and at times she could hear her mother's protesting cries. But eventually, amid all the degradation that was being inflicted on her, Debbie lost consciousness.

*

127

She was still spreadeagled when she became aware that it was morning and that the voices she heard chattering around her were those of the bush pigeons and parrots. She opened and then closed her eyes again. Her legs felt like huge pieces of lead. Then there was another voice, closer and more human. It was her mother's, dry, strangely desperate, demanding assurance.

'Debbie, Oritsha-Debbie, my daughter, we are alive!'

Debbie's head was scratching against the thorny bush in which she had been left. She wanted nothing but to lie there, to dream and die in her dreams. To get up and start living again after the experiences of the past night was going to be a Herculean task. She wished her mother would go away and leave her alone. She did not wish to live. She looked again at her mother, a well-kept woman fast approaching middle age, wearing only a lappa and torn blouse. Blood smeared the sides of her face and legs, but her eyes were dry; she was not crying, she was even trying to smile. Had she been raped too? That was a question Debbie would never ask. She felt guilty that, with all her education, she could not lift a finger to help her own mother. Had she been a man, they would have killed her outright; instead they humiliated her and left her to die slowly.

Stella Ogedemgbe was still talking: 'We are women, daughter, this is our lot. They have killed Ignatius and the other man and taken their bodies. And that poor girl with her baby . . . they just tortured her to death. They made me and her husband watch . . . oh, they were evil! It was terrible. But we must go on living, you and I. Remember the boys in the UK – how would they feel suddenly to hear that they had no family left? Please, Debbie, try to live.'

She half carried and half dragged her daughter along the path until they came near the main road. They hid there until it began to grow dark, then they were lucky enough to flag down an Igbo businesswoman taking her family home from Abeokuta. She too was running for her life after seeing her unfortunate neighbours beaten to a pulp and then burned.

The Igbo woman and Stella Ogedemgbe dug a shallow grave for the dead young mother and her two babies; the soldiers had cut her open and killed her unborn child, saying, 'Who knows, he might live to be another Abosi.' There was no time for prayers. Life was too precious and yet too precarious.

They were stopped at another checkpoint a few miles from Benin. These soldiers looked like proper militia. They were not preventing Igbos from going to their part of the country but simply checking to find out why they were leaving. Mrs Ogedemgbe described the nightmare she and her daughter had just been through.

'It's war, madam. I am sure those boys were only provincial militia. They did not know who you were. And you dress like an Igbo woman, with abada cloth, so don't blame them.'

'But a woman has been tortured to death, her two babies killed.'

'Madam, the dead woman was an Igbo, you said so yourself.'

'What of my daughter?'

'Give her hot water to wash herself. Hundreds of women have been raped – so what? It's war. She's lucky to be even alive. She'll be all right.'

'She'll be all right, she'll be all right – is that all you have to say? I'm telling you that my daughter has been ra – ' She could not bring herself to say the word. It was too horrible, too humiliating. She cried into the only lappa the soldiers had left her.

Debbie sat in front of one of the cars. She was still too numb physically and emotionally to say a word; but her brain was ticking like a tireless clock. She admired her mother, who could use her tongue to move the hardest of men. Those attacking soldiers would surely have killed her but for the fact that, even in their vile drunkenness, they feared Stella Ogedemgbe's tongue. But now Debbie wished she would stop. It would do no good going over all that had happened to them. Some people might sympathize, but many would snigger, she knew. She breathed in and with great effort called: 'Mother, Mother, that's enough now.'

The soldier at the checkpoint turned at her cultured voice. 'I am sorry, miss, but you do understand that there is nothing we can do at the moment. However, we shall report this. Many atrocities are being committed by our soldiers. I really don't know what is getting into the heads of these young people. Give us the descriptions of any of the men, and the details of what they did to you . . .'

Debbie raised her hand and shook her head. The sun was getting into her eyes anyway, so she closed them and turned her face to one side. She was not going to talk about it. It was bad enough her mother letting them know who she was, but no one was going to hear her tell all that had happened.

The soldier shrugged his khakied shoulders. 'Please yourself. It's a woman's world anyway. They get what they want.'

'What do you mean?' queried the woman who had given Debbie and her mother a lift to the Benin border. 'Don't you realize that she will never find a husband now that she has been raped by soldiers?'

'I did not rape her, so why attack me? She should go and wash herself and be a nun.'

It was then that Stella Ogedemgbe saw her daughter's point. They would become a laughing-stock. The pain and humiliation would forever be locked in their memories. She could not shut out the horrible way the Igbo woman with the child was killed, how they had pushed the butt of a gun into her, how they had cut her open, how the unborn baby's head had been cut off and the older child kicked to death . . . oh, it was too horrible.

But Debbie was alive, and that was everything.

10 *The Invincible Army*

The plane suddenly swerved to the right and, a few seconds later, a blood-curdling explosion followed. The passengers screamed and involuntarily lurched forward as the plane made another drastic dive into the clouds, and the 'Fasten your seat belts' sign flashed crazily.

'What's happening?' Alan Grey mouthed to his companion Giles Murray. He could feel the blood rushing to his head.

Giles, equally alarmed, shrugged his shoulders. Alan tried to stop a stewardess to ask her what the matter was as she dashed past, but she dodged him in her agitation to reach the pilot's compartment.

'I thought they were supposed to be calm and not show any fear,' Giles remarked. 'That one is more frightened that the passengers. Maybe she doesn't know what's happening herself.'

'Well, if that explosion had been inside the plane, we would all be goners. Something exploded outside, for sure.'

Alan Grey wiped the sweat of fear that was running down the side of his face. Fear contorted everybody's faces; the women who a little while before were screaming had now become fervent believers in the deity and were praying loudly to their various gods, and an imam was hysterical in his call to Allah as he told his black beads with shaking hands.

Then the cool voice of the Swedish captain came through the intercom: 'I am Captain Bengt. There is nothing to worry about. Everything is under control, ladies and gentlemen, and we are now free to land at Benin airport. Thank you.'

'Why do we need any kind of freedom to land in Benin in the first place? I've made this trip I don't know how many times,' Giles worried.

Alan chuckled nervously, to his friend's mystification. Then he whispered, 'I can guess what is happening. Abosi and his soldiers have taken Benin. Benin is now part of Biafra, and so this is an enemy plane.

131

We're very lucky to be alive. Maybe they didn't want to shoot us down because the plane will be useful to them. Whatever the reason for their not killing us straight away, all I can say is that we have been extremely lucky.'

He held tightly on to his seat and craned his neck to see what was taking place outside. The plane was plunging from side to side, now going up and soon afterwards making a desperate dive downwards. The passengers sat very still, all prayers said, tasting fear. Then at last the plane emerged from the clouds into broad daylight. Abruptly the runway was visible and it seemed as if it was running to meet them. There were more bumps and jolts, then a final big bump that made everyone gasp, and the aircraft touched solid ground. It taxied madly round, like a cock chasing after an unwilling hen, before it came to a halt. The passengers' grateful noises were deafening. Many didn't wait for orders but ran to the pilot. They hugged him, they cheered him, and he, with a foolish grin on his face, nodded limply.

As the two white men staggered out, they blinked in the sunshine, and Alan said, adopting a faintly paternal and contemptuous tone, 'Welcome to Benin, Biafra.'

They were not given much time to think, for four soldiers detached themselves from the other end of the tiny airfield and marched them roughly and unceremoniously to one of the little rooms used for luggage and passport checks. Everything was disorderly, and instead of travellers there were soldiers everywhere. Some were only schoolboys, excited to be in the uniforms of the conquerors and to have white men in their power. Alan and Giles could see that though their morale was high their discipline was rather dubious, so it was necessary to be calm. The firearms these soldiers sported were fully loaded, so it would be folly to annoy even the youngest of them.

The measured tread of men marching outside the door could be heard. Orders were shouted to the Englishmen in a language they knew was Nigerian, for they had heard it spoken so many times before either softly to welcome them or musically to wish them goodspeed, but now it sounded more foreign still, for they had never heard it spoken in this brutal guttural way. The Igbo language had become a language of war. An officer ordered them to strip, ready to be searched.

'Look,' began Alan, 'we are not here to spy or anything like that. We are on our way to Nwokolo's place – '

'So you think you are being taken for spies, eh? You have to be treated like everybody else.'

'But we are not Nigerians, we are English.'

'Yeah, so does your being English give you the right to lord it over us? We are friends of the British, we need your friendship, but that doesn't give you the right to play God. You are in Biafra now.'

Their clothes and passports were taken away and they sat on two straight-backed chairs in the bare room, looking at each other, ridiculous in their nakedness. They were not left alone for long. As word went round the young recruits at the airport that two white men were being held, soldiers would come in and, trying to suppress laughter, command them to stand up and then sit down again.

As unceremoniously as their clothes had been taken away they were returned within two hours.

'Now what the hell comes next?' Alan asked when they were fully dressed. 'Are we prisoners or what?'

'I think we are free to go. They can always stop us if they so desire. This is a crazy country if you ask me. Trouble is, who do you report this kind of treatment to?'

'Forget it,' Alan advised. 'Nigerian bureaucracy is impossible even at the best of times.'

Out on the main streets there was shouting and dancing. There was no doubt that people were very happy. They had been liberated, they chanted. Most of them looked curiously at Alan and Giles but felt so confident in their happiness that they did not think it worth their while to stop or molest them. At the motor park Alan got a copy of the day's Benin paper and was mildly surprised to see that a town in the Yoruba area called Ore had fallen to Abosi and his soldiers.

'If that nervous Momoh doesn't do something he'll wake up one day to find the whole of Lagos surrounded,' Alan said under his breath.

'Morale in this part of the country seems high, but it probably won't last. The tribes in this area – the Binis and the Urhobos – aren't so friendly with the Igbos. Maybe Momoh still regards it as an internal thing.'

'Which two tribes are ever really friendly?'

When the taxi that took them to Okpanam, John Nwokolo's home village, left the main road it gathered a thick cloud of dust as well as people in its wake. They rushed out of their corrugated-iron-roofed huts to watch and wonder what these '*onye ocha*' wanted in their village. Alan and Giles could not have chosen a more fitting day to arrive, for these people were happy to share with friends and visitors alike their joyful optimism that the Igbos were going to rule themselves at last, that there was to be no more Yoruba or Hausa domination and that they now belonged to Biafra.

133

Nwokolo had returned early that morning after the triumphant surprise entry and conquering of Ore. He, his subordinates and all with him were laughing almost hysterically at the ease with which they had taken the town. Celebrations and congratulations had been going on ever since the sounds of army trucks and motorcycles had woken the sleepy village just before sunrise. Many of the elders were sorry to be old now that at last Okpanam would be noticed, having produced a hero. Had not Nwokolo's little boy, this strong and handsome army officer, been the man of the hour in eliminating the Northern imperialists, had he not led the conquering soldiers?

The cries of '*Onye ocha, onye ocha!*' cut short further talk among Nwokolo and his relatives. Alan Grey and Giles Murray were welcomed enthusiastically and ushered into the front and best room of the house where the family had been sitting. People started to leave as the conversation was conducted in English. The senior Nwokolo tried to participate but he found he could not catch some of the sentences rapidly pouring out, so he too left in search of gifts with which to entertain his son's illustrious visitors.

'So you boys are making it. I see that Benin is now part of the republic of Biafra – congratulations,' Alan said benignly.

'I must say I am most impressed by the speed with which the whole operation was carried out,' Giles added.

'Yes, we may not have many arms or ammunition at our disposal, but we do have men and women prepared to lay down their lives for the cause, and that determines almost everything. We have to work fast and hope for the best.'

'Are you going to pursue the confrontation right up to Lagos?' Alan probed.

'I don't know. I haven't received my orders yet. In fact I hope to see the head of state this evening. Personally, I don't think we should rest on our laurels. The further we push the Nigerian army away from this area, the safer we will be.'

Food and drink were brought, and John Nwokolo's sixty-seven-year-old mother saw to it that the pounded yam she gave the visitors was very light and fluffy; her husband had warned her that white people's throats were not strong enough to swallow anything tough and that their delicate intestines would burst if the dough was too heavy. The fish soup was only lightly spiced with pepper. She really went out of her way to make the guests comfortable, as was usual; the fact that the guests were friends of her son – a son who had brought so much glory and honour to Okpanam – made the entertainment of these visitors a whole community thing. Everyone wanted to show them the best their village had, everyone wanted to feed them. And when word went round that all Alan Grey wanted were discarded articles of worship, all the huts, the big houses, the old public shrines dislodged their various carvings, mouldings, ancient animal ornaments which they now regarded as pagan objects. Most of them had been badly burnt or buried in the 'bad bush' with the dead, but the young boys of the village laughingly went and dug them up, wondering as they worked what the white men wanted with these discarded things. As far as the old chief Nwokolo, now a staunch Christian, was concerned they were losing nothing, in fact they could now reclaim the part of the compound that the hideous things had occupied. What was more, the 'onye ocha' paid – a pound to this head, ten shillings to that, a twist of tobacco to another one. Everybody was happy. The really good things seemed to be coming to the Western Igbos at last.

'You never know,' boasted Chief Nwokolo to his wife Ogoli-bu-uno that night after the heroes had gone, 'you never know, we may soon have water running from the taps, and electricity on our village roads, just like they have in the big cities.' To him, the Ibos' heyday was coming. His boy John had been responsible for the elimination of that feudalist overlord in the North, now he was the leader of the winning troops in Western Nigeria and would soon become a political bigwig, when peace was decided. The old man saw no reason why things should not go smoothly.

The drive to the East for Alan, Giles and Colonel John Nwokolo was a noisy and triumphant one. People all around had known that he was visiting his parents after he had stormed into Ore, and also that he would be going in person to Abosi to convey the good news and to ask for further directions. As their army cars roared through the dusty roads that led to the tarred ones, women and children shouted 'Hail Biafra!' and waved whatever pieces of cloth they could lay their hands on. The whole of Asaba market stopped and the name Biafra sounded from one end of the concourse to the other. Women composed songs on the spot, songs in which they wove John Nwokolo's name with that of Abosi, with the refrain 'Welcome Biafra'.

The untarred roads and bush paths gave way to the wide modern ones as they neared the Niger bridge that connected the Western Igbos with their brothers in the East. The further they went from the West, the louder and the greater the celebrations.

Their arrival at Aba, the then temporary headquarters, coincided with the time that Abosi was moving into a more permanent abode. He stood there by the piazza of the new headquarters, his beard more luxuriant than ever and his rare smile wider than many people had ever seen it before. Soldiers jumped to attention and flags were raised as Nwokolo's entourage passed. Abosi embraced Nwokolo, patting him on the back in a brotherly way. When he saw Alan and Giles coming out of the car, however, Abosi immediately froze.

'What are those white men doing in your car, Nwokolo?' he asked under his breath.

'Oh, it's only Alan. He came to my place to collect his 'primitive art' things and said he would come this way.'

'I keep telling you people to let me deal with these British whites. I know their games better than any of you. Why should he choose this time to look for his art treasures? We will have to see he leaves as soon as possible.'

John Nwokolo looked puzzled. The Englishmen, though ostensibly not looking in their direction, did not miss a thing. Alan pretended to be admiring the palm trees that had been strategically planted among some bright hibiscus bushes. The bright pinks and reds of the flowers glowed through the darkening light. Alan knew that Abosi was beginning to suspect him, especially since Aburi, but he was determined to bluff his way through.

With a fixed grin on his narrow face he said to Giles, 'We know nothing, remember, nothing at all.'

'Looks as if we are in enemy territory,' Giles acknowledged.

Alan was unnecessarily warm and exuberant in greeting Abosi. He shook his hand several times, repeatedly congratulated him on his recent successes and wished him luck in his new nation.

Abosi, with his head bowed, invited them in, but the joviality which had been there a minute before had completely disappeared, its place taken by his more normal grave demeanour. The building was a two-storied one painted all in white. It was heavily colonnaded in Victorian style but the arched windows were built wide to allow the cool breeze to blow through, although the newly installed air-conditioner made these windows rather redundant. Soldiers were everywhere like ants, busy putting up this and installing that. The general feeling was that Abosi intended to make this a place of permanence. The fall of Ore into Biafran hands, and the successes in the Benin area, left him in no doubt but that he would stay long as the undisputed head of the country he and his people had given birth to. It had at first been like a dream, then a realizable ambition; now it was actually happening.

This optimism in the air had a unique presence of its own. It was alive: people were breathing it in, eating it and at the same time feeding it. There was also an air of unmistakable condescension about Abosi's natural aloofness that the newly arrived men did not miss.

Nwokolo did not say much about the casual and somewhat cool reception he had been given. He was too aware of himself as a commanding officer in his own right to start whining about such a slight from Abosi. He did not anyway have much opportunity to speak to 'His Excellency' as he noticed everyone was beginning to call him, for Abosi had made an inaudible excuse and taken himself away, promising to see him later.

A soldier came up to Nwokolo as he was saying goodbye to Alan and Giles and offered to show him to his apartment.

'Thank you, soldier,' he said promptly. And he asked Alan, 'How long will you be staying in the East?'

'We're leaving as soon as possible. His Excellency is rather busy, as you can see. I shall call you again as soon as I return to the country. When you go back to your people, let them know how overwhelmed we were at their hospitality. I mean that.'

'I will. As things are, I may be seeing them very soon. This place needs only one army head, not two.'

The men laughed.

The way Nwokolo spoke betrayed his feeling that Abosi was being unfair. It did not occur to him that Alan Grey, who only a few months before had been one of their closest friends, could no longer be trusted.

'After all, I have been at the front fighting,' Nwokolo went on, 'I did not know what administrative changes had taken place. That man's pompous air will alienate him from his fellow officers. The sooner Abosi realizes that he can't afford to make a blunder, the better for everybody. After all, I am the man on the field; I tell the soldiers what to do, not him. See the fight we put up at Ore and Benin. Well, I'll have it out with him this morning.'

Nwokolo paced restlessly up and down his suite. A feeling of unease had descended on him and clung like a wet cloak that he could peel off. He could not help thinking of the past. The pathetic figure of the dying Sardauna loomed in his mind's eye. The man had knelt to him, begging him, promising him everything, but he knew he was doomed. Nwokolo had had to shoot him quickly and decisively, before his Hausa soldiers could change their minds; he could not underestimate the risk he ran in trying to convince those faithful Moslem Hausas to believe him, a Southerner, when he told them that their spiritual leader was an ordinary person, and a corrupt one at that. He had managed to win them over only after lengthy explanations, and that was the only break he needed. He had had to kill the man . . .

And all for what? For this spoilt arrogant brute? Come to think of it, what had Abosi and Onyemere done themselves? Had they really led the coups? They had only given instructions without risking their own persons. Maybe the Western Igbos were going to be second-class citizens in the new Biafra; maybe it would have been better for them to remain Nigerians. Alan Grey an enemy indeed. He was their friend. A friend for freedom.

There was a hesitant knock at the door. Nwokolo ignored it at first but the knock persisted, so he asked sharply, 'Who the hell is it? Speak up or I'll shoot.'

'It's me, sir. This is Biafra, we don't shoot each other here.'

'You, who? What is your name?'

'Ugoji, sir, Ugoji from Ibuza, a town very near your own.'

'I know where it is. Come in,' John Nwokolo invited. His gun was positioned and it was only then that he relaxed and watched Ugoji come in. Somehow he was beginning to distrust people. He had seen Ugoji once or twice when he was working at the bank, though there was no need to ask him what had become of his job. 'Welcome, but what can I do for you at this late hour? I only arrived here today, and I need some sleep.'

'I know that, sir. Congratulations on what you have done. But, sir, I think we may be backing the wrong horse. I've been here three weeks now trying to enlist, at least to be given some arms so that we can guard our towns in the West. Many of the people killed in the North were from your place and mine. They were stupid enough to hope that Gambari soldiers would discriminate between the Eastern and Western Igbos – '

'That was their own fault,' Nwokolo cut in sharply.

'I know that, sir.'

'Then what is it you want me to do? There are no arms to go round every Tom, Dick and Harry who wants to join the army just because he has lost his job. We are all one Igbo people. There is no division, and I don't want to hear such petty talk again. We cannot afford to divide now.'

'I know, sir, but recent rumours say that the federal forces may retake Ore at any time. I understand that you did not leave enough soldiers to guard the place. If they retake Ore and Benin, sir, our place will be finished. That is why I'm worried. We should have left a standing army, we should have our men guarding our towns, our wives and children, our young girls and old mothers.'

'What are you babbling about, man? And who sent you here anyway? Do you believe we would sit here and let the federal forces retake Ore, then all the Urhobo towns, then Benin, then Agbor, then come to our part . . . Wake up, man. I shall talk to the head tomorrow and we will make sure we consolidate our victories and put enough men to defend our property rights. I don't know where you heard that rumour about federal forces.' John Nwokolo laughed uneasily and then added: 'Federal forces indeed!'

'But, sir, wasn't that the same mistake we made about the Hausas, that they were nothing to worry about?'

Nwokolo looked intensely at the fair-skinned fellow Western Igbo standing in front of him, but if he was beginning to entertain the same doubts as Ugoji about the position of Western Igbos he was not going to let it show. He was grateful, however, that among all these Eastern Igbos there were a few from his own area, and he was equally gratified that they were beginning to ask questions. It was too late for him personally to go back: whenever people remembered the successful Northern coup his name would always be linked with the death of the Sardauna, which meant that unless the whole of the federation was subdued he himself was under sentence of death, knowing the temperament of the Hausas. And now he had made his situation worse by taking Ore. He would not be surprised if there was a price on his head. He must convince the head of state of Biafra that they must continue to fight with self-sacrificing spirit in order to consolidate their conquests. He did not wish to know where Ugoji got his information from. This was war and he would not welcome wrong and weakening rumours into his thought.

'Don't go about spreading talk like this among the soldiers. You could have yourself court-martialled as a saboteur,' he warned.

Ugoji turned away, lamenting that their people were caught up in a war of this sort. They had no choice but to join their brothers, the brothers he suspected might not want them in time of plenty. He sighed as his bare feet crackled among the dry leaves that covered the footpath leading to the shacks which refugees like him were given as their temporary abode.

11 *Operation Mosquito*

It was a Sunday. The sun was shining pleasantly and the people, soldiers and neighbours around Saka Momoh's elegant white-painted abode were already moving about. Momoh watched from his bedroom window as the two heavily armed guards patrolled, never saying anything to one another as they passed. He sighed: the beginning of another day. Another Sunday.

Some hymn music floated from the dressing-room where his wife Elizabeth had been getting ready for church for the past hour. Then he heard an indistinct voice from the radio. The music had stopped, but he kept on humming the tune as he finished his toilet. He was stopped by his wife's angry entrance into the room.

'Honestly, these people! Have you heard the latest, Saka? They are now claiming to be the only Christians in Nigeria. Can't that man Abosi and those who spread his dirty news for him tell the truth for once, not even on a Sunday?'

A wry smile spread on Momoh's narrow face. 'Today being Sunday has nothing to do with it. Abosi can get in touch with the best brains in this art of propaganda. They are so good at it that it would not occur to many people to doubt their word. We are up against a formidable enemy on that score. But I still keep hoping that he will give in to common sense. Surely he can see that if the whole of Nigeria rose against him he would have no foot to stand on?'

Elizabeth shook her head, almost shaking out the headtie which she had laboriously taken the whole morning to arrange in place. 'Not from what I heard on the BBC Overseas Service. It seems people believe him just because he penetrated into Benin. Why can't people see that he is lying?' she cried in anger and near despair.

'Don't worry, you'll see that he's providing the very rope which will hang him, with all his clever ideas. He claims to know the British better than we do. But with this Christian thing he is landing himself in trouble.'

'How, Saka?'

'Because Britain is a Protestant country. Most of the Irish are Catholics. I understand that the nuns managing the Igbo hospitals and many of the priests still running their schools are Irish. Britain would be blind not to see that if they backed Abosi then there would be no reason for them not to look sympathetically on their own Irish problem.'

Elizabeth shook her head again. 'Sorry, Saka, but I don't follow you. All I know is that people who want to interfere in our affairs should check the truth first.'

Momoh knew that there was no point in blaming outsiders. It was their own affair. Then he whirled round. 'That over-ambitious Igbo man must not be allowed to rule Nigeria. The French might help him, yes, but not the British. The British are like the Yorubas – they can smile and smile and still be villains. So, Elizabeth, get ready and let us go to that church, but this is going to be a service with a difference.'

He strode angrily into the lounge and chose a quiet corner. Perching stiffly on the edge of an armchair he started to make frantic phone calls. He shouted down the mouthpiece to all the Lagos radio stations, he ordered all the top newspaper reporters, commanded all the television cameramen to assemble at once in front of Christ Church Cathedral in Lagos where he and his family were going to worship that morning. He informed the bishop that he himself was going to do the preaching and the bishop was only too happy to oblige and please the military ruler.

By the time Momoh and his family had driven to the church, the streets facing it were already filled with journalists, photographers and the usual loiterers. This latter group did not have to wait long to have their curiosity gratified. They 'oohed' and 'aahed' as they saw the young Momohs filing into the cathedral. Elizabeth walked with grace and dignity, wearing the latest and most expensive lacy material in town, and her husband wore an agbada of the same material. Even their small son had his little baggy trouser suit made from it. Everyone knew that such material cost hundreds of pounds to buy and some wondered how they had managed to get it into the country when there was talk of banning such ostentatious cloths. Even the bishop, who welcomed this kind of attention for his church, remembered that the army had said they toppled the old government because of its corruption and predilection for showy outfits. Now Momoh reminded him somehow of the late Ogedemgbe. But the bishop pushed such irreligious thoughts aside as he posed with the 'reigning king' for the photographs he knew would be shown the world over. As the Igbo saying went, 'Who would not chew a fish that he found in his mouth?' He smiled widely, rubbed his soft puffy hands in glee, and bowed to his illustrious worshippers in the sight of God.

It was not only the bishop who was enjoying his publicity. The journalists scribbled and scribbled, licked their pencils and wrote frantically to show how important their mission was. They followed the congregation into church and, while people sang as they had never sung before in the hope of being seen on television, the cameras buzzed and clicked and clicked again.

Momoh responded to the mood of the crowd as he swished his agbada behind him, as though he were still in uniform and holding his baton of office. He knew what they were thinking, that he was too slow in making decisions, and that those few that he did make were wont be woolly and indecisive. But people were fools. Did they not realize that he could bring Abosi and his breakaway Biafra down at any moment he wished? He did not need advice from anyone. Nigeria was like a soup which too many expert cooks might spoil. Let Abosi keep his advisers. He, Saka Momoh, would know when to strike. That English-man, Alan Grey, had tried on several occasions to make suggestions to him, as had some Eastern Europeans who claimed to be in Nigeria on business. Let them all mind their own business and he would mind his. Grey had taken it upon himself to travel to the Mid-West at his own risk, using his love of primitive artefacts as a pretext, and had promised to report back the lie of the whole operation in the East. Everyone knew of the man's obsession with those so-called art objects; no one would suspect him of anything. Even Abosi would detect no flaw in his excuse.

Saka had more hope in Debbie's mission. He had pressurized her to go, without making it obvious. She was to use her education; on that level at least Abosi could not talk about 'half-baked illiterates' as he had referred to many of them. Ogedemgbe's clever daughter would not hesitate to do anything to convince the trained propagandists who seemed to surround Abosi twenty-four hours a day. Momoh would wait for news of Debbie. If she gave any indication that Abosi was unwilling to budge, then he would send a conquering army into the Igbo heartland.

On this Sunday, however, he was going to play it Abosi's way. The sermon was about war. It was almost an explanation, an apology to the rest of Nigeria. 'We are still brothers, and we hope the devil responsible for this chaos will go. What is the point of killing more and more Igbos? Have they not suffered enough? They are being led astray by a few ambitious people. We want the whole world to see that the Christians in Nigeria are not just of Eastern origin. We have Christians everywhere. The fact that my first name is Saka does not make me a Moslem,' he went on, getting warmer as he preached his sermon of mercy and pleaded for understanding.

He was the first to see the two brisk-looking officers who hesitated only a few seconds by the door of the church. They took off their caps and pressed them to their chests and marched with slow deliberation down the aisle, past the chancel and the communion rails, looking uncertainly from side to side. Momoh froze, like someone seeing a ghost. All eyes watched the progress of the two officers. They stopped in front of him, then the senior one took a further step and whispered a few words into the ear of the Chief Military Commander of Nigeria. The knot of veins on Momoh's head had never shown itself larger before. He clenched his hands ready to hit out at something but he realized that he was in church and not making a political speech. He gulped and announced:

'It looks as if we are destined to fight each other. There is no going back now. Abosi is in the Yoruba heartland. Abosi has taken Ore. He is a few miles from Lagos. I'm afraid we have to end this service.'

He left the pulpit abruptly, swishing his crisp white lace agbada. Anger fuelled his speed and gave cause to his impatience. Not until he reached the church door did he remember his family. His equally agitated wife, pulling their confused little son along, ran after him, only just making it to the limousine before Momoh shouted, 'Drive on – what are you waiting for?'

The driver, like a robot, started the engine, and then the awful sounds came. They came through the air. It seemed as if the sky, which up till then had been so innocently clear and blue, was torn into two and the gaping hole between the parts coughed out some horrible black mucus of smoke. It was death coming from the sky. People screamed and shrieked, and called these fires 'bombs'. Aeroplanes were seen flying low in and out of the smoke and fire, belching out more and more of it.

Lagos, the capital of Nigeria, was under attack! The people in the whole island became confused, just like ants whose pathway had been mischievously disrupted. Market women left their stalls and in panic ran towards the sea, thinking that the water would put out the killing forces of the burning bombs. 'Bombu, bombu,' echoed from mouth to mouth. Many big men waddled out as quickly as their sagging bellies would allow them, from their places of worship, not going back into their cars in case they got trapped. Lagos had never seen such confusion and panic.

Momoh's military driver managed to get his master and family home, though badly shaken. Anger and fear burnt from Momoh's eyes and his mouth was dry. He could say nothing. He could do nothing, even when he got home. He could only wait, in the hope that Abosi would bomb himself out.

That was what happened. It was Momoh's guess that it would be some time before there was a repeat of this scare – for that was what it was, only a scare. He also knew that Abosi could not have acquired enough explosives to allow him to stay very long in Lagos. Momoh barked at anyone who dared to approach him. But his wife Elizabeth could not be frightened off.

'You must do something right now, Saka. If the Biafrans don't kill us, the Nigerian people will. You must at least show them that we are putting up a fight. No one likes to be frightened like this, on a Sunday at that, and to be made a fool of. Those people say they are Christians, yet look at them raining bombs on civilians on the Sabbath.'

'Why don't you shut up, for God's sake? What nonsense are you talking anyway? Put up a fight indeed! So you are beginning to doubt the might of the Nigerian army, my soldiers? You'll see. You'll see.'

'Yes, and by the time you are ready to show the wonders you and your soldiers can do, we will have died. Maybe he didn't kill many people today, but he scored a military point. He has set panic among the people of Lagos, and who knows what the next set of bombs will do?'

'He won't have another opportunity. Please go and see to the children's lunch. I want time to think.'

A few days after this incident, Captain Alan Grey arrived in Lagos on his way to London, where he was taking a haul of art objects. He sought and obtained an audience with Saka Momoh.

Since he had known that soldier from the Tivs, Grey had never seen him so worried, so frightened and so undecided. Nor had he ever felt so welcome. Saka poured out his woes, telling Alan how he was still treating the whole thing as an internal misunderstanding. But the few soldiers who returned from the front told him that they could detect foreign-made arms among the Biafran soldiers.

'I don't think so,' Alan said keenly. 'In the not so distant future maybe, but at the moment their arms are those they had before the onset of the war.'

He walked up and down agitatedly, then faced Saka squarely.

'Listen, Your Excellency – ' his voice, usually well controlled, now betrayed the mockery he felt as he referred to Saka thus; it alternated between high and low as he failed completely to keep it on an even keel – 'if you are not careful, Abosi will take the whole country from you.' Then he steadied his voice, realizing as if for the first time how sensitive and vulnerable this superficially stubborn man was. The situation had to be handled carefully, otherwise Saka would go against him and irreparable damage would be done.

'Do you know,' Alan went on, 'that no single shot was fired in defence of Ore? Your few soldiers fled at the approach of the so-called "invincible army of Biafra" – an army rotten to the core with pride and arrogance, though at least they could be called to order. Yours ran for their lives at the mere mention of a rumour of attack. Where, Your Excellency, is the Nigerian army? I have to be blunt. You must have the truth, Saka; you are strong enough to take it. This is your country, but Nigeria is a member of the world. Many countries are interested in Nigeria. I won't say more, but remember this as well. No one is indispensable. If you can't defend Nigeria, somebody else will.'

Saka Momoh gulped the truth like a bitter pill, but he kept up the pretence. He was the head of state. 'You were going to find out about Abosi's position and tell me whether he is prepared to talk. Now you are back wanting to tell me what to do. How many times do we have to tell you British that we are now a republic and will welcome your advice only when we ask for it? You go about wanting to tell everybody how to live their lives. Do we interfere with your government? Do we? Answer me – do we, enh?'

God give me patience, prayed Alan Grey inwardly, his grey eyes appraising the agitation of this man who was the leader of over fifty million people. His strict instructions had been to help on the quiet, without any attachment or obvious obstruction in any way. As long as British investment interests were safeguarded. And he was to show no emotion at all. But however much he tried to perform his duties to the best of his ability, he found that dealing with people like this had made it an almost impossible feat. How did this leader expect to keep his Nigeria united if after hearing of the happenings in Ore he still had not decided on what he would do? What a great actor this Momoh was becoming. At the church that Sunday, four days ago, he had given the impression of being so impatient to go out and fight Abosi that he did not even have time to wait for God's benediction.

Alan swallowed and tried again. 'Your Excellency, the situation is not as you imagined. If you are waiting for a written apology or for

Abosi to make any kind of verbal move, you are waiting for nothing, because I think Chijioke Abosi and his advisers expect the issue to be decided militarily. If you allow him to stampede the whole of the federation into admission, the settlement will be even worse than Aburi.'

Momoh strode up and down restlessly. 'That stupid man probably thinks I am a coward, that I am too frightened to fight.'

Alan Grey watched him but kept a studied silence.

'Well, maybe I am. You know how it is. You are in a good position, you want peace and security, you become maybe complacent. But this man has never stopped fraying my nerves. What does he want, enh? To rule the whole federation? He's mad. That man Abosi is spoilt, and he is mad. He thinks the whole country is his father's business. He has been wanting to rule Nigeria for a very long time. I remember he approached me about it once, about taking over the federation militarily. I refused, Alan, because I felt I was a soldier dedicated to protecting my country, not dividing it. Do you believe me? It's true, you know.'

Alan grunted. He did not know whether to believe this or not. If it was true, why had Momoh not said it before now? Anyway, that was not the present issue. The present issue was who was going to rule Nigeria – Abosi and his Biafra, or Momoh and his indecisiveness?

'We have more arms and ammunition than Abosi will ever have. But these internal battles and massacres have cost us dearly.'

'Oh, for God's sake, Saka. If you have more arms and ammunition than Abosi then use them. As for money and people, Nigeria is a great nation. I don't need to tell you that. The whole Mid-West is rich in oil; part of the breakaway state is very oily; I'd sign percentages of the oil revenue over to people who would help you win the war. The best combat would be heavy yet quick, an all-out thrust into the Igbo heartland. That way the suffering of the people would be minimal. You have nothing against the civilians, I understand?'

Momoh nodded. 'Only against that man, who is now making his people look like sheep with a bad shepherd.'

Alan Grey did not know much about the latter statement. All he knew was that if Chijioke Abosi was in such a unique position that few of his advisers and subordinates were strong enough to take up the mantle of leadership should anything happen to him. However, Abosi exposed himself very rarely to fighting at the front, so the possibility of his being killed was remote.

Saka stopped his pacing and suppressed the urge to ask Alan why he should be so interested in his success. He remembered Alan having said once that he was simply a lover of Nigeria. He was still being paid by the British as part of their aid to Nigeria, but he was employed as a soldier to help build up the Nigerian army. Yet this man was doing more than that. Momoh knew better than to trust him completely, but what choice had he?

That evening, in the presence of his supporting colonels Salihu Lawal and Tunde Oshoko, Momoh signed away the greater percentage of the oilwells to some Western powers, on condition that they settled the Biafran question quickly. It was also agreed that Tunde Oshoko, known as the 'invincible arrow' to his colleagues and the young soldiers under him, was to lead his men and enter Biafra through the Northern border by the Benue river. Lawal was to retake Ore and Benin in what was to be called 'Operation Mosquito'. To rid Nigeria of the national pests of mosquitoes had been a feat in which even the colonials had failed; now Momoh saw the Igbos as Nigeria's symbolic mosquitoes. After retaking the Western towns, Lawal was to continue his successes until he penetrated the Igbo heartland.

'They will have given in before then,' Alan Grey observed.

'You never know with that man Abosi. He could convince his people to fight to the last man, while making sure that his own way of escape was carefully worked out,' Salihu Lawal drawled in his Hausa-tinged English.

'I don't think he would be so naive. I still think Abosi loves his people; it's just – well, this is war,' Alan said noncommittally.

'Well, if he does love them, he is being given this opportunity to show it. All the food going into that part of the country must go through Lagos harbour. And I expect Oshoko to close the Port Harcourt opening soon. It's not a nice thought, fighting people through their bellies, but that will make their leader give up the struggle. His people will put pressure on him to give in after that.' Momoh said hopefully.

'Every little pressure adds up eventually. But, Captain Grey, what happened to your girlfriend? Was she not supposed to be making Abosi change her mind? Or has she changed sides on reaching Biafra?' Lawal asked, his brow arched mockingly.

Noting the challenge, Alan replied, 'I don't know, Salihu. In fact I thought she would be here in Lagos. She wasn't in the East when I was there. I hope she is all right.'

His listeners looked at him keenly, wondering whose side he was really on. The next morning two troops, each comprising a thousand of the best men Nigeria could produce, were ready to set out to try and teach Abosi a lesson.

Alan Grey inspected the soldiers before they left. He was dubious about the discipline of most of these uniformed boys. The rank and file in the Nigerian military were still those who had failed to get employment anywhere else; at least in the army they were fed. However, most of them were simply cannon fodder. This so-called civil war was costing the country dear in money and manpower, yet the two warring leaders seemed too blind to see. If one could not stop people bent on killing themselves, at least one could help them die with a smile on their faces. Alan did his best to encourage the excited young soldiers who thought Biafra was child's play, involving only a handful of Igbos. After all, they were the real Nigerians and their task was to keep the country one; and apart from their greater number they were better equipped. The whole operation should not take more than a month.

The soldiers cheered and marched optimistically to a military-tuned national anthem. Prayers were said by both a Moslem imam and a Christian clergyman. So encouraged, the Nigerian battalion went to face the forces of Biafra.

Alan Grey, on the other hand, left the country, with his collection of primitive art and a long document listing everything the Nigerian army would need for a quick kill.

A few weeks later, Alan and his father were in a train taking them to their quiet Devon home. Sir Fergus congratulated his son on work well done; his colleagues at the Foreign Office were pleased. They agreed that a quick kill would be the best solution to the Biafran crisis; it was worth investing in arms and giving aid to Nigeria in this time of trouble, now that it looked as if there was more oil in the country than they had imagined. It was decided that Alan should go to the surplus section of the Ministry of Defence and buy up the old unwanted ammunition that so much had been spent on during the First World War. However people might describe this conflict, it was still 'jungle warfare' as far as the members of the House were concerned. Sir Fergus's protests to the foreign secretary were of no avail.

'You want us to teach those Africans how to use the new sophisticated methods? Suppose they turn round and use them against us? This is a good opportunity to sell that outdated ammo. If we delay, that man may go to other countries for help. We must make the best of being there first,' had been the argument.

The summer rain made the beautiful Devon flowers seem to hang their heads in shame. It was raining as if it would never stop. When they reached the house Alan dropped languidly into an armchair by the fireside and switched on the television.

Then the news came on. The commercial channel showed Biafran soldiers fleeing for their lives. Salihu Lawal was seen giving his men orders to shoot to kill. The strategy must be working. Yet there were only a few Biafran soldiers in sight. Who were the Nigerian soldiers going to shoot since Ore, the town where the scene seemed to be taking place, was in Yoruba country?

He must cancel his holiday, Alan decided. Nigeria needed him. If he delayed too long, and Saka Momoh should realize that he could win without Alan's help and the British equipment, then the oil might be given to whichever country flattered Momoh the most. These Africans made and changed laws as it suited them. He was going back, to make sure of England's share of the booty. The war in Biafra would be won in no time at all.

Two days later Alan Grey landed in Nigeria in a plane loaded with discarded British armoury. A new trade, in ammunition and human blood, had begun.

12   *The Tainted Woman*

Debbie could hear the movements of people in her father's large Sapele compound. Another morning, the beginning of another day. From afar came the hoarse voices of the food-sellers calling people to buy their boiled beans for breakfast. She watched some ants crawling through a gap on the cracked cement floor. Life must go on. In fact it had never stopped, even when she had been not only physically but also emotionally battered.

How was she going to cure herself of the deep mental ache that overwhelmed her each time her mind went back to that incident? That she would have to live with it, make it a part of herself, part of life, part of growing up, she had told herself many a time. But if only she could talk to someone who would understand without making fun of her or repeating it to anyone else. Her mother tried to make her accept what had happened to her, saying, 'It's the fate of all women, Debbie, my daughter. Think yourself lucky, that you were saved. Think what would have happened if you had died. Think of your brothers.'

But how unfair, Debbie thought, to be the victim of the very people she was trying to help. If Biafran soldiers had done this, she might have been more able to understand. But Nigerian soldiers! It was Momoh who had sent her to Abosi in the first place. She twirled the whole painful issue in her mind again and she felt sick. She could find no answer.

She was grateful for having her mother around. Her mother had nursed, talked, prayed, then bullied, telling her daughter to put it all behind her, that she could still lead a perfectly normal life – this from a woman who for years had pretended to be so frail and dependent that tying her own headscarf was a big task. All that show of dependence just to keep alive her marriage and to feed her husband's ego; and to think she had played that charade for over twenty-five years!

The bell of the nearby school started to ring and children's voices floated in. There was a knock on Debbie's door. It was Dora, the seventeen-year-old mother of a child by an unknown soldier. She shuffled in as usual, dragging her bare feet on the floor like the belly of a snake. Debbie was used to this but it still annoyed her mother, who had been accustomed to being attended to by smart servants in over-starched white aprons. Well, they could not afford such servants, not now in Sapele where they were almost in hiding.

'I shall be up soon, Dora,' Debbie said without bothering to look at her.

'No, miss, you don't have to get up. The boy down the post office brought some papers. He said they were for you.'

Debbie came out of bed too quickly; the twinge of pain she felt in her womb was a constant reminder. A good gynaecologist was an unattainable luxury at the moment so she had made use of a friend of her mother's, a nursing sister, who had done her best to patch Debbie up.

'So the post office does work. I didn't realize that.'

Dora shrugged her skinny shoulders pretending to know more about the situation in town than she actually did. 'Sometimes they open, sometimes they don't.' She was ready to sit down and indulge in a long morning gossip with Debbie, whose question she felt gave her an excuse to do just that. Debbie never treated her like a servant, yet Dora had the nasty habit of bringing her news she did not care very much about. She was the one who kept telling her that everybody in town knew what the soldiers had done to her. The poor sad girl seemed to derive some kind of satisfaction from knowing that there were women worse off than she was.

Debbie now waved her away and having collected the post from her said, 'I'll call you when I'm ready.'

She immersed herself straight away in the newspapers that were already two weeks old. It was as if she had been imprisoned and was now allowed a little freedom. She laughed at the picture of Lagos women running for their lives, and sympathized with a beggar shown hiding behind a raffia mat, as if that would protect him from the Biafran bombs. Then as she went on reading her heart sank when she saw that Ore had been retaken by the federal forces. She saw from the photographs taken of Biafran soldiers leaving the battlefield that they were getting too proud, too complacent. Fancy taking a strategic place like Ore and leaving practically no one to protect it, and then making a thrust into Lagos. And on top of that, going to declare Benin, a place that they had not taken the trouble to consolidate, a separate state. No,

Abosi must be made to see reason. He must be made to give in, while his position was still respectable. Instinct told her that once Momoh had started conquering, the man would not stop until he had killed virtually all Igbos. She knew how humiliated Momoh must have felt when Abosi started bombing Lagos. Even though only one of the bombs fell on a house in which a few members of the family were injured and one killed, the low-flying planes were a masterly touch of Abosi's in terms of psychological harassment. Revenge would indeed be sweet to Saka Momoh.

Then Debbie saw the letter tucked inside the last edition of the Lagos *Times*. The papers had been sent by Alan Grey. So he was still in Nigeria. In the past weeks she had almost forgotten that other people were still living. She must get out of this place, she must do something to make her forget that now, in the eyes of the world, and through no fault of her own, she was a tarnished woman.

She read in Alan's letter that he had been to England and was now in Lagos. He did not say much, only wanting to know where she was and how they all were. It would be nice to see him once more, she thought; perhaps he would understand. When she sought her mother out and told her simply that she wanted to go on to the East, to Biafra, her mother protested, saying she must be mad to contemplate such a move.

'Why don't you stay here and get married? In marriage you'd have all the protection you need and no one would dare refer to what has happened again. If you go, fingers will always point at you. People will always say, there she goes, the Ogedemgbe girl who was raped by Igbo soldiers. An unmarried woman is never respected, Debbie. You know that. It is a man's world here. Even if you remain single by choice, nobody would believe you. I'm going to build a new image for you. After a few years, people will forget; and, with your dead father's name and money, the right man will soon come along. Don't throw all that away.'

'Stop, Mother, please stop. Those were not Ibo soldiers who . . . who – '

'I know they weren't Igbos!' Stella Ogedemgbe exclaimed. 'But you're not going to go about telling people you were assaulted by federal forces? No one would believe it. For your name's sake, that must be the story, though the less you refer to it the better.'

'Oh, Mother, sometimes I just can't make you out. So the Igbos are to be made the scapegoats – suppose they win the war?'

'Is that why you're going to the East? For Chijioke's sake? How many men do you want, Debbie? Do you think I have no eyes to see that, but for that feminine-looking white man, Abosi would have married you?'

'Mother, it would be rude to argue with you. But you must get one thing clear. If Chijioke Abosi had been parcelled up and given to me free I would not have taken him as a husband. I am going there because of his ideas. I don't believe this is the right time to fight for the concept of Biafra. Can you understand me, Mother?'

'Understand what? Understand that you are a madwoman, with mad ideas? What is there to understand?'

Debbie's patience snapped and she cried, 'I don't want the kind of life you are mapping out for me. I don't want to get married just for protection. I don't want anybody's pity. Do you hear me? I don't want to be pitied. You think this war is something between two ambitious soldiers, but didn't you see what it did to my father? Didn't you see what it did to our innocent guard in Lagos? Didn't you witness Ignatius's death, Mother, and the death of that Igbo woman? It is not a war between Abosi and Momoh. This is our war. It is the people's war. Our very first war of freedom. Momoh and Abosi started the purge, to wash the country of corruption and exploitation. Now there is a danger of the two men putting their self-interest foremost. If that is the case, the war will be taken out of their control and put into the hands of responsible leaders who will see the purge through and restore to us a new clean Nigeria. That is why I am going to Abosi, to warn him not to let himself be carried away by personal ambition to such a degree that he forgets his original aim. I must go there before he allows outside influences to get the better of him.'

'Debbie, Debbie,' her mother called in a tired voice, 'what are you talking about? These men, whether in uniform or not, will repeat the very mistakes the so-called politicians made. You mark my words. I can't stop you; you're a grown woman. Go to the Biafra of your dreams, and when you get there you'll find ordinary people. Not angels, just people. And where there are people there will be corruption and exploitation. You can't change human nature. But maybe we all need our Biafras to keep us going. I only hope you don't get too disappointed with yours when you find it.'

Debbie looked mutely at her mother. It had to be different with Abosi. He was an educated man, with a name. He couldn't just want power. He had enough money already, so why should he want more power? Her mother just could not understand.

Tears ran down Debbie's face as she hugged her mother, much later, ready to leave. Mrs Ogedemgbe looked at her only daughter dry-eyed. She knew she had to let her go.

'I will try to understand, Debbie, and I hope you find what you are looking for.' Watching her go, she muttered despairingly, 'I thank God I have those two boys. This child, born a girl, wants to be a man, and wants the men to know she wants to be like them, and still retain her womanhood . . . I don't know, I don't know. Most sensible men know our power, so why go to all this trouble to tell them what they know already? Debbie, I hope you don't get hurt in the process.'

Dora carried a few things Debbie would be needing to the motor park, where there were many mammy lorries and buses going to Benin. She wanted one that would take her straight to Asaba, but experience told her to be quiet about going to an Igbo town. As a young single woman, and a non-Igbo, she must have a real reason for wanting to go. She was at the motor park early, and she waited and looked in vain for a lorry announcing its journey as anywhere near Asaba. But there was none. The sun rose and it was getting hot. Lorries came and went, and Debbie sat there waiting. She was no longer wearing uniform, it hadn't done her much good so far anyway.

'I don't think any lorry is going to Asaba today,' Dora volunteered.

'You go home. Mother may need you. I'm sure I will find something to take me there,' Debbie replied, trying to hide her uncertainty.

'Suppose nothing turns up? You can't walk all the way there. And why are you going to that place, miss? They are fighting a war. That's why no driver will go near there any more.

'Everyone knows there is a war going on, Dora, but I have a reason for going. Just stay with Mother, and if there is a rumour of an army approaching, whether Nigerian or Biafran, run into the bush. Take Mama with you and your little girl. Do you hear me?'

Dora nodded and frowned a little, saying, 'But the Nigerian soldiers are our friends. We're not Igbos, we're not even Binis, we are Itsekiris. They can't harm us.'

'Don't stay to find out. As soon as you hear any of them coming, just run. Now go back. If I can't find transport, I shall return. Go home, Dora,' she said with finality, taking her bag and the few books the girl had been carrying.

After about another hour's wait, she was aware of an agent for a group of buses called Ericho looking at her.

'Waiting for someone, sister? I can take you anywhere – Warri, Buruti, Benin, anywhere,' said the man with a flamboyant bow.

'Can you take me to Aba in the East?' Debbie asked.

154

The smile evaporated from the man's face and he stood back as if to have a better look at her. 'To Aba,' he repeated. 'What are you going to do there? I can tell you are not an Igbo bastard. Or are you married to one of them? If you are, I advise you to stay here, keep his house and money and look after your children. What are you going there to do?'

'I am not an Igbo nor married to one. I just want to go there to see a friend,' Debbie explained.

'No good friend would ask another to make such a journey. Not now. How are you going to get through the fighting? Sorry, sister, I can't help you.'

He made as if to go away and Debbie ran up to him. 'I can get transport to Benin, can't I? My friend is very ill, you see.'

Now the man became suspicious and came nearer to Debbie looking very serious. 'I know your type of woman. You are running away from your husband, looking for army men. Now they own all the money in the country, you women are leaving your husbands and going after the soldiers. What will happen to you lot when the war is over? Have you thought of that? I would rather die than have anything to do with a woman who has been touched by those soldiers. Go to Benin, there are many of them there. The Biafrans are running back to their Igbo land, taking as many women and as much booty as they can lay their hands on. And what is left is a plaything for the Nigerian soldiers. That's how they are purging our nation.'

Debbie was tempted to ask him why he did not join the army himself. He looked healthy and sounded intelligent. But his clothes and sunglasses were too flashy to bend to army discipline. She suspected he was either a drug pusher or a dealer in illicit alcohol, behind his front of being an agent.

Debbie had remembered Benin as a lively and very cosmopolitan place, but nothing in her wildest imagination prepared her for what she saw when she arrived at the motor park. The whole place had the atmosphere of a playground that had been taken over by rough boys. She did not need to be told that Benin had fallen into the hands of the Nigerian army. There were soldiers walking leisurely about everywhere. The false jubilation which Debbie and her mother had witnessed only a few weeks before had given way to the mad joy of revenge, killing and acquisition.

It was almost three o'clock in the afternoon. Since she had left home so early in the morning there was no food in her stomach, but the food stalls in the motor park were deserted. The only people she saw eating

155

were strolling men who claimed to be soldiers, some of whom wore only shorts and khaki cloth caps and were bare-chested.

As the day wore on, many more people straggled into the motor park, fear and despair on all their faces. Debbie approached a family of five who were sitting in the shade with their few belongings, and asked where one could buy something to eat in that place. The father looked at his wife and spoke rapidly to her in Igbo, but not too fast for Debbie to understand his warning.

'I am not an Urhobo,' she said. 'I am half Itsekiri, and I am going to the East.'

She might have been speaking Greek, the way people stared at her as if she were a strange creature. She was very thirsty but did not want to go about looking for a hotel or inn; such places could be fraught with hidden dangers at a time like this. Keeping to the open, she walked round in search of a public water tap.

'What are you going to do in the East?'

Debbie turned abruptly. The man's voice struck through her inattention. It was the father of the family she had spoken to before. He had come to the tap to refill the water bottles he was carrying. Debbie knew that she had to invent a story fast; she would be stupid to say, 'I am going to see Abosi.' Wringing her hands of the dripping water, she avoided answering the man directly in order to gain time.

'So cool, this water, so very cool. I have had nothing to drink for hours.' He repeated his question. There was a kind of anxiety in his voice, but what Debbie noticed immediately was that he did not look her in the face. He was making a big show of filling his bottles, obviously trying to avoid being seen talking to her. An eel of fear started to crawl at the bottom of her belly. The experience of the Benin road was still too fresh. She intuitively respected the man's unspoken wishes and replied tactfully, looking into the distance where the half-dressed federal soldiers were walking about aimlessly.

'I am to go to my mother,' she lied. 'She is old. She is Igbo and my father was Itsekiri. He's dead, you see, killed. My mother is the only person I have. She left Lagos for her home town in Aba and I am going there to make sure she is all right. See?' She ended on an apologetic note.

The man's strained eyes rested perfunctorily on her and quickly looked away. He heaved a sigh and murmured, 'Ah, our mothers. Mine is very old. I know they will start bombing our place very soon but none the less I want to be by her side. She is very stubborn. Wouldn't run for any bombs.' A sad smile spread over his tired Igbo face. 'If they

156

are going to kill her with a bomb, I want to be there. I want to die by her side.'

'It can never be as bad as that. Who is going to bomb the East anyway? The Biafrans wouldn't bomb their own cities and the Nigerian soldiers won't smell such places. Haven't you heard how strong the Biafran soldiers are, how high their morale is?' She looked around her quickly and, controlling her voice the more, added: 'I know they have lost Benin to Nigeria, because Abosi didn't leave enough men to guard his conquest, but that doesn't mean they are going to repeat the same performance in the Igbo heartland.'

'Your enthusiasm is infectious, young lady. I gather that you are new in Benin. You must be a university student, judging from your articulation. But if you took a walk into the city, just a few miles from here, you'd see corpses lining the streets. You'd see houses looted and burned. Igbo corpses, and Igbo houses. Here in Benin.'

'What has gone wrong?' The fear now settled in her belly.

'Everything is wrong. The timing, the leadership, the soldiers, everything. Most of all, it's because of our unpreparedness and careless-ness and greed. How can you declare a war and hope to win it by fighting with bare fists? It's like suicide. Our morale may be high but that will not get us far when we come face to face with machine-guns and bullets.'

Another woman dragging a child came to the tap. Debbie noticed that one of the soldiers standing at an empty foodstall was looking at her and the Igbo man. He seemed to notice it too, for he collected his bottles abruptly leaving her to puzzle about what he meant by greed. Was he referring to greed on the Biafran side or in the Nigerians, or even alluding to the human hawks perching impatiently on the outside waiting to congratulate the winner, but meanwhile urging both sides on?

Who in his right senses could bear to make fortunes out of other people's misery? Unable to find an answer for that moment, Debbie looked up and saw her new-found Igbo friend making his way towards his family. He swung the bottles of water jauntily but his airiness struck a falsely optimistic note. Was it for the benefit of the shilly-shallying soldiers? To watch him gave her a feeling of hollowness.

Well, it was war, and like all wars it had no respect for anybody. At the mere thought of what war had done to her, the hollowness in her stomach got deeper, and bitterness came to her mouth. The faces of those drunken soldiers, the ridicule with which the story of her ordeal was greeted, the tarnished image she would carry for ever – all for what? Was there really any point in her mission? Or should she have stayed in Lagos and watched the stronger party win, if at the end of the day the result was going to be the same? But Abosi had said they had broken away because they believed in the right of the individual; that the country's money should not go into the pockets of the few but should be more equally distributed. He had said that he would help his people with his money, and there was little doubt that so far he had been doing that. And at least he had a plan, an ideology, where Momoh was still indecisive, busy getting angry and suspecting everyone, however well-meaning they might be. No, she would rather go on to the East to see Abosi. She had nothing to lose now.

'Are you travelling with us? It would be safer. It's no use going down the Benin-Asaba road alone in any of those lorries,' the voice of the Igbo man cut through her wandering thoughts. 'The more of us there are the better.'

'Thank you,' she said mildly, including the whole family in her appreciation. They all looked at her curiously and the wife's questioning smile lingered more than that of the others.

There were more families arriving with their few valuables hurriedly tied up on their heads. Apart from the occasional cries of infants there was a strange quiet on the group. One of the children piped, 'Why can't we go in our car, Papa?'

His mother hushed him and said in a low voice, 'You don't want to be killed, do you?'

'Don't frighten the children unnecessarily,' the Igbo man cautioned his wife. 'Those who left in the lorries yesterday were not molested, so why should we be?'

The statements were disturbingly illogical. Why was everybody coming to the motor park in the evening and not earlier in the day? Some of the families looked as if they could provide their own transport, yet they were not doing so. Debbie's thoughts were jerked back to the immediate present by the sight of a group of eight soldiers who marched by, wearing that distant look one usually associated with those who smoke cannabis. The soldier leading them pointed his short gun to the sky as if bent on shooting the clouds. He turned automatically, facing the small family clusters of terrified people.

'You all Igbos?' he asked, staring beyond their heads into the distance. He sucked a trickle of saliva that was escaping from the corner of his mouth.

Everyone was afraid to speak and the silence angered the soldier. His voice rose to a near-hysterical bleat: 'I say, are there no Igbos here or are you all Edos? Are you no longer Biafaaa Biafaaa . . .?'

At his mockery of the name Biafra the other soldiers seem jettisoned into wakefulness. They laughed, throwing their heads back, still toting their deadly weapons at dangerous angles. The thought that they might go off at any moment forced people to move apart at the most vulnerable targets, leaving open spaces here and there.

'What is this again, what is this?' murmured a man who stood holding on to his son a few paces from Debbie.

'If there are no Igbos here, then what are you doing at the motor park? The orders I have received are to let all Igbos go home. If you don't want to go, your townsman's lorry will have to go to Asaba with no passengers.'

Two empty lorries thundered in. The trader who owned them jumped down and patted the corporal on the back in a friendly way.

'Ah, Mr Nwafor, your people no wan' go. They are not Igbos today.'

The trader looked at the crowd with guilt-filled eyes and said nothing. Then the corporal ordered in his hysterical voice, 'Search the lorries! Quick, on the double!'

The soldiers stampeded into action. They pulled out the seating planks, then opened the engine of the lorry, they felt the tyres and scratched the floorboards. One really crazy-looking soldier eyed the tarpaulin roofing; the trader, suspecting what might follow, muttered what seemed to be a protest to the corporal. The latter nodded and barked, 'Enough!'

The soldiers tumbled to attention.

'Your orders were to drive the Igbos who want to go home, but these people say they are not Igbos. So you will have to take your lorry to the next station.' Then his voice rose again and he let out a long bray of rage at the people, 'Move on, go back to the city. Move on!'

'Corporal, corporal, sir.' The voice of the Igbo man Debbie had spoken to earlier cut through the threatening atmosphere. The voice was not loud; it was deep and had something of fear, defeat and resignation about it. Yet it made the noisy corporal involuntarily pay attention.

'You know we are Igbos, otherwise we would not be here. It is good of Colonel Lawal to give us this chance. We are taking it. What made us silent was the way you were pointing the gun. We are glad to be going home, in a countryman's lorry too. We are all Igbos and we want to go back to our homeland.'

'Search them for arms, search them for food! Let them go to their

Biafra and starve. Search them!' With that last order the corporal marched towards the jeep that was parked a little way from the motor park.

Then the young soldiers had a field day. They scattered clothes, valuables, even money all over the park. The owners made mild protests, but nobody wanted to be shot. Luckily the soldiers were simply keen on upsetting the Igbo passengers, not on really searching as such. A few kitchen knives were seized, two bottles of orange squash, which the soldiers started drinking at once. Debbie was afraid they would discover her diary and some of the jottings she had made about the basic points for discussion with Abosi; she determined to get rid of these notes if she survived the search. To tell these people that she too was a soldier would be asking for ridicule if not worse.

'Gwo, gwo, gwo to your Biafra and eat yam. Leave Nigeria, where we have given you English bread, gwo there and eat your Abakiliki yams and cocoyams.'

The insides of the lorries were rearranged and the passengers climbed in. Soon they were on their way to Asaba with sighs of relief.

'Thank God for that,' a woman cried from the corner of the lorry.

'You can say that again. I thought we would not be allowed to leave Benin alive, especially after all the killings of last night,' another woman's voice answered from the shadows.

'In the last few days they have been killing each other. Look at those poor Igbo soldiers left behind. They were all clubbed to death – nice, intelligent young men. What a waste!'

The second woman began to cry into her lappa. Nobody asked her what the matter was, for everybody felt like crying too.

Night fell soon. The lorry sped on. Despite the broken tanks and one or two rotting bodies they saw along the road, they would reach Asaba in time to arrange transport to the East. That should not be difficult; crossing the Asaba bridge to Onitsha was a journey of a mile.

'Our name is Madako. What is yours?'

'Mine is Ugwu, Deboo-rah Ugwu,' she replied, accenting the name to give it more Igbo pronunciation.

'Do they call you Debbie for short?' asked a young man who until then had said nothing.

'Ye-es,' she said hesitantly. Warning bells were ringing. If these people realized she was not really Igbo, she would have a great deal of awkward explaining to do. Her fears intensified as the young man added:

160

'Debbie ... Debbie – isn't that what they call that top society woman, Ogedemgbe's daughter? We read about her a lot in Benin.'

'But I don't think her full name is Deboo-rah,' Debbie put in quickly. 'It is Oritsha Debbie, you know – hers is a Nigerian name, mine is English.'

'Congratulations,' the young man said cynically.

'What for?' Debbie wanted to know.

'For bearing an English name.'

Everybody burst into jerky laughter. It was brief but tension-relieving and Debbie knew that the moment of danger had passed. Then an uneasy silence fell on the passengers, the kind one feels on walking through a graveyard or nearing a deathbed. But there was a taste of uncertainty to it that asked, 'What comes next?' Just as people felt the compulsion of this silence, so they felt the urge to stare ahead into the wide, dark road.

All of a sudden a speck of light, as from a torch, was seen to grow and become persistent. They were not imagining it; it was real. As it approached them, the passengers saw that there were many others. The leading torch was stronger and the others glowed gently and went off like the lights of many fireflies, like innocent twinkling stars. They had their beauty, those small lights, although the men, women and children in that lorry were far from noticing it. They were thinking about death, a fearful, brutal death. Debbie could feel and hear people around her gulping and swallowing; she could smell the sweat of fear. The palms of her own hands were clammy. She ran her tongue slowly round her lips, trying not to think that another rape might be in the offing. Well, if it was to be, let it finish her, please God.

The lorry stopped with a jerk. There were more soldiers, and in the shadows people stood like tree stumps, unmoving. The moon had completely gone from the sky and by the look of things would not be coming out for some time. Perhaps she was imagining that she saw these people standing there, staring, by the roadside, Debbie thought ...

The soldiers banged the butts of their short guns repeatedly on the sides of the lorry for a minute or so. The sound jarred into the very being of the passengers, giving them the feeling of being forced to chew mouthfuls of sand. With each bang they jumped, and the bitter taste of suffering and fear filled the back of their throats. One child was violently sick, vomiting his terror.

Then a rough voice commanded: 'All Igbo soldiers in that lorry, come down at once!'

No one moved or said a word. The still silence intensified, sounding loud in their ears as they breathed hard, wondering what their fate was. Even the retching child had stopped, his insides paralysed by fear.

But the night insects still buzzed. Crickets from the undergrowth cried, 'Shame on you, humans,' frogs from nearby swampy ponds went on croaking and owls drawled their mournful complaints. This was a place for animals, this was their time of day; humans should be in their own habitat, in their built-up homes, not in this belly of the thick African forest where it was impossible to tell people from trees.

'All right, if the soldiers don't move,' another voice of authority raged, 'we'll get them; they won't like our methods, but we'll get them.'

Another theatrical silence followed. These outbursts and silences were meant to rattle the victims, to let the depth of their danger and the precariousness of their hold on life sink into every fibre of their being, reducing them to pleading and confession. Indeed many of those standing already had their teeth chattering as if in a fever.

Then suddenly it was time for the threatened holocaust. Soldiers like bees from all parts of the bush swamped the lorry. People were thrown out, the lucky ones were pushed. Debbie knew from bitter experience the importance of obedience in a situation of this sort. She jumped out before the butt of a gun could force her to do so. She was not going to give any soldier the satisfaction of using her body for target practice.

Torches shone haphazardly here, there, over their faces. 'If you are a woman, stand on this side. If you are a man, this side. Hurry, move, on the double!'

There was pushing and jostling and stampeding and shouting. Children cried, mothers called, soldiers yelled orders. All the people looked like demented animals.

In that split second, a block of what had previously looked to Debbie like tree trunks extricated itself from the mass and catapulted into the thick of the bush. It was four men whose legs had been tied together with rope, and they now hopped, making a blind dash for freedom. But they had made a foolish calculation in this last desperate attempt to save their lives, and they lost. Shots rang out. Every part of the bush was alive with shooting. The Nigerian army had enough bullets to last them ten more Biafras.

People screamed, huddled together. Even five- and six-year-old children knew what to do. They placed their hands at the back of their heads; they crouched down, rolling themselves up like lumps of pounded yam, some with their mother's body protecting them. Then the voice of authority again:

'Enough!'

There was a nerve-racking hush.

'Bastards, bastards, Yarmirin Igbo bastards! Who do they think they are, enh, trying to escape like that?' the officer with the voice of authority was raging spasmodically; the way he spat out the words, almost stammering, showed him as a man usually of few words. As if ashamed of being caught talking, he turned abruptly and ordered, 'Get on with your work, and make it quick.' Marching a little way off, he watched as the soldiers under him set to work.

They swaggered up to women passengers, shouting, 'Are you sure you are a woman? Are you sure? Take your clothes off – quickly, I haven't got all day. Take your clothes off, I say! If you don't, you are a dead Igbo liar.'

The women stripped their clothes off. Thoughts of modesty did not come into it, perhaps because there were so many of them being thus humiliated, perhaps because they sensed from the impatience and urgency in the voices of these wild and inhuman men that they were looking for an excuse to shoot to death anyone who went against their evil wishes. Perhaps, most of all, it was due to their intrinsic will to survive. Life had to be preserved.

The soldiers were far from satisfied. They now had to touch, they had to squeeze, they had to slap even probe, as the whim took them, to make sure that these were really women. The clustering female bodies standing there felt disgusted yet sorry for these crazy men. Debbie felt that they might have gone further with more outrageous behaviour, but for the man with the high-stepping walk and commanding voice. He obviously held some high office, but the light was too dim to make out who he actually was. It seemed to Debbie that she had heard that slow, slurring voice before, though in the confusion of the moment she could not remember where.

Tired of watching the movements of his soldiers and the innocent victims, the officer, a young soldier following him like a shadow, moved straight-backed towards the men who had been pushed together on one side of the road, opposite those who had been proved to be women and their children. As he was about to issue an order, the sound of an approaching car was heard.

'Everybody stand still. If you move, you're dead, you hear?'

The car seemed to have seen the flashing torches, for it stopped slowly and would not come nearer. After a minute that seemed like eternity, the slow authoritative voice ordered, 'See who it is.'

Twenty or so soldiers ran out firing their guns. The air was filled with screams, and though it was not clear where they were coming from the officer seemed able to recognize the death screams of his own men. Snatching a loudspeaker from the soldier standing beside him, he ordered, 'Enough, you fools! You are killing each other. Fools, kaferi fools, shooting your own men!'

Debbie, grateful for the privacy the dark night gave, smiled wickedly at this and did not fail to note that some of the men who had not yet been bound were creeping further into the bush. She looked away quickly and noticed that the woman huddled next to her had seen them too, for she overheard her praying in Igbo, 'May your Chi guide you.'

The avenging soldiers soon returned, pushing the bullet-ridden car. It was packed with food and personal valuables, but there was no one in it. The owners, having sensed what the torches were, had fled, taking their lives with them. The car was soon pushed to one side and forgotten, just like the still naked women. One bold old woman went to the heap of clothes and took a lappa in which to wrap herself.

'What the hell are you doing? Stop, or I'll shoot,' a soldier said savagely.

'Cover my nakedness, my son. The night is cold and this mother of yours is shivering,' she explained as patiently as one would to a mentally sick child.

The eager soldier thus addressed by her grumbled incoherently and looked away. The other women followed the old lady's example and hastily covered themselves with lappas, headties, anything they could lay hands on. Many sat down, waiting for whatever orders the colonel was going to give.

Now it was the turn of those from the lorries to be questioned. They numbered hundreds and had all been brought from Benin, many having made more than one attempt to get to the Igbo area after the city's collapse. About fifty soldiers were asking questions all at once in harsh, angry voices.

'Name? I say what is your name, you bastard, have you no name? Your rank? You're a liar, I know you're in the army, yes, fighting for your Biafra for your Abosi. Igbo bastard – "I am only a clerk in Benin." Liar! Igbo bastard! Move, on the double. Next!'

It seemed the routine would go on all night. It was becoming chilly and the mosquitoes were having a good harvest since there was no protection at all. Some people tried to sleep, but Debbie made an effort to stay awake. Fear leapt into her mouth when she saw a soldier with a gun pointing in front of him approach her.

'You, you – up, move, quick!' he shouted at her.

164

She clambered up from the dewy undergrowth where she had been sitting resting her head against the trunk of a tree.

'You, I say move!'

'But I am a woman,' she shouted in protest. Surely even in a chaotic situation of this sort there still had to be a kind of order. The women had so far been left alone in a chilling suspense, so why start molesting them now?

Another enthusiastic young soldier lifted the butt of his weapon ready to land it on Debbie, but she was saved from this assault by the timely intervention of the first soldier. 'Wait for the command. Go!' Debbie had to follow like a zombie.

All the other women sat up expectantly watching, wondering. What were they going to do to her? The women became more fearful when they saw that she was being led to the secluded corner where the high-stepping officer with the commanding voice had been hiding. It was during the few strides to the place that recognition worked itself into Debbie's consciousness. The man was Lawal Salihu. Yes, she had heard that he was in charge of mopping up Igbos in the Benin area, that he was to restore Benin to Nigeria. He was the officer who had driven her to the army barracks in Apapa to kit her out in her new uniform, the man who had mocked her for being the white man's plaything, who had despised her so openly. Now she saw the arrogant and solid profile. His slow, slurred voice was almost plush. Would he be merciful now? How had he recognized her in this dim light and among so many women? Had he watched when she stripped herself naked, for the sake of dear life?

She tightened the cloth she had around her more securely as if she were feeling cold and as if she was going to face a war, a personal war for her womanhood. As she moved she became aware of herself as a woman, a body, different from the mass of all the other passengers in the lorry. She knew that hundreds of eyes were following and watching.

At a sharp turn from the main road, army jeeps and lorries were arranged in such a way as to look like a chief's small compound. They were so arranged in this out-of-the-way place in the middle of thick bush that those standing just a few minutes away along the main road could not see them; the tiny footpath that led into this open space would deceive anybody except the soldiers who knew their where-abouts. Three powerful gas lamps stood at strategic places but their light was shaded by some specially constructed dark army hoods so that it did not reach the main road. One or two soldiers stood at attention, their hands on their weapons, and Debbie knew that there were more in the shadows. Her attention, however, was directed to the one standing at ease, his huge body leaning by the open side of the jeep furthest inside the compound-like structure. The soldier who had brought her there saluted then turned sharply and went back to the road to join his colleagues.

There was a silence. Debbie knew she ought to have saluted since Lawal was senior in rank to her, but she knew how ridiculous she would look standing to attention and saluting in a lappa, one that did not even belong to her. Then Lawal laughed, in a stomach-rumbling fashion that reminded her of her father.

'I thought you were a soldier,' he said scornfully.

'I am still a soldier,' she snapped.

'Really? Which side are you on now? Biafra's? You must be, to be among those Igbos going home.'

'I am not on anyone's side. I'm on the side of Nigeria. I want Nigeria to be one as we have always been.'

This was greeted by another derisive laugh. 'You are wrong, young lady from England. Nigeria has not always been one.'

Debbie knew what he meant: Nigeria was only one nation as a result of administrative balkanization by the British and French powers. Still, for over half a century Nigeria had been one nation. However, she was at too much of a disadvantage to argue. She simply stared at Lawal who towered over six feet above her. He looked at her for a long time and then remarked, patronizingly:

'I admire your courage. Do you know you could have been killed? What are you doing here? I could have you arrested as a saboteur if you don't answer.'

'I am still on my mission.'

'What mission? The one you had weeks ago? We were wondering what had happened to you. I thought you had gone away with your white man, back to his country. He is such a coward. As soon as we started to retaliate against Abosi, he left us. I still wonder whose side those people are on.'

'He only went for a short visit. He's back now.' Debbie partially agreed with Lawal. On whose side were the British? On whose was Alan Grey?

'So he is back, enh? We've been out of touch here in the bush for over two weeks. You are still his plaything then, are you? You are all saboteurs, selling our country to the foreign powers. People like you!' As he became more worked up and enraged he started to stammer. 'Go in, go in there. I am going to show you that you are nothing but a woman, an ordinary woman.'

Debbie offered no resistance. She knew already that hers was a losing cause. In the end, who was she to complain to? A pain shot through her as the weight of the Hausa officer fell upon her. She smothered her urge to scream, for fear of the reaction from this very angry man. He groaned and thundered, he swore and pushed her around, but the uselessness of it all had made her indifferent. It seemed he could not satisfy himself, could not go on. In despair he got up and cursed.

'You are as dry as the desert and as unappetizing as a great-great-grandmother.' He swore and slapped Debbie.

She did not know what came over her; maybe it was a desire to humiliate this man with his holier-than-thou attitude, maybe it was the knowledge that she could never be moist and soft for any man again. She slapped Salihu Lawal back, and he fell back on the bunk bed, staring at her. He was dumbfounded. He was being confronted by a new kind of woman and he could not understand it.

'Three or maybe four weeks ago I was raped by I don't know how many Nigerian soldiers when I was on this mission. Now you are raping me too.'

Lawal stared. His hands frantically located his beads. Debbie's laughter was hysterical.

'I was raped by Nigerian soldiers, do you hear me?'

The huge man was telling his bead vehemently now. 'Allah, Allah!' he prayed.

'Allah will never forgive you now because you tried to violate a woman who has been raped by so many soldiers, a woman who may now be carrying some disease, a woman who has been raped by black Nigerian soldiers. You thought you were going to use a white man's plaything, as you called me, only to realize that you held in your arms a woman who has slept with soldiers.'

Debbie tied her lappa about her. She felt exhausted. She felt empty. 'I hope my mission is not too late. I hope I shall be able to talk that other silly man Abosi into giving in now and letting his people live. You intend to kill all those men, don't you? There must be more than a hundred of them, and you're going to kill them all. And you a devout Moslem. They are civilians, you know.'

'You can sleep here till morning,' he said, his voice very quiet. 'I am sorry; if you had told me before, I would not have touched you.'

She nodded. 'I know. But please, those people, those poor people – do they have to die?'

Lawal nodded slowly. 'Those were my orders. And their people have been doing the same to those they conquered. We heard rumours that Hausas trapped in the East were being killed every day. This is the only way to force that man's hand. If you could convince him to change his mind, many, many lives would be saved. But it is a dangerous thing to try. See what it has already cost you? What man in his right senses would ever think of marrying you now, Debbie? Maybe your white man; they have no sense of value in such things. My mother would die if she heard I had anything to do with a woman like that.'

'But would she think better of me if I was raped by white soldiers? Suppose you had been the first to touch me, what would some other person's mother think? You poor, poor men have so many problems to solve, problems you created for yourselves . . . Yes, I'll stay here till morning, so that your soldiers will continue to think of you as a real man. Do you want me to cry out for their benefit? Would that make you feel better?'

In the morning, Debbie joined about fifty other weeping women who were in the process of being packed into a lorry. Two soldiers were commanded to drive it to a place near Agbor and then return quickly. Debbie's mouth was too dry to ask what had happened or was going to happen to the men. Some of the males were only fifteen-year-old schoolboys and their mothers were howling the bush down. But the soldiers pushed them into the lorry. One man rushed out from the men's side declaring, 'I want to give my wife all the money I have for her to use to bring up our children.' He searched through his dirty pockets, brought out three pounds and handed it to her. She refused, screaming, 'I don't want your money. I want you. All the money in the world cannot replace you.' Her voice rang out like that of an agitated ghost.

They were still loading the women into the lorry when the shooting started. The air was again filled with the cries of men dying. The men were bleating like goats and baying like hounds. In no time, it was all over.

Women, dazed with shock, still stared unbelievingly as they saw Lawal ordering the jeeps, trucks and ambulances to run over the bodies of more than two hundred men.

'We don't want it known that they have been shot. Run over them many times and clean up the roads.'

Over two thousand Igbo men died along the Benin–Asaba road on 'Operation Mosquito'. But, as they say, that was war.

13 *The Scapegoat*

The morning sun filtered through the metal bars into the tiny cell. There was just enough room for a wooden platform which served as a bed and under which the night bucket was propped. There was no mattress and no sheet but there was a hard tarpaulin-covered pillow which shone from the grease of the many heads that had rested on it. Captain Nwokolo put four of his fingers out through the barred window to feel the sun. He was gratified to have this little freedom. He had given up fighting now. He had given up demanding his rights as a Biafran and then as a Nigerian. Those rights now seemed impossibilities.

It was a few days since an inconspicuous looking soldier had come into his room and said quietly, 'You have to follow me, sir.'

'Follow you? Why, it's barely five o'clock in the morning. Where are we going, soldier?'

The soldier, who Nwokolo suspected to be an undergraduate for the university of the East, saluted and explained in his uppish English: 'I am sorry, sir, but I am not permitted to disclose your destination. My orders are to escort you out, sir.'

'Do you know who I am?' he barked at the young soldier.

'Yes, sir. You are Captain Nwokolo, the conqueror of the Hausas in the North, the leader of the great Ore mission, the . . .'

'Enough! On whose orders are you acting?'

'I am not permitted to say, sir,' the soldier repeated like a wound-up machine, his face betraying no emotion.

That had been four – or was it five? – nights before. Nwokolo had been ushered rather apologetically by one soldier and then another into this cell. He had demanded to see his friend Abosi the head of state, he had demanded to see the representative of his own Western Igbo people, in desperation he had even demanded a line to the Nigerian enemy

General Momoh. All his pleas had been completely ignored. He was left on his own, given beans for breakfast, garri and soup for lunch and beans for supper, all served through the hatch behind the strong door that led to his cell. The question that kept repeating itself in his brain was, 'What have I done wrong, what have I done?' He had come here to claim the honour that was due him and instead he was thrown into this place. The memory of the simple but warm welcome he had had in his little village Okpanam brought hot unwilling tears to his eyes. He told himself not to despair, that this was a grievous mistake. Abosi could not know that he was in this place and be quiet about it – unless he and Alan Grey too were under arrest. Had there been another coup?

The thought frightened him. A coup would definitely mean death for him and many of those who had brought Biafra to this level. But much as he probed the soldiers who brought him his food and those who came to empty his night bucket, and the one who took him out for half an hour every morning, he could get no answer from any of them. The big prison compound where he took his exercise was usually empty when he was there. Yet he could hear human voices and suspected that automatic weapons were pointing towards him from many an angle. He clung to this idea of a coup. It was the only explanation that made sense.

Nwokolo did not know that a few hours before he arrived in Aba, expecting a hero's welcome from Abosi, an agitated soldier had crossed from the creek into the East. He sought an immediate audience with Abosi, who was as usual busy with plans and talk about Biafra's ideological stand. An African state had made a declaration recognizing Biafra. This was a great boost, and coupled with the fact that Benin was now a Biafran state it seemed that the taking of the rest of the federation was only a matter of time. He had called an emergency meeting of his close advisers to talk about the wording of the letter of gratitude to the African state that had shown such courageous goodwill in their liberation fight. 'We do not really want the whole federation, all we want is the implementation of the promise made to us in Aburi,' Abosi said richly. He was at his most imperious and arrogant. He had reason to be.

Dr Eze, one of the early politicians who had viewed the secession with doubt but was now one of Abosi's advisers, asked, 'What of the promise given by your friend Chief Oluremi Odumosu, did he ever contact you after that?'

Abosi looked at Dr Eze and then his eyes rested on Dr Ozimba's. The cynical reply he would have given died in his mouth. These over-liberal old politicians were waiting, just like the foreign powers, to see who was going to win, playing a double game; still, they were useful to make the rest of the population believe in the truthfulness of the military aim. But after this war . . . He smiled vacantly and said aloud, 'Odumosu is still worrying about the arms with which I would fight and win.'

'Oh?' queried Dr Ozimba.

'Yes, this is unofficial; I heard it from one of our boys. I was told that Odumosu did not declare the Yoruba kingdom as he promised because he was not sure where I would get weapons and ammunition.'

'How callous. Did he really say a thing like that to you directly?' Dr Eze persisted.

'He did mention it in joke at Aburi, and I told him immediately that in Biafra our men will fight, our boys will fight, our women will fight, and even the grass in our fields will take up arms to fight this battle for our liberation.'

A loud cheer greeted this glowing statement. Abosi looked around and added in a low tone, 'We have to forgive him, poor old Yoruba man. After all, he is a politician. What else does any sensible person expect of that race of men?'

Silence fell in the large room. Many of the older politicians sitting there shifted their positions slightly. The banging of the builders outside, who had been ordered to start rebuilding parts of the parliament area, could be heard. The whole city of Aba would be rebuilt as a showpiece for all the world to see.

When the timid knock came, the men were not sure that it was not from the builders. But the knock persisted.

'Come in,' Abosi said irritably, since he had given instructions that they were not to be disturbed unless it was a dire emergency.

A soldier entered, saluted and with head held high and chest sticking out announced, 'There's a messenger from Benin state, sir. He wants to speak to you privately.'

'Privately? Why privately? Let him come in here.'

'Sir, I don't think . . . er, by the look of him – '

'Your duty is to obey, soldier. Show the man in.'

'Yes, sir.'

The man who was brought in was in his mid-thirties, dirty and stinking. His head showed patches where his blood had flowed and dried. He had only one trouser leg. His eyes were red with tiredness and fear. It looked as if he had swum most of the journey back. One look at him told Abosi that this was not a bringer of good news, and being a proud man Abosi wanted to receive the news first and then see how he would translate it to his advisers.

'Come,' he said, his voice low.

The man limped and followed him into the next room.

When Abosi emerged a few minutes later, it was as if he had aged twenty years and he could not look directly at the faces of his advisers. One or two of them got up, wanting to rush to hold him, because despite his bulk it looked as if he was not only sagging but swaying and on the point of falling.

'This is a very, very bad day for us,' he said hoarsely. 'Very bad. But we must not let it continue so. We cannot afford to. Those responsible for this must be punished. A house divided against itself cannot stand. Nigeria has taken Ore, and Benin State has gone back to them. There was no single soldier there to defend Ore, nobody to raise an arm against them taking Benin. And I, Abosi, detailed men whom I trusted to make Ore – but look at what such men have done to our morale. What are we going to tell our people?'

The silence that followed was profound. Even the builders outside must have heard the sad news, for all went very quiet near and around the military headquarters.

'What beats me are these so-called Mid-Westerners. Have they got no loyalty at all? Only a few days ago when we took Benin they were shouting and claiming that we had freed them from the shackles of Momoh's Nigeria. Now with the fall of Ore they are screaming, "Kill Biafra and her Igbo people." We will show them; we must retake those places.' Abosi delivered this as he walked up and down the length of the room with slow, deliberate steps. 'We will show them.'

For the first time in the hours they had been in the room everyone seemed aware of the hum of the fan. Dr Ozimba's cough when it came made Abosi stand still in the middle of the room, his sad eyes lowered and looking imploringly at the painted cement floor.

'I don't think we can keep those places at the moment. Their geographical positions make it impossible. I think we should concentrate on keeping Biafra as she is, using the natural boundaries of the River Niger.'

This was an audacious statement, and even bolder when made at this time when all present were feeling so hurt.

'You never really wanted us to secede in the first place, Doctor. You were busy dreaming about your Pan-Africanism with your friend Nkrumah and those black Americans, while the problems next door to

172

you were shelved. Isn't that so?' Abosi asked rudely, his low voice sounding dangerous warnings.

'Like everyone here, I believe in the advancement of the black race. I don't believe in tribalism, but we in Africa are being forced to acknowledge it because the foreign powers are using those very divisive groupings to tear us apart. I cannot preach Pan-Africanism when we are still fighting for the basic survival of our people. We must survive today without losing too many of our people. That is all I am saying.' He bowed his skull-like head. He was on the defensive, knowing that the younger people did not trust him, but being a seasoned diplomat he also knew that his short statement would allay immediate danger. He was not unaware that in a situation like this scapegoats would be needed to explain the defeat to the rest of the people.

'Where were the rest of the soldiers detailed to conquer Ore and Benin then?' Dr Eze asked, bringing the talk back to the immediate problem.

'I'm not sure exactly, but I know Nwokolo was then in his village celebrating his victory and will be in Aba soon.'

'But who did he leave to protect the place he had taken?'

'A handful of young militia, who were slaughtered in no time by the Nigerians. What a loss of manpower and arms. We'll need more arms; Dr Ilogu will have to see to that. He speaks many European languages and is good at the psychology of those people. We can't afford a blunder like this at this time. It's unpardonable.'

'Your Excellency, what will happen to the Western Igbos? With Benin taken they are now exposed to the Nigerians' anger,' Ozimba pointed out.

'We'll have to leave them to their fate. We can't afford to worry about them now. Those of them who wish to cross the river into the East are welcome to do so,' said Eze.

Ozimba got up shaking in anger. 'Are they not Biafrans then? We've been telling them they are – isn't that why they fought for the cause?'

'Oh,' Abosi waved his hands airily, 'we'll solve their problems after the war is over. But we cannot afford now to claim that Biafra is only for us Igbos. A great part of our mineral resources is in areas where the ethnic language is not really Igbo ... We'll sort out those boundaries later ... Meanwhile, Biafra stands for freedom, freedom for the persecuted Easterners, most of whom are Igbos. Yes, let's leave it like that.'

Dr Ozimba left the meeting in a thoughtful mood. Had they been right to secede? Would the federal forces stop fighting now they had reclaimed Benin and Ore, or would they drive the Easterners further away into the Igbo heartland? Should he advise Abosi to count his losses and give in now that the tide was turning?

It was after this that the arrest took place of John Nwokolo and the others who had fought at Ore but not remained there to prevent its recapture.

Rumours started infiltrating about the advance of the Nigerian army up the Mid-West. In the heat of that moment a large group of the student population made a big protest march to Abosi, shouting, 'Give us arms, give us arms, we wish to protect our heritage. We want to be given a chance to play our part. We cannot study in this uncertain atmosphere. Give us arms, give us arms!'

Abosi came out from his large mansion in Aba personally to thank the students who had travelled miles from their various educational institutions to make their point. He agreed with them, saying that he would rather the enemy took Biafra in ashes than in slavery. The setback was only temporary and in a few days, before the uncouth Nigerian army could come anywhere near their university, the arms would be ready. A crash training programme would be launched to prepare the students. Biafra's invincibility in the airfields would be re-established. And in less than a week, all the saboteurs who had been rounded up were going to be executed by firing squad. The names of the traitors would be released when the time came. He thanked them once more and declared that they had humbled him by their determination to fight for their heritage.

The students, over six hundred of them, returned to their colleges and university. They hid their books in the earth, in the bush or in their villages, and took up sticks, machetes and cudgels in the crash military training course to save Biafra. Every student, male and female, was encouraged to take part.

Those working in the kitchen were among the first to note that the war was going to be a lot more bitter than they had all envisaged. Apart from a few bags of mouldy garri, no food was forthcoming, while Radio Biafra kept pounding in people's ears how their soldiers were annihilating Momoh's soldiers.

'We'll have to fight with empty bellies,' one of the girls remarked, laughing sadly.

'But why can't we get food?' another protested. 'And there's no salt in the market.'

'If it's true that our soldiers are invincible, why can't we get medicine for our children's malaria?'

174

Abosi and the members of his inner war cabinet knew what was happening: Nigeria and Momoh were trying to starve them into surrendering, but to admit this at this time would only incense people the more.

The much publicized day of the execution of the so-called saboteurs drew nearer. Nwokolo was like someone in a daze when the reverend father came into his cell to give him the last rites. That he had been tried and found guilty of being a traitor, an agitator, of killing the Sardauna, were things he failed to understand. He was blindfolded and all hopes he had for his new country went through his mind. When the burning shot went through him, it was as if he saw the figure of the dead Sardauna in his night covering cloth, having the last laugh.

They were quickly buried, and the clamour of the Biafran people for Abosi to do something died down, just for a while.

But Mrs Ozimba was worried for her husband. 'We must leave. If things keep going this way, they will start killing the old politicians. See what they are doing to each other?'

'But I can't escape, my dear. The road from the West is blockaded. And it's too chancy to fly, with our planes being bombed. Besides, everyone knows who I am. We're stuck here. We simply have to wait and see. If the starvation continues there'll be no option for us but to call a halt.'

That night, all seemed calm; there was no moon and no firing of any kind. The people of Biafra had learned to shade their lights so darkness reigned.

It was in the middle of this calm night that the Nigerian soldiers invaded the university town. The hungry student soldiers, who were still waiting for the sophisticated arms promised them, rushed almost bare-handed to face the automatic weapons of the Nigerian army and they died in their tens and hundreds. Many more were maimed for life; the lucky few fled into the bush. It was a gallant suicidal move. But it did not change the fate of Biafra. The revolution was turning sour.

The inner cabinet again met. It was then established that this was not just a war that the rest of Nigeria wished to win, it was genocide. Had not thirty thousand Igbos been killed in the North? Had they not been hunted down in the country's major cities? This was a fight for survival.

'There is no question of giving in. We can still win. But if we make the mistake of giving in . . . look what they did to our university town in Nsukka. They will do the same here.'

'All I want is that we should be allowed to live in our native land in peace. We've sent pictures of the mutilated bodies to Dr Ilogu in Geneva; he will spread the news. As soon as the media in Europe takes it up, you'll see that public opinion will be on our side. The few arms captured from Nigerian soldiers were made in England. We will invite the British press and their diplomats to come and see what the guns they sell to Nigerians are doing to our people.'

Arrangements were made to boost internal farming and to protect the hospitals and encourage home products. They would stop making attacks outside Biafra but would concentrate on defending the natural boundary, a boundary that was shrinking by the minute. They were going to be self-sufficient; while Dr Ilogu and those Biafran diplomats sent abroad were busy convincing the world of their plight, those at home would work at the grass roots.

It was in this optimistic mood that Dr Ozimba, who knew that his popularity was waning, brought out the poem he had written about Biafra. He suggested that instead of the soldiers singing 'In the name of Jesus we shall conquer' they should have their own national anthem.

This was greeted with a loud cheer. Nobody doubted his sincerity, not after this.

14 *Refugees of the Darkening Night*

The women passengers were packed to the tailboard of the mammy wagon that was taking them to Agbor. There was hardly any room to move. Children were squashed between the adults and whimpered in pain as the lorry jolted from side to side. The road was normally smooth, but the receding soldiers had dug holes here, laid wooden trunks there, and scattered stones everywhere to make the journey of the approaching Nigerian soldiers as difficult and as delayed as possible.

There were two pregnant women among the crowd. One had not stopped weeping since they left Benin. Other women gave vent to spasmodic yells and cries for their murdered men and then lapsed into silent thought. But this pregnant woman kept calling her husband, asking him, as if he were there with her, what she was supposed to do with the child she was carrying. Her non-stop wailing and the occasional show of sorrow of the others made the drive uncomfortably noisy.

'If you don't stop your Igbo wailing, we'll make sure you do,' one of the soldiers threatened.

There was a little silence as the women digested what he said, but after only a few seconds the pregnant woman started again and the other women now joined in full force. The driver got angrier and jolted the lorry even more fearfully.

'Now he wants to kill us too,' one woman shouted, and the others took up the sentence like a folk song.

'It's not me, it's the fault of the roads your menfolk left. See how they have ruined everything. Wait until we lay our hands on those Igbo bastards,' the driver bawled through the partition that divided them from the women.

The lorry swerved and avoided hitting a tree by sheer luck. Children started to howl and the women shouted in horror, nerves taut with anger and fear. The driver straightened the lorry and warned that if they didn't stop babbling, he'd drop them there and go back to his regiment. There were shouts of 'You can't do that!' in various languages: Hausa, Yoruba, Edo, Igbo and pidgin English. The driver got the message but still maintained, 'If una no keep quiet, I go stop una here, now.' The pregnant woman, however, still went on crying as if all around her was happening on another planet. She was very young and having her first baby, and was so skinny and pathetic-looking that the nerves of her hands and neck stood out in knobbly relief like those of a starving old woman. She soon began singing a mournful, meaningless song.

When the lorry came face to face with a huge felled tree in the road, the driver and the other soldiers with him got down. It was evident from their jumpy attitude that they were afraid. They held their automatic weapons by the side of their bellies, fingers on triggers, and milled about the huge tree, for a moment not knowing what to do. Fear had now taken over the women and they held tightly on to the children. The bold old woman who had previously dared to go for her clothes along the Benin road whispered to the pregnant girl: 'My daughter, you have to stop mourning for the dead now. We here are still alive. If those madmen really get angry there is nothing to stop them shooting us all. I don't mind for myself, but what of these tiny children?'

The girl was either too far gone to understand or she did not care, until the old woman made her way to her and slapped her on both sides of her mouth. The girl fell back on another woman sitting behind her who let out a scream.

What followed was another nightmare. Suddenly gunshot whistled from all sides of the bush and the driver was soon lying by the tree trunk dying. One soldier was shot in the leg but dragged himself to the front of the lorry to get what looked like a dark ball. This he threw in the direction of the shooting and there was a mighty explosion. There were screams and cries, and Biafran soldiers in tattered uniforms with leaves tied on their cloth hats came out from the bush. Only one of the six men who had left Benin with the women was still alive.

'Come out, all of you, come out,' said the gentle voice of an Igbo soldier. 'Where are your husbands? How come you are travelling with no men to guard you?'

'They have killed them all, including our grown sons,' replied the old woman.

There were about fifty Biafran soldiers who had been left to guard this road leading to the Western Igbo towns. They looked at the haggard women standing in front of them and could offer no explanation as to why they should lose their men. They were not given much more time to brood, for the pregnant girl began to cry out in pain.

'She can't be in labour, can she?' asked a soldier, bewildered by the baying animal noises she was making.

'Well, I think, she is, Sergeant,' Debbie said, before checking herself, as she realized that her accent might give her away. She could not bear to think what would happen to her if these people guessed that she was not Igbo.

'What part of Igboland are you from?' the sergeant asked her sharply.

'My mother is from Onitsha but my father is dead. I was born away from our land, so I am going to my mother.'

'Mmm,' grunted the sergeant. 'All these young things who were taught so much English that they speak with the accents of "been-tos".'

The others laughed. Debbie knew that the less she said the better. To distract attention from herself, she dashed to the pregnant girl's aid even though she had no idea of what to do. But she sensed that they must hurry and leave this place. The token soldiers along this border would not be able to defend and hold this place long, against the heavy armoured cars she had seen hidden in the bush. The bold old woman, who because of her age and fearlessness was becoming their leader, went with Debbie to the side of the bush path to help the young girl who was now screaming uncontrollably in labour.

'But she can't have her baby here, sir,' protested a young soldier, looking lost and embarrassed.

'We have no choice as to where we are born, do we, soldier?'

'No, sir, it's just that we can't afford to stay here long enough to see her regain her strength.'

The young soldier was speaking the truth. The lorry was in no fit state to go on, though every vehicle they could commandeer would be of some use; so the soldiers were ordered to tow the mammy wagon behind the jeep that had brought them to the Mid-West. Most of them would have to risk walking the remaining distance to Asaba. The Nigerian soldiers would be after them in less than four hours if they realized their men had been killed and the lorry taken. The captured soldier, stripped to his underpants, was being questioned and he now was the one crying and bleating for mercy, begging for his life.

Weak laughter from the women at the edge of the bush announced the birth of a baby boy. 'Oh, you have a ready-made name – Biafra,' chanted the old woman as she spanked the child into life.

His mother whined for some water to drink; the water available had been used in the birth and she was not strong enough to walk, so it was decided that she should be put in the towed lorry. The jeep itself had been badly damaged by the hand grenade carried by the dead soldier.

'We don't know exactly where we are . . . somewhere between Agbor and Benin. We'll have to keep to the road as long as possible, but if you hear any vehicle approaching, take to the bush. It will be some time before we're anywhere near the stream at Ologodo, so it's going to be a very long day. I'm sure that when we get to Agbor we'll be able to get new tyres for the lorry and maybe repair the jeep. It can't be more than about twenty miles, so we should make it before the Nigerians realize what's happened to their men.' So saying, the sergeant and the other soldiers heaved the tree trunk more into the centre of the road. 'That alone should take them two hours to shift,' he remarked confidently.

They set off, a straggling group of refugees, with the strong soldiers pulling and pushing the heavy mammy lorry. The sun came up and the children started to cry for food and water, but there was none to give them. Their progress was slow.

After only about four miles, it became clear that the young mother had died; her baby cried and she did not pick it up.

'Do any of you know the name of the father?' the harassed sergeant asked.

No one did. The sergeant suggested that when they reached the East the baby could be cared for by the Irish nuns.

'I will give him my milk, meanwhile,' another young mother volunteered. 'He can share it with my baby.'

'Good, daughter of the Lord. Your baby will not suffer. This new one will not take too much from you,' the old lady said.

Debbie resolved that if no one else took the baby, she would. He was not going to any orphanage. In an Igbo family there was always room for one more mouth.

The soldiers buried the unfortunate girl, and hurried their tired refugees on. Many were beginning to lag behind, not much caring if they stayed with the group or not. Debbie found herself once more moving slowly in the company of the old woman and the wife of Madako, who seemed to have aged in only twenty-four hours. Her two children tugged at her side and the third baby was securely tied on her back. Debbie looked at her and smiled weakly, perspiration running down her nose.

'I am sorry about your husband. He was a good man. He talked to me as if he had known me all my life. I'm so sorry.'

The woman nodded. 'Thank you. I still blame myself for allowing us to leave Benin. We could have hidden somewhere. Hmm, maybe he is luckier than the rest of us. I wish Abosi would call it a day. What difference does it make to us who rules up there? We still have to work, pay our taxes – why make us suffer like this? Now I have to bring up two boys and a girl alone . . . if we survive, that is.'

'I'm sure we will all survive. With people starting to starve, Abosi would be stupid not to give in. I'm sure he'll give in.'

'Hmm,' sighed Mrs Madako, 'you don't know our people. Do you think those at the top will starve? No, they are probably there drinking champagne. And as for the businessmen, they don't want this war to end. You see that driver who brought us to the Benin–Agbor road? Well, he used to be an ordinary poor lorry driver, now he's a very wealthy man. He got a contract from the army to take his people across to Asaba.'

'But he must have known that most of the people he was carrying were going to be killed,' Debbie said.

Mrs Madako shrugged her shoulders. 'Who can tell? He probably didn't. Even if he did, he would convince himself that since he did not kill them he had nothing to worry about.' She sighed.

Debbie offered to carry one of the Madako toddlers, though she had not backed a child in her life. She was clumsy in tying the oja round the baby so the mother suggested she should use only one wrapper to hold the child on her back. Still Debbie was nervous and the baby had to be held firmly for her to knot the cloth round her waist. A soldier was watching and he could not help laughing and remarking:

'What type of women is Africa producing? That one can't even back a baby. How will you carry your own child when you have one?'

'Her type will push hers in that keke thing they call a pram,' another woman put in.

Debbie made light of it. But as she walked down that dry road in that heat, with the weight of the child almost breaking her back, it struck her that African women of her age carried babies like this all day and still farmed and cooked; all she had to do now was walk, yet she was in such pain. What kind of African woman was she, indeed?

She wondered the more, since she had never been to this part of the country before or seen the type of vegetation through which they were passing, the small bush tracks which other women knew would only lead to someone's farm and nowhere near the water they were dying for. On looking back, she saw that many people were lagging behind, unable to keep up even their slow progress; but they dared not stop until they arrived at a town or village. They were tired, hungry and thirsty. The child Debbie was carrying had gone to sleep and was becoming heavier and heavier.

'I don't know if that old lady will be able to make it,' breathed Mrs Madako, dragging her unwilling eight-year-old along.

'I doubt it, but what are we to do? If we wait for them to catch up, those Nigerian soldiers will kill us all,' Debbie replied.

Mrs Madako looked at her closely. She wanted to say something, it seemed, but was not sure how to put it. Debbie guessed that the woman did not trust her completely. Debbie had a kind of foreign look about her. She was too thin to be a typical Igbo girl, and then there was her accent. Mrs Madako did not know how to place her. Debbie had told them earlier that her mother was in Aba, then she had told the soldiers she was in Onitsha.

'They won't kill you,' Mrs Madako said. She had seen the soldiers call Debbie into the bush the night before and knew that it was the colonel himself who had wanted her. 'He won't let that happen. But I don't know why you chose to suffer with us.'

Debbie was quiet for a while then asked faintly, 'How do you mean? Why do you think I am going to the East?'

Mrs Madako smiled wryly. 'You over-educated people. Who knows why you do anything?'

'You are not such an illiterate yourself,' Debbie observed.

'I had enough training to qualify me to be a good wife. I wonder where I can go to learn the art of being a good mistress or a second wife, since that is what is being thrust on us women. What I don't understand is why you chose to be one of us.'

'Oh, come on now, Mrs . . .'

'My name is Uzoma.'

'Thank you, Uzoma. You know that mine is Debbie.'

'Why, you even anglicize Uzoma. Are you putting it on, or is that really the way you talk?'

'I went to college in England. But please don't repeat that. Such knowledge wouldn't be helpful here, would it?'

The sergeant leading the refugees stopped to wait for those lagging behind. When Debbie and Uzoma came up he warned, 'We will have to leave some of you behind. There is a good hiding place a few yards from here; we'll hide those of you who can't walk fast. The Nigerian soldiers will be here in no time; they must have missed their men by now. So the choice is yours.' He waved them on as he waited to convey the same gloomy message to the slow walkers still far down the road.

'I'm not staying here,' Uzoma murmured. 'I'll keep up with them if it takes my last breath. We have no other protection.'

Debbie looked back and saw the tired women talking and arguing with the sergeant. Then he left and trotted to the front. The message was clear; follow if you could, or be left along that road. The soldiers promised to return with water as soon as they reached the Ologodo river, which they said was only a few hours' walk away. Much as people pitied the old woman, the second pregnant woman and many others who could not make it, they knew they could not wait. A woman ordered her four boys to go along with the soldiers and not to wait for her, and it was only after some tearful exchanges that they did so. The sergeant told them: 'The Nigerian soldiers will not kill your mother but they might kill you because you are boys. Besides, Biafra needs strong boys like you.' With that, he swung the youngest, a plump five-year-old, on his shoulder and moved on.

Debbie and her group had started trotting ahead, aware that that was the only way to survive. They lost a few more people on the way, before they sighted the Ologodo river, bright and glittering in the pale evening sun. They rushed forward to drink their fill. And for the first time in over seven hours they saw other people, who lived in nearby villages and had come to the stream to fetch their domestic water. They were not unfriendly and did not run away, for they had seen many refugees crossing their villages in the past months, though not refugees with this type of urgency in their behaviour. The villagers wanted to know if Benin had really fallen; they wanted to know first-hand what was happening to the Igbos in Benin.

'You must all disperse into the villages,' the sergeant advised. 'Don't cluster together. Just go to your villages.'

People said quick goodbyes to each other and took up different footpaths that led to various parts of the town of Agbor. Debbie kept with the Madako family, and the new baby 'Biafra' was almost forgotten in the rush until, giving Uzoma back her toddler, Debbie took the new child. The young mother who had breast-fed him all day came along with them too, as did the four boys whose mother had stayed behind, and the woman with her six children. There were eighteen of them, including Madako's three children. There was little time to choose which route to follow; they walked up the nearest path. None of them knew anything about the area, so it was a matter of luck that they found a sheltered grove off the footpath in dense forest. It was mutually agreed that they needed a shelter in which to gain their breath back before facing the villagers. They could still see the stream and the tarred road, but they remained well hiddden.

'They are working on the lorry,' announced Ngbechi, one of the boys, peering through the leaves into the fast approaching night.

'It will be something if they can use that to take people back to the East. It's best for us to wait here and see what happens,' Uzoma suggested. 'If they can get the lorry going, we will be able to travel with the soldiers.'

It was a brilliant idea. They waited and prayed while the soldiers worked, not knowing they were being watched by the women. Soon the lorry started to quiver, ready to go. Ngbechi was sent to the soldiers and returned to report that they were first using the lorry to take water to those left by the roadside, including his mother. So the group waited with bated breath.

The loud bang that sounded only about twenty minutes later woke almost the whole village. The women refugees and their children jumped into wakefulness. Some of them had been sleeping off their weariness. Quickly, Debbie tied the new baby on her back again, Uzoma picked up her toddler, the other mother marshalled her six children and they dashed out of their hiding place on to the main bush track. The rat-tat-tat of gunfire sounded so near, it seemed to be right at their heels. Then there was a big explosion which lit the sky like storm lightning.

It was clear what was happening. The Nigerian army with their superior armoury were taking revenge. Debbie allowed her mind to dwell a little on the Biafran sergeant and his men and asked as they puffed their way to the village:

'Do you think he sent all his men back to those women?'

'He'd be a fool to do so,' replied the nursing mother.

'Only the young privates would go on errands like that. The senior ones don't suffer. Some of those poor boys could hardly hold up their trousers, let alone heavy guns.' Uzoma touched her breasts in a pained gesture of sympathy for the mothers of the unfortunate young soldiers who had been blown to pieces.

The door they decided to knock on belonged to a middle-aged widow. She was pleasant but afraid and ill-at-ease because she had no food to give to her visitors.

'Our Obi has declared us neutral. We can't afford to take sides, since we are on the border. I don't know why they should be shooting here at all. Did you hear the bangs? Why can't they take their war to Biafra or Lagos, why come here to Agbor?'

They calmed the woman down and reassured her that they were harmless. She checked her akpata shed and brought out the left-over pounded yam which she kept for her breakfast. A piece of dry fish too was found. The children were given one lump each of the yam and the adults shared the dry fish. Before long they had all fallen asleep on the mud floor of the front room, only waking when the morning cocks began to crow.

Debbie had never felt so rested. She remembered nights when she had tossed and turned in her soft-scented room in Lagos, she recalled occasions when she had stayed with her parents in three-star hotels in England and had been given some hot drink to induce sleep, and she thought of her places of rest in the past two nights. Why had it come to that? When the history of the civil war was written, would the part played by her and women like Babs, Uzoma and the nuns in Biafra be mentioned at all? Had her original aim of pleading with Abosi not become redundant? How many Igbos were killed yesterday? How many Nigerians? As far as she was concerned, they were all Nigerians. She knew that Lawal's Operation Mosquito was just one of four major ones. How many people were dying every minute on other fronts? She sighed, wondering if the plight of people like them, trapped in the bush, was noised abroad. What a mess!

Her thoughts were sharply brought back to the dangers of the moment by the sounds of grenades. They were similar to the shots and bangs and horrible blood-curdling sounds of the previous night. The Nigerian soldiers were probably on the main road although so persistent and loud were the sounds that they seemed to be where the women were sleeping. Mrs Madako grabbed her youngest baby.

'We must leave at once. We will endanger the life of this kind woman if we stay any longer.'

The widow, shaking with fear, came from the smaller room where she had slept with some of the children and protested, 'I heard that. My ancestors would never forgive me if I let you go now. You'd be caught in the cross-fire and what would happen then? And what will the children eat? Don't you know that Asaba is about forty miles away? How many days do you think it will take to make the journey with no food and so many children?'

'Thank you, mother,' said the young woman with the milk. 'I know there is a way to ferry us to the smaller Igbo towns in the West. You are too near the road. As for food, we shall buy as much as we can, and hope for the very best. Many of those approaching soldiers know us. They stopped us along the Benin road, they packed us into the lorry, after they'd killed our husbands. If they fail to find the Biafran soldiers they are looking for, they will pounce on us. We have no defence.'

'You will go to your deaths if you leave during the day. If you have money I shall go to the village market and get you yams, fish and garri. At least that will help you keep alive.'

The women brought out their hidden money. Some had large amounts of Nigerian currency tied into their scarves, some in the edge of their lappas. The woman with six children had lined her baby's hat with the money and covered the inside in plastic. The kind widow set out to the market with two of the children. When she returned from the market, she was not the same confident woman who had left them.

'You are right,' she breathed, 'they are everywhere – searching, questioning. They say they want to kill every Igbo. Every Igbo thing that moves must be shot. What does not move must be shot as well. They are even combing the bush. They will kill anyone who harbours anything belonging to a Biafran.'

'And, Mother, we saw "Tyrone Power",' said Mrs Madako's twelve-year-old Boniface, wide-eyed, 'it's completely burned to the ground, everything is burnt.'

'Who is Tyrone Power?' they asked the boy.

'The lorry, that lorry that brought us from the Benin–Asaba road, the one the Biafran sergeant was repairing, remember? That's its name. It was written on its forehead.'

Debbie could not help smiling, wondering at the way children noticed such minor things at a time like this.

When it was completely dark, and it was apparent that the soldiers bent on purging the country of Igbos would soon be calling, the four women backed the babies and led the older children into the bush, but not before the widow had fed them hot yam porridge spiced with pepper and laced with chunks of bush meat. That, at least, would last them through the night. They had plenty of matches for lighting a fire and a big tin bowl contained the cooking-pot and stones for cooking.

'Goodbye then, and may God go with you,' said the woman.

They hugged her and left in single file, refugees of the darkening night setting out on their long journey through the thick Mid-Western Nigerian bush to Biafra.

Two hours later, Nigerian soldiers kicked the widow's door open, demanding to know where the Biafran soldiers she had harboured had gone. She did not disappoint them. She said they had come to her hut, threatened to kill her so that she had to feed them. But, she said, they had gone through the bush on the Umunede side – exactly the opposite route to that which the women and children had taken. She urged the Nigerian soldiers to hurry, for she was sure they would catch up with the Biafrans. So they thanked her and left her in peace, giving her two tins of corned beef.

She went on her knees and prayed to God to forgive her for telling so many lies. Her prayers must have been heard, for the soldiers never again throughout the duration of the war knocked on her wooden door.

15   Outside Help

Alan Grey had been expecting the sort of lavish dinner party that befitted the Nigerian head of state. But that was not the case. He had been invited as a personal friend of Saka Momoh and his wife, and was being informally entertained in this simple, homely manner, with the young children of the master and mistress even allowed to run between their legs. They were being attended by servants from Momoh's own tribe, servants who were so unsure of themselves that they giggled nervously behind the partition on seeing a white man sit down at the polished mahogany table.

Grey had had some strange welcomes in different parts of Nigeria. He had been welcomed with kolanuts in the North, he had been welcomed with nanny goats in Benin and Asaba, he had been welcomed with exotic fruits and farm produce in many Yoruba towns. But this welcome was most strange to him, in that he knew that Momoh's winning the war was only a question of time. The Biafran soldiers had been blasted out of Ore, they had been wiped out of Benin and were now being driven far into their homeland. The boundary of that new country was shrinking by the minute. Everyone except the leaders of Biafra could see that this was a revolution that had turned sour. But Alan was a friend of both leaders. To his way of thinking, he had not betrayed Momoh, neither had he betrayed Abosi. The arms he had promised Momoh helped in retaking Ore; and Abosi had been impossible to reach when he was there. The man was still smarting after the defeat at Ore and was in no mood to rationalize on any point; as far as he was concerned, he had declared through a messenger, the Ore mishap was just one of those temporary setbacks that could happen in wartime, and Alan had agreed with him.

Alan's eyes roamed around the fairly large but sparsely furnished room, and his host's eye caught him doing so. They both smiled noncommittally. Momoh was smiling at the foolishness of the maids but Alan was recalling the last time he had been in this part of the building. It seemed like centuries ago that the Ogedemgbes lived here.

'This is all I ask of life, you know,' Momoh began, holding the plain serviette as if he was not sure what to do with it. 'I am glad we are to have peace at last. A little while ago we were all scared, and I was particularly worried when the rebels started harassing the people of Lagos. They are not used to that kind of attack. If he had kept it up much longer, we don't know what would have happened.'

'We don't know what would have happened,' echoed his wife Elizabeth, parrot-like.

'He will give in soon,' Alan said, 'but if not, it would be a good idea for you two to get together again and decide on something.'

'Decide on what? Hmm, you don't know that man. Nothing will move Abosi except our side's complete victory.' Elizabeth suddenly came to life, almost standing up in her exuberance. Alan noticed that she was very pregnant and that there was a kind of unhealthy brilliance in her eyes. Her voice had a forced, sharp edge to it. She must have been under tremendous strain. Was that why Momoh had arranged to meet him in this relaxed and undemanding atmosphere?

'My guess is that he will lose many lives if nothing is done soon,' Alan said slowly, his eyes resting on the table cloth.

'Then it is their own fault! The fault of the Igbo people. Can't they see? Why should they support Abosi blindly like that? He doesn't even belong to their world. He is too rich, has too much education and belongs to too many exclusive international clubs.'

Momoh laughed dryly, embarrassed for his wife. 'Elizabeth has not been well. The strain, you know. The child is expected any minute now. In fact I may not be able to go to the big celebration on Sunday. It's so near her time.'

Elizabeth looked from one to the other. She knew she had said too much, but surely Alan was someone she could be frank with. She had known him for a long time; a man like that would not expect her to talk only about babies and clothes. None the less she took the hint from her husband and kept quiet. She directed the hovering girls who were serving the food silently, as if she were a deaf-mute.

Afterwards Momoh led Alan to the other part of the open room where children's toys littered the floor. He had a glass of orange juice while Alan had a cup of coffee. Elizabeth waddled to a large chair.

'As I was saying, the only thing that will bring this trouble to a quick end is not just arms but more people to fight. Even though we are winning, it's costing us the lives of a lot of young people. Mothers are refusing to let their sons go into the army. There's now a song that says "It is easy to go to Biafra, but to return is the problem". Another six hundred privates left Lagos this morning to go and help Lawal along the Benin–Asaba road. He had a thousand before. These figures are never written down, because they would alarm people. As far as people on this side of the country are concerned, the war was over when the Yoruba town Ore was retaken.

'But we need men, mercenaries. You can get them for us, Captain Grey. We will pay. Nigeria is rich. And while I am alive I won't forget those who help us in time of trouble. We must blast Abosi out of his proud complacency. He must be forced to know who is the leader of the two of us. That man must be taught a lesson. If only he could be captured, his people would give in.'

'Many of his people believe that if they gave in ... Well, many of them think that this has become a matter of genocide, judging from what Lawal is doing in the Benin area,' Alan said hesitantly.

'Well, can you blame the Hausa man, since his Moslem spiritual leaders were killed in cold blood. Have you forgotten Nguru Kano and the great Sardauna? However, I am going to issue an order to stop him killing civilians. Will you help us get mercenaries?'

'They cost a great deal of money these days. And to get white mercenaries to come and fight a war like this will be complicated.'

'White mercenaries will do anything for money. I saw some of them in the Congo. Are you going to help? If not, the war will cost more lives. And you know that last time I met the businessmen from your country I told them that the whole operation would only take three to six months. I was wrong. That man is determined to take the whole of Nigeria.

'So many orphans, so many children will die.'

'Oh, God,' Elizabeth burst in, 'those that will die in Biafra are only babies, Captain. Think of the sixteen- and seventeen-year-olds we Nigerian mothers are losing. Anyway, don't you know that those people breed like rats? They will soon replace their dead babies.'

'You should go in and rest now, don't you think? Captain Grey and I are going to stay up late into the night. We still have to make plans for the ceremony in which I am to be promoted General. So go to bed, Elizabeth.'

She had to be helped up. She had been dismissed and she giggled like her maids, apologetically. 'You will help us, Captain Grey. If it goes wrong, they will kill him. I am sure they will. Please help us!' she begged. She burst into tears and cried in low, spasmodic gusts. Momoh led her towards the inner room.

'I'm sorry, Elizabeth is worried about many things. This child is coming too soon after the other two. I guess at a time like this one never knows when one is going to be murdered in one's sleep.' His laughter was short and mirthless.

'Trouble is, in a military situation like this, all the responsibility rests on very few men; on one man, in your case,' Alan said. 'I wonder about the morality of your paying white men to come and shoot your own people for you.'

'What other choice have I? African states are one by one beginning to recognize his illegal country. And do you know the latest? Help is being offered him from South Africa – yes, South Africa. Think of that! Since when have white South Africans had the goodwill of the black man at heart? Abosi would be a fool to accept help from them; but if pushed to the wall he'll say, "It's war." '

'Hmm, I can't promise anything. The best way may be to get a few white mercenaries to lead some black soldiers trained in England. We have many West Indians in London who look up to Nigeria as one of the most important black nations on earth. They wouldn't be fighting just for the money but because they want to see Nigeria great again. And because they're black, Abosi's soldiers would think they are Nigerians.'

It was agreed that Momoh should pay a large deposit, which he did not possess; that, however, did not worry Alan Grey. The oilwells in the Mid-West had been liberated since the Nigerian army had sent the Biafran soldiers flying to their homeland, and a British oil company could now go there and pump enough oil to pay for the war. Captain Alan Grey left the next day promising to get the mercenaries within a week.

Saka Momoh suspected that the birth of their third baby would coincide with the day he was to be honoured as General of the Nigerian Army. The day started well enough, with no more than Elizabeth's usual groanings. But by breakfast time it was clear that this day was to be special not for her bad temper but for the birth of the child. With luck, she would have the child before the marching up and down of the token soldiers left in Lagos started.

Soon Elizabeth's groans progressed into bays of pain. She was whisked into a lush apartment in the island maternity hospital. Nurses and doctors busied themselves; it was not every day one was privileged to be present at the birth of a child of the head of state. Some of the junior nurses who were off duty refused to go home and loitered round the hospital's large net-curtained corridors. Journalists had never been so fortunate; news was just making itself these days. Life was easy since they did not have to rack their brains in search of anything creative to write. First came the fall of Ore, which was acclaimed as the turning point of the war; then Benin fell, like a priceless diamond added to Momoh's crown. It had been soon after that that his few close army colleagues had decided it would be an approporiate gesture to make him a general. He was going to win the war, it was clear that his foresight and tenacity had routed the rebels from Benin. He had to be honoured. Flags were flying all over Lagos, the island's major central square was decorated just as it had been for the Independence Day celebrations. And now came the news that not only were all these things taking place, but the First Lady was going to have a child on that day as well. It was to be a day of double joy.

Elizabeth lay on the narrow bed and laboured for the birth of her child. The sweat of pain and agony poured from her body as it swelled and contracted alternately. She agonized for hours, and as evening drew near even the Nigerian doctors who believed very much in letting nature do its work knew that something was wrong. One minute they were sure the child was coming and they urged the tired mother to bear down. She would comply, and the very next minute the child had retreated again, swelling the upper part of the mother's abdomen. Some of the doctors who had been so keen to be associated with the birth this morning no longer were. Who wanted to be known as being responsible for the death of the child of the head of state, or, worse still, the death of its mother?

Momoh in all his elasticity and impatience marched in towards evening wanting to know what was the matter. One look at his wife told him that this was not a case of ordering nature to act quickly. Neither was it a case of being able to use the money from Nigeria's black gold. The thought that each child who had died in Biafra may have cost its parents this much or even more did not cross Momoh's mind. All he wanted was the safety of his own wife and child.

He looked wildly at the white-coated figures around him and signalled to the head gynaecologist to follow him. The latter did so with bowed head, behaving as if Elizabeth were already dead.

'What is it? If it is a question of money, I'll pay anything. Save them for me, please, and do it quickly. She is very tired, can't you see?'

'Yes, Your Excellency. The thought of operating had occurred to us, but we were not sure how you would feel. You may not want a wife with a scar.'

'Hmmm, I see. That is serious. How big would the scar be? Would it disfigure her much, enh?'

'The scar would be in the lower part of her belly, but she would always cover it anyway. It's just that her being the wife of the head of state . . .'

'Suppose you don't operate?' Momoh snapped.

'They'd both be too tired to live, Your Highness.' The bewildered surgeon was unsure of the correct title to use. Today a soldier might be a major, tomorrow a captain, the day afterwards a general; the way they piled honours on each other made it difficult for one to keep up to date.

'Then operate, and make it quick.'

'Yes, Your Excellency.'

A Caesarean section was performed, but the child did not survive. While Elizabeth was still under anaesthetic Momoh was shown the monstrosity that had been inhabiting his wife's body. It resembled a giant frog more than any human he had ever seen, he thought. It must be a curse. He could not have been responsible for this thing. The deformed piece of humanity was wrapped with its afterbirth and quietly destroyed. All Elizabeth was told when she came to was that her baby had died during birth, and had been buried. Like a good wife, she knew she should not ask why she had not been able to see the body.

Momoh ordered the ceremonies for his promotion to go ahead as planned. People were full of anticipation, expecting him to announce that this was a day for double celebrations; but he did not. He said nothing about it. And the unfortunate doctors knew better than to open their mouths. Only a stupid person would argue empty-handed with a man with an automatic weapon.

Momoh had intended to send a special message to Lawal that the civilians he had captured were to be spared, but events had completely pushed this out of his mind. When he did recall his promise, Momoh decided that it would antagonize the Hausa man to suggest that he did not know what every soldier knows, that in war one fought other soldiers, not civilians. Telling him would be as insulting as reminding him to blow his nose.

The people of Benin were not too surprised to see a jet plane landing in their airfield and swarms of young recruits dashing out like green locusts in their camouflage uniform with matching steel helmets. They were to swell the ranks in Operation Mosquito. For days their lieutenant drilled them in jungle warfare.

'Those Biafran rebel bastards, you know them, don't you?' the lieutenant bawled at them. 'We are starving them out, and their one or two tanks are being operated with palm oil.'

This brought cautious laughter among the new soldiers. One murmured to a colleague, 'If they use all their palm oil to work their machines, what do they use for eating their yams?'

'Quiet!' demanded the stiff lieutenant. 'So you must learn to crawl in the bushes, you must learn to fight with clubs. Don't be surprised if some of them have spears like our great-grandfathers. You must expect that. But whatever they use, we are here to clean up after Colonel Lawal, to purge the country of the Yanmiri bastards. Do I make myself clear? Any questions?'

'Sir, what do you do if the people surrender?' asked a soldier obviously new to the art of killing, looking rather sick.

'Surrender? Let me tell you once again: the only good Igbo is a dead one! One minute they will surrender, the next minute the very person you have just been merciful to will stick his knife into your unsuspecting back. Anything that moves must be shot, and anything that doesn't move must be shot too, to make sure it can never move again. It may be necessary to keep a few of them alive to help run our country, but those orders have not been given yet. We are to familiarize ourselves with this part of the country and wait for some white professional eliminators who will lead us in our operation. So train hard.'

Alan Grey was a man of his word, particularly when Britain's interests were at stake. He did not disappoint Momoh. He had been able to get four white mercenaries. Hawkins, a square-bearded veteran of the Congo and minor uprisings in South Africa, had jumped at the offer of four thousand pounds Alan had made him. Life in England was too orderly and boring for him; he had no family, and although the money was always useful he would have fought such a war for nothing. He had been fighting such wars for almost two decades, since his first experiences with the East African Mau-Mau, and the excitement of it was in his blood.

His second-in-command, Ennis, was tall, lanky and seemed to be hastily put together. He used his wide, innocent smile a lot, but he was a man who had killed over fifty people with direct shots; he himself could not guess the number he had shot in the air. He was a clever pilot, but his inclination towards suicidal flying had very early prevented his career from following more honest lines; it was too risky to entrust the lives of innocent people into the hands of such a man who in his fits of deep depression could not be held accountable for his actions. But he was an expert at dropping death from the air and at dodging death when retaliation came from the few Africans who could aim anything from the ground. It always excited him, like deer-hunting in the forest; in fact he could kill without a qualm of conscience, telling himself that at least the black people could retaliate. Half his payment on these missions was given to his wife, who lived in the English countryside with their two children. They had a lovely house, the children were in a private school and when Ennis was home he played the organ in their church.

The third man, Pascoe, was to be dressed as a vicar throughout the operation. He was the oldest of the group, a perfect shot and very good at supporting both sides in a jungle war. He would shoot one minute and the next pray for the corpse he had helped on its passage to heaven. He was in his mid-forties, with a broken marriage, grown-up children and a boring 'holiday job' in an assembly plant. Because of his slurred speech some people said he had originally come to England from Greece, but like most of those who lived as mercenaries he was an international person. Anywhere was home for him.

Clemens, the fourth man, was the most junior. He was only thirty, but a keen learner. He had only the experience of the Congo to draw from but he would help Hawkins keep an eye on the sixteen hastily put together black soldiers, most of them of West Indian origin, who had been told that Nigeria was being infiltrated by the Russians, that the Russians were using the Biafrans to break the country into two and would be turning Nigeria into one of their communist strongholds in Africa against the people's wishes.

These sixteen young men ranged in age from nineteen to twenty-five, and even though some of them had not finished their basic army training Alan Grey knew that they were worth more than most of the indigenous Nigerian soldiers, to say nothing of the emergency breed called the militia. After their initial welcome to Benin, Operation Mosquito was set in full force. The war was to be ended in two months to prevent ordinary civilians suffering further.

For days, life was not very exciting for these privates. They fanned out and started marching slowly towards the Igbo lands. There was little to be seen. The thickness of the bush, the strangeness of the language and the friendliness of the soldiers kept the mercenaries and the new black soldiers of the liberators busy. They progressed deliberately, sometimes on foot, making sure that no Igbo was left behind. Not that there were many to be found. Those left swore that they were not Igbos and had changed their names. Those who were too late in changing their names had fled into the bush. The soldiers burned some of their houses and looted others; yet what they were agitating for was direct action.

16 *Women's War*

The crickets' buzzing was rather muted; the birds were silent. Even the fireflies were not too busy, twinkling almost half-heartedly. The snakes and the other animals that moved on their bellies had retired for the night. Only the owl let out its occasional drone.

Inside this thick forest was a deserted farm, for people in this area of Igboland believed that the further their farms were away from their homesteads, the more fertile the earth would be. Also the further away from one's family one went the more one could work and not be troubled with everyday complaints. There were signs that the farm was still being worked on; the young yam stalks looked well tended. In the middle of the farm was the usual resting hut known as *uno ogo*. Every farm had one of these, where the farmers gathered in the middle of the day to cook the fish they caught on their way to their farms and to roast the yam taken from their apata. They would eat, and drink and drink and then gossip. Although they claimed to be running away from women's gossip at home, yet more gossip took place at the farms than in the homesteads. Now that it was night and the farmer had gone home, there was no one in this hut. There was no moon and there was an atmosphere of mystery; it was a very suitable hideaway for the wandering refugees of the night.

Debbie, Mrs Madako, the other adults and the children could not afford to move during the day in case they ran into soldiers. Intuition told them that since most of the soldiers were strangers to this part of the country, where one had to use a machete to cut one's way through the forest, they would not dare to prowl at night. Their intuition guided them in other ways, too; when in the belly of the bush one could only guess which direction was which. So even though this was their fifth day they did not know whether they were anywhere near the town of Asaba. Their friend at Agbor had said it was only three nights' trek, less if they could walk in the early mornings as well. At least they were near some human habitation, though the town could still be seven to ten miles away.

They trooped into this small resting place and almost collapsed on the beaten earth. Mrs Madako, not letting her tiredness get the better of her, soon set a fire going in front of the uno ogo and one of the big boys put down their movable kitchen – the metal bath containing cooking stones and pots – and before long the unfortunate frogs they had caught earlier in the evening were bubbling in water collected from a nearby pond. Boniface, the eldest Madako son, had asked his mother whether drinking from that pond was safe and she had retorted that it was all water and they had to drink it or die. However, Debbie urged them to wait until the water was boiled. They gobbled down the frogs, not caring that some might have been poisonous, and ate the remaining yams they had brought from Agbor.

Dorothy, the woman with milk in her breasts, crawled to a corner to feed the babies. She put hers to one breast and gave the other to the baby called Biafra.

'Is he sucking well?' Mrs Madako asked.

'No, he's too tired, and I don't think he is getting enough from me.'

'Poor child. He was so still on my back all day today,' Debbie put in. 'He's not gaining weight at all.'

'I pray to God we reach a village or town tomorrow. We've eaten the last yam and you can see from the soup tonight that we ran out of fish a long time ago,' Mrs Madako pointed out.

'We can't be far from a village. We have to find a village and send someone to look for our mother,' Ngbechi said pluckily, as he cradled the head of his young brother in his arms. 'I'm sure she is hiding in the bush along the Agbor road.'

The others stared blankly at him. Their vacant eyes said things which their mouths dared not utter, things they nevertheless knew in their hearts to be true. Surely Ngbechi had heard the explosion that blew up the mammy lorry on its way back to fetch his mother and the others? Yet he refused to believe it. He still believed she was alive. But miracles could happen, and who were they to dispel the faith of a child?

They all dropped off to sleep on the earth, except Ngbechi who was keeping watch for the first part of the night. Boniface would take over after him and Debbie would take it from there until morning.

Ngbechi could hardly keep his eyes open. But these last days since his father's death had matured him and he knew that the lives of the others depended on his keeping good watch. To keep awake he moved around the hut, hoping that his canvas shoes would protect him from snakes. His step soon acquired a rhythm that harmonized with the noises of the night as he lost himself in thoughts too deep and too adult for an adolescent. Then gradually foreign noises began to work themselves into the now familiar ones. At first Ngbechi thought he must be dreaming. He forced his eyes wider with his fingertips and stopped to listen again. Yes, there was no doubt about it, new movements were coming nearer the hut. He walked back quickly, almost tumbling over the sleeping bodies on the floor.

'Wake up, wake up! Quick!' he hissed.

As if in reply to his pleadings, the recognizable rat-tat-tat sound of shooting followed. He did not need to persuade the others to wake, for they all shot up, their subconscious evidently very aware of their danger. Dorothy snatched up her baby, Mrs Madako did the same to her youngest and pulled the youngest boy of the parentless family towards her, while Debbie slung the tiny baby Biafra on her back and led a few other children with her. They all hopped, jumped over thick bush and entangled yam stalks as they ran and ran until they were plunged into a deep muddy swamp. The mud reached the waists of the adults and the unexpected chill of the slimy water made Dorothy who was in the lead scream. But her scream was too late to warn the others who followed her in.

'Oh, my God, what are we going to do?' gasped Debbie.

'Just prop the little ones up and pray they don't drown in this mud,' replied Mrs Madako.

'Let's go back, please, Mama,' Boniface cried, 'let's go back.'

'We can't go back, the shooting is coming from behind us,' his mother said.

'I think they are shooting from the left,' corrected Debbie.

They stopped to listen. The shooting was now much more spasmodic and, yes, it was coming from the left.

'We can't stop. They are still not far away,' Ngbechi said.

'Yes, we have to go forward,' Debbie agreed.

'But it's so swampy, we'll be buried alive,' Dorothy whined. The trouble was Ngbechi and his brothers. But the big boy solved the problem by carrying the five-year-old on his shoulders while giving as much help as possible to the middle ones.

'I am the only one who has nothing to carry except this kettle,' Boniface announced.

'Look at this boy,' his mother said, 'he talks about a kettle, an empty one for that matter, when we are talking about people and our food. We have even left our portable kitchen at that farm.'

'That's why we must move away,' Debbie said, 'because if the soldiers see it, they will know that people have been there very recently.'

The ominous truth of Debbie's statement hit home. They were all quiet as they plodded on. The children wisely kept their mouths tightly shut, not for fear of being heard but because sometimes the mud reached their chins and might enter their mouths. Without any warning, they suddenly plunged into a deeper area, and there was much screaming. In one desperate moment Debbie let go of the hand of the boy she had been holding, as she tried to steady herself and prevent baby Biafra from being drowned on her back. Panic-struck, she saw Boniface climbing up a tree which, although its stem looked solid, like most trees of the bamboo family growing along the Nigerian creeks, was not deeply rooted. Boniface had scarcely climbed it when it came crashing down on all of them. There was shrieks of 'My baby! The children!'

'We must go back. Let's go back!' Her voice rang out, the voice that had once been used to giving orders. And the others, still stunned, obeyed.

They worked hard to rescue the Madakos' daughter and disentangle Boniface from the thorny branches. Ngbechi proved a tower of strength, carrying his young brothers on both shoulders and helping the not so young. Slowly they waded back, taking one step at a time.

Debbie stopped in her stride and a chill ran through her like an electric current as she felt some warm liquid running down her legs. It surely was not the swampy water for that was very cold since it was still virtually night. Then something like a small weak hand gripped her side. It was that poor baby Biafra. She could not stop to see what was happening to him. Her hands were not free even to give him an encouraging hug; if she did that the two boys she was holding would drown. She shook herself from side to side to give the baby at least the rhythm of life; that was all she could do for him. There was no time to stop, no emotion to waste. They must go on.

When they came to a portion of the creek where the mud was not so deep, where every child's head was clear, they waited, resting, gasping for breath. Then Ogo, Ngbechi's five-year-old brother, said what sounded so remote and yet so prayerfully desirable:

'When we get to Biafra, the land will be dry, my mother will be there and my father, and my mother will cook us fried plantain and chicken stew, won't she, Ngbechi?'

'Yes,' his brother replied. 'When we get to Biafra, all our troubles will be over.'

Debbie, her hands going numb from holding the children tightly, looked around. This swampy grove was the type the sun never reached. Thick green vegetation hung over head, and around them were many creeping plants with superficial roots. They all kept very still, holding their breath. Though the sound of shooting had stopped they could not tell where, let alone who, the soldiers were. Were they Nigerians or Biafrans, how far were they from the village or town that owned the farm? And what village or town was it anyway, Yoruba or Igbo?

'Let's move to the drier bit. My legs are stiff with mud,' Boniface said.

'We should wait a bit longer to be on the safe side,' Debbie advised.

They spent the rest of the night on their feet in the swamp, holding tightly on to one another so no one would be lost. What looked like a gleam of light worked its way through the intricately entwined tropical forest. Yes, it was getting slightly lighter; new sets of morning creatures that lived in this grove were coming alive, waking and struggling forward on tired legs.

The adults let go their grip on the young ones, who could now manage by themselves. They all looked like masqueraders covered in chalky mud as if ready to celebrate some festival. In normal circumstances the mere sight of them would have sent anyone into a fit of uncontrollable laughter. But nobody laughed spontaneously, though the mischievous Boniface could not help remarking to his new friend Ngbechi, 'You look like death.'

'Look who is talking. Your face looks like the devil,' Ngbechi retorted.

They tried to laugh, but the sides of their mouths were so caked with mud that the movement of their lips sent pieces of disturbed dried mud flying. This triggered in Debbie memories of a face-pack she had once applied when she visited a beautician in London. Now she tentatively peeled mud from her face and felt the skin underneath. It was as smooth as it had been on that day many years before, when she had had to pay a large amount of money to get the same effect. Now she paid nothing. She smiled, wanting to share the irony of it with the other women; but she could not, for she knew they would think her arrogant to bring up such topics when they were not even sure that they would live to see the next minute. It was at moments like this that Debbie really felt lonely, surrounded as she was by other women. Her education, the imported division of class, still stood in the way. She was trying so hard to shake it off, to belong, but at times like this she knew that achieving complete acceptance was indeed a formidable task. These women would only accept her if they did not know her real background, so she had to keep silent about her store of past experiences.

Her mind was forced back to the present. She had to see to the baby on her back. First she helped the woman with six children settle them by the side of the swampy creek which would give them a kind of protection. They suspected that, whatever happened, no soldiers would come from that direction. The creeks gave them the only escape route they had, even though they knew it could mean a short route to muddy death.

Debbie loosened the caked cloth that tied the baby Biafra and her wad of papers to her body. She intuitively knew what she was going to find, though she hoped her fears were unfounded. Even when she was releasing the tiny stiff body from hers, she refused to look into its face. The small body, no more than a shrunken lifeless skeleton, fell out. It was then that Debbie noticed the other women watching her. There was no doubt that they felt as she did. On this issue their common Africanness came to the fore; a child was the child of the community rather than just of the biological parents. Their eyes met hers. What was there to say? The baby, their baby, had died.

Uzoma Madako straightened herself from the crouching position in which she had been for the past half-hour. Looking at the shrivelled body of the baby boy only days old, she advised, 'We must bury him quickly, and start thinking seriously about our position, before we all become like him.'

Dorothy, the young mother who had been feeding him, began to cry, and the others looked at her as if to ask: 'So you still have tears to shed?'

'Is our land Biafra going to die like this baby, before it is given time to live at all?' she sobbed. 'He only lived for a few days! He only lived for a few days! I think the death of this child is symbolic. This is how our Biafra is going to fall. I feel it in my bones.'

'Don't talk like that. You'll make us all more miserable. Biafra will pull through, you'll see. It's always like this in great wars. Today victory is on one side, tomorrow on the other side,' Debbie tried to console her.

'That may be so. You talk like that because you have no husband and no child. What of my husband? What of my many brothers who are fighting inside Biafra and who may all be dead by now? Will they come back to life when Biafra's fortunes change? Oh, I don't want to go on. I want to go into that mud and die. I can't look after my children by myself. I want to die.'

Uzoma Madako walked up to Dorothy and hit her on her right ear, releasing particles of mud.

'Shame on you, woman. Shaaaame!' she fumed. 'What type of Igbo woman are you? Which bush community did you come from? What unlucky woman raised you as a daughter? Since when have men helped us look after children? Have you not old people in your cluster of homesteads, to do their job of bringing up the younger ones.'

'Ah, I wanted to say something like that too. After all, the children are ours. I remember when I married,' reminisced the quiet woman with six children, 'I remember so very well. My husband came to our village to marry me in our village church. My mother said that I was lucky. That I was going to be given children, and money to look after them. That I was going to be given housekeeping money. My mother had never left our village and we could not imagine what it would be like to be given money for looking after the house and your children. It was going to be so nice. Now I am going back to be just like my mother. But my lot will be worse than hers because I have no husband to go to the farm and bring back yams, or to mend the roof of our cottage.'

Uzoma was determined that no one in that company was going to wallow in any kind of sadness. She listened sympathetically, then said with little preamble: 'Your husband must have been a very nice man. Mine gave me housekeeping money but I had to sell things to make it up. He was a big man, but I still had to do something. I was hoping to go back to teaching in a few years' time. Our men were useful, yes, very useful; but they have now been killed by other men. We have children to look after. Just like our grandmothers. They looked after our parents who had us. So I don't know why Dorothy should want to die, when her days are not up yet.'

Again Debbie marvelled at the resources of women. She had seen Uzoma Madako with her husband in Benin, seen the way she sat, her head resting passively on a pole that supported one of the sheds at the motor park; Debbie had seen the way she lifted her eyes as if they were so weighty, had heard the way she spoke in a whisper. And now look at the same woman, a few days after the death of her husband, she had the courage to slap another woman, to tell another woman to stop indulging in self-pity.

'Your husband has given you two children, this baby boy and the girl at home with your old mother. Don't you think you have to make sure you live so that you can look after them? Because the men also gave us their name, you forget your father's name, and in the process of letting your husband provide for you, you have become dumb and passive. Go back to being yourself now. If you are too lazy to farm, you may have to sell your body. But what is so new about that? Your children have to live. Get up, women, and let us bury the son of another sad woman.'

'That mother is better off. At least she is dead and does not have to worry about anything now,' Dorothy continued mournfully, picking pieces of caked mud from the dirty body of her child.

'How do you know she is better off? Have you been dead before? How do you know all these people dying before their time are happy where they are? Our men! A few years ago it was "Independence, freedom for you, freedom for me." We were always in the background. Now that freedom has turned into freedom to kill each other, and our men have left us to bury them and bring up their children; and maybe by the time these ones grow up there will be another reason for them to start killing one another.' Uzoma Madako rambled on as she dug a tiny grave with a bamboo stick she had picked up. 'Let's put a cross here and move on,' she sighed.

They inched on, staying away from the main bush tracks since they did not know which might yield a group of soldiers. Near sundown, they saw what used to be a cassava farm though now it looked like a battlefield. There were rotting corpses and trampled cassava plants. They did not have time to worry about the dead; the only good thing was that this farm indicated that they were close to a village or town. Hope gave them more energy and they walked on. It no longer mattered whether the village was that of a friend or enemy. What mattered was that at least they would see other people.

They had not gone much further before they heard the noise of dancing. The whole town seemed to be celebrating something. The women waited cautiously by the track that joined into the main road.

'I wonder what day of the week this is? Is it an Eke day or a Sunday? It can't be Christmas. What have people to be so joyous about at this terrible time when there are corpses rotting in their cassava farms?' Mrs Madako muttered.

'It looks like an Igbo farm,' Dorothy said.

'Yes, and if my guess is right we're on the correct track to Asaba. Listen carefully to the wind and you can hear the sounds of their beaded gourds. I still don't understand why they should be so happy.'

'I think I know, I can guess,' Boniface started to shout. The others tried to cover his mouth so that he would not bring trouble upon them.

204

'We've won the war! The war must be over. Why else would an Igbo town be celebrating like this? We've won!'

The women looked at each other. The boy had a point. Should they risk going out into the open? They were very hungry, thirsty and tired, and Ngbechi's little brother's stomach had started to run because of lack of food. Mrs Madako's daughter could not last another day in the bush. And where would they hide if they decided to stay? Someone would have to go and find out what was happening.

As if he read everyone's thoughts, Ngbechi said, 'Miss Debbie, you take my other two brothers as well as Ogo, I will find out what is happening. We must get some food for Ogo.'

They all looked at the five-year-old Ogo who only a few days before had been bouncing with life. Now he was like a wet rag. Somebody would have to go, but definitely not Ngbechi, who was like mother and father to his brothers.

'No, son. How would I be able to face your mother in heaven – I mean, in Biafra . . . if anything happened to you? We will all have to go together,' declared Mrs Madako. 'If they are shooting, they can shoot us all.'

'No, Uzoma, I will go,' Debbie said. 'Just stay here. I know some of the Nigerian soldiers, remember? That may be useful if they are holding the town. But if we really have won, there will be no trouble since the soldiers will be Biafrans.' She looked around her. 'I need something with which to give you a sign in case of danger. I can't think of anything right now.'

'I can – my kettle. If we are in danger, beat it loud so that we can hear you.'

'Suppose they kill you, how will we know?' the pessimistic Dorothy asked.

'Oh, keep quiet, Dorothy, and be sensible. How can they kill her? And if we don't see her then we'll know that . . . but, Debbie, nothing will happen to you . . .' Uzoma's speech was cut short by a heart-rending whine from Ogo. The boy was in agony. He twisted and turned and clawed at his big brother, and then a foul-smelling dark liquid began to run from his dirty khaki shorts.

'Oh, no, God, don't let it happen, not to this poor child,' Debbie prayed, and losing no more time she dashed out of the bush on to the main path. Somehow she did not think of fear. The last few days had taught her that death could be a welcome relief. She walked on and soon saw people in ordinary everyday attire. They all seemed rather tense; one or two looked her way, wondering where she came from.

That main centre of Asaba was usually very cosmopolitan but since the start of war the Eastern Igbo traders had gone, the Hausa cloth-dyers had fled to the North and the few foreign firms that opened small stores had sold up and returned to their countries. A few white Syrians, known locally as 'Koras', who had long forgotten their place of origin still remained, as did the stubborn Irish priests and their nuns. The latter group stayed in their mission stations, keeping the dispensary going and helping babies who were determined to be born, war or no war, to come safely into the world. The Anglican priests had long left, feeling that the church and the state went hand in hand.

The track widened into a full road. The road to her right wound gradually uphill and on both sides were vacant stores and sheds that had seen former busy days. Many people were coming from the inner part of the town and going up towards what she guessed was the centre of town.

The sun was still hot and its rays went into her eyes. Using her palm as a shade, she looked up the hill and managed to make out the pointed steeple of a church, at the top of which was a cross. It looked quite a small cross from where she stood but none the less it was one. She had never been a religious person, yet she smiled at the thought that a Roman Catholic cross had become to her a sign of hope. She walked towards it.

Groups of dancers came out in what was obviously their best Western Igbo white otuogwu. She noted that most of them looked haggard and hungry. Opposite the church was another big building, standing there on the hill looking very significant and proud, and it was here that most of the dancers were making their way. Debbie watched, and what she saw made her heart sink. For just behind the building, which she now realized was the city hall, was the very armoured personnel-carrier she had seen in the bush along the Benin road. It had looked like a caravan then, in the middle of the night, yet Debbie knew that it was something which meant untimely death to many. Now on this clear early evening its ugliness was the more pronounced. A chill ran through Debbie.

She stood there wondering what the meaning of all this was. Should she go back and tell the others to run for it? But the other side of the road would only lead to the River Niger. How would they be able to cross it to the East? From the beginning of the war, that part of the river had been a focal point and the Asaba people guarded it with their strongest men. But if the Nigerian soldiers were already in, who would be guarding the place now? No, it was best for her to go on to the mission.

As suddenly as she had discovered the armoured personnel-carrier, she saw another tank almost hidden further on, around which were soldiers. Soldiers were everywhere, clustered together in groups, some playing draughts, some dancing with the townspeople, showing the kind of forced joy that any onlooker could tell was too loud to be true. Debbie went straight into the church, but there too were soldiers, not praying but resting from the glare of the sun. Debbie looked away, in search of any priest or nun. Seeing none, she walked out again, and behind the church was what she was looking for, the mission house.

An old and very wrinkled nun with skin burnt red by the sun saw her.

'We are in the bush,' Debbie began, 'some of the children are dying ... What is happening – the Nigerian soldiers here and everyone dancing?'

The old nun was joined by another nun, and for a while they listened to Debbie speaking. They had seldom heard Africans speak English that way.

'Look, you're not Igbo, what are you doing here?' the old woman asked.

'I was originally going to see Abosi ...' But as she said it Debbie knew it sounded insane even to her own ears.

The nuns calmed her, gave her some water and told her that three days earlier the Biafran soldiers had fled, leaving the Western Ibos to mind their towns. Some who still believed in Biafra had gone with the soldiers, including many of the convent girls. But the majority had stayed. After a while they had known that they could not hold Asaba and that it was a question of time before the Nigerian soldiers came and bombed the town. At first it had seemed a good thing that the Biafran soldiers had gone without staying to fight it out, because at least that way very few people were killed.

'You see, the Biafran soldiers were hungry; they had nothing to fight with but their enthusiasm, and even that was on the wane. From what we hear, they had started committing atrocities with young girls and bulldozing the people into giving them their food. Some unfortunate people were even shot as saboteurs. So when these people came in, these Nigerians, they brought lots of food and came to "liberate" Asaba, we were told. Hmmm, some liberation! What you see going on is meant to be a liberation dance. They've been urging everybody to come out and dance, and since today is Eke market day – even though there's no longer any market to speak of – people are out dancing. They are tired of hiding in the bush, afraid for their lives.'

'We must go and get the others. One child is very bad,' Debbie urged.

'If you can tell us the place, we will go and get them. You are tired and you badly need a wash. Daughter, let me ask you again, what are you doing here?'

Anger which Debbie found difficult to control was fighting inside her. How could a foreigner ask her what she was doing in her own country? Because she was well-educated these do-gooders obviously did not expect her to soil her fingers helping her own people. What hypocrisy, what a sham! Debbie could see about eight nuns milling about in their long white habits – did these women sincerely believe in what they were doing, or did they still subscribe to the old idea of helping the savages? Oh, her thoughts were in a muddle. The Nigerian soldiers were on one side of the road with their Russian-made armoured cars and British tanks, and here were these women on the other side, nursing the dying and saying Mass. It was impossible to make sense of it, but in times as desperate as this any help was better than none.

'Like you, Mother, I want to see what help I can give,' she replied.

The reverend mother shook her old head and blinked in the sun.

'Moder, Moder Superior, where are you going this time?' an enthusiastic soldier who gave the impression that he did not care for anything in this world enquired. He muttered something in Urhobo which made the soldier beside him laugh hysterically.

The old nun pretended not to notice. All the people of Asaba had to pretend not to notice the jeers.

'I am going into the bush to get some dying children out. I have to hurry.'

'These people, we told them that they should come out of the bush, that we are now one Nigeria. And we promised not to harm them and yet they still stay in the bush among snakes and scorpions. Will you be needing our help, Moder?'

'No, I think we can get these ones.'

'Are there any more? How did you know they were there? Some of them could be hiding those bastard Biafrans,' another hefty soldier said, walking up.

'Don't worry, the Biafran soldiers have all gone,' one of the nuns said.

'None the less, some officers must follow you,' ordered 'Hefty', at the same time calling the group of loungers to attention. Six soldiers with guns marched Debbie, the mother superior and three other nuns down the road to the path that led to the dense forest beyond.

Debbie wondered desperately how she was going to convince the others from a distance that all was well and that they should come out of hiding. The sight of the gun-carrying soldiers would give them the wrong impression. She confided her fears to the aged nun, who argued and bargained at length with the officer in charge of the little army. She assured him that if there were any Biafran soldiers around she would alert them, and if they found she was covering the Biafrans they could shoot her dead.

'What do you think we are?' asked the enraged officer. 'We are not white people, you know, who kill for killing's sake as they did in Auschwitz. We are Nigerians. We are not killing mad. We kill for a reason.' He emphasized this credo by swinging his fully loaded automatic to and fro in front of the unarmed women, who did not know what to make of this outburst. They only knew the best thing was to remain quiet.

'All right, go, but we shall stay here and watch. And you'd better tell your refugees not to play any hanky-panky by trying to run away. Because if this machine coughs once, it's death. We are not killers . . .'

'I know, you are not killers like those who performed in Germany,' the mother superior intervened quickly before the Urhobo officer continued. She smiled wryly, intensifying all the age lines on her gaunt face, and added: 'You know a lot of history.'

'Yes, Mother, that Catholic college down by the river, the great St Patrick's of Asaba, was my Alma Mater,' he announced proudly.

'Is that why you people were specially chosen to guard Asaba, because you were schooled here?'

'Yes, Mother, something like that. Many of us went to St Thomas's in Ibuza, seven miles from here. We know this area very well, and our knowledge of the place and customs of the people is useful.'

'My son, I hope you use that knowledge to the benefit of the people you grew up with.' The old nun looked him straight in the eye, her own piercing blue eyes almost completely hidden by a crinkled overhanging brow. Her look was so fierce that the officer at once lowered his gun and began to shuffle his feet aimlessly. Debbie began to suspect that all was not what it seemed. These people, mainly Urhobos and soldiers from Benin, had a nasty surprise for their neighbours, the Asaba Igbos, she was sure.

They were cornered, but they simply had to take their chances. If the women and children were left in the bush they would surely die. At least if they were brought out they would be fed, and could take their chances of life like the rest. At least the children could be given immediate comfort.

Ngbechi was the first to emerge, peering this way and that from behind a tree whose branches spread wide shade in its surrounds.

'It's all right, it's all right,' Debbie whispered, hoping and praying that she was right. 'Asaba has fallen. The people are celebrating One Nigeria.'

Ngbechi called to the others and between them they carried the now unconscious Ogo. The nuns poured some water into the child's mouth but most of it dripped from the corners of his lips. Ijeoma, Mrs Madako's daughter, was beginning to have the same symptoms of dysentery that had killed baby Biafra and seemed to be killing Ogo. The nuns, however, seemed familiar with the malady and did not wrinkle their noses at the stench of these rotting pieces of humanity.

'I hope we are not too late,' the old nun prayed. 'O Holy Mother, help your children.'

'Where is their mother?' asked the third nun, not grasping the whole situation.

Nobody answered and Ngbechi looked at the faces of the women around him, begging for the assurance that they could not give him. Reality was beginning to set in. They were orphans, like hundreds of other children who were victims of the decisions made by adults of whom they had never heard and would never see.

'The Holy Mother of God will look after you,' said the third nun. 'You will soon be a man, so you'll be all right.'

Ngbechi suppressed the urge to cry, and carried his sick brother across his shoulder, while Debbie pulled the middle ones along with her. Boniface, slightly weakened, trudged along. It was a group that looked innocent enough, especially with the nuns holding the other children and supporting Dorothy and Uzoma. In their rush to save life, Debbie and the nuns had forgotten to mention the hiding soldiers or explain the details of their presence.

Ngbechi, determined to reach the mission hospital quickly, had made long strides along the steep hill. He had paused to gain breath in the fast disappearing sun when he caught sight of the armed soldiers emerging from the bush where they had been waiting.

'Soldiers!' he gasped. 'Nigerian soldiers!' And before anyone could stop him, he made a U-turn, bent on carrying his sick brother into the safety of the bush.

'Stop, Ngbechi, stop!' Debbie shrieked.

But it was too late. The observing officer's gun coughed once, and Ngbechi lay on the tarred road bleeding to death.

Debbie, Dorothy and Uzoma left the children in their care and ran up to the soldiers, screaming: 'Go on, shoot all of us! Shoot us too, please shoot us!'

Debbie did not realize what came over her. She jumped on top of the bewildered officer and began to wrestle with him. She was badly torn and beaten before she became too exhausted to cry any more.

The nuns dragged and half carried the three shaken and tired women to the mission with the children. Ogo had died and so had his big brother Ngbechi.

'I must cross into Biafra,' Debbie told the mother superior an hour after they arrived at the mission. The others were trying to sleep but their eyes would not close. No one could imagine what was going to happen. The shooting had occurred too far down the hill to be heard in this part of town, where the people were dancing as if intoxicated. The mother superior said that it was because of the tensions of the past year, when they had no food to buy, added to the general problems and fear of refugees running in from other parts of the federation; the people of Asaba, placed strategically by the gateway to the main Ibo heartland, wanted nothing but peace, peace at all costs. The Nigerians had won, and it would surely only be a few days before things returned to normal. So they were dancing to show the liberating soldiers how grateful they were.

But the giddiness of the whole town shocked many of the newly arrived refugees who still found it difficult to regard themselves as Nigerians after all they had suffered in the name of freedom.

'I hope history will be able to chronicle all this,' Uzoma Madako said.

'Chronicle what? That a few days ago there was a Nwoba family, in which there was a healthy mother, a well-to-do father and four boisterous sons? Now there are only two boys aged ten and eight, both half dead from dysentery. And that the eldest son Ngbechi was shot when he was running away from the most wicked man I have ever seen in uniform? O God, revenge the death of this brave, innocent boy.'

Debbie relived the memory of Ngbechi comforting his brothers, of the heart-rending decision he had had to make to take his brothers away from his mother so that they could survive, of the quiet tears she had seen him shed, and of his fears about not knowing much about the relatives who would look after them. Would the two living boys ever make it? And if they did, would they know the name of their parents'

211

village? Debbie looked at them lying there on the mat with other parentless children, and wept.

The sounds that cut into her sorrow came like palm kernels falling on a corrugated-iron sheet, non-stop, persistent and becoming louder. Human voices bayed like hounds, brayed like horses, croaked like dying goats being slaughtered. Debbie, Uzoma and the others ran out. Debbie ran back in to snatch the two sleeping Nwoba boys, dipped her hand into a nearby food shelf and took a loaf of bread. Then she ran. She looked once, only once, at the town hall across the road where she saw hundreds of male dancers in their dazzling white robes being shelled from all sides. Soldiers were shelling the trapped people inside through the windows, through the doors. Other soldiers stood a little way off to make sure no one escaped. Debbie dashed into the bush and stuffed the ears of the frightened Nwoba boys with rags, while she listened to the cries of dying humanity.

Very much later, she heard the cries of women from the mission house, the nuns who felt they were doing God's work and that that would gived them immunity from the soldiers. Debbie guessed what was happening and shed some tears for the octagenerian Irish nun.

She looked towards the East, and there was another glow. Then followed a big explosion as the bridge towering the great River Niger erupted into the air and everywhere was aglow in the cloud of fire. So the Nigerian soldiers' suspicion was right. Asaba people had been hiding Biafran soldiers, who had just successfully crossed over and were blowing up the bridge behind them. What an expense, what a waste, Debbie thought, remembering how many millions Nigeria had paid for that prestigious bridge, how many people had died during its construction. All in the name of freedom.

She looked away from the glow and stared with pity at the town of Asaba. Its people had been mercilessly exposed. The brothers they had been hiding in the name of 'tribe' had left them at the mercy of the conquering Nigerian forces and these very brothers had even blown up the bridge behind them. The Asaba people were trapped in their once beautiful town, and a mockery had been made of their brotherhood.

Debbie recorded all this in her memory, to be transferred when possible to the yellowing scraps of paper she dignified with the name of manuscript. They had survived with her so far, because most of the incidents were written down in her personal code which only she could decipher. If she should be killed, the entire story of the women's experience of the war would be lost. A great deal of what was happening was too dangerous to write down so she had to make her brain porous enough to absorb and assimilate, writing down only key words to trigger off her recollections when she finally sat down to put it all into plain words. She must try to live, not just for the women but for the memories of boys like Ngbechi.

Meanwhile, she would have to somehow cross over to the other side. She would see that Biafra, that idyllic land of hope which had cost the black race so dear. She had to make it. She must.

A sound like a huge snake crawling on the dry leaves grew louder. Instinctively she covered the mouth of the eight-year-old, and the older boy knew that it was time to be quiet. The sound stopped momentarily and Debbie asked with fear, 'Who is it?'

'It's me, Miss Debbie, Boniface.' He came out of hiding looking like a shrunken old man. He smiled in the faint light of the young moon. 'My mother and Dorothy are over there. They are not hurt . . . I mean, Dorothy's baby was shot on her back. And that family, the woman with her six children, they ran into the bush. We don't know where they are, but Dorothy said they stayed with the nuns.'

'With the nuns? All of them?' Debbie cried. She shook her head. 'They must have escaped like we did. They couldn't have stayed with the nuns.'

Boniface shrugged, looking so much wiser than his age. His mischievousness had gone. 'We hope so too. Mother refused to believe it. Dorothy is very confused. Come, let's join them.'

Silently, through the thick bush with crisply dried leaves underfoot, they went singly, listening, crouching, ready to run at the slightest untoward sound. They made a few turns at the least expected places and Debbie marvelled at how Boniface was able to find the way. Finally they saw the women. They could not exchange words, but their eyes said a lot.

Only much later did Uzoma Madako remark, 'Even that old mother superior did not escape. They did it to her and then killed her.'

'No, they did not kill her, she just bled to death. They killed the young nuns and many others, but they did not kill Mother Francesca,' Dorothy insisted, in a vain effort to wash away the sins of the men of her race who wore borrowed army uniforms, promoting an equally borrowed culture. A culture that did not respect the old.

'She just bled to death. They would never rape an old woman, never . . . she just bled to death,' she continued, accepting the death of her child, but not able to understand the abuse of the helpless old.

17 *The Sons of the Rich*

It was a quiet evening in Biafra, the type that was becoming the norm. People were too afraid to leave their houses in daylight. The experience of the past months had showed that the Nigerian soldiers seldom missed their targets during the day. At night, once one did not carry any kind of light, one was comparatively safe.

Mrs Ozimba looked at her husband of several decades, and straight at the back of his now hairless head. When she was young she used to tell herself she would marry a man with lots of hair and a beautiful set of teeth. Now her husband had none of those things, though his artificial teeth fitted him so well that no one ever suspected their falseness. She wanted to say many things to him, but she knew from experience that when his neck was stooped like that she was not supposed to say a word.

She got up and switched on the radio. She dared not turn to Radio Nigeria or the BBC, for fear of hearing demoralizing news. One must listen to news that gave one hope. It must be Radio Biafra.

The National Anthem which her husband had written came on. In fact it was sung at every opportunity by school children, soldiers in the bush, even some housewives planting their own farms in the drive for self-help. It had become a symbol of unity and of hope. But the Ozimbas knew that to them, their children and immediate family it was a symbol of their coming destruction. If the Nigerian army should ever capture them alive they would not survive for a trial, for did not the Biafran national anthem bear the stamp of the great Dr Ozimba? It was ironic that, only a few months before, the same words had meant his survival from the wrath of Abosi who was looking for scapegoats to blame for the negative turn of events.

The announcer started in a high voice full of buoyancy. Biafran soldiers had done it again, they had captured and killed one thousand

Nigerian soldiers on the Western front – 'our invincible army has immobilized the Nigerians on the Western front, our loyal men have retaken the bridge and that market' – then the national anthem again.

'For God's sake, can't these announcers give us a little relevant news? Don't they think there are some of us who can face the truth?'

'Look, I keep telling you. You have to be strong and loyal. This is war and you are the wife of one of the people's leaders. You must have faith. Some people have even been killed by their friends for listening to foreign news. Even if our news is biased, it is our duty to try to believe it and make others believe. What is left for us to do? If we give in . . . haven't you heard what they did in Asaba? What of Nsukka – all those innocent young people?' Dr Ozimba stormed angrily. 'I don't understand you women. We are looking for the best way to get out of a very tricky situation and all you can think of is ways of muddling us up.'

As she looked at her husband, fury swelled her throat, making her look momentarily as ugly as a toad. Many, many things which she would have liked to tell this man forced themselves back into her belly like a lump of vomit that would not come out. She listened to more misleading reports of how people were clamouring for Biafran currency which was worth several pounds, and to the voices of people claiming to be well fed on the proceeds from their 'Operation Feed Biafra' project, and the news of some wedding with a description of what the bride was wearing and a list of the celebrities at the reception.

'I suppose it's all right to tell people what they want to hear,' she sighed as she got up to make her way to the other room of this emergency abode.

Mrs Ozimba had wanted to plan with her husband how to get their two sons out of this trap, but how could one discuss such a thing with a man who seemed to think that divine wrath would descend on them if she made the mistake of listening to world opinion on their plight?

They were eating their cornmeal bread by candlelight when a persistent knock told them that someone determined was at the door. An armed bodyguard answered, and in came Mrs Eze. She looked rather sheepish on seeing Dr Ozimba at the table; she had calculated on his not being home. Ozimba smelt a rat, for he knew that when women of the same educational background who married men in the same profession were together, a great deal of husband-tearing was bound to take place. Only Mrs Ogedemgbe was needed to complete the trio. He wondered where the poor woman was now, as he quickly made a muted excuse and disappeared into the other room. Coping with one over-educated Igbo female whose only outlet was her husband was enough for the evening. He would rather face an angry Salihu Lawal than two such women.

The two women exchanged pleasantries to gain time. Then Mrs Eze brought out a wrinkled paper which had evidently passed through many hands. In the dim light Mrs Ozimba read a hopeful letter from Mrs Stella Ogedemgbe. She wrote that she was sad to hear that kwashiokor was killing hundreds of children and even adults. Nigerian soldiers had occupied her area of the Mid-West. She urged the wives to remember that the only thing their politician husbands gave them was their names. And because she was Mrs Ogedemgbe she could send them food through the creeks via the Mid-Western towns. She would accept Biafran money, and that way they could get a business going. She had four strong canoe men in her employ. And had they heard anything of her daughter Debbie? She had not seen the girl for months. Her two boys, thank goodness, were safe in England and the elder had entered university. They should reply through the same Biafran soldier who brought the note, and please not report him to their husbands. She had paid heavily to convince him that he would come to no harm. She was still their loving friend and sister, Stella.

Mrs Ozimba breathed deeply and said, 'Thank God. Oh, thank God.'

'I've already made a list of what we need. Bags of salt and garri. And on the first trip I am exporting my son. If he stays here, he will die with us all. After that Nsukka business, I feel guilty looking other mothers in the face.'

'My neighbour, Mrs Akabudike, lost three sons in one day. All at the same university, God help us. That woman will never recover.'

Luckily, the two women's sons listened to their mothers, and left Biafra along with the list of goods and bags of Biafran money. They wrote to their fathers soon afterwards to say that they were safe, and Dr Eze and Dr Ozimba both shook their heads and remarked, 'These women, what they can do.' When the second sons left, and Abosi began to be suspicious, Dr Eze claimed that his two sons had suddenly disappeared. This caused panic inside the cabinet for it was thought that enemies had infiltrated, abducting the sons of the top men. But both Eze and Ozimba slept better, and meanwhile their wives carried on a very lucrative trade.

The ordinary Igbo family still had to send their sons to the front to fight the war of liberation, their children and old people still died of malnutrition as the war continued and Abosi kept reminding them on

216

Radio Biafra, 'We will not give in. It is better for us to die standing than to be tortured to death by those bent on genocide.'

In an emergency meeting of the Biafran inner cabinet, he had to confess that their boundaries were shrinking fast. He suspected that people were beginning to question his authority – was it not said that authority forgets a dying king? The refugee problem had become almost insurmountable. They swam and rowed across the River Niger into what was left of Biafra, refugees from the conquered villages and refugee children, mostly orphans, who were the greatest headache of all. Abosi wanted to know what to advise people whose villages had been taken over. Should he tell them to remain there and die of gunshot wounds, or advise them to come to what was left of Biafra and die of hunger?

'What annoys me is that Momoh denies the fact that his soldiers are killing innocent civilians. The whole world knows that is not so.'

'Are you sure the whole world knows?' Abosi asked Dr Eze. 'If they did know they couldn't be this indifferent.'

'They aren't indifferent. The Red Cross have units in the Mid-Western Igbo towns. I understand that our friend Alan Grey is helping as well.'

Abosi smiled, fingering his beard which was beginning to have strands of grey in it. When he spoke, he spoke for all of them. 'Alan Grey . . . Alan Grey. He is England in this war. He arranges mercenaries and arms to be sent to Momoh, then comes to Red Cross our people. He wants to fatten us up for the slaughter.' He shook his head. 'Some people have no conscience. This war is Britain's greatest shame. I hope the world never forgets that.'

None of the men sitting there with bowed heads said anything about the possibility of losing the war. But it was suggested that they should hold a consultation with the few lieutenants and sergeants they could find, so that they could be put in the picture.

One look at the soldiers, who were grateful to leave the hazardous life of the bush, was enough to tell the ideological leaders that the war was over. The men looked starved, their once spectacular jungle green uniforms were mostly in shreds; some had only their soldier's cap to proclaim their occupation. There was little to fight with, there was no food. Though the only airport was still in use at night for bringing in a small amount of ammunition and medicines, even that strip was likely to be closed at any moment. However, Dr Ilogu's letter from Geneva said that the world was learning of their fate. He was arranging for some European journalists to come and see their plight. And the international outcry was curtailing Momoh's butchery. With more men, and the promised new ammunition, it would be possible to hold Nigeria at bay until talks were arranged between these two leaders.

It was decided that able-bodied men should not be left in the occupied areas, but should come into Biafra and join with the standing soldiers to put on a series of surprise attacks, using the biological warfare tactics which the few remaining scientists inside Biafra perfected. Four soldiers were delegated to go by night into the Mid-West and get young men; conscription should be enforced, since most of the young men inside Biafra had stopped volunteering. Some even poured ash on their heads to make themselves look old.

A few days after this meeting, hundreds of Nigerian soldiers were trapped and killed by the biological method known locally as 'Ogbunigwe', killer of the crowd. This boosted everybody's morale, and the villages along this route became Biafran again after being Nigerian for a couple of months. But with each engagement, the number of orphans doubled.

Dr Eze and Dr Ozimba had assured Abosi that they would get the four soldiers out to the Mid-West; they were tied, like bags of the Biafran money which was fast becoming of little value because of the high rate of inflation, and the soldiers were dropped at the far side of the river, where they quickly merged into the forest. After walking for only a couple of hours, they scared the living daylights out of some women who were in a makeshift market in the bush, all armed with clubs, prepared to kill a soldier before being killed themselves.

'We are Biafrans, Igbos like you. His Excellency Abosi sent us to you. Look at our uniforms.'

The women looked blankly at them, as if they did not understand what was being said. They would have run in all directions had they not thought the soldiers would shoot anyone who ran. The soldiers began to sense how really hostile some Western Igbos had become to the name of Biafra.

One woman stepped boldly forward and said, 'Biafra, Biafra, what is Biafra? You killed our man from this part, Nwokolo; the Nigerian soldiers came and killed what your soldiers left. We are Ibuza people, but we now live in the bush, thanks to your Abosi and your Biafra. Our town is now a ghost town. Go there and see Hausa soldiers killing and roasting cows. They shoot anything on sight, and kill anyone who gave shelter to your people. And when we needed you, where were you? Where was your Abosi when our girls were being raped in the market places and our grandmothers shot? Please go back to your Biafra. You call us Hausa Igbos, don't you? You call us fools because we fought your wars for you, and you are well protected in your place, claiming the glory? Please go away before you bring us bad luck.'

'Wait, Emiliana,' said another woman. 'If Abosi sent them, let them go and see our soldiers. They may have something to say to each other.'

'Your soldiers? You have your own soldiers?' asked the leading Biafran soldier.

'Yes, we became tired of being in the middle. Your Biafran soldiers killed our men and raped our girls, because you accused us of harbouring enemy soldiers, then Nigerian soldiers would accuse us of the same thing even though we were innocent. There was nobody to protect us, so we formed our own militia.' The women looking darkly at the four men nodded with determination.

'Can you take us to the men then? We are glad you can defend yourselves. When the war is over, His Excellency will reward everyone and this nightmare will be a thing of the past.'

'Yes,' said Uzoma Madako who was standing by, 'including my husband and my child.'

'Yes, a thing of the past.'

Watching, Debbie knew that the unsuspecting soldiers had touched a very sore spot. Nearly all the five hundred or so women hiding here in the bush had lost someone dear. In this bush, miles away from the main road, they were surviving on the fast disappearing fishes and crabs from the nearby stream, and many had even started to cultivate new farms. It went through Debbie's mind that she should volunteer to take the soldiers, and find out in the process how they managed to find this hidden place. It was obviously not as attack-proof as people thought.

When she announced in pidgin English her offer to take the Biafrans to the Mid-Western Igbo soldiers, the leading Biafran looked at her closely. Her face was vaguely familiar but he could not remember where he had seen her before. Uzoma Madako, who suspected the reason why Debbie was taking this gamble, would have followed but she knew the children would suffer if anything happened to both of them.

'Take a bigger club with you, Debbie, so that you can defend yourself,' she said in a low voice.

People smiled, and went back to their buying and selling.

'I'm not from this part,' Debbie said. 'I am trapped. I'm not the only one; there were eighteen of us when we left Agbor, I don't know how many weeks ago. Now we are only six left: two women and four children. We wanted to get to Biafra, but the Asaba massacre . . .'

'You mean you saw the Asaba massacre?' the soldier asked in horror.

'Yes, and many others since. These people here have suffered more than you in the East will ever imagine. The real war is being fought here. I'd like to cross over with you. When do you leave?'

'Tomorrow evening. But things are no easier in Biafra. At least here people can sell bush rats and live like a community.'

'It's not safe. A family down the other side of the bush were killed only yesterday, for no reason. The father was a solicitor from the North, the first son was a medical student in Ibadan. They were having their evening meal.'

'All right. You can come to Biafra and join the army anyway. Who are your people?'

Debbie did not have to answer because as they turned into a particularly thick part of the bush, in their walk to where the militia were hiding, a voice hissed:

'Stop! Hands on your head, or you are all dead.'

'And don't look round,' ordered another.

'Put down all your guns. You are fully surrounded.'

The Biafran soldiers did as they were told. Then Debbie announced:

'I live in Abala Ime with the women. These are Biafran soldiers who came to speak with you. Abosi sent them. I was only bringing them to you.'

'Yes, comrades, His Excellency sent us.'

There was the rustling of leaves and the sound of many voices. Debbie dared not look back. The militia was full of bitter and angry men.

'You,' one of them addressed her, 'take your women friends to Abala Oja. We shall meet them there.'

One of the soldiers bent to retrieve his home-made gun but was ordered not to.

'But we are all Igbos,' the senior officer protested, 'aren't we brothers any more? What is this?'

'Just go on. We shall see about the brotherhood later.'

As Debbie, Uzoma and her two surviving children and the two Nwoba boys were munching cocoyam bought from the makeshift market, she told them they might have to move to Biafra the next evening. No one protested. They knew the Nigerian soldiers were busy looking for this hiding place, and with people as hungry as they were, one crazy person might reveal the secret for the sake of a square meal. The women would have to make their way to Abala Oja, where the canoe would come for the Biafrans.

Debbie held tightly to the Nwoba boys while Uzoma did the same with her two. They crawled and slithered and walked. Luck was with them because there was no moon, and many of the women had crept into the main town to bury a chief who had been shot in broad daylight. An old woman had come into the bush to tell the younger women, so that they could do the digging. They would never allow any man there because the Nigerian soldiers would shoot men on sight. So that night the bush was busy. They arrived at Abala Oja without any molestation.

They hid in the nearby creek holding their breath, praying that their plans worked out. Debbie knew that she and Uzoma had overstayed their welcome at Npkotu Ukpe, where most of the women from Ibuza were hiding; she and Uzoma did not belong to their town although mutual distress had brought them all together for the sake of giving each other comfort.

Some of the men from that place were still trapped in Lagos. They had sent their families home, hoping to join them later; but when the war escalated, 'Operation Mosquito' turned the roads to the Igbo towns into death traps. The women and children, most of whom were born in the cities and had no idea how to live in the villages to say nothing of surviving on tree roots in the bush, did not know whether their husbands were alive or dead. The men who were already in the villages left and joined the Biafran army. But this arrangement started going sour when the Biafrans were leaving, on hearing that the Nigerians were steadily gaining back lost ground. If they had left as they came, the local people would not have been so offended. But they did not.

This young and irresponsible wife would leave her children in the care of the dedicated Irish Catholics and take after a young soldier who had promised her regular meals on top of everything else. That young schoolgirl was pregnant with a soldier's baby, for soldiers had the food, having been given the right to distribute the supplies that filtered in from Europe through secret channels. Many Biafran soldiers made illegal profit from this food. Girls who refused to go with them were cornered and raped. Many women, however, were willing victims. They saw life as purposeless anyway. They decided to enjoy their freedom while they had it, and why not with a strong young soldier who could fill one's belly? Tomorrow would take care of itself, and besides there might never be a tomorrow anyway.

The local men despaired and gritted their teeth. They could not stand this kind of behaviour from their fellow Igbos. To make matters worse, some local men were openly shot by Igbo soldiers for harbouring Nigerian soldiers or giving them information. When they eventually left, many men, frightened of what would become of them, joined up with the Biafran soldiers. They crossed into the East and burned the connecting bridge behind them. They had no choice.

Now the Mid-Westerners were fed up with serving Abosi and being betrayed. If the Nigerian soldiers were coming to kill them in their homeland, they would first of all have to cope with their own guerrilla militia. Abosi had sent his four-man delegation to cream the men off and convince them to come and man the diminishing Biafran army; but the Ibuza and Asaba people said, 'Enough is enough. You may rape and humiliate our wives and daughters, but when it comes to your doing the same to our mothers, we would rather die.'

Debbie, Uzoma and the children heard the crawling that sounded like the gentle wind ruffling dry leaves. It came and it stopped. Then it came again. The children instinctively crouched by a nearby tree and held their hands at the back of their heads to protect their brains from whatever blasting was coming.

Then a voice croaked, 'It's me, the lieutenant – you remember me.'

Debbie recognized the voice, though now it was that of a damaged man. When he made himself visible, tears were running down the crevices of his dirt-stained face. Debbie ran to aid him.

'Come on, come on, Uzoma. There are four of them.'

The Biafran soldier's parched voice gave out a hysterical sound that was half a bleat and half hyena-like laughter. The children jumped, ready to take off into the belly of the forest but Uzoma restrained them. No sane human could emit a sound so unreal. What he had to tell them made their skin grow goosepimples in that humid heat.

'They clubbed us down with the handle of their women's odo. I am the only one alive, because I fell down first and the others fell on me. I'll never be able to use some parts of my body again. They are dead, all of them.'

'Killed by Nigerian soldiers?' Uzoma gulped.

'No, there was no Nigerian in sight. Killed by Mid-Western militia.'

'You mean we're killing each other? I can't believe this. Why, why?'

'Haven't you heard the latest then? They made us listen to it over their bush radio. You haven't heard that Dr Ozimba has defected? He's now advocating "One Nigeria".'

'What?' Debbie cried. 'Oh, my God! That man is a liar and a cheat.'

'Since he is alive and still has money, he can deny anything. Politicians are good at denying what they said yesterday. If he can't deny it, he can always explain it away. But it's too late for those whose lives have been lost,' Uzoma sighed.

'I just can't think of any reason he can give to justify this step at a time like this. The man has ruined his political future; no one will ever respect him again.'

'Poor Abosi, that he trusted such men,' Uzoma whined.

'We don't know yet but I don't think he'll let us down. He believes in what he's doing, and I am still solidly behind him. I wish he had not ordered Nwokolo's death, though; that mistake alienated the Mid-Westerners from us. They are good and loyal fighters. We could have used them for a long time yet,' the Eastern Igbo soldier said. 'After the war was won we could have decided how to deal with them then . . .'

The two women ignored him and let him ramble on until they saw the canoe silhouetted in the dark night.

Abosi had provided two large canoes to ferry in the Mid-Western recruits he expected, but the canoe men who made the trip at the risk of their lives were annoyed to find that there were none waiting for them. They asked the wounded man several times about his other friends and were shocked to hear what had happened. For a long time they refused to take the women and children. How could they be sure they were not Mid-Western women trying to infiltrate Biafra just to cause more trouble? Uzoma Madako described the village she came from, she described her parents, she begged and cried, but the canoe men refused to budge. Debbie suspected that some payment might work, but she had little money on her. Then she touched her ears and realized that despite the ups and downs of this long journey to the East the gold-stud earrings which her father had bought her and which her mother had insisted on her wearing were still in place.

'Come here to this corner, I have something to show you,' she said to the chief canoe driver.

The man stretched out his hand and pocketed the expensive and well-cut earrings in his damp and tattered khaki shorts. He agreed to ferry them across. So this is Biafra, the two women thought, numbed with shock.

Debbie observed wryly to Uzoma, 'To think that all this ballyhoo started because people thought our politicians were corrupt and accused them of taking bribes. An ideal place where righteousness would rule, where there would be no bribery, was to be created, and that place would be Biafra . . . And now even the canoe man asks for a dash. Do you know what he told me? He said, "We are not Red Cross people, you know. We are soldiers."'

'Ridiculous. When you see things like this, you don't know what to believe any more.'

'I still believe in what Biafra stands for; that's the only way I can accept the brutal killing of my father, and the deaths of Ngbechi, Dot and her baby and all those innocent nuns.'

'I didn't know you had a father . . . oh, nonsense – I'm putting it badly. I didn't know your father was recently killed. Who was he? You only ever speak of your mother in Aba and Onitsha.'

'We are friends, aren't we, Uzoma? Whatever happens in the near future I would like us to keep in touch.'

'You sound as if you're going to outer space. Who are you, Debbie?'

'I am Debbie Ogedemgbe.'

Uzoma opened her mouth and closed it again, swallowing the night air.

'Chief Ogedemgbe's daughter? Oh, my God, what are you doing here?' she hissed desperately.

'We've been through many ordeals together. Don't you know that there are even Yorubas who support the idea of Biafra? I'm still on your side, believe me. I'm trying to prove that beliefs can go beyond tribes. Abosi is our family friend, yet he is Igbo. I am going to see him.'

'Oh, I am sorry, Debbie. I hope all this suffering is worth it. I hope you are not going to be disappointed in the end.'

They touched the East before long, and Debbie kissed the ground.

'I'll take these two boys, in case their mother happens to be alive. If not, something will be done for them. I still have friends,' she said.

'Thank you, Debbie.' They embraced, then walked their different ways in the dead of the night, one of the canoe men going with Debbie as her guide when he heard that she was going to see Abosi.

The surviving lieutenant did not reach Biafra again. He died in the second canoe.

So closed another route that connected Biafra with the outside world through the Mid-West.

18 *Face to Face*

The security men guarding the makeshift imperial building housing Abosi and his family had been briefed to expect a group of fighters coming from the Mid-West in the company of four uniformed Biafran soldiers. Not in their wildest dreams would they have connected that information with the funny lot standing before them and saying that they were there to report to His Excellency about the mission.

The canoe man was well known in his area as a very wealthy man, who would smuggle out the sons and daughters of rich people to other parts of West Africa for a large price so that they avoided conscription. He was huge and dark, and his arms hung loosely at his sides like the fronds of a giant coconut tree. His over-exercised shoulders were square and broad and seemed to dwarf his head. He made up for his small head by the sharpness of his eyes. To make matters worse, his voice was quiet and caressing which, coming from a man of his size, made the security soldiers even more suspicious.

In contrast to the overblown canoe man, the woman by his side was like a witch, all eyes and head. Her hair had gone a pale brown not unlike that of the children she was holding. She was dry and almost fleshless, just skin and bones, yet the lustre in her eyes was enough to tell the soldiers that she was not an old woman but a comparatively young one, albeit of uncertain age.

They were hustled into a smaller house outside the walls of the imperial building. Not knowing what to do with them, the soldiers made Debbie and the canoe man repeat their stories several times. They made them strip to make sure they were not carrying any arms. The canoe man did not have much clothing in the first place, but Debbie's wallet of loose and tattered papers attracted a great deal of attention. They wanted to know what they were, and when she said that she was scribbling down events of the past years in a kind of diary, interest in her intensified and they took the flat wallet. She would be sorry if those notes were destroyed, although most of her experiences had become such a part of her now that they haunted her night and day so that she could never forget them. One thing she had been careful of was not to write her name on them. In a law court, she could always deny ownership – if given such a chance. But these men made and abided by their own laws, without the knowledge of Abosi who was only a few yards away.

Then she begged one of the officers, 'Will you let me write a note to His Excellency? If after reading it he does not send for me, then do with me whatever you like.'

After much debate, a piece of paper was produced. Debbie simply wrote: 'Chijioke, I have to see you. Debbie Ogedemgbe.'

She begged the officers not to read it because it was private, though she knew it was a hopeless request as there was no envelope and the soldiers were burning with curiosity. A few seconds after the note was taken, one yelled in:

'So you are the daughter of Ogedemgbe. What are you doing in Biafra? Come to spy on us? Isn't it enough that one of your father's oldest friends defected a few days ago? So you have the courage to come here?'

'Shoot her,' commanded one.

Debbie watched the home-made Biafran version of a shotgun cocked. Just in time another voice came in.

'Oh, leave her, she's only a woman. What harm can she do, and how could we explain it to His Excellency?'

The gun was lowered and Debbie was able to breathe again. Then they faced the canoe man and kicked him.

'Why do you come here with her? To get a dash for being a good boy? Well, take this – another kick.' The man howled and the soldiers laughed.

'You can't be the same Debbie,' came Juliana Abosi's voice in a shocked whisper, all of a sudden. 'What have they done to you? I can't believe it.'

They embraced and soon Debbie was given the first good meal she had had for months. She asked Juliana to help her get the two Nwoba boys from the security soldiers. Debbie had to wait until very late in the morning, however, before Abosi could see her. He expressed sorrow at her father's death.

'I thought you were safe in Lagos while we here were fighting for survival. I thought all was well with you.'

'You won't believe this, Chijioke, but I was originally sent – or let me say I volunteered – to come here to convince you to stop this war. That was months ago when things were not so good for Saka Momoh. Now I think my mission has come too late. Many people have died and still hundreds die each day, and yet it continues . . . this war, I mean.'

Abosi was tense; but Debbie could not doubt the squareness of those shoulders. She knew then and there that her suffering and her self-imposed crusade had been for nothing. She felt like hating all men, but she had been drained of emotion.

'I haven't much time,' Abosi was saying. 'But I am sorry if you've risked your life for nothing. What good could you have done, just you, little you?' He smiled.

'I am me. Debbie, the daughter of Ogedemgbe. Tell me, if I were a man, a man born almost thirty years ago, a graduate of politics, sociology and philosophy from Oxford, England, would you have dismissed my mission?'

'You are brave, but you've answered the question yourself. You are not a man.' Here he laughed. 'Momoh would have his joke, sending you to ask me to change my mind, when underneath it all he was using your English boyfriend to supply him with arms and mercenaries with which to kill us.'

'Abosi, surrender now and make peace with Momoh. Your independence will be given to you. I am sure of it. If you go on, you will lose everything, including self-respect, and you may be the last man standing to fight. I am not doubting your aims and your powerful ideas. But you were ill-prepared, and the Western world isn't ready to give us that kind of independence. Not yet. Momoh is a willing tool, as many of our leaders are. I forgave those who killed my father because I thought that from the deaths of men like him would rise a new African nation. But that is not to be. So give in, Abosi, now, and do it with pride.'

'Hmmm, what a lovely speech. But, Debbie, what would become of all these people if we gave in? Don't you know what they would do to them?'

'Believe me, Momoh didn't start this genocidal thing, but the officers fighting for him have turned the whole thing into one big blood bath. By continuing, you give them an excuse to go on killing innocent people, starving them out. Oh, Abosi, I wish you'd seen a tenth of what I have seen. You would believe me then.'

'Hmmm, you are enjoying a woman's privilege. If you were a man, you would have been shot this minute as a traitor. So you see, being a woman has its advantages.'

'What are you fighting for, then, if at the end of the day there's only you to populate Biafra?'

'You're still naive. Woman, we are fighting for the right to live in our homeland. The right to be ourselves, the right to live. Is that too much to ask? If we are promised that right, of course the war will end at once.'

'Abosi, I have an idea. Let me go to Britain, and stir the consciences of people over there. I will show them pictures of dying children, mutilated bodies and bloated corpses. I'll tell them, I'll tell the world that you are not fighting only over the oil but for what you've just told me, the right to live.'

'You think they don't already know?'

'Ah, but they haven't heard it my way. They haven't heard it from a neutral Itsekiri woman, not an Igbo. People will believe me.'

Abosi smiled and promised to discuss it with his inner cabinet. Meanwhile, he advised Debbie to get some sleep.

The plane that took Debbie away from the secluded airport inside Biafra had no lights. Trying to suppress her fear, Debbie clutched her wallet of notes to her breast as the supply plane shot up into the dark night. Many people in the plane were on different mercy missions for Biafra, but no one spoke, except the reassuring pilot. In less than twenty minutes the lights went on, and all breathed again. They were out of danger, out of the range of the Nigerian bombers that paraded the sky like vampires in search of blood.

In London, Debbie soon got in touch with one of the leaders of the Igbo community, and in no time a big demonstration took place in Trafalgar Square. Thousands of student sympathizers turned out, urging the prime minister to end the war. Some delegates were sent to America, where the war became one of the major issues in the re-election of the President. The communist world, especially China, jumped on the bandwagon. If Nigeria was buying arms from Britain and Soviet Russia, the Chinese would help Abosi. However, Abosi, being an Englishman in all but his colour, found it impossible to trust anything with a communist flavour.

He pressurized Debbie and all those waging the ideological warfare to make sure the pictures of dying children appeared every day in the media. 'People must never forget about us. Show them what with their help one black man can do to another, show them how they are helping our children die.'

Debbie and two other eye-witnesses were given a free hall in which to address a group of journalists interested in making the dangerous journey to Nigeria to see exactly what was happening. The moving talk went on for hours, and at the end of it many present had their faith in the fight for freedom confirmed.

She was returning to her father's Mayfair flat when a familiar voice cut in from behind her: 'That was very moving, Debbie.'

Spinning round, she saw Alan Grey standing there in the late summer sunshine. She simply started to laugh and so did he, glad to see each other.

'Debbie, where've you been all these months?'

'You heard what I said in the hall this afternoon; those were personal experiences, not tales.'

Alan considered this for a while, the stories of torture, of rape, of mass murder, and he looked again at her, but found it difficult to relate such happenings to Debbie. Surely she was being over-dramatic; she had been under great strain. He shrugged.

'And you, what are you doing here, buying arms for your friend Momoh?'

'No, not really. I'm helping the Red Cross getting aid.'

Debbie stopped in her tracks and placed both hands on her hips, laughing loudly enough to turn the heads of a few people sauntering down Park Lane.

'You mean you send arms to Momoh and food to Abosi? Well, I've heard of hypocrisy, but to see it practised this way is something else.'

'We're on the same side of the fence, you know.'

'How?'

'You want the war to end quickly. We want it too.'

'Oh, I get it. I understand that you arranged arms for Momoh and even enlisted mercenaries to help him make a quick kill, to safeguard the businesses of your entrepreneurs. But your quick-kill theory didn't work, because the Biafrans put up stronger resistance than you expected. So now you've changed from being a killer to a healer, all in a lifetime – oh, Alan!'

'I don't blame you for interpreting it like that, but few people in their right senses want to kill other people.'

'Well, most of the Western world must be crazy then. You claim to have rescued us from killing each other as sacrifices, but for all your Christianity you seem to be killing more.'

'Human error,' Alan said in a low voice, and for once he looked vulnerable. Could all this have been a mistake resulting from human greed and miscalculation?

Inside the flat which her late father had kept for his girlfriends, she forgot herself for a while and engaged in a rambling monologue that was becoming part of her since her recent stay in the bush. Alan was immersed in the colour magazine of the day's Sunday paper, looking at the pictures of children emaciated beyond recognition, at pictures of bleeding wounds and decomposed corpses that gave a tragic impression of Biafra.

Then Debbie's voice cut through: 'After all, we are a sovereign state. We've been an independent nation for the past nine years. Maybe the fault is more ours. We invited them to come and settle our trouble for us, so they started to take sides to their own advantage. We only can save ourselves. I wish Momoh and Abosi could see that . . .'

Alan walked up with the quietness of a cat and held her by the waist, making her tip the spoon of instant coffee she was going to pour into a cup. 'Do you do this often now, talk to yourself? You know what they'd say in Africa?'

'Yes,' she laughed, 'they'd say I'm a witch.'

'Debbie, how did those torrid photographs get into the Sunday papers?'

'Your pressmen took them. Didn't you read the photographers' names? Did they sound African?'

'Tell me, Debbie, when you said you were speaking from personal experience this afternoon, you didn't really mean yourself, did you?'

'Oh, white man, don't you understand your own language now? What does the word personal mean?'

'You mean you were . . . I mean – '

'I mean I was raped, several times, Alan, in the bush, I don't even know by how many men, I didn't count – '

'Stop, stop, for God's sake. Must you go into details?'

'You asked me.'

Debbie was not surprised that the conversation was changed and became very abstract and political. Alan would see to it that certain pressures were brought to bear on the Government so that the Biafran case would be debated. The suffering people would get food, clothing and medicine. Alan Grey would not be able to prevent the sale of arms to Momoh, because top people were involved in it; besides if Britain stopped, there were many other countries willing to sell him arms on credit, because of Nigeria's oil. They both agreed that if all failed,

Abosi should somehow be eliminated, since without him many hero-worshippers would stop fighting. But Momoh must be made aware of the killing of civilians.

Alan soon got up to go, and as if in a dream Debbie felt him brush his cold lips on her cheek. He was so distant, so English, such a gentleman. Debbie's smile wobbled on her lips.

'What do you advise me to do? Ring a bell and cry, "Beware, here comes a leper"?'

'Don't be silly. We have much more important things to worry about now.'

'Funny, I had expected the son of Sir Fergus Grey to behave differently from an unsophisticated Moslem African, but you reacted exactly like Salihu Lawal. Tell me, would it have made any difference if I had been raped by white soldiers?'

'I don't know what you're talking about. Stop being ridiculous.'

Debbie did not stop him. He left. Somehow she felt that a formerly useful door had just been slammed in her face. She cried all night, not because she wanted him but because of the uselessness of the whole charade.

Word came to her a few days later that the British Prime Minister would be visiting West Germany, and it occurred to Debbie that this would provide an opportunity for her to give vent to her bitterness.

The British Prime Minister saw a few Igbo students demonstrating there, but that was to be expected; he was confident that the Germans would give him all the protection he needed during this short visit. What he did not bargain for, however, came when he opened his mouth to speak. A leather full of animal blood exploded in his face, covering his lips and soiling his suit, and the accusation 'Murderer!' rang out from the Ibo students. The message went home. A quick debate took place on the prime minister's return and he agreed to visit Momoh personally to see to it that the civilian killings were stopped.

The night when Debbie returned from Germany and was having coffee with some old college friends who had kept the student Biafra movement in London lively, Alan Grey telephoned.

'I'm at the airport. The PM has gone to Nigeria. I told you I would pull strings. Get your Abosi to agree to any ceasefire arrangement they propose. He's losing anyway.'

Later the telephone shrieked again, and this time it was Abosi. He told Debbie that it did not look as if the British PM would be visiting Biafra to see the situation for himself. His spies told him that Momoh had promised to see that no civilian killings would take place, but

Abosi was sure some pockets of killings were still going on. Did she remember that bush where she had been hiding near Ibuza? Well, the people had been bombed out and now were forced to stay in their town. Ibuza had lost over two thousand people.

Debbie sighed disconsolately.

'If we ever give in at all,' Abosi went on, 'we must do so with weapons in our hands, honourably – not begging to be spared. We have pride, we have dignity.' He told her that arms had been specially made for the Biafrans in a particular English town whose name he would give her later. Her instructions were to go and collect them and see that the next Red Cross supply plane carried arms, not food. She should not worry about the Red Cross people; they knew all about it.

'Suppose Momoh does stop the killing and there are UN soldiers on the spot to see that the ceasefire is enforced, would you stop fighting then? Because it's likely that that's what is going to happen.'

She was reminded that she was a woman and that a good woman should do what she was told and not ask too many questions. The conversation was over.

'That man intends to fight to the last. He still thinks he can win. He"s living in a dream world.'

She stared pensively at her London friends. Could she trust them? If Abosi thought he was going to use her to get arms into Biafra because as a woman she would be less conspicuous, she was going to give him the greatest shock he had ever had in his luxurious life. She had known these student friends, Ronald and Jill, for over ten years; she would risk taking them into her confidence.

She told them what Abosi was planning. She feared that if news of the planned attack should leak out, the Nigerian soldiers would start killing again; but she had to see that the English public was not deceived. After all, the supply plane was being maintained by public contributions. What right had Abosi to use it to carry arms?

In the event there was no need for any action from Jill and her student protesters, who were going to announce what Abosi planned to do with the relief plane sent to the orphans. Debbie simply told the pilot that orders had been changed. Food and not ammunition was to be flown over after all because the press had been alerted. Not wanting to be involved in a scandal, the pilot agreed. And the students who appeared from nowhere helped load the bags of stockfish, rice and clothes into the plane.

The arms, grenades and other instruments of killing were transferred to the house of one of the leading Igbo Biafrans in London. He too was becoming disenchanted with Abosi's plan.

To say that Abosi was furious was the understatement of the age. He raved madly.

When Alan Grey telephoned Debbie from Lagos a few days later, it was to tell her how pleased Momoh was with the good job she had done. She was instructed to return to Biafra but to stay in the occupied part of Iboland. She was to be a guest of her father's former friend and colleague, Dr Ozimba, and his wife, and would be told when to make the necessary move with her special equipment of elimination. Even the Ozimbas were not to know what she was carrying, and she was to be careful, very careful, because such deadly weapons could kill both the operator and the target. He wished her luck.

A hooded car was waiting when she arrived at the second airport now in the hands of the Nigerian soldiers. Mrs Ozimba was incoherent with joy at seeing Debbie alive.

'We must send for your mother. She must come here to see you.'

'No, I'll write to her, and eventually I will travel to the Mid-West myself to see her. Meanwhile I'm very busy here.'

'Busy doing what?'

'Writing a book.'

'Hmm, will it be interesting?'

'Oh, yes, it will be very interesting. I think I'll call it *Destination Biafra*.'

19 *The Holocaust*

Momoh was hysterical in his denials. He waved his hands appealingly in the air to convince his listeners; he swore volubly by the soul of his dead father, and he gambled with the heads of his young sons, all to press home his claim that no civilian had ever been killed by the Nigerian soldiers except those caught in the cross-fire. The British delegates sympathized with him and told him they understood, but maintained unequivocally that the killing of women and children must end.

Momoh got angry and lost control. What right had the British Prime Minister to tell him what to do? Was he not the head of a nation? He had given them his word and they could take it or leave it. Had not the British been supporting Abosi? And now they were here pleading for the Igbos.

'You sit there,' he continued after taking a needed deep breath, 'you sit there smoking your pipe of peace, wanting me to do what you like, enh? What happened to all your big talk about the intelligence of the Igbos? Why can't their intelligence save them now? It's all at an end now. I am not a murderer . . .' He went on for quite a while longer, though most of the foreign listeners could not make out what he was trying to say.

The delegates could not believe their ears when they learned that the general would not be coming to dinner that night because he was offended at the way the British Prime Minister had treated him. The prime minister pleaded his way to Momoh's apartment to explain that he had meant no offence. After all, was the general not the head of the most important all-black nation in the world? That really brought a smile to Momoh's face. He made more oil concessions, promised to halt killing and make it one of his most important duties to capture Abosi, since without him motivating the revolution the Igbos would give in. The two leaders parted as friends.

Salihu Lawal and his two-thousand-strong regiment, still in the bushes surrounding Nsukka, a few miles from the Igbo heartland, heard all about this conference and the promises made by the head of state.

'Who the hell does he think he is?' Lawal fumed to his subordinate Aminu Latifu. 'He stays there among soft cushions in the company of his wife, ordering us what to do. Does he think we are butchers? We don't kill anyone except those who attack us.'

What annoyed Lawal more than anything else was that he too was tired of killing. He felt he had revenged the death of his spiritual leader enough. He had issued orders to the few armed officers left in the occupied area to treat the Igbo people humanely. He was tired of the smell of burning flesh which seemed to reach them wherever they went. He was tired. He wanted to go home to his wives, he wanted to hear the noise of his many children. He wanted proper Hausa food and a cool goatskin, not this makeshift life. Why keep over two thousand men hiding in this bush for weeks with little food and nothing to do? Yet that man Abosi would never give in. So what was one to do?

The decision was made for him the very next afternoon. Two soldiers stationed at the outposts brought two whimpering young men. They were naked to the waist and their khaki shorts were not too faded to completely hide the jungle pattern of the Biafran forces. But they were swearing and protesting that they were not Biafran soldiers. Lawal looked at them with detached boredom.

'What do you want us to do with them, sah?' asked the sergeant who had brought them.

'Do what you bloody well like with them,' snapped Lawal.

'Only, sir, they say not to kill civilians.'

Lawal covered his face with his cloth army cap and laughed. 'If you think these well-fed Igbo men are civilians, you'll believe anything. They feed their army men with the food from the Red Cross that the world is told is for their starving children.'

The sergeant smiled a malicious, sadistic smile, which triggered off new pleas from the Igbo men when they saw it.

'Please, sir, Lieutenant, spare out lives and we'll tell you when the attack is going to be, we'll tell you everything, if you spare us. Oga, sah! Your Honour.'

'You know, you are beginning to amuse me,' Lawal said. 'What is you name, Biafran soldier?'

'Michael, sir. My friend is Emmanuel.'

'So, Michael, who is going to attack whom?'

'We, sah, we are going to attack you, sah, and kill all of you.'

'Really, with those weapons you all made in your mothers' cooking stones?' Lawal asked, pointing at two pathetic-looking guns that might have been soldered together by a blind man. Yet he knew that they worked and he did not underestimate the Biafrans' capabilities. 'Thank you, soldier, a group of ten men from my regiment can settle fifty thousand Biafrans using these things you call guns.' He spat.

'No, sir, we have sophisticated guns, very sophisticated ones, sir.' His friend, Emmanuel, looked at him curiously, opening and then shutting his mouth again.

Lawal got up and slapped both men's faces. 'If you lie to me, I'll give you the type of burial you deserve. So you'd better speak the truth. You, Emmanuel, where are the arms coming from?'

He shook his head. 'I don't know, sah.'

A shot rang between his legs, missing him by a fraction of an inch. He jumped and cried out for his mother.

'The next one will burst your testicles,' Lawal warned. His face was glowering and his behaviour menacing.

'Yes, sir. From abroad. From abroad, sir.'

'Liar! How from abroad? The only plane that comes to your airstrip is from the Red Cross to bring food. No other plane is allowed in. How do you get your arms, soldier?'

'From abroad, on the Red Cross planes,' Emmanual said.

Lawal looked unbelievingly at Michael and asked, 'Is this true?'

'Yes, sir.'

'Allah,' gasped Lawal. 'Now I know that this man is crazy. And those white people . . . I don't understand them. Only a short while ago in Lagos they were telling us to end the war, and now for the sake of a few thousand pounds they are selling arms to Biafrans using the Red Cross mercy planes.'

'They may not even be Red Cross planes. You can't trust these Igbos. A red cross can be painted on any old plane.'

'Take them away and kill them,' Lawal ordered.

'But, sir, you promised us our lives, you can't go back on your word. We are harmless to you now.'

'All right. Spare them. How many of you were sent out to spy on us?'

'Six, sir,' replied Emmanuel, happy that they had been given at least a temporary reprieve.

'So the others have gone to tell Abosi of our position. When is the attack?'

'We don't know. His Excellency did not tell us when.'

The two Igbo men were pushed away.

Lawal dispatched a quick message to Momoh to report what he had heard and to advise him not to withdraw the Nigerian Queen's Own Regiment in the northern part of Biafra as he had promised the British. Lawal would await his orders and start moving in two days' time, but he would send the white mercenaries to the north of Biafra. What he did not tell Momoh was that he had been wanting to get rid of these people. He found them a thorn in the flesh and ridiculed them for coming to fight in a war that was not their own simply because they were paid. To a certain extent he respected their courage, but to put them in their place he never consulted them on anything.

He also pointed out to Saka Momoh that the small strip of land which now constituted the whole of Biafra was the home of over five million people. It would be impossible not to harm civilians if the military attacks were stepped up.

Momoh called the British shameless murderers. There was no time to find out whether the Red Cross relief plane was genuine or not. The Nigerian side had been winning and must now take immediate action to consolidate their conquests.

At five o'clock the following morning, Lawal stretched and breathed in deeply, preparing to do his morning exercises. As he looked into the hazy early air, he wondered perfunctorily why all was so quiet. There were usually soldiers in the camps nearest to his who were up by this time, when the cramped atmosphere beneath the tarpaulin sleeping enclosure which protected them from malaria mosquitoes became too oppressive. The possible ignominy of a soldier dying from malaria rather than in action forced them to comply with these sleeping arrangements, but many like Lawal would come out for a breath of fresh air at the earliest opportunity.

After a while Lawal became curious at the uncharacteristic silence. He padded back to his own private enclosure and ordered his personal assistant Aminu Latifu to go and wake the men.

'To think that we may be going into action tonight, and there they are sleeping like pregnant women.'

Aminu Latifu yawned his way outside to alert the soldiers. After only a few minutes, however, he came tearing back in, and shouting with two officers from another camp.

'Sir, sir! I've never seen anything like it before. All the soldiers in the camp, all dead! All of them . . . in their sleep! Come, Lieutenant, just come and look,' Latifu cried, while the others wrung their hands as if they had suddenly been struck dumb. 'Come and see – I have never seen anything like this before . . .'

The Hausa lieutenant allowed himself to be dragged along to the big camp like a sleepwalker. He could not take in what he was being told. How could over five hundred men die in one night in their sleep?

But that indeed was what seemed to have happened. He saw the men, and the white soldiers of fortune too, lying side by side in their light sleeping-bags, apparently asleep; but it was a sleep from which they would never wake.

'What is this?' Lawal asked with panic in his voice. 'What exactly is all this?'

'Ogbunigwe, sah!'

'Ogbunigwe, the killer of the crowd . . .' Lawal repeated slowly.

'It was those two Biafran soldeirs, sah, they brought it in, sah. And yet they managed to escape,' Aminu Latifu lamented.

'Stop saying "sah, sah" to me!' Lawal yelled his frustration at Latifu. 'All of you get into your uniforms. I can face the bullet, but not this deadly biological thing. I don't understand it.'

Mrs Elina Eze was surprised to see her husband at home at two o'clock in the afternoon. His eyes were bloodshot and his face ashy. He looked ill.

'Now what is up?' she asked.

Dr Eze shook his head. Then he collected himself and said briskly. 'You must leave. Take those two boys Debbie left with you and our young daughter and make for that canoe you and Mrs Ozimba patronized. Leave quickly. Now, in about an hour. Quick.'

'What are you talking about? Are the Nigerians here? Surely you don't think they will go back on their word not to kill civilians?'

'Elina, listen to me. Abosi took me and some soldiers and about five hundred saboteurs who had committed some sin or other against the state of Biafra . . . most of the men had been caught trying to make themselves look older so they wouldn't have to go to the front and risk not returning like most of their friends and relatives. Well, Abosi showed them some bodies floating on the stream and said these were Nigerian soldiers who had just been killed. I didn't count them but there must have been more than a hundred. Poor men . . .'

'Yes, poor men,' echoed Elina, at the same time wondering why her husband should be so upset; after all, the Biafrans had killed many more before. 'Never mind, though, it is war.'

'I wouldn't mind if those men really had been Nigerian soldiers. But they were all Igbos. I could tell from their singlets and loin cloths. They were village men.'

'What are you trying to say, Doctor?'

'That our soldiers killed our own people for refusing to join up and fight for Biafra.'

'How could Abosi do a thing like that?'

'There was one bold man among the prisoners who asked what the exercise of showing them dead bodies meant. And the reply was that if they tried to avoid joining up for the final push, their fate would be the same. Then the man retorted, facing me, "It's all right your forcing us poor people to fight and lose our lives for your dreams, but, Dr Eze, where are you sons? Should they not be here setting the example we the common people need to follow, instead of pursuing studies in Britain and America?"

'Abosi didn't say a word. He was too shocked to speak,' Dr Eze said, after a long pause, during which husband and wife looked at each other in fear.

'We must go away. I wish we had defected with the Ozimbas.'

'Yes, Elina. Abosi did not say a word to me on our drive back, but I know what he was thinking.'

'That man is isolating himself more and more. He will not win this war,' Elina affirmed. 'That I know.'

'I don't know. His latest plan is so foolproof that his chances of success are greater. You know what our people are, they support the winner. Oh, I feel so crushed by his mere presence. But he still has followers, all right. Last night about eight or nine hundred Nigerian soldiers were killed without his firing a single bullet!'

By six o'clock, obeying the desperation in her husband's voice, Elina had packed enough food to last them a while. She knelt on the floor and begged her husband to come with her.

'They will kill you, I know that. Come and let us escape together. It wouldn't be a betrayal. He has lost. We have lost. Let us save our lives for our children's sake.'

'No, I will see this thing through. Our new tactics are bound to be successful. With this surprise method coupled with our biological eliminator, the Nigerian soldiers have no chance. They've been trained the British way of fighting to order; our way is different. It's called guerrilla warfare.'

Elina stared at him as he looked into the distance like someone hallucinating. These men really believed that they were still going to win. She tried once more.

'But they have taken all our oil lands, and it's said that they're already drilling some of the wells. Even if we win now, how can we maintain a Biafra without a drop of oil? Wasn't the oil the reason for all this mess in the first place?'

Eze turned to his wife. 'Is that what you are going to tell your children and granchildren, that we men plunged our nation into chaos because of oil? Let me tell you, woman, we are fighting for the right to live like everybody else. And the rest of the world are now coming over to our side. If we effect this final win, they will grant us what we want.'

Pity at the shortsightedness of her husband and his sex came over Elina. How could grown men make such blunders, and yet elevate themselves with such arrogance that one could not reach them to tell them the truth? She did not want to perish with him; she intended to live to see her children settled in life and if possible to see her children's children and tell them the story of Biafra. Dying this way was his choice. She would leave, using the creek way she and her friend Mrs Ozimba had perfected, then she would make her way to either Upper Volta or Gabon. But she was not going to die for another person's bad dream.

She hugged her husband, knowing that he had been conditioned to be too cold and self-assured to value any demonstration of affection from her. Yet the maternal thing inside her made her pity this childish man who thought he knew all. She forgave him his foolishness, just as she would many times forgive her own sons.

Dr Eze was startled, not knowing how to respond. But it did not matter; it was too late now to realize the value of Elina. She pulled the Nwoba boys and her little twelve-year-old daughter, and walked quickly out of the house.

Her husband still stared into the distance, seeing the Biafra of his dreams which would be the richest land for black people, where he would be so wealthy that he would not know what to do with the money, where he would be so powerful that Europeans from all over the world would come to seek his friendship . . .

'You are under arrest, sir, you, and anything you say may be used against you.' This was punctuated by a slap from a soldier standing behind him.

Eze collapsed on the floor spluttering. He heard one man say, 'Don't kill him, you fool. His Excellency wants him alive.' He also heard the angry reply from another voice: 'I don't care if he is dead. They led us

240

into this holocaust, and now they're all sending their children out of the country, leaving people like us to fight their dirty war. Soon we'll be rid of all these greedy old men, Abosi and all. They think only they can organize a coup? We want a share of the oily national cake too.'

As Dr Eze lost consciousness, he remembered his wife's voice saying, only an hour or so before, 'Was not the oil the reason for all this mess in the first place?' All women were witches – how did she know?

An agitated Alan Grey called at Dr Ozimba's house to see Debbie busy typing on an old typewriter bought from the now shanty Onitsha market. She was surprised to see him. But he was not in a happy mood and, as on the last time he saw her in London, he was detached. Now there was an urgent mission.

'You have to achieve this in less than forty-eight hours, not four months like the last time,' he said. 'Tell Abosi to surrender, because Momoh and Lawal are in a very murderous mood. It would be completely senseless to wait until there's a new massacre. Remind him that over five million Ibos are packed into the little place that is now Biafra. And that they are completely surrounded. He can never escape.'

'You're making a mistake if you think Abosi is the type of man to give up his post and run,' Debbie warned.

'If he wants to die fighting, why take millions of his people with him? If he surrenders, Momoh has agreed to a peace treaty. If not, many innocent lives are going to be lost in the next few days.'

'Why this sudden change of plan?'

'You still have the mini land-mines?'

Debbie nodded.

'Abosi's biological method killed hundreds of soldiers in one night without his firing a single gun. If that continues, he will never surrender. And Lawal is enraged at being left in the bush with thousands of panic-stricken men. So they are giving you three days to talk Abosi into surrendering; after that, there'll be a once-and-for-all descent into what's left of Biafra. And with powerful land-mines and thousands of hand grenades and all the Russian automatic – '

'And the British ones,' Debbie put in.

The ghost of a smile spread on Alan's face but he checked himself, then added: 'You can't blame us now for not trying to save lives, can you?'

He came nearer to her, his lean body towering over her, his grey eyes boring deeply into her brown ones, his teeth gritted with tension. Then he hissed, 'So are you going to do it then?'

'I'll do it.'

'Good. Do your woman bit tonight,' he said. 'Abosi used to fancy you, I used to see the desire in his eyes when he talked to you at Government House in Lagos . . . well, use that part of you to make him do what you say.'

Debbie walked up to Alan Grey and slapped him on both sides of his face.

'That is for the way you and your country have fallen in the eyes of the black nations. This war is one of your greatest shames.'

As usual inside Biafra everyone was hurrying to finish their daily tasks. People still took no chances. At night most families left their houses and took shelter; those in hospital would lie under their beds. The rumour of the dead eight hundred Nigerian soldiers had spread and gave some hope, but recent events had taught the Igbos to be modest in their victory. It was at this time of nightly preparation that Debbie came into the town and went straight to Abosi.

Again, however, her mission failed. Abosi simply would not give in. He felt he was already winning. If millions of people had to die, that was war. He wanted a separate nation, even with his last breath.

Alan Grey shook his head when he heard this news from Debbie, and before long the two men who were going to help plant the land-mines at about evening meal time arrived. Debbie prayed to God to forgive her. If Abosi was eliminated, she reasoned, millions of lives would be saved. But while he was still there the war would go on, a war that had become his personal war and no longer the people's war. She soon left her hiding place when the evening grew dark.

The quiet town was suddenly startled by the resumption of bombs falling, raining on to Biafra. People were screaming everywhere in pain and terror. The way the bombs and grenades were exploding, it seemed the Nigerian soldiers had determined finally to wipe out whatever remained of Biafra.

Debbie ran. Another shock awaited her and her two companions. There were no guards by Abosi's door. His Excellency's abode was completely empty. They went from one room to the other and saw that apart from the fixtures and a few chairs everything had been cleared. Had Abosi and his family been kidnapped? They must have been forced to leave, for they could not have anticipated that Lawal was going to attack this night. Debbie became desperate. Why had Lawal not waited for her to complete her mission before launching this heavy offensive action against a defenceless city packed full of starving refugees? Where was Abosi, the symbol of Biafra?

She dashed out of the house and made for the multiple garage at the back. It was empty. Abosi's oversized white Mercedes had gone, as had Juliana's mini and his mother's red Toyota. They could not have been kidnapped; they had left willingly. Had Abosi suspected that he was going to be forced to surrender? Would she have been able to harm him personally if he had refused? Was her love for Nigeria greater than her admiration and suppressed love for this man? Her feelings were mixed. Let her find him first. He owed her – he owed all of those who had believed in him, in his burning zeal, in his ideal – an explanation.

'To the airport, the airstrip,' Debbie ordered. 'Quickly. I'll direct you.'

Bullets sang over them as they drove crazily in the dark. Debbie was more frightened in case any flying grenade should fall on the explosives they were carrying, and blow them to bits. It soon became too dangerous to drive, as they neared the airport, so they parked the car and took to their feet, carrying the deadly explosives gingerly.

Screams of the dying and the terrified filled the air. The airport was well-concealed and known only to a few elites as their ultimate escape route, yet the bombs haphazardly raining from the dark sky were alarmingly near it. They crawled into the tunnel that ended with the airstrip.

Debbie wished that she had been wrong about Abosi leaving, but she was not. For there, preparing to take off, were two planes. From where she was crouching she could see that one was a South African aircraft and the other French. They were definitely not Red Cross planes. Should she come out of her hiding place and ask the whispering men standing by the planes what they were doing, why they were there? Should she approach and have a closer look to find out who those people were?

The decision was taken out of her hands. A bomb whizzed overhead and landed only a few yards from where she crouched. Screams rang out. Many people had evidently taken refuge there and were watching as well. To think that this place was meant to be secret! Rubble filled her lungs and she coughed and choked. One of her eyes seemed to have closed forever, but with the other she saw the white Mercedes being hurried into the plane, followed by the other Abosi cars and several hurriedly tied packages and bundles.

A hot uncontrollable anger enveloped her, making her sweat and shiver at the same time. To be so betrayed, by the very symbol of

Biafra! She remembered the pitiful baby Biafra who stretched and died on her back; she remembered the image of the young mother who was raped and then pounded to a pulp by those inhuman soldiers; she recalled the death of Ngbechi and his little brother Ogo, who had wanted plantain and chicken stew and could take no more . . . She had always known herself to be impulsive and that in this particular case circumstances would dictate her actions. Abosi must not escape! He must not be allowed to escape and leave all the believers of his dream to face Lawal and his crazy Operation Mosquito campaign. Like a good captain, Abosi should die honourably defending his ship. Her mind was made up. No man, not even Abosi, was going to make a fool of her, a fool of all those unfortunate mothers who had lost their sons, the hopes of their families.

She ran. She called on her two companions, but only one moved; the other had choked to death in the explosion.

They took the land-mines and hurried and hurried. And in the desperation they fumbled. Hatred and the urge for revenge drove reason from Debbie. She cursed under her breath as they scrambled in the dark. Then came the sound that put an everlasting hole in the pit of her stomach: the sound of a plane taking off. The land-mine had failed her, it had not gone off. She was about to try and get the second plane when all of a sudden the land-mine went off. It threw her from her hiding place, as it did many other people from theirs, but she was alive.

She saw people who perhaps had been waiting to go into the other plane running this way and that. The shrieks were deafening. And in the middle of it all she saw him too, the white man. How did he manage to be here? Was there anything, anything at all, black people could not hide from these white people? She wanted to die at that minute.

'Debbie, Debbie, you miscalculated,' he said, 'even in the job of eliminating Abosi. But he has eliminated himself. You know what he was telling us? He said he was going outside Nigeria to negotiate for peace. That men has become a seasoned politician.' Alan Grey laughed hysterically. 'We must give him elbow room to escape. The war is over, Debbie. It's all over.'

He looked up at the still smoking sky and went on: 'But it will take another twenty-four hours before those men dropping the bombs get the message. Unfortunately hundreds of people will die before they are satisfied. They've got too many bombs to use up. Come on, let's go to that waiting plane. It will take us to England in no time. This is one of the worst places on earth to stay right now.'

'Why, why should you want to take me along with you? To start patronizing me with your charity all over again? You forget I have the plague, you forget that I was raped – '

'Oh, forget all that. We've been through a great deal together. I'll marry you if that's what you want. But for God's sake, you must leave this Godforsaken country. If Abosi could leave, why not you?'

'I see now that Abosi and his like are still colonized. They need to be decolonized. I am not like him, a black white man; I am a woman and a woman of Africa. I am a daughter of Nigeria and if she is in shame, I shall stay and mourn with her in shame. No, I am not ready yet to become the wife of an exploiter of my nation,' Debbie raved.

'You are mad, Debbie. What are you going to do after all this? There's no place for you here, you know that.'

'There are two boys, the Nwoba boys, and many other orphans that I am going to help bring up with my share of Father's money. And there is my manuscript to publish. I shall tell those orphans the story of how a few ambitious soldiers from Sandhurst tried to make their dream a reality. Goodbye, Alan. I didn't mind your being my male concubine, but Africa will never again stoop to being your wife; to meet you on an equal basis, like companions, yes, but never again to be your slave. Look, we even have a South African plane here offering the same help you are offering. But how did they know about tonight? And how did you know, white man? Oh, Abosi, I wish I had succeeded in killing you. To make us sink this low! If future generations should ask what became of Biafra, what do you want us to tell them?'

A larger bomb exploded, and Debbie swallowed more debris.

Alan Grey could plead no longer. It was too dangerous to stay and talk. Chaos was reigning, but instinct urged him to make for the quivering plane. He boarded it with many other expatriates, not caring where the plane took them as long as it was out of Nigeria.

After all, his mission was complete. Nigeria had been successfully handed over to the approved leader, Saka Momoh. The fact that he came from the minority tribe, and had an ample supply of guns and bombs, would stabilize his position. Nigeria badly needed that stability to allow foreign investors to come in and suck out the oil. Nigeria would need the money, too, to repay the debts she owed the 'friendly nations' for their generosity in supplying her with arms, during the time when one tribe was fighting against the other.

Alan Grey boarded the plane, leaving the Nigerians to go on killing each other if they so desired. He had done all he could. As for Debbie, he did not mind either way. The choice had been hers. But the silly woman had refused his help. That was the trouble with these blacks. Give them some education and they quoted it all back at you, as if the education was made for them in the first place.

He shrugged his shoulders. In a few hours' time he would be landing in England. 'That's life,' he said to himself. 'Nigeria will learn one day. See how long it has taken us.'

He was right, it was all a part of life.